Billionaire
BOSSES

OFFICE SCANDALS

KIM LAWRENCE
MAUREEN CHILD
CATHERINE MANN

Printed and bound in Spain
by C.P.I. Barcelona

MILLS &
BOON

First Published in Great Britain 2016
By Mills & Boon, an imprint of HarperCollins*Publishers*
1 London Bridge Street, London, SE1 9GF

OFFICE SCANDALS © 2016 Harlequin Books S.A.

The Petrelli Heir © 2013 Kim Lawrence
Gilded Secrets © 2012 Harlequin Books S.A.
An Inconvenient Affair © 2012 Catherine Mann

ISBN: 978-0-263-91791-8

24-0316

THE PETRELLI HEIR

KIM LAWRENCE

Kim Lawrence lives on a farm in Anglesey with her university lecturer husband, assorted pets who arrived as strays and never left, and sometimes one or both of her boomerang sons. When she's not writing she loves to be outdoors gardening, or walking on one of the beaches for which the island is famous—along with being the place where Prince William and Catherine made their first home!

PROLOGUE

London
June 2010

Izzy let out a startled yelp as her heel caught in a hole in the pavement and brought her to an abrupt stumbling halt. Wincing, she flexed her narrow ankle experimentally. Fortunately it held her weight when she put it back down again.

No damage but her feet hurt.

Why?

It took her a few moments to connect the ache in her feet with the time she'd been walking. She glanced at her watch, scrunching her eyes to read the face concealed by the cuff of her thin jacket. What time had she started walking?

Her smooth brow furrowed as she tried to sort out the confused sequence of the day's events in her head. It had been afternoon when she had shaken the hand of her mother's solicitor and thanked the funeral director. There had been no one else to thank, no one else to exchange amusing anecdotes of the departed with.

Her mother, Dr Ruth Carter, famous in the academic world all her professional life and famous outside it since her one attempt at a populist book landed her with an international best-seller that had broken all previous records for a non-fiction book.

The royalty cheques still kept dropping on the door-mat—Izzy's doormat now. She was almost rich… Was that a bit like being nearly famous…? Izzy shook her head. For no reason at all she suddenly wanted to laugh or was that cry? No, not cry, she didn't think she had any more tears available to shed. They were all frozen in the lead weight that lay hard and heavy pressing against her breastbone.

Dr Ruth Carter had enjoyed her fame as a celeb-rity psychologist, and had become a firm favourite on breakfast television shows. There were probably many people who would have liked to come and pay their last respects, but Ruth Carter had had firm views about funerals.

No religion.

No fuss or flowers.

No wake.

No fuss and no tears.

Her only child, actually her only living relative, Izzy had respected her wishes and she hadn't cried. She hadn't even cried when she had found her mother's body and the neat handwritten note, written as she spoke in that distinctive bullet-point dogmatic style.

In the weeks that followed both the police and then coroner at the inquest had praised her composure and bravery, but Izzy hadn't been brave. She had been numb, and now, today, she was…angry, she realised, identi-fying the emotion that was making her chest tight. She had kept walking because she was afraid that if she stopped all that anger would spill out and she had a mental image of herself enveloped in an angry toxic cloud.

She wasn't angry with her mother for choosing the time and manner in which she died. The insidious terminal disease that had slowly been robbing her mother of her ability to function independently, keeping her locked in a helpless body, had been terrible. No, her mother had made her choice in her time, the note had said.

And to hell with everyone else!

Her mother hadn't said that, but during the clinical goodbye today Izzy had thought it. So, yes, she was angry! The doctors had said her mother had at least another twelve months of relatively normal life, months when Izzy could have said all the things she would never say now.

Not even goodbye.

And now today her mother had reached out from the grave and... Izzy unfolded her stiff fingers from the typed letter that lay scrunched in her pocket and lifted a hand to her head. The dampness on her skin and her hair came as a surprise and she stared at the wet shiny pavement. She hadn't even realised it had been raining.

She didn't even know where she was! Or for that matter who she was...? She knew she wasn't the product of a contribution by an anonymous sperm donor.

It turned out she had a *real* father, one who was right now receiving a similar letter to the one the solicitor had handed her this afternoon. Apparently, the poor man had been an eighteen-year-old student at the time, selected as a suitable genetic father and seduced by her forty-something mother, who had been reacting to her ticking body clock.

Why had her mother lied?

Why had she told her now?

Why had she left her alone?

Izzy straightened her slender shoulders and gave herself a strong talking to. *Focus! You can't fall apart, you're capable—everyone says it, so surely it must be true.*

Where are you, capable Izzy?

As she looked vaguely around a door opened to a nearby building and sounds of people talking and laughing spilled out, all so normal…how weird.

Without meaning to she followed the sound and found herself in a bar. She loosened the button on her jacket, aware that she was thirsty. It was warm and humid and crowded as she began to work her way through several groups of people standing; all the tables were full, except one.

Izzy's restless gaze was drawn as if by some invisible magnet to that table or, more specifically, to the man who sat at it.

He was the most beautiful man she had ever seen!

The sheer awfulness of the day fell away and she stood stock still, oblivious to the curious stares she drew. As she stared at the man her heart hammered against her ribcage, her throat became dry and her knees were quite literally shaking, but not with exhaustion. She no longer felt weary but energised, her body taut and tingling with a squirmy, stomach-clenching excitement.

The man put down his drink and stared back, dragging his dark hair from his wide bronzed brow. Izzy shivered, as if the man had touched her, which was crazy, and she pressed a hand to her stomach where the fluid heat was spreading outwards.

On a purely aesthetic level he was someone people would always stare at. His face could have belonged to a classical statue and was a miracle of classical symmetry. He had incredible carved cheekbones, an aquiline nose and sculpted lips that were both sensual and cruel...?

Izzy shivered again. Just then a group of noisy, slightly the worse for wear young men bumped into her, the physical jolt wrenching her from the bold, overtly sexual scrutiny of those dark eyes. She turned her head sharply and thought, *My God, I'm panting!*

A man had never looked at her that way—as if he wanted her—or if one had Izzy hadn't noticed. Not enough to do anything about it anyhow. Not a sexual creature, Izzy's mother had proclaimed—her professional opinion—after first ruling out the possibility her daughter was actually gay, but in denial about her sexuality.

My mum, the big fan of plain speaking; my mum, who respected honesty; oh, yes, my painfully honest mum. Izzy felt the letter again—the bombshell honest Dr Carter had exploded when she was no longer around to answer for the biggest lie of them all—and felt her anger rise up once more. Well, maybe she could, just for once, prove her mother wrong?

Just because she'd never experienced blinding lust before didn't mean Izzy didn't recognise it when she felt it. She dabbed her tongue to the moisture that had broken out along her upper lip, still staring at the man even with a solid wall of people between her and those dark disturbing eyes.

The crowd of men jostled her again, moving in close

and delivering a few good-natured comments that Izzy didn't even register. As she approached the bar she was still seeing those dark hungry eyes. She focused on them—it wasn't hard—and seeing them, feeling them, she didn't have to think about anything else.

'Are you eighteen?' the barman asked for the third time, studying the young woman's glazed blue eyes and wondering if she was on something.

'No, yes…I mean, I'm twenty-one…almost.'

Izzy was not surprised when he asked, 'You got some identity, miss?'

Flustered, she reached into her bag and found her driving licence, holding her thick wavy chestnut hair back from her face with her forearm when it flopped in her eyes.

The barman raised his brows as he scanned it before producing her drink and an apologetic, 'We have to check.'

She jumped when a beefy, slightly clammy hand landed on top of her own, pressing it into the surface of the bar. 'A beautiful woman should never pay for her own drink,' the owner of the hand slurred.

Oh, God, and the hits just kept coming, she thought, her nostrils flaring in distaste as she inhaled the beer-laden fumes of her admirer.

'Thank you, but I'm meeting someone…excuse me.'

The man didn't move. If anything, egged on by his mates, he moved in closer. Izzy hunched in on herself defensively.

Not a violent or angry person, diplomatic Izzy balled her hand into a fist in her head. She could hear her mother saying, *When you have to shout, Izzy, you have lost an argument.*

But her mum wasn't here.

'Go away, you creep!'

I just yelled, and it felt good.

'*Cara*, I'm sorry I'm late but...' The men crowding around her suddenly parted to reveal the unbelievably attractive lone wolf from the table. Lean and broad-shouldered, all hard muscle and sinew, he was a head taller than the drunk pestering her and he had the entire mean, brooding hungry look going on, boosted by the combustible gleam in his narrowed eyes.

Izzy couldn't tear her gaze away from his face and she wanted to touch him so much it hurt, which was crazy. She was gazing with helpless admiration at the long curling ebony lashes that framed those spectacular eyes when with zero warning he fitted his mouth to hers as though he'd done it a hundred times before and kissed her hard, full on the mouth.

It was only when he lifted his mouth that he even appeared to notice the other men.

'Is there a problem?' No longer languid and warm, his deep voice was layered with icy hauteur.

Problem? she thought, swallowing a bubble of hysteria. Did standing there staring or not being able to breathe count? His kiss had tasted of whisky, she thought as she ran her tongue across the outline of her own trembling mouth. The younger men almost fell over themselves to assure the stranger that there was no problem at all as they vanished like mist.

'You looked like you were about to deck him. You're a feisty little thing, aren't you?'

Izzy unclenched her fist. 'That was very resourceful of you, but I didn't need saving.' *I'm feisty!*

This close, the raw maleness that had given her a hormone rush from across the room was a million times more intense.

'No…?' His shoulders lifted in an expressive shrug as he stared at her, dragging his hand back and forth across the dark stubble shadowing his square jaw. His eyes slid to the glass in her hand. 'You were planning to drown your sorrows?' His mouth curled into a self-derisive sneer as he added softly, 'Stare into the bottom of a glass and feel sorry for yourself?'

Izzy looked at the glass in her hand… Was she?

'I wish you more luck than me.'

Was he saying he was drunk? He didn't look drunk. He didn't sound drunk. In fact his rich, gravelly, slightly accented voice was delicious—he was delicious.

Her heart raced; the sexual tension between them was like a wall cutting them off from the rest of the room. The reckless exhilaration fizzing through her bloodstream made her feel dizzy.

'I don't want a drink any more,' Izzy said breathlessly, at the same time wondering what she was doing.

Whatever it was it felt good.

His dark eyes didn't leave hers for a moment. 'You don't? What do you want?' His brow furrowed. 'How remiss of me. I'm—'

'No!' Izzy reached up and pressed a warning finger to his lips. Once there she found herself tracing the firm outline, fascinated by the texture and warmth of his skin. 'I don't need to know your name. I need—'

He caught her hand and held it by his face and slurred throatily, 'What do you need, *cara*?' His thumb stroked a line down her cheek as he bent in close and whispered, 'Tell me…'

His gravelly accented drawl made her insides dissolve.

'I've had a very bad day and I don't want to think about it. I need...' She paused. Life-changing revelations or not, twenty years of sensible caution did not give up without a fight. The man could be a homicidal maniac...he could...he could...he could...

Izzy closed her eyes and opened them again. She needed not to think, she needed to feel...his skin. Desire washed over her like a flash fire, dragging the breath from her lungs and making her skin prickle.

'I think I need you.' *Is this really me saying that?*

'Think?'

'I need you.'

It was definitely her leaving a bar with an enigmatic, beautiful stranger.

CHAPTER ONE

Izzy hurried up the aisle, her heels clicking on the marble floor as she went. She pretended to be unaware of the scattering of nudges and not so discreet whispered comments that followed her progress. She pretended extremely well—she'd had practice.

It would have been nice to think people were riveted by her stunning fashion sense, but the reality was that, while the misty blue silk chiffon dress did bring out the blue in her blue-grey eyes and made her rich chestnut hair look more auburn than brown, it was a little too snug across her post-baby bust. And besides, the church was filled with a lot of women who were better dressed and, in her opinion, better looking—short and skinny with freckles was an acquired taste.

But the attention she garnered had nothing to do with the way she looked and everything to do with her being there at all, because everyone there knew that Izzy was not a real Fitzgerald!

Two years ago when Izzy had first arrived in the small Cumbrian market town, her appearance had attracted much more attention, but happily she was yesterday's news. The pregnant illegitimate daughter that Michael Fitzgerald had not known he had was a scandal still, but no longer one that was likely to steal the show. And things were improving.

Izzy's expression softened as her thoughts caused her glance to drift to where her father sat talking to his brother, the father of the bride. The two men with their leonine heads of grey-streaked strawberry-blond hair were alike enough to have passed for twins, though Jake Fitzgerald was older by three years.

As if feeling her gaze Michael turned his head and winked at her and Izzy grinned back. Her father was a remarkable man. How many men receiving a letter telling them that they had a daughter from an affair twenty years ago would have reacted the way he had?

Not many, she suspected. But Michael hadn't even wanted the DNA test! In fact the entire family had been great and instead of treating her like a cuckoo in the nest they had opened their collective arms and drawn her into the protective inner family circle.

She had been a stranger to these people, yet when she had been at her most vulnerable they had been there for her. After a lifetime of believing it was a weakness to rely on other people Izzy had initially found it difficult to accept their help, but their warmth had thawed her natural diffidence. Asking for help was still not her first instinct, in fact she hated it, but she was learning that sometimes there was no choice but to grit your teeth and swallow your pride. A lot of things changed when you had a baby.

Izzy's attention suddenly turned to her auburn-headed young half-brother, handsome in his morning suit and deep in conversation with someone sitting next to the aisle in the row behind. He really needed to take his seat. 'Rory, come on. She's here.'

Rory straightened up with a grin. 'Chill, Izzy. Anyone would think you were the one getting married.'

'Cold day in hell,' Izzy murmured without heat. Good luck to Rachel and her Ben, but, though having a baby had changed her view on some things, her certainty that marriage was not for her remained unshakeable. She had read the statistics and in her view you'd have to be a gambler or a hopeless romantic to take those sorts of risks and she wasn't either.

It wasn't that she didn't believe in soul mates, but in her view if two people were meant to be together they shouldn't need a piece of paper to keep them that way.

'Don't worry, your Prince Charming is out there somewhere, Izzy—always supposing you don't take the treat-them-mean-keep-them-keen thing too far.'

'I don't!'

Unable to defend herself further because an expectant hush had fallen, Izzy slid into her own seat and waited as the other seated occupants passed her daughter along the row, like a smiling parcel. Lily landed in her lap happy and smiling.

Izzy glowed with pride as she received a gummy grin. Her daughter really was the most perfect baby.

Beside her, Rory's mother, Michelle Fitzgerald, looked amused as Lily made a bid for the blue feather fascinator it had taken Izzy half an hour to attach attractively in the chestnut brown hair she had pinned up in a simple twist. But even with a dozen hairpins the artistic loose tendrils had been joined by numerous wispy strands despite a double dose of hairspray. Her hair just had a mind of its own.

'Rory!' Michelle snapped, turning her attention to her son, who had still not taken his seat.

'All right, Ma,' he soothed with an eye roll as he dropped down into the pew next to Izzy.

'Rory, perhaps we should swap?' Izzy suggested as she abandoned her attempt to secure her headgear to the slippery surface of her shiny hair. Instead she shoved it in her pocket and offered a toy duck to Lily to distract her. 'In case Lily kicks off and I have to make a quick exit.'

She would have hated her small daughter to ruin the bride's big moment and, though she was for the most part a sunny baby, Lily was capable of some seismic meltdowns when thwarted.

According to Michelle it was just a phase all babies went through, and as much as Izzy respected the older woman's knowledge of all things baby she privately wondered if it was possible her daughter had inherited her volatile temperament from her father.

But that was one thing Izzy would never know, because although she knew every angle and shadow, every curve and plane of his face, as page after page in her sketchbooks filled with his likeness attested, Izzy didn't know the name of the man who had fathered her child.

She had not thought seriously about the day when Lily asked about her father—nothing beyond its inevitability. Maybe she would get her sketchbooks out on that day and show her daughter. Would she say, *'This is how he looked. He was possibly the most handsome man ever to draw breath...oh, and he smelt good too...'* Who knew? Since Lily's birth Izzy had adopted a one-day-at-a-time approach to life.

In the meantime she viewed the sketches as a cathartic coping mechanism. Her sketches were her therapy and one day presumably she would draw him out of her system.

'Sure, if you like.' Rory stood up, ducking his head in an attempt to appear inconspicuous, hard when you were a lanky six four. 'You two haven't met, have you?' he added, turning as he spoke to let Izzy shuffle along the wooden pew. 'Izzy, this is Roman Petrelli. He's here to buy some horses...Dad hopes. Do you remember Gianni arranged for that placement for me with Roman's Paris office last summer? Roman, this is my sister Izzy.'

Last summer she had been knee deep in nappies and night feeds and pretty much everything else had passed her by, but she did find it easy to place the handsome half-Italian Gianni among the plethora of Fitzgerald cousins. And there were a lot of cousins—her father was one of nine siblings.

'Hello.' A distracted smile curving her lips, she turned her head, following the direction of Rory's introductory nod, and her eyes connected, her smile wobbled and vanished.

She had walked right past him. How did that happen?

He was not the sort of man that under normal circumstances would be overlooked—Izzy hadn't the first time she had seen him.

Now he was here the breath left her lungs in a silent hiss of shock.

'Hello.'

The voice awoke dormant memories and sent a flash of heat through her body. Incapable of speech, she nodded and thought, *He really does have the longest eyelashes I have ever seen.* And there was no discernible recognition in the pitch-dark eyes those lashes framed.

This wasn't happening.

But it was! It was him—the man she had spent that night with.

Two years later and Izzy had rationalised the reckless impulse that had made her act so totally out of character. There was probably some psychological term for what she'd done when she'd been half out of her head with grief, exhaustion and shock, but Izzy had not continued to analyse it, she had simply drawn a line under it.

You could only beat yourself up so much and, as she had felt no desire since that night to rip off any man's clothes and ravish him, there had been no lasting consequences to her actions—except one, which she could never regret.

How could she regret something that had given her not just her much-loved daughter but a new and wonderfully supportive family? There was a strong possibility that, if she hadn't found herself alone, pregnant and very aware how fragile life was, the letter sent by the father she had never met might have stayed where she had initially thrown it—in the bin.

Tapping into reserves of self-control she didn't even know she possessed, the silly smile still pasted on her face, Izzy broke free of the pitch-black mesmerising stare and turned away. Outwardly calm, at least to the casual observer, her body was gripped by a succession of deep internal tremors as she hugged her daughter.

Her shoulder blades ached with tension as she buried her face in Lily's soft dusky curls. People often remarked on her vibrant colouring, marvelling at the peachy glow of her skin and her liquid dark eyes. The less tactful asked outright if she looked like her father.

Izzy never reacted to the question and her silence had given rise to a great deal of speculation. There were currently several theories in circulation about Lily's father, which ranged from him being a dead war hero to him being a married politician. But whatever people thought, the generally held opinion was that Izzy was the innocent party, the girl who had been abandoned, because apparently she came across as a nice girl.

The irony was not lost on her and Izzy detested the undeserved victim status that had been thrust on her, but, short of publicly announcing that she was actually a shameless trollop, what choice did she have?

It was actually a relief when someone chose to take her to task about her single-parent status. Just the previous evening Michael's great-aunt Maeve had exclaimed, 'A child needs two parents, young lady.'

'In a perfect world, yes, but the world isn't perfect and neither am I.'

Izzy's quietly dignified response had taken the wind out of the old lady's sails, but she had made a quick recovery. 'In my day a girl like you wouldn't be wandering around as bold as brass like she has nothing to be ashamed of.'

'She doesn't have anything to be ashamed of, Aunt Maeve.' It was her father who came to Izzy's rescue, putting an arm around her and drawing her in close.

'Don't you go looking at me like that, Michael. One of the few good things about being old is being as rude as I like—would you deprive me of one of my last pleasures?' She held out her empty glass and glanced at the whisky bottle on the dresser. 'So, girl, who is the father?'

Izzy had not satisfied the old lady's curiosity. She hadn't told anyone the identity of the father—how could she?

Izzy's blue eyes were shadowed with shamed anguish as she responded to Lily's cry of protest and loosened her grip just as the organist pulled out all the stops. Izzy knew better than most what it was like to grow up without a father and it was something she had always vowed not to do to a child of hers should she ever have one.

With the rest of the congregation Izzy rose to her feet. Were his eyes trained on the exposed nape of her neck or was it her guilty conscience that made her skin prickle and tingle? Tingle the way his long fingers had once made her—she pushed the thought away and took a deep breath. With Lily on one hip, she stared blankly at the service sheet clutched in her free hand, knowing she was a whisper away from tipping over into outright gibbering panic.

She had to stay calm.

She had to think.

The father of her baby was sitting behind her. What was she meant to do now?

Take a leaf out of her mother's book and write him a letter?

Casually drop into the conversation, *Oh, by the way, this is your daughter*? Now that would be a real ice breaker, but could it be listed under small talk?

She choked on a bubble of hysterical laughter, the sound drowned out by the hymn being sung.

Realistically Izzy knew, always had known, that should this unlikely event occur she had to accept the real possibility that he might not even remember that night two years ago. So maybe doing nothing was a possibility? Just wait and if he said nothing leave it…?

She reluctantly discarded the tempting idea. This was Lily's father. What had Rory called him…Roman? At least she had a name now and knew that he was Italian, although she'd already had an idea about his nationality. During their night together he had whispered wonderful things to her in throes of passion; she might not have understood the things he had said, but she had recognised the language.

She remembered everything.

She tried to push away the hot, erotic images crowding in—she had to focus.

On what, Izzy—your impending public humiliation?

Her chin lifted. She would take what was coming, but not Lily. She would protect Lily.

Lily, who looked so like her father, which was good news for her because she'd grow up to be the female version of him—stunning—but bad news because surely everyone seeing them together would know.

And he'd seen Lily.

He had to know!

Was he sitting there in shock?

No point speculating; she just had to stay calm and play this by ear. A wedding was hardly the place to introduce a man to his daughter.

Was there a good place?

He might be here with his girlfriend or wife even...! Feeling sick now, Izzy closed her eyes and tried to remember who had been sitting next to him, but couldn't.

Could things get any worse? She'd slept with a stranger and got pregnant—please let him not have been married!

A question that might have been better asked before you ripped off his shirt.

Ignoring the sly insert of her conscience or what was left of it, Izzy touched a protective hand to her nape.

Nothing in his expression had suggested he even recognised her. Was it really possible he didn't remember their night together? Or maybe he might have developed a convenient amnesia to avoid embarrassment. If so should she play along with it? Everything in Izzy rebelled against the idea.

Why was she torturing herself? He might feel even worse and as embarrassed about that night as she was, sitting there now wondering if she was a potential bunny boiler about to mess up his life.

If so he'd feel relieved when he realised she didn't want anything from him. Rich men could be pretty protective of their wealth and she could recall now the word billionaire coming into the conversation when the family had discussed Rory's good fortune at securing a placement within the Petrelli company.

Great, she couldn't have had a one-night stand with a teacher or a plumber. No, she had to pick out a billionaire Italian!

At the end of the ceremony Izzy got to her feet when everyone else did, clutching her daughter to her chest. She slung a furtive look over her shoulders but chickened out at the last minute and tucked herself in between Rory and Emma in the slow-moving file of guests leaving the church, doing her best to be invisible. When she finally worked up the courage to look again Roman Petrelli was gone, the occupants of the pew behind having already vacated their seats.

She touched Rory's sleeve. Her half-brother turned his head. 'Your friend…is he?'

'Friend…? I do have more than one…?'

'Duh!' Emma, who was eavesdropping, inserted

with a roll of her eyes. 'Who do you think she's talking about? The utterly gorgeous hunk, Roman, of course! Such a sexy name, but not as sexy as the man himself. Did you get a look at his eyes?' She pressed a hand to her heart and sighed dramatically. 'You know, I could really do with a walk on the wild side.'

'Izzy isn't as shallow as you,' her brother retorted, adding, 'Could you do with a hand there, Izzy?'

'Thanks.' Izzy slanted a grateful smile at her half-brother as she relinquished a squirming Lily to him. 'She wants to get down and she's really strong.'

'Me, shallow—I like that,' Emma interrupted, adding with a warm look at Lily, who was pulling her uncle's nose, 'All the Fitzgerald women are strong.' She sent a conspiratorial grin to Izzy. 'The only place Rory is Roman Petrelli's friend,' Emma confided, directing a sisterly smile of sweet malice at her brother, 'is in his dreams. Rory only asked for him to be invited because he wants to suck up. Do you really think he's going to give a geek like you a job, Rory?'

'I'm a geek with a mind like a steel trap and great charm—why wouldn't the man give me a job?'

'As if!'

'Let's put it this way, little sister, I'm more likely to get a job off him than you are a night of passion.'

'Wanna bet?' Emma drawled, her eyes sparkling challenge.

'Like taking money off a baby.'

Izzy shook her head to clear the images flying around like a swarm of wasps in her brain. Images that involved her lovely innocent half-sister and a predatory Roman Petrelli. The sick feeling they left in the pit of her stomach had nothing to do with jealousy, she told herself in response to the nip of guilt. She was simply looking out for her sister.

Emma was only eighteen and was not nearly as sophisticated as she liked to pretend, and Roman Petrelli was…an image of him lying on the bed, the toned musculature of his bronzed torso delineated by a sheen of sweat, flashed into her head and the word that came to her was…perfect.

'Please,' she reproached. Her laughter sounded forced to her own ears but the squabbling siblings didn't seem to notice. They just grinned and continued the argument until they got outside into the fresh air and the stakes in their bet had reached the extreme scale of silly.

'Let me have Lily,' Emma begged as they stepped aside to join the other guests in the sun.

'No, better not, Emma—she'll ruin your hair, and that dress…' Izzy pointed out, holding out her arms to take her daughter.

'Good point!' agreed Emma. 'I must look beautiful for Roman… How old do you think he is?'

'Too old for you,' retorted her brother austerely. 'And actually, Em, we're both out of luck. He's not coming to the reception so neither of us will be able to use our lethal charm.'

The reprieve might be temporary but the relief was so intense Izzy laughed out loud, drawing a questioning look from her siblings.

'Don't look now—Aunt Maeve is heading this way.' Not a lie as such, more an inspired distraction, and it worked perfectly. At the mention of their elderly relative the sister and brother act adopted the attitude of sprinters under starter's orders.

'Just us again,' Izzy said, rubbing her nose against

Lily's button nose and breathing in the sweet baby fragrance of her shampoo.

A wave of love so intense that she could hardly breathe closed Izzy's throat as she whispered softly, 'I'll never let anything hurt you. I love you, Lily baba.'

Izzy had known she had been loved, even though her mother had never said the words and not encouraged Izzy to be sentimental. A mother herself now, Izzy found it sad, but was relieved that her own fears that she might struggle to express her feelings had been unfounded. Since the first moment she had held her baby in her arms they were words she couldn't stop saying.

CHAPTER TWO

ROMAN'S intention when he'd walked into the church had been to skip the wedding reception—the deal for the new stallion had been done with Michael Fitzgerald and there was no longer a need to hang around. But his plans had now changed.

The adrenaline that had been dumped in his bloodstream when he'd recognised the slim woman walking up the aisle was still making him buzz, and, conscious of the fine tremor in his fingers, he pushed his hands deep into the pockets of his well-cut trousers.

She had been sitting right in front of him and all he'd had to do was reach out and he could have touched her. He knew who she was now, she had a name, and this time she wouldn't be able to vanish. Anticipation made him feel more alive than he had in…?

With a frown he blocked the thought. He'd been given a second chance on life and admitting he was bored seemed terminally ungrateful.

And in truth he wasn't bored. The mystery woman who was no longer a mystery represented a challenge— unfinished business.

Challenge, he decided, was the operative word. It wasn't as if she had occupied his thoughts to the exclusion of everything else since their night together, but her unexpected reappearance had resurrected the frustration her vanishing act had inflicted two years earlier. But he'd had more to worry about at the time than a one-night stand slipping away. Maybe his overreaction had been in part bruised ego or maybe she had become the focus for all his frustration at the time?

But then what man wouldn't feel frustrated when, having discovered the girl who ticked just about every erotic fantasy box he had, and some he didn't know he had, vanished off the face of the earth leaving nothing but the elusive fragrance of her warm skin on the bed sheets?

Roman had felt robbed and cheated. It had not even crossed his mind that he would not be able to persuade her to spend the rest of the day in bed with him. The idea that she wouldn't be there when he returned with coffee and croissants had not occurred to him.

Conscious of the heavy heat in his groin, he waited for her to appear again, his impatience growing until he began to wonder if he had imagined the whole thing.

It wouldn't be the first time.

There had been a couple of occasions when he had thought he had caught sight of her in the distance only to get closer and discover that the rich chestnut hair and slim petite curves belonged to someone else, someone who didn't have a mouth that invited sin.

This time, though, it was different; she was no figment of his imagination and she had recognised him. Admittedly her reaction had not quite been the one he normally got from women—none, as far as he could recall, had ever looked as if they wanted to crawl under a pew.

She had blushed…actually blushed! His expressive lips quirked into a sardonic grin aş he remembered her total lack of inhibition, her throaty little gasps and greedy clever hands. His mystery woman was the last person he would have imagined capable of blushing!

But the blush was in keeping with the entire freshly scrubbed, wholesome, sexy thing she had going on. Roman shrugged, closing off this line of speculation. He didn't care if she led a double life; he just wanted her, wanted to see her soft creamy body in his bed, feel her hands on him and feel her under him. He half resented wanting her, recognising that not having her could transform her from a missed opportunity to a mild obsession.

But something about her reaction still nagged at him. Why had bumping into an ex-lover thrown her into such a state of obvious confusion?

Unless she had a jealous partner around—even sitting next to her?

Who had been sitting next to her?

Roman, who was famed for his powers of observation, scrunched his brow in concentration as he tried to recall, but came up empty. He could remember the nape of her neck pretty well and the fall of the wisps of her hair around her face. The truth was he hadn't been thinking straight in the church and he'd needed the fresh air and distance to get his brain back in gear and his hormones on a leash.

Was she concerned he would not be discreet?

If so she needn't have worried. The only thing that Roman was interested in was having her in his bed again, not advertising the fact. Would the reality live up to his dreams or would he be disappointed? The anticipation of having his sexual curiosity satisfied on this point sent his level of arousal up another painful notch.

Roman continued his vigil of the guests from under the canopy of a leafy oak tree a safe distance away from his fellow guests clustered now in laughing groups around the newly married couple. His new vantage point gave him a clear view of the stragglers emerging from the church.

His tension and frustration grew with each passing moment, until Roman began to think somehow she had escaped him again. But then he saw her emerge.

Lust slammed through his body with the force of a sledgehammer. Watching her with the intensity of a hawk observing its prey, Roman felt his anger surge along with his appetite for her as he recalled the morning after their night together...

He had been so eager to get back into bed with her after his quick trip to the coffee shop that he had left his discarded clothes in a trail from the front door to the bedroom, only to find the bed empty and the sheets still warm—he had just missed her!

No woman had ever rejected him and now twice within the space of twenty-four hours a woman had walked out on him. Literally speaking he'd done the walking on the first occasion, and bizarrely it had been this second act of rejection that had got to him more. It had propelled him out into a city of millions of people to find her, which was either a measure of the sexual spell this woman had cast over him or a measure of his emotional stability at the time.

But he hadn't been insane when he'd walked into the crowded bar that night and the last thing he had been looking for was sex. His hand slid to his leg as he again thought back to the events of that night. He'd been licking his wounds and feeling pathetically sorry for himself.

Oh, God, yes, he had been pretty mad at the world, life and women as he'd sat at that table with a drink in front of him. He'd lost count of how many drinks had gone before it, when she had walked in.

He had sworn off women, but he'd noticed her, as had half the men in the room. He had drunk too much, but hadn't been drunk enough not to appreciate the shapely length of her slim toned thighs and the lush curves of her pert bottom in the dark pencil skirt she had worn. As he'd watched her move across the room he'd tugged the tie around his neck loose and thought, *One door closes and another opens*. Love had no longer been an integral part of his plan for the future, but he'd realised there was still sex.

It had been a cheering thought, one that might make a man get out of bed in the morning. For the months of his illness and subsequent chemo his libido had lain dormant, he hadn't even thought about sex, but things had woken up dramatically—he had wanted her from the moment he saw her.

She had great legs and a great body—slim and supple; that much he could tell even though she'd had more clothes on than ninety per cent of the women in the room. The skirt she had worn reached her knee and her elegant cream silk blouse had been more office wear than nightclub, yet she had exuded some innate sensuality—he hadn't been able to take his eyes off her.

Their night together had been incredible and the fact that he had experienced more pleasure making love to a woman he felt nothing for than any before or since had proved to him that emotional involvement did not enhance sex. His recent disastrous engagement only illustrated that it was actually an encumbrance.

Roman had never managed to recreate anything approaching the hot, sizzling sex he had enjoyed with his mystery woman. And he hadn't had sex for…not since… His brows lifted in surprise—he hadn't realised it had been that long!

He'd just been too busy with work lately to notice. The six months he had taken off on medical advice as he'd gone through his treatment had always seemed excessive and had necessitated him delegating areas of responsibility.

He had adopted a less hands-on approach that should have given him more time to enjoy his life—a healthier work-leisure balance. In reality he'd found himself unable to let go. Spare time was for people who didn't enjoy work or people with families and that was never going to be him.

On an intellectual level he knew that not being able to father a child did not make him any less a man, but it was not something a man felt on an intellectual level. When Roman had been given the news he had felt it in an icy fist in his gut, and even worse had been the prospect of telling his fiancée at that time, Lauren.

His lips twisted into a sardonic grimace as he played the scene over again in his head. Her understanding and support at the time had made him feel he might have misjudged her, but later he had discovered that not having children did not fill her with nearly the same sort of horror as the thought of how much weight she might put on during pregnancy.

Roman clenched his jaw and pushed away the

thoughts—they belonged in another lifetime. His hungry gaze riveted on Izzy Fitzgerald again. She belonged in another lifetime too, but the memory of their night together had not faded, instead it had become something of a standard that he had measured every sexual encounter against since, and none had come near...

Would the memory have exerted the same sort of fascination if he had known her name back then? He didn't have a clue, but he knew that he wanted her. He didn't waste time trying to figure out why. Time-wasting was anathema to Roman, who knew better than most what a precious commodity it was.

He could see the dark hair of the baby in her arms. Was it hers?

Roman did not do single mothers. Call him a cynic, but he could never quite believe that they were not out to bag a father for their child. Besides, he would be expected to pretend an interest in their kid and that just wasn't his thing. The fact was there were a lot of women who didn't come with the added complication of a child—so why complicate life?

But if Izzy Fitzgerald had a kid, would that be a deal breaker?

He smiled to himself as he watched her move, the wind plastering the blue dress she wore against the slender line of her legs. His temperature climbed several degrees as he remembered those legs wrapped around him, her nails digging into his shoulders, the expression of fierce concentration on her face as she fought her way towards climax.

He expelled a deep sigh. *Dio*, there were definitely exceptions to every rule. Did she have a husband? His brows twitched into a heavy frown; some rules he would not break.

But, God, it was going to kill him to walk away from this.

She had been the best sex he had ever had.

Izzy was about to get into one of the waiting cars that were lined up to whisk them to the reception when she realised that she didn't have her handbag; her keys and phone were in it.

'Damn, I think I left it in the church.'

Emma, who was standing with a shoe in one hand while she rubbed the toes of her shoeless foot with the other, looked up. 'Have you lost something, Izzy?'

'My bag—I think I left it in the church.'

Michelle, who was already in the car, leaned out with her arms outstretched. 'Give me Lily while you go and get it. You only have yourself to blame, Emma. I told you those heels were too high.'

'Thanks,' Izzy said, handing her daughter over to the willing hands. 'Don't wait for me.' Izzy blew a kiss to her daughter and mouthed, 'I'll catch up,' through the closed window.

Michelle nodded, and her father, who was strapping Lily into a baby seat, waved. Izzy grinned in response before she began to retrace her steps back to the church. The hotel where the reception was being held was only a gentle stroll down the village high street and it wouldn't take her long to meet up with the rest of the family.

Izzy pushed open the lychgate and ran on into the churchyard, which was totally deserted but for a solitary figure, the vicar, who was making his way on foot to the reception. She exchanged a few words with him before she went back inside the church, the quiet of the building acting as a balm to her frayed nerves.

The prospect of contacting Lily's father and telling him she existed filled her with total dread, and then... then what? How would he react? How did she want him to react? Izzy clenched her hands into fists and wished fiercely that she had never learnt of his identity, that he had remained some dark dream, and felt immediately guilty for being so selfish. Of all people she should know that it was wrong to deprive a child of all knowledge of her father.

She breathed a slow deep breath. She'd do the right thing—whatever that was—but not today. Today she would party, dance and enjoy herself.

Izzy laughed, the sound echoing back at her as she thought, *Who am I fooling?* She could almost feel the draft from the proverbial sword hanging by a thread above her head.

Her handbag was not on the pew where she thought she had left it, but a quick frantic search revealed it on the floor where it had fallen and, other than a dusty footprint, it was none the worse for wear.

She dusted it off and once outside opened it to check the contents. She was just refastening the pretty pearl-encrusted clasp when a prickling on the back of her neck made her pause, and slowly she turned, lifting a hand to shade her eyes from the sun.

Somehow she wasn't surprised at all to see Roman Petrelli standing only a few feet away.

Her heart was thudding like a sledgehammer against her ribs as she straightened her slender shoulders and lifted her chin. That fictional sword suddenly felt very real indeed!

Her earlier glimpse of him had left her with the impression of extreme elegance and raw male power, and now she could see that he possessed both those qualities in abundance. She could also see just how breathtakingly handsome his classically cut clean-shaven features were.

Of course, she already knew he was good-looking. That night in the bar he had been elegant, but crumpled in a dark, brooding way, his jaw shadowed and his hair worn a lot shorter then, sticking up in spiky tufts.

Izzy had no idea what demons he had been struggling to contain, but she had seen it in his taut body language and the vulnerability she had sensed was there behind the hard reckless glow in his eyes.

She recognised it was possible that she had been imagining something that had never been there, because she had needed an excuse for jumping into bed with him. But Izzy liked to think that she had been drawn to him, had felt that weird connection to him, because she had been fighting her own demons too.

There was no trace of vulnerability, hidden or otherwise, in the man who stood before her now. Here was a man definitely in control, a man who did not inspire any stirrings of empathy.

His eyes were sensuous, but cynical and hard. There was a hint of cruelty in the sculpted curve of his lips and she felt a shudder run down her spine. The only emotion this impeccably dressed, effortlessly elegant stranger inspired in Izzy was a deep unease that bordered antipathy. Her skin prickled with it.

'It was a lovely wedding,' she heard herself say inanely.

Roman studied her, searching for signs of the forthright, bold woman who had delighted him in bed with her directness. Many women had thrown themselves at him, but she had been different, or so it had seemed to him. She had seduced him, not just with her delicious body, but with her generosity and a rare utter lack of self-consciousness.

His jaw tightened and he realised that she could not even meet his eyes. He felt a stab of disappointment.

'We have been introduced—you probably don't remember. I'm Izzy.' She thought of holding out her hand but changed her mind and rubbed it up and down her thigh, the friction creating a static charge that made the fabric cling. Forget touching him, just being this close to him was painfully uncomfortable and her skin tingled with awareness, the muscles in her stomach quivering like an overstrung violin. Touching…no, not a good idea!

His sensually moulded lips thinned. How long would she continue with this little charade that they were strangers?

'I remember.'

The throaty comment was open to interpretation, but Izzy, struggling to stay in control, chose to treat it at face value. 'I believe Rory worked for you. He really enjoyed it.' Her jittery glance encompassed the empty churchyard; anything that meant she could legitimately not look at him was good. 'Everyone's made their way to the hotel.' Good manners made her add, 'Do you know the way? Can I help you?'

'I really hope so, Izzy, or is that Isabel?'

Her eyes flew to his face. She moistened her lips nervously with her tongue, struggling against the sensation that she was sinking beneath a wave of sexual awareness that was wrapping itself around her like an invisible straightjacket.

Breaking contact with his sardonic glittering stare, she conjured up a smile of sorts. 'Nobody calls me that.' She made a show of looking around. 'It's Izzy. Looks like we're the last...or are you not going to the reception?' she asked hopefully.

'Wild horses would not keep me away.'

'Really...oh, well, it's not far. Do you need a car?'

Without meaning to she dropped her glance to his leg. She remembered the red livid scars she had seen gouged into the muscles of his thigh during their night together. She had been conscious of a slight limp when he had approached her in the bar, but had dismissed it until she had seen the cause. The scarred tissue had shocked her, causing her sensitive stomach to quiver in reaction to the obvious pain they represented.

'Thank you, but I think I can make it under my own steam,' he said. Instantly he was catapulted into the past as he remembered her gasp when she had first seen the scars that night two years ago.

Survivor's scars, he called them. They were not pretty now, but two years ago they had been relatively fresh; the livid purple puckered tracks gouged in his flesh had been the thing of horror movies. In his head he had anticipated her revulsion to them and had schooled himself not to care. It had only been his desire to see her that had stopped him turning off the light.

He had offered but she'd refused. She had lain on the bed where he had left her as he had removed his clothes. She had been laughing throatily after the shoe he had flung over his shoulder had hit a mirror, cracking it in a zigzag from top to bottom.

But when she had seen his scars she had stopped laughing and he had tensed. Pity as a reaction was even less attractive to him than repugnance.

Holding his eyes, she had flipped sinuously over onto her stomach and grabbed his wrist. Shaking her head, she had pulled his hand away from the lamp.

She had looked at the ugly red line that began high on his thigh and ended a few inches above his knee and asked, 'Does it hurt?' adding huskily when he shook his head, 'Can I touch…?'

'Touch?'

Roman had taken an involuntary step back. He had always taken his body, the perfect symmetry of his strong limbs and his naturally athletic physique, for granted, but all that had changed overnight. His body had betrayed him and become the enemy and though not a vain man he accepted that others would be repelled by his scars. For him they were a constant reminder not to take anything for granted—ever.

'Why would you want to? Morbid curiosity?'

Her astonishment had been too spontaneous to be feigned. 'Don't be stupid.'

'I am normally considered to be above average in the brains department.'

Her slow wicked smile had made the lust in his belly grip hard. 'I'm not that interested in your brains.'

Her blouse, unbuttoned to the waist, had billowed out as she'd pulled herself up onto her knees. He had been unable to take his eyes off her, the tantalising shadows of her nipples through the lace of the bra that matched her pants, as with sinuous grace she had risen from the bed and come to stand beside him. Barefooted she had come up to his shoulder. 'Are you hiding any more of those?'

He had been unprepared and shocked when she had reached out again and touched him, lightly running a finger down the raised scar tissue.

He had caught her wrist, unable to keep the bitterness from creeping into his voice as he'd asked, 'Isn't that enough?'

'No.' Tilting her head to look at him, she'd pulled her hand from his grip. 'Not nearly enough. I want to touch all of you,' she'd whispered. 'I don't want to miss any place out.'

Roman felt lust clutch hard and low in his belly and was dragged back to the here and now. A faint growl worked its way upwards from his chest before he managed to push the images away.

'We could always walk together.' Of all the things they could do together, walking was not high on his list, but he was not about to let her escape.

'Actually I'm in a bit of a hurry.'

He felt his exasperation climb. Dismay was not a response Roman was accustomed to from attractive young women, and he suspected the novelty value would wear off quickly.

'And you think I can't keep up?' He might not be taking the lead on any climbs, but his limp only manifested itself now when he was extremely fatigued.

'No, of course…' She took a deep breath and sighed. 'Fine.' Said with all the enthusiasm of someone who had just agreed to give up her place on the last lifeboat.

Roman was torn between amusement and annoyance at the grudging concession. His annoyance would have been a lot greater had he not known that she was as aware of the chemistry spark between them as he was, but for some reason she was reluctant to acknowledge it...

He was confident that whatever the reason for fighting the attraction she would lose the battle, and he relished the prospect of seeing the confident bold woman he knew was there under her diffident, fresh-faced exterior.

'A pleasant stroll down a leafy village road on a sunny day—what could be nicer?' murmured Roman as he fell in beside her, matching his stride to hers.

'The inn is fourteenth-century.'

'Is the tour commentary optional?'

She slid him a sideways look of dislike. He had no manners at all but a great profile. Her glance drifted lower. Actually he had a great everything. 'I thought you might be interested. My mistake.'

'I'm fine with the charming company and the leisurely stroll,' he murmured, adding drily, 'Very leisurely stroll.'

Izzy compressed her lips, and, to squash any suspicion he might have that she wanted to prolong this walk, lengthened her stride. It was a struggle, despite his comments to the contrary, to believe that his mangled leg did not give him pain, but he showed no sign of difficulty in matching her pace.

As they continued down the steep, winding village street a silence developed...not of the comfortable variety. In the end and despite the risk of drawing another of his rude comments, Izzy cleared her throat. She had to do something to drown out the silent tension.

'It was a lovely service... Rachel looked beautiful, didn't she?'

Roman, who thought one bride in a meringue dress looked much like any other, gave a non-committal grunt. The main event had not been what he was watching, or thinking about. 'Her father is Michael's brother?'

Izzy, happy to discuss this safe subject, nodded. 'Yes, they moved to Cumbria about twenty years ago. They bought neighbouring farms and married sisters.' Both brothers still retained the Irish accent that Izzy found so attractive.

'So the bride is your cousin?'

'No…well, sort of, I suppose. Michelle isn't my mother—I'm not a real Fitzgerald.' Not something she normally said, actually not something she ever said except to herself, but he made her nervous and she babbled when she was nervous. He made her a lot of other things but Izzy didn't want to go there.

Roman registered that this was an odd thing to say, but as his interest in the Fitzgerald family and how she fitted into it was at best minimal he did not react to the information. Instead he suddenly stopped in his tracks. While it had been entertaining to a point he was tired of this fencing.

'How long are you going to carry on pretending we are strangers?'

Izzy took another few steps before she slowed and turned to face him, her face flaming. His elevated brow and his dark eyes mocked her.

'I didn't even know your name until five minutes ago. We are strangers.'

'Strangers who have had sex,' Roman retorted, his impatience wearing paper thin. Her innocent wide-eyed routine was beginning to irritate him. 'Was the child yours?' He had a vague recollection of dark curls and a pink dress, so presumably a girl, but he had been concentrating on the woman holding her and the way her already beautiful face had been transformed when she had smiled at the kid.

He'd said *yours* not *mine*. So maybe he hadn't guessed that Lily was his daughter. Feeling her panic subside from red alert to amber and fighting the lingering urge to run, Izzy veiled her eyes with her silky lashes as she fought to regain her composure.

'Yes, she is.'

'Are you married?'

Izzy was too startled to respond to his abrupt question. 'I beg your pardon.'

'I'd prefer you answered my question.'

There didn't seem much point lying. 'No, I'm not married,' she admitted.

He tipped his head, some of the tension in his expression fading as his eyes continued to sweep her face. 'And you're not with anyone?'

Izzy framed a cold smile in response to his continued abrupt questioning style. She was suddenly conscious of being very hot. The silk chiffon dress clung uncomfortably to her skin and beneath it her bra chafed her nipples.

'Is this you making small talk or is there a reason for this interrogation?' It was hard to tell if he knew how rude he was being.

'You didn't answer my question.'

She gave a small smile. 'You noticed.'

He clenched his teeth in a white smile that left his spectacular eyes cold. 'I can do small talk. I can even tell you you're the most beautiful woman here today.'

Izzy was desensitised to insults after being the focus

of gossip for so long, but compliments always threw her off balance, even one delivered in such an oddly dispassionate way. Or maybe it was the person doing the delivering.

She moved her head sharply to one side, causing the loose tendrils of her hair to move over her face, partly to hide the juvenile blush she felt burning. She looked at him through her lashes and achieved a negligent shrug that managed to deliver a level of indifference she was a million miles from feeling.

'You could? But your innate honesty prevents it?' she suggested.

'I could, but—' He shook his head and his hooded gaze skimmed the pure lines of her oval face, lingering on her soft full mouth, taking pleasure from her beauty on a purely aesthetic level. His pleasure tipped over into the carnal as the image of those cool lips moving over his body sent his level of arousal up several painful notches.

'After that build-up this should be good.' Her amused smile faded as their glances locked. The rampant, hungry gleam in his eyes made her painfully conscious of the ache between her thighs.

'It will be,' he promised modestly, adding in a low throaty drawl that made her heart kick heavily against her ribcage, 'I thought you'd prefer a more direct approach.'

She had been very direct the last time they'd met, and it had saved a lot of time. He really wanted that bold seductive witch back. What would it take to cut through this act? 'Maybe,' he mused, appearing to consider the question, 'I haven't been direct enough.'

Before she could digest his comment, let alone respond to it, he was right there beside her before she was even conscious of him moving. Then without a word he framed her face with one hand, fitting his thumb to the angle of her jaw, and tipped her face up to him. His other hand moved over the curve of her bottom, his fingers splayed across the firm contours as he dragged her closer to him, then in one smooth, seamless motion he fitted his mouth to hers.

Izzy froze at the contact, her body stiffening in tingling shock. Then as his tongue insinuated itself between her lips, forcing them apart, a low tremulous moan was wrenched from deep inside her. He was hard and hot and she closed her eyes, stopped fighting and grabbed for him, her hands circling his neck as she opened her mouth, inviting him to deepen the slow, sensual exploration.

The devastating kiss seemed to go on for ever, or was it seconds? Izzy had no idea. When he released her her head was spinning and she was shaking and struggling for breath. Blinking, she took a shaky step back, falling inelegantly off one heel in her agitation.

'No!' she cried, avoiding the steadying hand he had extended as she regained her balance—her pride and dignity would take a lot longer. What was it about this man that seemed to awake her inner cheap tart?

Shock and shame rippled through her as she stood there wanting to hit his smugly complacent face, wanting to curl up and die from sheer shame, wanting not to be here.

Shame or not, Izzy knew with despairing certainty that if he touched her she'd react the same way. She wrapped her arms tightly around herself as she shivered and blinked to clear the last remaining shreds of the hot haze of lust fogging her vision.

When she made herself look at him she felt something inside her snap. Not the same something that had snapped when he had slid his tongue into her mouth, not mind-numbing lust—this was mind-awakening fury. Two years…two years of coming to terms with that night and in a few seconds she was right back to square one!

'Just what was that meant to prove?' she yelled at him as her conscience criticised her. *You are such a hypocrite, Izzy. You are angry with him when you should be angry with yourself.* As she was hit by a fresh wave of shame her eyes fell. *He might have instigated the kiss but you sure as hell did your best to make sure it didn't end!*

'That we are wasting our time talking when we should be in bed,' he answered calmly.

A gurgling sound of sheer disbelief escaped her clamped lips as the haze of lust descended again like a blanket. Furious with herself for inviting his response, she painted an expression of distaste onto her face while struggling to push away the images his words had planted in her head…sweat-glistening golden skin, tangles of limbs pale and dark intertwined…moans… She wasn't even sure if the moan was part of her torrid imaginings or real. All she cared about at this point was keeping him ignorant of what was going on in her head.

'My God, you do love yourself, don't you?' Her haughty scorn was paper thin; scratch the surface and her entire body was suffused with burning heat. Her insides shuddered with the aftershocks that still made her shake.

At least no one had seen them; that was something. The thought was barely formed before a frantically barking dog ran out into the street. Izzy immediately recognised it as the shop owner's excitable terrier.

Afraid that the noise might bring someone out of the shop to investigate, she snapped a desperate, 'Hush, Bella,' which the dog ignored as she ran barking towards the village shop where she continued to bark as she danced around the feet of the figure standing in the doorway.

Izzy's heart sank to her knees as she registered the familiar figure of Emma, her eyes round with shock and her mouth open.

'Izzy!' she said as though she expected to be contradicted, her glance moving repeatedly back and forth between Izzy and the tall figure beside her.

'This isn't what it looks like, Emma.' Except it was, it was exactly what it looked like, and this time she didn't have trauma or alcohol to blame. It had been all her. Biting her lip, she turned to Roman, her blue gaze willing him to back her up. 'Tell her,' she snapped.

'I don't know what it looked like. I only know what it felt like—rather good. You haven't lost your touch, *cara*.'

In one sentence he had managed not only to confirm Emma's suspicions, but also leave the impression that this wasn't the first time they'd kissed.

Her eyes narrowed with dislike, and to rub salt in the wound he looked utterly cool, except for the dark bands of colour that drew attention to the slashing angle of his sculpted cheekbones.

Emma shook her head as though she were just waking up. 'Wow, you and...' She inhaled and suddenly grinned, approval beaming all over her face. 'I said you needed some fun but I never...' She looked at Roman and shook her head again, framing a silent Wow! behind her hand as she looked at her sister.

'Emma, no, I—'

'It's fine, Izzy, totally cool. The man obviously prefers brunettes. Carry on, pretend I was never here.' Throwing a quick cheeky grin over her shoulder, she set off down the hill as fast as her incredibly high spiky heels would take her.

'Emma!' Acting on an instinct that told her she had to stop Emma and explain to her that she couldn't tell anyone what she had seen, Izzy hit the ground running, but she had barely covered a yard before she was physically hauled back.

Slapping at the restraining hand on her shoulder, she spun around furiously. 'What do you think you are doing?' she snapped.

He released his grip on her arm but took both her hands in his, pulling her around to face him. 'What are you doing?' he countered, struggling to drag his eyes above the level of her heaving bosom.

'I've got to stop her before she tells someone that she saw us.'

Under his olive-toned skin the fine muscles along his jaw quivered and clenched. 'You have a baby so I'm thinking people might have guessed you've been kissed before,' he drawled.

'I'm sure you thrive on notoriety, but I'll still be living here tomorrow.'

'Why do you assume I thrive on notoriety?' Roman worked very hard to protect his privacy.

She shook her head stubbornly. 'You're a billion-aire p-playboy.'

The term made Roman's firm lips twitch with amusement. 'Playboy?'

'All right, maybe not a playboy,' she admitted. Did she even know what a playboy was? 'But you are a bil-lionaire.'

Roman blinked. He had been referred to as such before but never so accusingly. 'Which means I don't value my privacy...?' The furrow between his dark brows deepened as he tacked on an abrupt question-ing, 'And why?'

She looked at him blankly. 'What do you mean why? Why what?'

'Why will you be here tomorrow? Didn't you live in London? Why have you buried yourself out here in the middle of nowhere?' Unless she had followed the father of her child?

'You can't bring up a child in a flat...' *Why am I defending my life decisions to him?* 'And anyway, this happens to be a very good place to live.'

'So this is a permanent arrangement?'

Her eyes slid from his. 'My family lives here.' She lifted her hands, still confined in his. 'Do you mind? I need to catch up with Emma.'

He let her go and watched as she rubbed her wrists even though he had not been holding her tightly. 'You catch her and what? What are you going to do to her if she doesn't keep your dirty little secret?'

For the first time she picked up on the anger in his voice.

'What's going to happen if she does tell? Is the sky going to fall in?'

Izzy loosed a scornful laugh. 'Oh, I'm sorry, I wouldn't want to hurt your ego by not telling the world what a great kisser you are. Would it help if I gave you marks out of ten?' She rolled her eyes. 'Oh, for goodness' sake,' she snapped. 'Get out of my way. I have better things to do than pander to your massive ego. I have a baby who needs feeding.'

The reminder of the child situation brought a frown to his broad brow. If he could not have a child of his own Roman did not want to play father to some other man's…but he was willing to concede that all rules had exceptions.

'Look, two years ago I was a very different person. Let me spell it out for you: I don't have sex with rude, incredibly arrogant bores.'

'You did.'

She gritted her teeth. 'I must have been very drunk.'

'No, you weren't, but you were incredible.'

Furious with herself for reacting to his smoky voice, she screened her eyes and took a deep breath, exhaling it slowly before she reacted.

'Really.' She gave a rueful grimace. 'I'll have to take your word for it. I'm afraid that it's all a bit hazy for me.'

'I am happy to refresh your memory. I've wanted to repeat the experience for a long time.'

The man had an extraordinary ability to say the most outrageous things the way other people commented on the weather.

'You want to get drunk and jump into bed with a total stranger? I don't suppose there's anything stopping you, but personally I like to learn from bad experiences, not repeat them.'

'Bad experience? How would you know if you don't remember?'

'I've met you now, so let's call it a lucky guess.' Izzy's hands balled into fists at her sides as she struggled to breathe past the anger building in her chest. Did he really think she was that easy?

No, he knows *you're that easy.*

'Anyway, what are you suggesting—the shrubbery?' She flicked the bush to her right with her hand, causing scarlet petals from the rhododendrons to rain on the floor. 'Or is that too romantic? What about the back seat of your car?'

One expressive brow lifted. 'I have a perfectly acceptable hotel room, but I'm always up for a new experience.'

Izzy looked at him, achieving a look of amused contempt, then spoilt it by choking out, 'You're totally disgusting!'

He looked taken aback by her reaction. 'I thought you liked me that way.'

Like! Like had nothing whatever to do with the feelings this man evoked in her. 'I didn't say that or anything like it!'

Again her lie returned to taunt her. 'How would you know, if you don't remember anything about it? I'm not quite sure why you're getting so worked up. I thought you were a girl who liked to cut to the chase.'

'I know you think you're totally irresistible, but for the record I find you crude and crass and quite frankly I wouldn't touch you with a ten-foot pole!'

'Actually, I'm thinking more hands-on, *cara*,' he drawled. 'So you're not interested?'

His amused disbelief made her long to slap his complacent, beautiful face. 'Absolutely definitely not.'

He shrugged. 'A pity.'

Izzy couldn't decide if she was relieved or insulted that he wasn't pushing the idea. The fact that she had doubt at all proved that her judgement was seriously flawed around this man.

CHAPTER THREE

Izzy walked into the hotel foyer, aware that Roman was following a few steps behind her. She stopped and turned. 'Will you go away? Or I'll call Security.'

'I was invited, remember!'

'You…'

'All right, I'm going, but if you change your mind I have a room…'

She ground her teeth at his deliberate provocation. 'I'm never going to be that drunk.'

'Izzy, dear, did you find it?'

Flustered, Izzy turned to find Michelle with Lily in her arms, walking across the lobby towards her. 'Find…? Oh, yes, my bag, thanks, Michelle. None the worse for—' She stopped and dropped her hand, realising that she had found her bag, but she didn't have a clue where it was now. Although she wasn't much concerned compared with the presence of Roman Petrelli, who was now standing just a few feet away from his daughter. 'Sorry, it took me longer than I thought.' She knew he hadn't moved; even with her back to him she could feel the waves of raw male magnetism he radiated.

'Oh, don't worry about that, the reception isn't for another hour.' Michelle's expression showed her opinion

of this break with tradition. 'All at the behest of that ridiculously expensive photographer Rachel insisted on.'

'Well, thanks. I didn't mean to dump her on you.'

'You know I love having her, the little angel. Actually she fell asleep in the car and she's only just woken
up. Have you got her…yes?' Michelle relinquished her
hold on the baby and took a step back to grab a glass of
champagne from the tray of a passing waiter.

'Have you seen Emma?' Izzy asked casually.

'No, she must be around somewhere. Are you feeling
all right, Izzy? You look rather pale. You haven't got
another migraine—' She broke off, her quizzical gaze
shifting to a point behind Izzy. Even without the eyes-
widening moment that Izzy presumed was the normal
response for any female with a pulse when they saw
Roman, she knew what was coming next, but even so
she still flinched when she heard his voice.

'Excuse me, ladies.' Moving into view he divided
his smile between Izzy and Michelle, giving the older
woman the lion's share and conscious in his peripheral
vision of Izzy's expression of panic. What the hell was
her problem? Did she really think he was about to tell
the world they had shared a night of passion? Being associated with him had never done any woman's social
standing any harm. 'But I think this might be yours…?'

If her back hadn't been literally to the wall Izzy had
no doubt she would have run, but as the tall, elegant
and devastatingly handsome figure approached, with a
smile that could have charmed a steel bar into malleable
submission, there was nowhere for her to go.

Izzy took a deep breath and lifted her chin. This
was face-the-music time. She stared at the handbag
dangling by its decorative metal chain strap from the

long brown forefinger of his right hand, but before she could respond Michelle exclaimed, 'Oh, look, Izzy— it's your bag!'

Izzy, who had never seen Roman turn on the charm before, was not surprised to hear the older woman give a girlish giggle.

'Oh, yes, so it is. I must have dropped it again or something, thank you.' She waited, her eyes conveying cold disdain as she shifted Lily's weight to her left hip and in the process partially shielded her from view before she extended a hand to receive it.

Roman held the bag just a little away, prolonging the moment before he threaded it over her wrist. His lips twitched appreciatively; managing to make 'thank you' sound like 'go to hell' was quite an achievement.

He dipped his dark glossy head. 'You're welcome.'

'Well, isn't that lucky you found it, and realised it was Izzy's?' From Michelle's expression it was clear that she was not immune to his high-voltage charm.

'Very lucky.' He extended his hand towards Michelle. 'Roman Petrelli. We have met at Gianni's wedding.'

For once Izzy was able to place Emma and Rory's handsome older cousin as the son of her father's eldest brother. He was here today with his gorgeous, red-headed, very pregnant wife.

'Of course, you were his best man, but no.' Michelle tilted her head a little to one side as she studied Roman's handsome features with a frown. 'That's not it. You remind me of someone...?'

Izzy knew exactly who he reminded her of and stared at the floor. This was probably what it felt like to act normally in the middle of an earthquake when you knew, you just *knew*, that any moment the earth was going to open at your feet.

'Your son Rory worked for me last summer...we were impressed. He's a young man with promise.'

The perfect way to a mother's heart—say something good about her son, Izzy thought, a cynical smile twisting her lips.

'Thank you. I'm prejudiced, of course, but I know he really enjoyed working for your firm. He was so enthusiastic when he got home. He's waiting for his results at the moment. It's such a tough job market out there.'

'Has he put in many applications?' Roman asked, not thinking about applications but the slim figure standing a few feet away. He could feel the inexplicable anxiety rolling off her in waves.

'He's waiting for the results of his finals.' Michelle gave a rueful smile and admitted, 'He was aiming for a first, but he thinks he messed up a paper.'

'Well, exams are useful but I think enthusiasm and ambition are equally important.' Struggling to maintain a level of appropriate interest, Roman fished a card out of his pocket. 'My PA will be expecting his call.'

Izzy was amazed that Michelle, normally a very moral person, saw nothing wrong in this piece of blatant bribery thinly disguised as generosity.

The man clearly thought he could buy his way in or out of any situation. He probably heard no as a response once every ten years or so and then it was probably incorporated into, No, I don't mind if you wipe your shiny handmade Italian shoes on me, Mr Petrelli. It would be an honour.

Izzy endured this conversation with gritted teeth. Without asking someone to move out of her way she could not drift unobtrusively away without drawing un-wanted attention to herself and, more importantly, Lily.

She was cornered and couldn't even access the glasses of champagne, she mused as another waiter drifted by, and she could really do with a drink. She had always known Lily looked like her father but until seeing them virtually side by side she had not realised how much. She couldn't see how anyone would not be struck by the uncanny likeness.

He had to notice... It was inevitable. She was amazed they weren't already the focus of finger pointing.

This was the last place in the world she wanted the big reveal, right here with a captive audience. It was going to happen; it was just a matter of when.

It was Lily herself who eventually kick-started the event. Tired of being carried and ignored, she let out a yell, shouting loudly, 'Want go down, play...now!'

Roman winced in response to the sudden high-pitched ear-piercing squeal.

Michelle saw his expression and said, 'She does have a temper!' as she gazed with a fondness he struggled to understand at the red-faced bundle who was struggling like a demented demon to escape her mother's arms.

His glance moved on to the small demon's mother, who looked self-conscious, pink-cheeked and actually far too young to be a mother as she struggled to soothe the child, whose tantrum was causing a good deal of attention.

Roman might have expected to feel a certain amount of satisfaction witnessing her discomfiture. He did not consider himself a vindictive man, but he was a man who believed strongly in the old adage of 'what goes around comes around', and she had left him feeling a different and extremely painful type of discomfort. Her hypocrisy was staggering. First she had responded to him in a way that had fanned his smouldering desire into a full-scale conflagration, but had then acted as if he had somehow insulted her by suggesting they get reacquainted in bed! She had somehow managed to offend his masculinity and his intelligence in the process!

Double whammy!

Roman knew the signs when a woman was interested in him, and she was, so why was she acting as though there was some sort of stigma attached? It was as if she had undergone some weird personality transplant. Maybe taking her out of this environment, where relatives lurked around every corner, would bring back the erotic, uninhibited, adventurous lover of that night? He had a private jet on standby...and the villa on Lake Como... He smiled, seeing the plan formulating in his head coming together.

The opportune timing of the child's sob meant he did not have time to consider why he felt such a strong need to construct an elaborate plan to get this woman into his bed, when he could achieve the same result without any effort on his part at all and with a woman who did not act as though he were a social liability!

As he watched Izzy cope with the distressed child and display a level of patience that was staggering, Roman found himself experiencing a sudden and inexplicable desire to help her.

He didn't, of course. He didn't have a clue about children, especially loud, screaming ones. His critical glance slid back to the child, who appeared to have been pacified slightly and was not so red in the face any more. He could see that she was not so... He stopped and looked closer. The child had dark hair, with blue-black curls, huge chocolate-brown eyes and skin the colour of rich honey. His eyes followed the suddenly very familiar shape of a jaw and eye…the mouth.

'Dio!'

Izzy was alerted to the impending scene by his raw gasp. Her glance flew to his face in time to witness the stunned recognition. Both shock and denial were written in the strong sculpted lines of his patrician face.

'How is this possible?'

Unaware that he had voiced the question out loud, Roman half expected to hear an answer in his head, but no reply was forthcoming. His brain, unable to cope with the shock, had closed down.

'Were you off school the day they did the birds and bees?' She regretted the comment the moment she said it, but flippancy was one of her coping mechanisms.

Jolted back to reality by Izzy's comment, Roman glared at her. What was she now…the mother of his child? It didn't seem possible, but instantly he knew it was. He looked at her and then at the baby, then back at the mother, who looked away guiltily.

'Isabel?'

His voice made the fine downy hairs on her body tingle… 'Izzy,' she corrected, staring at his chest. Almost without thought she saw herself unbuttoning his shirt and peeling back the fabric to expose the smooth, golden tautly muscled flesh beneath. Taking a deep breath, she closed the door on the memory.

His dark, heavy-lidded stare zeroed back in on her face. 'I think we need to talk.'

She gave a grudging nod, but was saved the need to respond by the appearance of a suited usher who had been sent to corral the stragglers and drive them into the wedding breakfast.

He consulted a seating plan in his hand and said, 'Come on, ladies, we need to get you in first. It's a tight squeeze and once you're at your table it's kind of hard to get out without a lot of hassle.'

The last sight Izzy had of Roman Petrelli's dark head was in the distance as she joined the file of guests who were waiting to be greeted by the happy couple.

He looked like the living, breathing incarnation of retribution.

The wedding breakfast seemed to go on for ever, but when the opportunity arose during a gap in the speeches Izzy made her move for the fire door and escaped into the hallway.

There was no one in sight.

Then she spotted his tall distinctive dark head at the same time a waiter extended a tray of champagne her way.

With a groan of, 'Oh, God, no!' that made the waiter withdraw his tray, she began to weave her way through the crowd, her aim nothing more complicated than to put as much space between herself and the tall Italian as was humanly possible. She walked through the first door she came to and found herself in an orangery that was for the moment blissfully empty except for an elderly man with a red nose and large moustache who was dozing in one sunny corner, and the pianist playing the baby grand in one corner of the room.

The pianist smiled at Izzy and glanced towards the sleeping figure before miming an ironic hushing motion with his finger.

Izzy smiled back and set her struggling daughter on the floor, rotating her neck muscles, which ached from a combination of extreme tension plus the extra pounds her growing daughter had gained.

'Careful,' she cautioned absently as Lily grabbed a chair leg and pulled herself to her feet.

Izzy leaned back in the wrought-iron chair and sighed as her daughter eyed a plant several feet away and launched herself towards it, managing half a dozen steps before falling on her well-padded bottom. The startled expression on her face drew a laugh from Izzy.

'Oops!'

Her daughter's lower lip stopped quivering and the tragedy vanished and a moment later she sent her mother a sunny grin and continued across the room on all fours this time. As she watched her progress Izzy's smile faded; she knew she was hiding and that she couldn't continue in this way.

What was she avoiding? She couldn't run away; she had to face him—he was Lily's father. The image of his expression when he had looked at Lily surfaced, the shock and disbelief etched in his strong-boned features still fresh in her mind. She doubted many things in this supremely confident man's life had shaken him, but seeing Lily had.

Izzy suddenly felt an unexpected stab of sympathy for Roman. She had been shocked too, but she had had nine months to get used to the idea of having a child. He'd just had the facts thrust live and kicking under his nose.

God only knew what was going through his mind.

She took a deep calming breath. It felt like the first time she'd really thought clearly since she'd felt herself sinking into those deep dark eyes on that night two years ago.

That one night when she had been someone else, but a night she was reminded of every time she looked at her daughter. Sure, this had been a shock—massive understatement—but might it not also be a positive thing…a good thing? It was a massive disruption of the comfortable status quo she had been enjoying, but surely her daughter having a chance of something she had never had the opportunity to experience was worth some disruption?

'Lily, no!' Izzy raised her voice in warning above the soft piano music in the background.

Her daughter's head turned at the sound of her raised voice, but she did not halt her shuffling progress towards the tall cactus sporting scarlet blooms along its spiky stem that had caught her eye.

Before Izzy or her daughter could reach the spiky cactus the pot was blocked by a tall figure. A frustrated Lily treated the tall figure to a glare and, thrusting out her lower lip, yelled, 'No!'

Izzy took a deep calming breath and scooped up her daughter, sweeping her wriggling and kicking off the floor. 'Her favourite word.'

'She's determined, isn't she?' Roman observed, staring at the red-faced baby who was his daughter—how was it possible? He pushed away the question that had been running on a continual loop since the baby had looked at him.

He had always acknowledged a comment that a baby looked like one parent or the other with a certain degree of polite scepticism. In his, admittedly limited, experience all babies looked much the same with their indistinct unformed features.

He had never had reason to change his mind about this until half an hour ago, but he could have been wrong—he had to be wrong.

Was it coincidental that the subject had been much on his mind since he had updated his will? He had no child to pass his wealth on to but there were good causes and not all of them were females with a taste for designer shoes.

As he had left the lawyer's office the older man had shaken his hand warmly and said with a smile, 'No doubt the next time we see you will be when you marry or have your first child?'

Roman prided himself on focusing his energy on things he could change, not lost causes. Anyone who got to be thirty and didn't realise that life was not fair was either very stupid or very lucky. He was neither, so he had not wasted time bewailing the hand fate had dealt him. He got on with life—a life that would not contain a family. He'd thought he had come to terms with it, but now…?

Had he only been seeing in Lily what he wanted to see? he wondered. Did he imagine the resemblance the child had to his family line? No, he dismissed the possibility almost immediately.

After his parents' deaths he had discovered a box of photographs and one among the dozens of images had been of him on his first birthday. The likeness between that image and Lily was not just striking, it was almost identical.

He'd had sex with her mother and now two years later his mystery woman turned up with a baby who looked impossibly like him. It did not take a genius to do the maths…

'Michelle said that Lily was fourteen months old, but she must be nearly fifteen months…?'

'Fourteen, she was premature.' The long labour had ended in an emergency Caesarean when the baby had become distressed.

The silence stretched between them, broken finally by Roman's hoarse voice. 'Were you ever going to tell me?' He could feel the vibration of a dull roar in his ears as his stunned gaze narrowed and swung her way. She'd had ample opportunity to come clean and she hadn't.

Izzy registered the accusation in his glare and let out a grunt of sheer disbelief. How dared he act like some innocent victim? Presumably he had conveniently absolved himself of all responsibility!

'Telling you was never an option—I didn't know your name.' Hard not to say it out loud without feeling shame.

'You were the one who insisted on anonymity,' he reminded her grimly. She was not the one who had encouraged him to have unprotected sex, though, reminded the voice in his head. In his defence, in a brief moment of sanity he had made an attempt to ask her if she was protected, but it had been an attempt he'd abandoned when she had touched a finger to his lips, encouraging him to be silent. 'And I meant today, or didn't you recognise the father of your child?'

Oh, yeah, because there was more than one man out there that looked like him.

'Oh, so now it's *my* child…' She smiled and had the satisfaction of seeing his jaw clench. 'Make your mind up, Roman.' His flush suggested she had made her point.

'And when was I meant to tell you about her? In the middle of the marriage service perhaps? Or during our delightful walk back here?' she snapped. 'It was kind of hard to get a word in edgewise while you were so charmingly propositioning me. Tell me, does the *I need you* line normally work for you? *I want you, really*?'

'It worked with you. No, I take that back, you were the one that said that, weren't you?'

The seamless comeback sent a flush of shame to Izzy's pale face. 'Look, I know this was a shock for you and I'm trying to make allowances—'

'That's really good of you,' he said in a voice like dry ice.

'Well, one of us has to act like an adult!' she snapped back.

'I'm struggling here, but what exactly is adult about hiding from me?' he drawled sarcastically.

She cast a quick furtive glance over her shoulder. They were alone but for the pianist and the dozing guest, but that situation could not last. 'Yes, I was avoiding you, because I didn't want this sort of public scene. I just knew you'd react like this...' She stopped, the anger fading from her face as she finished. 'Actually I didn't have a clue how you'd react. For all I knew you'd prefer to ignore Lily's existence.'

'And that would have suited you?' He watched the way her expression changed as she glanced towards the happily playing tot, the slow smile that transformed her face.

Izzy hesitated. This was a subject where her opinions were still lurching dramatically from one side of the argument to the other. She voiced the one thing she was sure of, though he might not agree. 'It would have been your loss.'

Roman could not argue with this assessment and quite suddenly he felt his anger towards her dissipate. He was blaming her for something that was not a curse, but a blessing.

'I'm a father… *Madre di Dio…*!' It shouldn't be possible but it was. Roman felt a fresh explosion of wonder but it still didn't fully sink in. 'Did you try and find me?'

'How could I? Where would I have started?' He took a step closer, a tall and overpoweringly male presence that made her feel trapped. She lifted a hand to her throat to cover the pulse she could feel beating there.

'Do I make you nervous, Isabel?' He stepped closer again, his nostrils flaring as the scent of her perfume brought back memories his body responded to hungrily, making him uncomfortably aware of the heaviness in his groin. 'Isabel. I like that name, it suits you…'

His husky voice sent a secret shiver down her spine. Her pale skin was dusted with a layer of perspiration from the effort of concealing her emotional turmoil. 'Not Isabel, Izzy. People call me Izzy.'

'I'm not people.' *I'm the father of your child.*

His facial muscles froze as he fought an internal battle to regain control of his feelings. He focused on the positive: his child would not grow up not knowing he existed.

The sheer breathtaking arrogance of this pronouncement made Izzy blink, and yet it was hardly surprising if he had such a high opinion of himself.

Her eyes drifted over the carved contours of his chiselled cheek to his sensually sculpted mouth and the mole just visible in the carved contours of his cheek. She expelled a long shaky sigh. He was the most handsome man she had ever seen. His charismatic sex appeal was off the scale and his amazing looks must have always made him the focus of attention in any room he occupied.

CHAPTER FOUR

'FOR the record, I'm really not the nervous type.' But Izzy was the type to find Roman's sexual aura of masculinity totally overwhelming. Though that could hardly make her unique; his sexual charisma meant that every woman in the room stared at him.

He had been the one asking the questions but there was one that was troubling Izzy.

'Were you…are you married?'

'It's a bit late to develop a moral conscience.'

She narrowed her eyes. 'Were you?'

'I've never been married, but I had a close shave.'

She was relieved. At least that was one thing she didn't have to feel guilty about, though more from luck than good judgement.

'You got cold feet?' She didn't blame him. The idea of committing to one person for the rest of your life was a scary thought.

He gave a sardonic smile. 'No, I got dumped.'

She waited for the punchline. When it didn't come her eyes widened. 'You're not serious!'

'How good you are for my ego,' he drawled. 'However, not everyone finds me as irresistible as you do.'

His ego was titanium coated, she was sure.

Responding to the tug on her skirt, Izzy bent down and picked up Lily.

'She is a pretty baby.' He softened his voice and said, 'Hello, Lily.'

Responding to her name, Lily reached out, her chubby fingers closing around his pale grey silk tie. Chuckling, she pulled and Roman didn't resist. His face came in close, so close that Izzy could see the fine-pored texture of his skin, the gold tips to his long sooty lashes...smell the cologne that elicited a rush of memories.

'I'm sorry,' Izzy muttered, her face flaming as she tried to unpeel her daughter's fingers from the fabric. She was unable to stop her eyes sliding sideways to his taut aquiline profile and her quiet desperation grew.

Roman could see the stress in the skin stretched tight across the fine bone structure of her face, but felt little sympathy. 'That's something, I suppose.'

Izzy pretended not to hear the muttered comment as her breast brushed his arm. This was not the time or place for any sort of confrontation and she had enough on her plate coping with being this close to him. The scent of his lean, hard body continued to trigger all sorts of memories that she had imagined she had deleted. Heat travelled in a wave over the surface of her skin, causing the silk of her bodice to cling to her damp skin.

'She looks like me.'

Breathing far too hard, actually panting, Izzy gave a grunt of relief as Lily loosened her grip and she took a step backwards. 'At least she missed out on the freckles,' she said, directing her gaze at his crumpled tie.

His hooded gaze moved upwards in a long assessing sweep from her feet and stilled on her face. He felt the kick of desire in his belly and for a moment the strength of the raw physical attraction swamped the anger and resentment he was containing. Barely.

'She's beautiful.'

Normally when anyone commented on her baby's remarkable beauty Izzy glowed with pride. On this occasion she stiffened. 'I know.'

In the periphery of her vision she was aware of a group of laughing guests entering the room, their chatter drowning out that of the pianist playing in the corner. She felt a stab of relief, as Roman surely wouldn't continue this conversation in the middle of a crowd… would he?

She didn't have a clue.

He might be the father of her child, but she didn't know him at all and she had no idea what he was capable of, at least outside the bedroom. The mental addition caused a memory to surface and desire to pound through her blood, pooling hot and achy in her pelvis.

'She looks like you.'

'I have been called many things, but not beautiful.'

If that was true then she was amazed, because he was the epitome of male beauty.

'Is she a happy baby?'

Izzy glimpsed a yearning in his face as he stared at Lily that made her look away quickly, feeling like an intruder.

So far she hadn't spent much time wondering how he was feeling. Anger and suspicion would both be natural responses for a man who realised he had fathered a baby, but was he resenting being landed with a responsibility that he hadn't planned or asked for?

'Look, I know we need to talk, but not here…*please*.'

For a moment she thought he was going to refuse her request, then he nodded and she felt a rush of relief. 'I'm not staying here. I'm in the Fox—do you know it?'

Izzy nodded. The new manager who had been recruited by the boutique hotel had been asking her out on a weekly basis since she'd dined there weeks before. Izzy had not accepted his offer, though she hadn't ruled out the possibility she would in the future. She liked him and, as Emma said, being a mum was not the same as being a nun.

'I know it.'

'I'm in the garden suite. Meet me there at...' his eyes narrowed as he did some mental calculation '...eight tonight.'

Her reaction to the order wrapped up as an invitation was immediate. 'I'm not coming to your room.' She intercepted his look and, lifting her chin, added, 'I'd prefer somewhere more public.'

'I'm not trying to get you into bed.' When was a fling not a fling? He now knew the answer: when it was with the mother of your child.

Izzy matched his sarcasm. 'Imagine my disappointment.'

'Bring the baby if that makes you feel any better,' he suggested, sounding bored.

'I can't. She'll be in bed.'

Roman clenched his jaw. She might be being deliberately obstructive or she might be stating the truth. With his zero knowledge of child care he was in no position to judge. 'All right. Tomorrow morning.'

He watched as she licked her lips and ran the tip of her tongue across the soft plump contours before catching the full lower lip between her white teeth and chewing. She nodded and his heavy eyelids drooped partially, concealing the gleam that had lit them.

'Nine-thirty?' he said, still staring at her mouth. Tomorrow when he'd had time to calm down and get things straight in his head might be better, he told himself. *Who are you fooling...?* It would take a hell of a lot longer to get anything straight. Finding himself face to face with a child who was unmistakeably his had been the most shocking experience of his life, which in itself was quite shocking considering this was a man who had sat in a doctor's office and been given a fifty-fifty chance of surviving to his next birthday.

'The park that the hotel backs onto, I walk there with—' Izzy broke off, bending her head as she winced and began to free the strands from the tenacious little fingers that had grabbed her hair. 'No, Lily, that hurts.'

The baby ignored the plea, seemingly fascinated by the glossy mesh of her mother's hair as she sank her chubby fingers deeper. Roman could identify with the fascination. He could remember burying his face in the soft, sweet-smelling chestnut waves, feeling them whisper across his chest and belly as she'd slid down his body. He inhaled and pushed the thought away, but not before his body had hardened helplessly in response to the image. 'Let me...' he husked.

'No!' She jerked her head back, causing her eyes to fill with tears of pain as her daughter's little hand came free with several strands of her hair.

Roman's hand fell away in a gesture of exaggerated surrender. 'Anyone would think you're afraid of me.' The idea bothered him more than a little.

Her chin tilted an extra defiant inch. 'I'm not afraid of you.' More afraid, quite irrationally, of herself.

Crazy! It wasn't as if his touch were going to turn her
into some wild, wanton creature with a moral compass
wildly out of whack.

He'd kissed her and she had walked away. *Round of
applause, Izzy.*

'Just one thing I need to know.' He hadn't intended
to ask, but it was out there now and a man had a right
to know if he'd been used.

'Did you do it on purpose?'

She looked at him, her blue eyes narrowed, her
smooth brow creased in furrows of incomprehension.
'Do what?'

'Get pregnant,' he said bluntly.

The possibility had not occurred to him until the wedding breakfast, when he had been seated at a table with
his old friend Gianni Fitzgerald and his lovely wife.
Roman had struggled to tune out the slightly tipsy
woman sitting opposite him without being outright rude
and her anecdotes had become more scurrilous as the
interminable meal had gone on.

He had managed tolerably well until he'd heard the
name of Michael Fitzgerald's older daughter mentioned
and after that he had unashamedly egged the woman on.

'Of course, Michael was young and this woman was a
real man hater. She never told him she wanted a baby…
planned it all in cold blood.' The woman, speaking behind her hand, had paused for dramatic effect or possibly
to catch her breath before continuing. 'But it's Michelle
I feel sorry for. Of course, she puts on a brave face, but
to have the girl living in the village! And now there's
the baby and no father, it makes you think, maybe it's
a family tradition…?'

Her laugh had been cut off when Gianni had at this

point picked up on the conversation and intervened, closing down his garrulous relative smoothly, but not before the seed of suspicion had been planted in Roman's brain.

The blood drained from Izzy's face as his meaning sank in. She gave a shrug, choking back the anger and glancing over her shoulder to make sure their conversation wasn't being overheard.

'For the record, no, I did *not* plan to get pregnant. And if I had been looking for a perfect genetic specimen to father my child I would not,' she gritted through clenched teeth, 'have chosen one who thinks he's God's gift…an arrogant, humourless, bossy idiot who—'

'You have forgotten the limp,' he drawled, cutting off her diatribe.

Izzy threw up her hands in angry exasperation. 'I don't give a damn about your limp.' And neither did any woman she had seen today, she thought, recalling the lustful female stares that seemed to follow his progress. 'But I wouldn't deliberately lumber my kid with a dad as stupid as you are. I always thought that when I had a child it would be with someone who—'

She took a deep breath and, aware of the curious glances their impassioned exchange was receiving, she lowered her voice to a husky murmur and added, 'I didn't plan anything. I was…' Her eyes fell. 'I don't normally…'

'Jump into bed with a total stranger?'

The interjection brought a flush of shamed anger to her cheeks. 'I really don't think you're in any position to occupy the moral high ground…or is it different for men?' she snipped back sarcastically.

His face darkened with annoyance. 'This is not about blame.'

She elevated a delicate brow. 'Just as well, because from where I'm standing you don't come off very white-knight-on-a-charger in all this.'

Roman watched her walk away, the child in her arms, her narrow back straight and proud. She was right: he was in no position to throw stones; his behaviour had been totally indefensible. So he had genuinely believed that there was no chance of him getting her pregnant, but, unwanted pregnancies aside, unprotected sex with a stranger made him criminally stupid.

It made him the man he had always despised. Someone so selfish he was unable to think about anything beyond his own pleasure.

CHAPTER FIVE

For the sake of her sanity, when Izzy left the reception she blocked everything out and tried to think of nothing beyond a quiet night at home with Lily. She had to try and regroup and get her head back together. Tomorrow would be time enough to worry about what she was going to say to Roman Petrelli.

That was the plan, but as with most best laid plans it went sadly awry.

Izzy's went wrong in a major way the moment she opened the door of her cottage and found Michelle and her father standing there.

'I had to tell him,' Michelle said.

Izzy sighed. 'Of course.'

It was after midnight before they left and at least by the time they had left her father was no longer planning to confront Roman Petrelli.

Izzy was touched that he wanted to protect her but she struggled with the idea of anyone fighting her battles for her, having always been taught not to rely on anyone but herself.

On the other hand she had been grateful for the help her father had provided when Lily had been born. It had been Michael who had suggested she stay permanently in Cumbria with them—after all they were her family.

Izzy had been touched by the offer, but she could think of no surer way to destroy the delicate new relationship she had found with her new family than imposing herself on them with her new baby. Besides, Izzy needed her own space too.

It had been Michelle who had come up with the compromise that they could all live with, and Izzy had moved into the cottage on the edge of the village a mile or so from the family farmhouse where her half-brother and -sister had spent their childhoods.

It was hard sometimes not to contrast their lives with her own. Her mother had taught her some valuable things like independence and self-reliance, but had not taught her about casual physical demonstrations of affection or the teasing that went with life in a close-knit family group.

But despite the acceptance of the family Izzy still felt an outsider at times. Not because they excluded her, but because she recognised a need to maintain her own distance.

But living in the cottage she was close enough to enjoy the support of her new family and far enough away to maintain her independence, and it gave everyone the space they needed.

After her father and Michelle had finally gone Izzy went to bed herself, but she slept badly. But it wasn't a hunting owl or a fox that had kept her awake or even the darkness. It was the thought of meeting Roman Petrelli this morning.

Lily, normally a fairly sunny baby, seemed to have picked up on her mother's mood and was cranky this morning too. She had taken hours to eat her breakfast and had fought every step of the way Izzy's attempts to dress her. By the time she was finally ready to leave, a good ten minutes later than planned, Izzy felt drained.

Glancing in the hall mirror, she saw that she looked even worse than she felt, with violet smudges darkening the underneath of her eyes.

Izzy was tempted to dash back inside to at least apply some blusher to alleviate her sleep-deprived pallor and give her confidence a bit of a boost, but she had no time. Instead she manufactured a smile for her reflection and reminded herself that Roman probably wouldn't notice her less than yummy-mummy appearance and so what? She wasn't out to impress him anyway.

A brisk walk up the hill meant she wasn't pale when she arrived at the hotel, her cheeks flushed with the exertion of pushing the buggy.

As she struggled to push it across the gravel forecourt a tall figure emerged from the side of the building. Unlike yesterday she was prepared for his appearance, but even so her heart started pounding like a hammer and her knees started to tremble.

'I'm sorry I'm late.' The breathless quiver was, she told herself, nothing to do with the fact that he radiated an aura of raw masculinity—he really was breathtaking!

'No matter.' His dark glance slid to the sleeping child and he tried to analyse the emotions that tightened like a fist in his chest. Once he had taken having a child for granted. Now it seemed more miracle.

'Would you like a coffee?'

'Actually it might be a good idea to walk and talk. Lily will wake up if I stop pushing her and she's quite cranky this morning.'

They did walk but there was no talk.

She endured the silent attrition for ten minutes, during which time her apprehension had increased tenfold until she could bear it no more.

They had reached the footpath that circled the lake when Izzy had had enough. 'Let's sit, shall we?'

Roman tilted his head. 'Fine.' With one hand in the small of her back he guided her towards one of the benches beside the lake.

Izzy sat down, resisting the impulse that made her want to shuffle to the far end when Roman sat down beside her. He was a man with an overpowering presence and the sort of sexual charisma she had thought was an invention of romantic fiction.

He took a bag out of the pocket of his long black trench coat and tipped the contents on the ground, giving an awkward grimace when he caught her astonished stare. 'I bought some food for the ducks. I thought Lily might like...?' He nodded to the sleeping child.

'That's very thoughtful of you,' she said. 'She's tired...and it's probably easier to talk without...'

She stopped and raised her voice above the squawks of the ducks who had mobbed them. 'I have to be back by twelve. Emma is picking Lily up. She goes back to university tomorrow and she wants to spend some time with her.' Her half-sister was a doting aunt.

A nerve clenched in Roman's lean cheek as he turned to look at her. 'So do I.'

His direct stare brought a flush to her cheeks. 'Oh, of course...I didn't think...'

'She's my daughter.' If he said it out loud often enough it might start to feel more real.

Izzy nodded tightly.

Roman swallowed and dug his fingers deep into the dark pelt of hair on his head.

'I appreciate all this must be a shock for you.'

Roman's hand fell away, leaving his sleek hair standing up in spiky tufts on his scalp. 'Shock!' He gave a twisted smile and laughed. 'You have no idea.' He stretched out his long legs in front of him and loosened the button on his coat, the fabric parting to reveal the dark cashmere sweater he wore underneath.

Izzy felt the muscles in her stomach quiver. He really was an extraordinarily attractive man.

'I thought Lily was a grumbling appendix until I was six months pregnant.'

Her attempt to inject a note of levity—good timing never had been her strong point—was greeted with an incredulous stare. 'Seriously?'

'No, not seriously.' She had known immediately, even before she'd done the test. She had simply felt different.

He turned his head. 'I never thought I'd have a child.' He still struggled to get his head around the idea.

So children did not figure in the glamorous life of this man. No real surprise there—it was hard to imagine him welcoming grubby fingerprints on his shirt.

'I suppose not everyone likes children.'

She felt herself relax slightly. Was that what this meeting was about—a warning to tell her not to expect him to be a hands-on parent? He needn't have worried; she didn't need or want anything from him. As far as she was concerned her daughter had all the positive male role models she needed.

'I'll let you know how Lily is, a yearly update if you like.' He was looking at her oddly so she shrugged and added, 'Or not.' Then looked away because those spooky silver lights deep in his dark eyes made her feel dizzy.

Had she assumed too much? Did he want to walk away and act as though nothing had happened?

'Though it would be useful to know if there is any significant medical history on your side…?' This practicality was the reason her mother had decided to give her the details of her biological father, in case after she was gone Izzy found herself in a situation where such information would be useful.

His thick, strongly defined sable brows knitted together as he stared at her as though she were talking gibberish. 'I didn't say I didn't like children. Actually I don't know any.'

Unlike the large and noisy Fitzgerald clan, he had been an only child and there had been no cousins to play with. His parents, madly in love and totally wrapped up in one another, had never intended to have children, and resented the intrusion of a third party, and at an early age Roman had been shipped off to school. He hadn't minded. He'd liked school, excelling academically and at sports, though not team sports—Roman with his lone-wolf tendencies had never been a team player.

'Though I was one myself once,' he added with a half-smile.

'You don't have brothers or sisters…?' Izzy asked and he shook his head. 'Neither do I, but then I'm sure the grapevine gossip told you that.'

Instead of reacting to the charge he picked up on the previous statement. 'Actually I was told that I couldn't have children, or at any rate it would be unlikely.'

But unlikely had happened, a miracle had happened.

Did she really think he'd be content with yearly updates on his child's life?

Izzy was confused by his admission. She knew he was not impotent so that left what…?

'Three years ago I had chemo.' He offered the additional information in the manner of a casual afterthought.

Her eyes flew to his face 'You're ill?' Beneath the calm surface Izzy could feel the ice forming…counting, she waited for the next breath. 'You're not dying? God, no!' She took a deep breath, let it out in a long hissing sigh and made a struggling attempt to breach the social chasm that had opened up at her feet.

His broad shoulders lifted in a fluid shrug. 'We are all dying, *cara*.'

Izzy, conscious that her knees were shaking, flashed him a dark look, annoyed that he was making light of a subject that was anything but. 'You know what I mean.'

He conceded the point. 'I had the all-clear, but surgery…well, you saw the scars.'

He watched as she closed her eyes, her long curling lashes fluttering like butterfly wings. Her eyelids lifted. 'Well, you might have said that straight off instead…'

'Sorry.'

Two years ago he had been in remission and the doctors had been cautiously optimistic, explaining that if he went another two years then his chances of suffering the disease were no more than those of any other member of the population. If it did return then worst-case scenario would be to amputate the leg.

Roman touched his leg now at the thought. The metal inserted to replace the diseased section might give him pain and preclude him enjoying some of the athletic pursuits he once had, but it was a hell of a lot better than the alternative!

He had cheated death, but for a while it could just have easily gone the other way. Life was that fragile. Not that he had dwelt on the possibility of death for long. What would have been the point? Such things were out of his hands and if he had learnt anything from the experience it was not to waste time worrying about things over which you had no control.

Izzy released the breath she had not been aware of holding. 'You were awfully young for...'

'Cancer? Yes, I was twenty-eight.'

God, so young at a time when a man like Roman would think he was invincible. 'But they must have...I mean, don't they...freeze your...?'

'Are my future children in a test tube in some laboratory somewhere?' His eyes flashed as she blushed and nodded.

'Yes, but due to a technical glitch they got thawed prematurely.'

Her eyes widened. 'That's terrible! You said you were dumped. Is that why...?'

'The beautiful Lauren gave me back my ring? Actually she kept the ring, but, no, she was fine with the idea of a baby-free life. Unfortunately, I made the mistake of admitting to her that if the cancer returned then there was the possibility that they might have to amputate my leg. Poor Lauren couldn't stand the idea of being stuck with a cripple.'

Izzy's contempt for this woman knew no bounds.

'She sounds like a total and complete idiot!' she fumed, wondering if underneath the cynical, amused façade he wasn't still in love with this prize bitch.

Probably—men had no judgement when it came to beautiful women.

She caught him looking at her oddly and added quickly, 'I'd have thought they'd have had all sorts of backups to prevent that kind of thing from happening?'

'They do, but they also have human error.' The sympathy in her wide clear eyes was genuine, as was the dismay when he added, 'Lily might be my one chance to be a father and I intend to be fully involved in her life.'

Fully involved. The words made her uncomfortable. 'I get that…I see, but I'm sure you'll have your own family.'

'I already have a family.'

'We're not…' Izzy took a deep breath and forced herself to speak more moderately. 'In what way, fully?' she asked, struggling not to sound defensive and knowing she hadn't succeeded.

Roman held her eyes and set out his intentions so that there was no chance of her misunderstanding. 'In every way…'

He saw her blue eyes flicker and the muscles beneath the pale skin of her throat ripple as she swallowed, probably wondering what he knew about being a father. But what did he know about being a father?

Refusing to acknowledge the rare voice of silent self-doubt, Roman pushed it away.

'I hope you'll help me.' Roman felt he was being pretty fair given the circumstances, but he would learn with or without her help. 'I've already missed out on the first months of her life.' Roman stifled the resentment that made the muscle in his cheek clench. What was important, he reminded himself, was the future.

'And for that you blame me.'

'I'm trying hard not to.' But her attitude was making it increasingly difficult; she was so spiky and damned confrontational.

Sensitive to the thread of accusation in his voice, Izzy raised her chin. She was perfectly willing to take responsibility for her part. She'd had sex with a stranger and had got pregnant—not something she was proud of—but she hadn't done so alone.

'I realise it might be difficult for you to share Lily...'

Her eyes widened and she shifted uncomfortably in her seat. Holding the buggy handle, she used her free hand to lift the collar of her jacket against the chill breeze that was blowing.

'And why the name Lily?' Roman asked, looking at the sleeping child.

'Why. Don't you like it?'

The suggestion of a smile vanished from his sensual lips as he turned his attention back to Izzy. 'Do you have to be so defensive? Look, if you want a fight I can do that,' he said, now visibly exasperated.

'Of course I don't.'

'Actually, I like the name...' A name he had had no part in choosing. He pushed away the thought and the anger that came with it.

'Roman, I would have told you about her, but I had no idea how to contact you.' She gave a laugh to hide her embarrassment and managed to inject a note of rueful amusement into her voice as she added, 'I didn't even know your name.'

'You could have hung around to find out.'

'When I woke up you were gone.' Izzy closed her eyes, feeling the familiar sick churning of shame and self-disgust in her stomach as she relived the moment she'd realised that her lover of the previous night had not waited for her to wake up.

That had been the grim reality for her in the early hours of the morning after she had fallen asleep in the arms of her lover, believing this was perhaps the start of a love affair between two people destined to be together.

Even the memory embarrassed her now.

Now she knew it had just been sex. Casual sex.

'I'd only gone across the road to...' Izzy shrugged and lowered her gaze, still able to recall the guilt and self-disgust she had felt when she had woken up in that strange room alone. She intended never to forget it.

'It doesn't matter now, Roman. It was such a long time ago.'

'And you have so many meaningless affairs that you might have me mixed up with someone else?'

'Hardly an affair,' she countered calmly. 'More a one-night stand.'

'I have no taste for semantics.'

'Well, I like things to be clear...and clearly I'm not your family.'

'You're the mother of my child. That makes you my family.'

Izzy's teeth clenched in frustration as she watched his dark eyes follow a young woman wheeling a pushchair along a path that ran parallel to the lake. She released a hissing sigh and dragged a hand down her cheek, tucking the stray shiny strands of hair behind her ear.

'You can visit Lily any time you like.'

'I don't want to visit Lily.' His dark eyes held hers as he dropped the bombshell so casually that she barely heard it go off. 'I want to watch her grow up. I want to help her with her homework. I don't want to visit her—I want to live with her. Support her…'

'I support her. I've been supporting her for the past fourteen months.'

'How?'

His scepticism irritated the hell out of her.

'What do you want—a report? A letter from my bank manager or my CV?' She gave a snort at his expression.

'You work? You're an academic like your mother?'

'No, I'm not an academic.'

His brow lifted. 'Have I touched a nerve?'

'No, you have not touched a nerve!' she yelled, then, encountering the ironic glitter in his eyes, bit her lip. 'I did an interior design course at college and got a place with Urquarts.'

'Impressive. It must have been hard to leave.'

'How do you know I've left?'

'You are living in Cumbria,' he pointed out. 'Not really commutable distance.'

'Oh, yes…well, actually I've done a couple of small commissions the past few months on a self-employed basis… It's simply a matter of juggling.' Ten balls in the air but she wasn't about to admit to him how difficult it was.

'It is wise, no doubt, for you to keep your hand in, considering how hard it will be for you to get your feet back on the career ladder, but I'm sure you already know that.'

'It is possible to have a career and be a mother.'

'Of course it is.'

Her eyes narrowed. 'Are you patronising me?' she asked in a dangerous voice.

His dark brows lifted. 'I am admiring you. Clearly

if you got a job with Urquarts you are good at what you do and ambitious…?'

Izzy responded to his quizzical look with a blank expression, determined not to give him any ammunition to use against her.

'It is good for a woman to be ambitious and stimulated by her work, but the balancing act will be much easier to achieve when you have support…when you are not living alone.'

Izzy just stared at him for a speechless moment. Had he heard a thing she had said? Finally shaking her head, she surged to her feet. 'That isn't going to happen. Lily lives with me…she needs me…I need her… no…no…no!'

She reminded him of a tigress defending her young as she positioned herself between him and the buggy. 'Calm down. I'm not trying to take Lily off you. There are ways around this.'

She folded her arms across her chest. 'Amaze me.'

'We both want to live with Lily, so the obvious solution would be to cohabit. Another option we should not discount out of hand, of course, is marriage…a definite possibility.'

Izzy stared at him and thought, *My God, he's insane! My baby's father is a lunatic. Marriage, he actually said marriage!*

'You're joking, right?'

'I'm deadly serious.'

Izzy grabbed the buggy. 'Just keep away from me and Lily.'

'You're being very emotional about this.'

'Too right,' she said, turning the buggy around.

He rose with a curse. 'Look, you're not letting me

explain this properly. You're not going to deny that a child needs two parents.'

'Not if one of them is insane.'

'When I said marriage I was simply referring to a contractual arrangement, not a romantic one.'

'Love and marriage, now who ever heard of such a crazy idea? It'll never catch on.'

'I'm thinking of Lily. Who are you thinking of?' he yelled after her, smiling despite himself when without turning she made a rude gesture over her shoulder.

'I'll be back!'

She did turn then, yelling, 'I've heard it before and the other guy was much more impressive.'

CHAPTER SIX

THE only person Izzy had confided in was Michelle, whom she described the conversation to over coffee and cakes the next morning.

She laughed about it and made it sound like a joke but in truth she was really anxious. Would he try and take Lily from her?

Then Michelle reacted in a way Izzy had never anticipated and instead of condemning Roman she actually defended him.

'Well, I'm not saying it wasn't over the top, but at least he isn't trying to dodge his responsibilities, which a lot of men in this situation would, you know. Did he actually propose? It's actually rather romantic when you think about it...'

'Well, not actually propose in so many words,' Izzy admitted. 'And believe me, it *wasn't* romantic.'

'So has he been in touch since yesterday?'

'No, and he's booked out of the Fox.' Izzy hoped she had seen the last of Roman Petrelli...didn't she?

Later that day Izzy was interrupted from her power walking back home by her phone ringing. Chest heaving, she stopped to pull the phone from her pocket halfway up the steep country lane. The calm objectivity she was trying to exhaust herself into still eluded her.

Roman's *I'll be back* threat still haunted her.

It was all about what he wanted, and, yes, today he wanted to be a father, but what did he know about being a parent? Nothing, he had said as much himself, and would he be equally enthusiastic when the novelty of the situation wore off?

'Yes!' she breathed into the phone.

'Izzy, is that you?' Layla, the owner of the interior design agency she had worked for straight from college, sounded startled...and small wonder.

Izzy took a deep breath. 'Yes, Layla...sorry, I was just...'

Layla as always got straight to the point. 'I've got a job for you, a big job. It's perfect, it's... I've got it down somewhere, but it's in the middle of the country—you like the country, darling.'

'That sounds great, Layla, and I appreciate you thinking of me, but until Lily is older and at school it's difficult. The commission in Keswick last month was great, but anything bigger...?' The older woman had continued to put some part-time commissions her way and Izzy was grateful.

'Oh, I didn't think about you, darling—the client specifically requested you.'

'Me?'

'Seems like he saw the Dublin town-house project you worked on before Lily was born—did you know it was on the market? Anyhow, apparently he was blown away.'

Izzy felt a stab of pride. She had been pretty pleased with the project herself. 'So the client is Irish?'

'Not a clue, darling.'

Izzy frowned and glared at the nail she had just caught herself nibbling before thrusting her hand in her pocket. 'So you don't actually know who this client is?'

'What does that matter? A film star, a royal, an oil-rich sheikh—he won't be there. Apparently there's just a skeleton staff. The point is he's got pots of money, expense is no object and he'll give you a free hand.'

'Free hand? There must be a remit?'

'Nope. He's apparently willing to put himself entirely in your hands. The only stipulation is that it is a suitable family home to take his bride to...lucky girl. Oh, yes, it is a he.'

'It sounds too good to be true...' Izzy found herself almost hoping that there would be a catch; it would make it easier to justify refusing it.

It wasn't that she regretted her decision to take a career break, but the sense of guilt she felt lingered.

Her own mother had worked up until the day before Izzy's birth and had returned to work two weeks after. She had always encouraged ambition in her daughter and instilled the importance of having a career and being independent, and she would have been appalled that Izzy had taken even a temporary career break to look after her baby.

Ironically it was thanks to her mother that Izzy was financially able to take time off at all to spend with Lily. Izzy was still receiving healthy royalties cheques from her mother's successful writing career.

'A gig like this could make your career, Izzy.'

'True.' And two years ago Izzy would have jumped at the golden opportunity. 'And I appreciate the offer, but the timing's not right,' she said firmly.

'Is this about leaving Lily? Because, you know, you don't have to. Part of the remit is to make the place child friendly, not just a show house—a family home. Lily could be your guinea pig!'

'Really?' Izzy's thoughts raced. That did put a different slant on it.

'I'd say go and think it over but the only problem is—'

'I knew this was too good to be true.'

'They want you to start immediately.'

'How immediately?'

'Right away…as in tomorrow.'

Izzy was shaking her head. Organising Lily for a trip to the local supermarket took her an hour. 'Well, that's just not…' She stopped, an arrested expression stealing across her face as she thought, *What am I doing?*

Suddenly she felt her excitement growing. Far from being bad timing, this could actually be perfect timing! 'Tomorrow?'

'You'll take it…' The relief in the older woman's voice was unmistakeable.

'Where is this place?'

'Oh, you won't need directions,' Layla replied when Izzy asked for the address and a contact number. 'There will be a car to pick you up at the station. It couldn't be simpler. Just let me know what train you'll be on and I'll pass on the details. And don't forget to keep your receipts. The client is willing to pay all travel expenses and I didn't even have to ask.'

Simple—if she didn't already know that Layla was childless this phrase would have cleared up any confusion, Izzy decided as she disembarked from the train with a baby buggy and her baggage.

She felt hot and sticky as Lily's beaker of juice had spilled down her linen trousers. On the plus side the stain distracted from the creases in her trousers and she decided that linen had perhaps not been the best choice. But she had wanted to make a good first impression and the wide-legged trousers teamed with her favourite silk shirt had seemed to say professional competence. Ah, well, fingers crossed her new client was not someone who judged by appearances.

It wasn't until she exited the railway station that it occurred to Izzy she had no idea where she was going, let alone who was picking her up. A situation a normal person could be relaxed about, but not one with a baby.

As she manoeuvred the buggy laden with bags she saw a silver four-wheel drive taking up several parking spaces. As she approached the door opened and a man wearing a dark suit got out from the massive car with blacked-out windows.

The man did not hesitate, but approached her directly. 'Miss Fitzgerald?'

Her brows rose. She hadn't been expecting the strong Italian accent. 'Yes, that's me.' She tipped her head in acknowledgement and nodded, registering the width of his shoulders. 'How did you know?'

The man removed his dark glasses and shot out a hand to stop the holdall balanced on top of her case from falling to the ground.

'The boss described you.'

Presumably a woman with a baby.

'Here, I've got it,' he added, taking the buggy she

had lifted Lily from and snapping it closed with an expert action.

'You look like an expert, Mr...?'

'Gennaro, miss, just Gennaro. Grandchildren,' he added by way of explanation.

'Hello, Gennaro, and thank you,' she added as he tossed the heavier of her suitcases into the boot space beside the buggy with impressive ease. Those shoulders were not just for show, it seemed.

He flashed her what she presumed passed as a smile in his world, but might have been a grimace. The man had a face that made a granite rock face look expressive.

'Is it far?' Izzy asked as she settled herself in the back seat. Lily was strapped securely into a baby seat beside her, her lavishly lashed eyes already closing.

The driver glanced at her in the rear-view mirror. His shades were back in place. 'No.'

Izzy didn't press him for more information, partly because he was negotiating rush-hour traffic through a busy market town and partly because he did not look a man who wanted to chat. She leaned back in her seat and decided to enjoy the journey.

Once they had left the town behind the countryside in this area proved pretty. As she gazed at the passing scenery her thoughts began to wander into territory she had been avoiding.

Would Roman have fulfilled his threat of 'I'll be back'—expecting her to give ground? What would he do when he discovered she was gone?

The thoughts going through her mind made Izzy frown. She chewed her lip and tried to summon some of the defiant certainty that she had begun the journey with.

Relax, she told herself. *This is the right thing to do.* Annoyed that she felt the need to justify her actions, she shook her head and with a spurt of defiance said out loud, 'What could he do?'

Embarrassed, she looked around. Lily was still sleeping, her face flushed, and the driver gave no hint of having heard her, concentrating hard on the road ahead.

Izzy lowered her rigid body back into the leather seat, not realising until that moment how knotted the muscles in her neck and spine were.

Your trouble, Izzy, she told herself, *is that you worry too much and have a tendency to overanalyse.*

She had taken a job, not made a life-changing decision! True, she would feel better about it if her father and Michelle had not expressed their concerns over her decision to take the job, or at least the timing.

They had reluctantly agreed to her request not to give Roman any information about her whereabouts if he asked. In retrospect she could see that it was unfair of her to put them in that position. This was her problem, not theirs.

As her mum would have said, *Your mess, Izzy, you clean it up.* And she'd have been right.

Izzy exhaled a long gusty sigh, finally acknowledging the voice in the back of her mind she'd been trying very hard not to hear all day. When she rang the farm this evening to give them the address as promised, Izzy decided she would tell them they didn't have to lie for her. She leaned back in her seat, feeling some of the tension leave her shoulder blades. She felt a lot better having made that decision.

She would contact Roman herself and explain the situation. She recognised the real risk he'd come rushing down here throwing around his ultimatums and trying to take over her life, but it was one she felt she had to take. He did have a right to know where his daughter was.

She chewed her lip, fretfully gnawing at the soft flesh. Running away from her problems was just so not her. It made her seem…spineless, but the timing of the perfect job offer when she had been feeling so cornered by Roman had been too much of a temptation.

Well, the job was still perfect and on the plus side it might make Roman see her in a different light. This was an opportunity to show him she could have a career and be a good mother, that the two were not mutually exclusive. She needed to establish from the outset that she wasn't someone he could push around.

Izzy spent the next fifteen minutes of the journey working out what she would say to him, mentally rewriting and editing the conversation in her head, anticipating all his comments and coming up with some killer comebacks. By the time the car pulled off the highway and onto a long straight driveway lined with copper beeches she was confident that she had made her argument forcibly but in a calm, reasonable way.

And she would not make the mistake of apologising. Roman was the sort of man who equated apology with weakness. She had a perfect right to take a job without consulting him and she would make that quite clear.

As they reached the rise in the drive she leaned forward, looking through the windscreen anticipating seeing a house, but the drive just stretched on bounded either side by parkland grazed by sheep and a few cattle. 'Are we here?'

'Next bend you'll see it.'

Izzy sat up straighter in her seat, holding on to the

door as the four-wheel drive negotiated a wooden bridge. 'Does all this land belong to the house? Oh, my goodness!'

'*Sì*, it is a bit of a dump,' came the dour response to her amazed gasp.

Izzy couldn't decide from his expression if he was joking or not because the dump he spoke of was an enormous golden-stoned mansion.

Izzy took a deep breath. 'It's beautiful.' Actually beautiful did not do the building justice; it was stunning, with mullioned windows and mellow golden stone— totally breathtaking!

Gennaro brought the car to a halt on the gravelled area in front of the house. 'The boss said—'

'Where is…?' Gennaro pulled open his door and she raised her voice, adding, 'When will I be meeting him and his wife?'

It was fine by her if the elusive clients did not want to be hands-on, but, as she had told Layla, it was essential that she at least meet them. Her job was not about ticking off a list of requirements or filling a place with the current fashionable must haves; a home had to reflect a person's personality.

'The boss isn't married—'

Izzy frowned as the man crunched around to her side. 'But I thought…' She accepted the hand he offered as she jumped down.

'And I'd say you're about to meet him.' In response to Izzy's questioning frown, he nodded his head to a point behind her. 'Here he is now. Don't worry about the baby. I'll get her out.'

Izzy turned around to face the direction the burly Italian indicated in time to see a tall, lithe figure vaulting over the six-bar gate that kept the sheep from stray-ing into the garden.

'Oh, my God!' Izzy felt as if a giant hand had pushed into her chest and for several heart-thudding moments she literally couldn't breathe. *How do I get out of here?*

Roman, seemingly oblivious to her state of near col-lapse, walked straight up to the older man, who nod-ded and removed his shades. 'Any problems, Gennaro?'

'No, boss, the train was actually on time.' Gennaro unfastened the baby seat complete with baby and lifted it out.

'I'll take that.'

Izzy watched, too stunned to protest, as Roman took hold of the baby carrier.

'Should I take the bags up?'

'If you would. Oh, and could you ask Mrs Saunders to send some coffee through to the library, and maybe some sandwiches? Then I won't be needing either of you until tomorrow.'

Gennaro nodded his thanks at Roman and tacked something on the end of his conversation in Italian that made Roman laugh.

Izzy wasn't laughing.

She wasn't even capable of acknowledging Gennaro's nod as, with a case under each arm, he walked up the shal-low flight of steps towards the open front door.

'Good trip, Isabel?'

He spoke as though this was a prearranged meeting, which of course it was—only she hadn't been kept in the loop. She had stepped right into the trap he'd so cleverly baited. He knew exactly what her weakness was; she'd told him about her guilt at being a stay-at-home mum even if she could afford it financially. And he had sown the seeds of doubt when he had suggested that it might not be so easy to step back into the job market after a lengthy break. This was the set-up to end all set-ups!

Why hadn't she seen it coming? The too-good-to-be-true offer…why hadn't she smelt a rat?

Possibly because she wasn't twisted and sneaky. She wanted to laugh or throw something at him or both. Instead she stood like a rabbit caught in the headlights, thinking, *Any moment now I'll wake up and realise this was all a dream—a nightmare.*

'So what do you think?' he asked, gesturing towards the building behind them, but looking at Izzy.

She shivered at his voice. The dictionary would sound like an indecent proposal when read in that deep, husky, dangerously seductive timbre.

'This is your house.'

'I knew you'd get there eventually, *cara*.' He watched the two spots of angry colour appear on her smooth cheeks. 'So, what's your opinion…professionally speaking? Does it have potential?'

'Professionally?' she echoed, thinking very unprofessional thoughts as she fixed him with a murderous glare. Just how long was he going to insult her by pretending this job offer was anything but an elaborate hoax?

'I realise it's all subjective, but do you like the place? Could you see yourself—?'

'I can see myself pushing you off a cliff!'

She sucked in a deep breath, causing Roman's glance to drop. Having a baby changed a woman's body and though Izzy was lighter and more fragile-looking than he recalled, her breasts were definitely fuller. His eyes darkened as he remembered how one had fitted per-

fectly in the palm of his hand. Now they would over-
flow, the soft, silky, milk-pale flesh… He took a deep
breath and pushed away the tactile image, but not before his body had hardened helplessly.

His sculpted lips twisted in a smile of self-mockery.
For some reason around this woman his normal iron
self-control took a holiday. What was it about her? It
wasn't as if she were overtly sexual. She had a great
body, as he knew only too well, but she didn't flaunt it.
Look at the way she was dressed today, the shirt but-
toned up to the neck, baggy creased trousers, and not a
scrap of make-up. It was something elusive and intan-
gible about her that, like smoke, defied his attempts to
pin it down, control it.

As he scanned her tense features he wondered why
he looked at her and saw something different from everyone else… How many times at that damned wedding
had he heard her referred to as serene?

She had not been serene that night they had spent together. He saw an image of her sitting astride him, her
smooth thighs locked tight around his hips, her head
thrown back and the sheen of sweat making her pale
skin glisten in the darkness. She didn't look serene right
now either; she looked like an exhausted young mother
who had just received a nasty shock.

A beautiful but exhausted young mother. It would
take more than lines of exhaustion bracketing her soft
full mouth and dark shadows under her stunning blue
eyes to diminish her looks.

He was in part at least responsible for putting the
shadows there, he thought, and pushed away the stab
of unaccustomed guilt. This was a situation that needed
resolving. He had already missed out on the first pre-

cious months of his daughter's life and he was not going to miss out on the next while they bargained out a deal.

'Sorry, no cliff, but you could always improvise.' She liked to project the cool and calm image, but he had caught her off guard and people revealed more of themselves when they were off guard.

Izzy felt her anger drain away and with it her taste for this conversation. After all the heart racing she felt horribly flat. 'You got me here, but what I don't understand is why you went to all this effort. Did you really expect me to stay? I'm taking Lily home, but don't think I won't send you the bill for this wasted journey, because I will!'

Even while she was hating him, at another level she was noticing the shadow of purple-black growth on his jaw and lean cheeks, the air of restless male vitality he exuded and how incredibly sexy he looked in the black jeans that clung to the long, muscular lines of his powerful thighs.

'Why not look around first? You might like what you see,' he drawled.

Izzy, refusing to acknowledge his reference to her drooling contemplation of his lean, muscle-packed body, met his knowing gaze with a defiant glare.

'Think of my home as your own.'

Home had a permanent sound and Roman had never actually had a home as such. He had over the years owned various properties because he liked the space and privacy and hotel suites gave little of either.

The only home he had known had been the town house near the university where his parents had worked and lived during term time, but his recollection of it was dim. Vacations had been spent on various digs in various far-flung corners of the globe, and when he was small he had been dragged along but usually left in the hotel room.

Then as he'd got older and bigger he had spent his summers either staying with friends' families or with a distant aunt of his father's in Tuscany.

'I thought you lived in Italy.'

'I do for a large part of the year, but recent developments make it necessary for me to have a British base, and I have never thought that the city is the best place to bring up a child.'

Izzy maintained her scepticism and filed away the statement to deal with later. Any spare energy she had was being used to stay upright. 'So you just popped out yesterday and bought this place?'

'Obviously not.'

A tiny gurgling sound quickly escaped Izzy's throat. The surprises just kept coming. *Roll with the punches, Izzy,* she told herself. *Tomorrow this will all be a memory.*

'I've owned it for…' he screwed up his eyes and glanced back at the building as he made the mental calculations '…two, almost three years now?'

Her sapphire eyes regarded him with disbelief. 'You're asking me?' How could a person own somewhere like this and not know how long they'd owned it for? If she had needed proof that Roman Petrelli lived in a different world than she did, she had it.

'Is it important? It's structurally sound and actually in better condition than I thought it would be.'

'I'm really not interested in your…' She stopped and directed an incredulous look at his face. 'You make it sound like you've never seen it before.'

'I haven't.'

'You bought it without seeing it?' The idea seemed utterly preposterous to Izzy, who felt herself sinking back into a numb state of disbelief.

'It's what I do. It was a speculative purchase—the price was good.'

In other words, she thought scornfully, he had profited from the misfortunes of others.

'And I could afford to sit on it until the market—'

She cut across him, her voice flat as she asked, 'Why?'

'The place was bought at the height of the property boom by a—'

'I mean, why am I here?' Not that she would be for long. If it weren't for Lily being asleep, she would already have been trotting down that winding driveway, but if it weren't for Lily she wouldn't be here anyway.

She glanced towards her sleeping daughter cocooned in the baby carrier and experienced the familiar, almost suffocating swell of love, so intense that she felt light-headed. Although the light-headed feeling might have something to do with the fact that she hadn't been able to force down more than a couple of bites of the unappetising sandwiches she had bought on the train, and breakfast—God, that seemed like a lifetime ago—had been a slice of toast. She lifted a hand to her head and tried to remember if she had actually swallowed any of the toast.

'You look as if you're about to fall down.'

Izzy read the concern in his rough tone as criticism and her chin came up. She might look awful but it was damned rude of him to point it out.

And to add insult to injury he looked incredible, as

always. He didn't seem capable of looking bad, no matter what the situation.

A deep visceral longing she refused to acknowledge twisted itself like a vine around her resentment as she made the journey from his booted feet to his glossy head… Somewhere around his taut middle her fingertips began to tingle.

By the time she reached his face other parts tingled too, her cheeks were flagged with rosy heat and she was having a problem regulating her breathing. Long, lean and hard, he was more male than any man she had ever encountered.

She had always been dubious of the theory that in some throwback to a time of hunter-gatherers women chose an alpha male to father their children, but maybe…? Not that she had been looking for a father, just a lover, someone who could make her forget. Her blue eyes glazed as her thoughts drifted back.

And he had.

He had made her forget her name. She had taken pleasure from his body, revelling in a sensuality that she had not known she possessed. As the buried memories surfaced the past and present collided and for a moment she was looking at Roman and hearing, not the words coming from his lips, but a deep animal moan of pleasure that had been wrenched from his throat when she had curled her fingers around his silky, throbbing shaft…

CHAPTER SEVEN

'I SAID are you all right?'

Izzy blinked. This time there were no extenuating circumstances; this was simply unvarnished lust. She dodged Roman's gaze, denying the feelings, ignoring them in order to stay sane, stay safe.

'Fine.' Other than the ripples of hot sensation spreading outwards from a core that lay low in her belly. 'Will you stop looking at me like I'm some sort of specimen you want to dissect and pick apart?'

'If you'll stop undressing me with your eyes.'

Shame washed through her like icy water. Instead of remembering the sex between them, she should be remembering the awful hollow feeling she had felt the morning after. She was never, ever going to feel like that again; she had learnt the hard way.

'I was not!'

He arched a brow and grinned. 'My mistake.'

Only it wasn't; he knew it and so did she.

'You wouldn't look so hot either if you'd just travelled on public transport with a small child. I suppose you think it's easy?' She slung him a belligerent glare just in case he thought she was canvassing the sympathy vote.

'I hadn't thought about it.' But he was now.

'You have no idea, do you?'

The mild contempt in her superior little smile would have irritated him had he not realised she was right. He glanced down at the sleeping child. Izzy was the one who had spent the sleepless nights with Lily, which made it doubly frustrating because she was resisting his attempts to make up for that now.

He put the carrier carefully down on the ground. 'Then tell me,' he suggested. 'I want to know.'

His focus had been totally on what he had missed out on, and not how different her life must be as a single mother from how it had been as a single girl. She had once been able to walk into a bar late at night and see someone she liked and now she could not just act on impulse. Maybe this was not such a bad thing. He had always considered himself pretty broad-minded and not a possessive man, but the idea of the mother of his child spending a night with a man, any man, filled him with a violent revulsion.

So far he had been preoccupied with resenting the time he had missed with his daughter and planning for the future; now for the first time he was realising how much her unplanned pregnancy must have changed her life too.

'I should have sent a car for you. Whoa, easy, let me…'

'What are you doing?' she snarled, backing away, dragging the handle of the folded buggy with her as the wheels gouged grooves in the thick gravel before it was removed from her grip.

'I thought you were going to faint.' He remained ready to step in because she had definitely swayed.

She narrowed her eyes. 'I don't faint.'

Roman controlled his growing irritation with her belligerent independence with difficulty. 'Fine, you don't faint,' he said, sounding bored. 'But wouldn't you be more comfortable continuing this conversation indoors, in the warm?'

'I'm not a child. You don't have to humour me.' Her eyes slid from his. She had no idea what it was about this man that brought out the very worst in her. She took a deep breath. 'All right.'

It was the practical response because she would not be comfortable continuing this conversation anywhere, but the wind had picked up while they were standing there and the chill would soon start to penetrate Lily's cosy padded jacket. She bent forward to pick up the baby carrier.

'Let me.' He paused, his hand above her own.

Izzy's fingers tightened over the carrier handle. After a brief internal struggle she stepped back, tucking her hands into her pockets. After all, it was only the carrier she was relinquishing to him. To make a fuss would only serve to highlight the insecurities she was struggling to hide. Roman's next comment suggested she wasn't doing this very well.

'I'm not trying to steal her, just helping.'

She knew he was looking at her but with her jaw set she stomped up the steps, her eyes trained on her feet. 'Steal her over my dead body.' She paused as she entered the hallway, unable to repress a startled admiring intake of breath.

'This place must have quite a history. Is the panelling original?'

'I wouldn't know.' His taste ran to the modern, and

convenient. If they had been talking a private up-to-date gym, and the latest in computer technology, both items that this place lacked, Roman would have been interested.

'But just think about all the people who have lived here over the centuries.'

'I'm more interested in the plumbing, which is a bit basic. This way—the library is the second door on the left.' He nodded and stood to one side to let her go ahead of him.

Izzy, who would have liked to linger in this magnificent space, followed his directions and found herself in another equally pleasing room. It was being warmed by a fire burning in the massive stone grate and was lined with a row of south-facing mullioned windows that filled it with light.

'I thought nobody lived here,' she said, staring at the book-filled shelves.

'They came with the house.' His gaze moved over the book-lined walls. It was actually quite a pleasant room. 'Sit down, before you fall down.'

'I'm…' She responded to the pressure only because she couldn't stop her knees from trembling.

She sat there, her arms primly folded in her lap, and watched as he set the baby carrier down carefully and strolled across the room to the console table where a tray of coffee and sandwiches had been placed.

He pushed down the plunger of the cafetière, turning his head to enquire, 'Black or white?'

'White, no sugar.'

He piled a plate with some sandwiches and carried them across to where she was sitting, along with her coffee.

Her skin, dotted with freckles that stood out clear against the pallor, had an almost transparent quality. 'I don't want to get blamed if you pass out.'

'Are you going to stand over me while I drink this?'

'Yes.'

Pursing her lips she picked up the china cup. 'Anything for a quiet life.'

He laughed. 'Not so that you'd notice…and a sandwich,' he added when she put the cup back down.

Izzy slung him an irritated look, but she actually had three sandwiches, discovering she was starving. 'Satisfied?' she asked sarcastically as she pushed the plate away and sat back in her seat, folding one leg under herself. 'Do you have to stand there like some guard dog?'

She kept her expression neutral as his narrowed dark eyes moved over her face, but it was a struggle.

He didn't respond to her question, but his mouth did lift up at the corners as he flopped with languid grace into an armchair. Izzy felt the tension in her shoulders lessen as he stretched his legs out in front of him and crossed one ankle over the other. It was easy to feel at a disadvantage when he was towering over her.

She began to tap her toe on the polished wood floor as he set his elbows on the aged leather armrests.

'Some people would call this kidnapping.'

'A bit over the top, don't you think?' he drawled.

Her fury shifted up several notches as she folded her arms across her heaving chest. She sketched a smile and gave him a flat look.

'Oh, yes, I'm definitely overreacting.' The man was unbelievable, as well as being totally unscrupulous and manipulative.

His dark brows lifted. 'The job is genuine. I offered it

to you and you could have refused, but you took it.' He rose in a graceful fluid motion and angled a questioning look at her face. 'There was no coercion involved.'

Izzy wished he would stay in one place or at least keep sitting down; the man was like some prowling jungle cat, all restless energy and unpredictability. In some ways she would have felt more relaxed with the animal he reminded her of in the room rather than the man himself!

'Genuine!' She almost choked over the description. 'But I wouldn't have taken it if I'd known…known…'

'That you'd be living with me?'

The helpful insertion drew a gasp of horror from Izzy. 'Live with you?' she echoed.

Roman laughed.

'Or have you realised that this is too big a job for you?'

She struggled not to rise to the taunt and failed miserably. 'I'm up to the job.' It was her dream job and he knew it. She eyed him with seething dislike before squeezing her eyes closed as she made an attempt to regain some control of the situation and herself.

'This is a totally preposterous idea.' The tingling on her exposed nape made her open her eyes with a snap. Her radar had not misled her. He was close, too close, and crazily as she stared up into his deep-set, mesmerising eyes with those impossibly long lashes she wanted to step into his lean, hard body.

The effort not to made her shake, though she couldn't be sure that was the only thing making her shake. The fact was, physically he was like a narcotic to her and she had a terrible suspicion that, like any addict, one taste and she'd need a regular fix.

She dragged her gaze from his mouth, where it had drifted. *Don't taste, or look.*

'I hoped I'd be able to like you because you're Lily's father, but—'

'It is not necessary that you like your employer, and, speaking of Lily, it might be a good idea to keep your voice down if you don't want to wake her.' His sardonic mocking smile was briefly genuine as his glance touched the sleeping baby.

He was right, not that she'd admit it, but she did lower her voice as she snapped, 'I'm not working for you, end of story. And as for live with you, I'd prefer to live with a snake...' Izzy stopped. 'You're a cold, manipulative—'

'That's the façade. Deep down I'm soft and fluffy.'

She flung up her hands in a gesture of frustration and, fighting an urge to smile, sprang impetuously to her feet. She took a couple of steps towards the baby carrier before twisting back and facing him, her head thrown back, her eyes darkened to emotional navy as she glared at him.

'Do you take anything seriously?'

As if a switch had been flicked his sardonic smile was gone. He said nothing while he watched her chestnut hair bounce and settle silkily around her shoulders, then took a deliberate step towards her.

Her feet wanted to shadow the action, but she forced herself to step forward, not back, determined not to allow herself to show...fear? No, that was the wrong word. What was she feeling? What were the emotions swirling through her bloodstream? Excitement, loathing... She lifted a hand to her head, the contradictory mix making her feel light-headed. It would serve him right if she fainted. But in reality the idea of showing any weakness in front of him was terrifying.

Izzy shook her head, tuning out the distracting internal dialogue to think past the buzz in her head.

'I take being a father very seriously.'

His voice was low, almost soft, but the lack of emphasis only intensified the emotion behind the statement, causing Izzy to feel an irrational stab of guilt.

'And I will not be sidelined or fobbed off.'

'And I will not be pressured,' she threw back. 'This isn't about you and what you want. It's about what is best for Lily.'

'And that's you?'

'I'm her mother.'

'And that automatically makes you the best carer for her?' He elevated a dark brow and, shaking his head slowly from side to side, clicked his tongue in mock disapproval. 'Isn't that a rather sexist attitude, Isabel?'

'I'm not being sexist, I'm stating a fact—' She stopped abruptly mid-flow, the colour draining from her face so dramatically that he thought she was about to pass out. 'Are you suggesting...?' Her voice faded as jumbled images of lawyers and court hearings flashed through her head.

'Are you talking about contesting custody?' Legal battles did not come cheap and Roman had a lot of money. In theory she had faith in the legal system, but the thought of losing Lily made her feel hollow and more afraid than she ever had been in her life.

He opened his mouth to say he'd do whatever it took to have his daughter, then met with her stark blue gaze. Suddenly emotion kicked him hard in the chest; she looked so damned vulnerable. This situation combined with a chronic lack of sleep might have made his temper short, but Roman had never been a bully.

'No, I'm not.'

He had seen custody battles from a spectator's viewpoint and found them petty and distasteful. To use a child as a bargaining chip had always struck him as being abhorrent and in his new role as father he found the practice even more disagreeable.

'But I don't want my daughter raised to think a man's contribution to the bringing up of a child ends at the moment of insemination.'

Unable to shake the images of court battles, despite his denial, Izzy blinked up at him still feeling physically sick. 'Neither do I.' Her confusion was genuine.

He arched a satiric brow. 'Really? I'd assumed that you'd be carrying on the family tradition. You've got to hand it to your mother—she did at least practise what she preached.'

'If you want to know what I think, I suggest you ask me, not base your assumptions on the snatches of my mother's books you read.'

'Actually I read the entire book.' And having done so he had been amazed that her daughter was as relatively normal as she seemed. The woman had been a total zealot.

From his expression she was assuming Roman was not a fan. 'She wrote twenty.'

His lips tightened in a spasm of impatience. 'I think we both know which book I'm talking about. Did she actually believe all that drivel she wrote or did she just have a mortgage to pay off?'

Izzy took a deep breath and calmed her breathing. While she did not agree with a lot of what her mother

had preached, she was not about to stand there while
he sneered. 'My mother's book is considered a modern
classic. She sparked debate, which can only be a good
thing.' There was nothing her mother had liked more
than a good argument.

'Do you make a habit of rubbishing people who are
no longer here to defend themselves?'

The contempt in her voice made him flush, the colour running up dark under his golden-toned skin. 'So
what did your mother teach you?'

She tilted her chin to a proud angle. 'My mother
brought me up to make my own decisions.'

'Like having unprotected sex with a total stranger?'

He clenched his teeth, recognising the utter hypocrisy of his below-the-belt jibe the moment it left his lips.
He still could not believe that he had been so criminally
reckless; the only time in his life he had had unprotected
sex had resulted in a child.

Izzy sucked in a breath. 'If you're trying to make
me feel ashamed, don't waste your breath.' Her voice
quivered and she bit her lip before husking, 'I already
do.' She moved her head slowly from side to side in
an attitude of bewilderment. 'I can't believe it was me
that night.'

She had coped with the memory by treating it like
some surreal, erotic, out-of-body experience. The
wheel had fallen off that coping mechanism the moment Roman had appeared in her life. All the pent-up
passion she had successfully denied had surfaced, no
surreal dream any longer.

Roman's expression hardened. She was talking as if
she'd been some awkward adolescent instead of a sensual woman who had known exactly what she wanted

and had not been afraid to ask. 'Don't tell me,' he drawled. 'You didn't know what you were doing.'

She coloured angrily at his sarcasm. 'I'm not trying to deny responsibility.' In response to a faint whimper from the baby carrier she took hold of the handle and, on autopilot, began to rock it back and forth rhythmically. 'But I had just buried my mother, and I'd never actually done it before. What's your excuse, Roman?' Izzy froze and thought, 'God, did I say that out loud?'

'Yes.'

Izzy's eyes widened with shock before she pressed a hand to her mouth—a classic ease of too little too late. In the stretching silence the sleeping child's regular breathing drew Roman's attention. He was still staring at his daughter when he finally spoke.

'Buried your mother?' His research had of course told him the woman was dead, he might even have read the date, but he had not made any connection.

Roman turned his head in time to see Izzy biting her lip. She met his eyes and tilted her head in acknowledgement. 'Cremated, actually.'

An image of her face that night floated into his head. He had been unable to take his eyes off her from the moment she had walked into the room, him and half the men in there. Amazingly she had seemed utterly oblivious to the lustful stares that had followed her.

He could still recall exactly what Isabel had been wearing when she'd walked into that bar. He could close his eyes and see the smooth oval of her face, her incredible skin, her startling sapphire eyes. So why hadn't he recognised something wasn't right?

When she'd kissed him, she'd been trying to forget. He should have seen it. Hadn't he been trying to achieve the same thing himself with the aid of a bottle and failing miserably?

'That day?'

She nodded.

Roman ground his teeth together and pressed the fingertips of one brown-fingered hand to the pulse spot throbbing in his temple before spearing both hands deep into his short sable hair.

She had used him!

And you didn't use her?

He closed his eyes and expelled a sharp sigh through clenched teeth. The truth was he *had* used her, sought to escape the total mess that was his life for a few stolen moments and find hot oblivion inside her. She'd been tight as a glove and they had shared a night of raw sex; her response had been uninhibited, elemental.

'How is it possible?' His dark brows flattened into an accusing line above his deep-set eyes. 'On such a day you should… Why were you alone? Someone should…' He stopped, a nerve in his lean cheek clenching.

'There wasn't anyone.' She seemed oblivious to how heart-rending that statement sounded as she related, 'That was the way she wanted it. She didn't want anyone, no sentiment, no ceremony, no service or wake.'

'And no closure for the loved ones left behind,' he rasped hoarsely. 'Though why am I surprised? Such a request is typical of a woman who never thought of anyone's needs but her own.'

The blighting condemnation of her dead parent drew a shocked gasp from Izzy. She let go of the handle and took a step towards him, her hands on her hips.

'Have you got a problem with strong women, Roman? Is that it?'

'You think your mother is a person to be admired?' Roman was bewildered by how protective Isabel was of the memory of someone who had lied to her all her life, deprived her of a father and, as far as he could see, been a friend, not a mother. 'You put your career on hold to spend time with your daughter. Did your mother ever put your needs above her own?'

'That wasn't a sacrifice,' she said quietly. 'I wanted to spend time with Lily. I didn't want to miss out on these early months. You have no idea how—'

'Precious they are? I think I have.'

Her eyes fell from his steady stare. 'She would probably have been equally happy and contented with a nanny.'

'I doubt that. You're a good mother.'

Izzy, conscious of a warm glow that shouldn't have been there—his approval meant nothing to her—took refuge in antagonism. 'And the point is I could do that, spend this time with Lily because the book you despised gave me financial independence. I appreciate you feel responsible,' she said stiffly. 'But I don't need your money and Lily and I are fine...'

'So what do you expect me to do? Walk away and say ring me? What happens when Lily gets ill or hates school? Do you really want to face those things alone?'

'If I need it the Fitzgeralds give me all the support I could want.'

'The Fitzgeralds? Do you think of yourself as one of them? Don't you feel an outsider?'

Alarmed by his perception, she lowered her gaze, allowing her dark lashes to screen her eyes from him.

'My independence means a lot to me and they respect that.' Which was more than he did. His constant prodding and prying were making her feel under siege and what was it about? All she'd been was a cheap one-night stand; the fact she'd had his child did not alter that.

'You must have been terrified when you found your-self pregnant and alone.' Roman struggled under the weight of unaccustomed guilt he felt when he thought of what she must have gone through. He saw her sitting there alone and afraid... His jaw clenched.

'I wasn't alone. Michael contacted me the same week I discovered I was pregnant.'

And what a week! In the space of two days she'd discovered that her wild night of passion with the hand-some stranger had left her pregnant and received the letter from the man who was her father, inviting her to meet her new family.

'If I hadn't been pregnant...' She stopped as a sudden stab of emotion made her eyes fill. She blinked hard before adding with a hint of defiance, 'And, yes, feeling alone, I might not have agreed to meet him, but I did so my story had a happy ending.' She took out a tissue and blew her nose. The prosaic action touched Roman more than any tears would have.

'This story is not ended, Isabel. Our story is not ended.'

She shook her head, knowing he was right but still fighting it. Life had been simpler without him but here he was and he showed no signs of going away. For Lily's sake she knew she should make an effort, but they had nothing in common. He didn't even live in the same world as she did, but she could try at least not to be enemies.

'We don't have a story. It was just sex.' Staring at her clasped hands, she didn't see anger that flashed in his eyes. 'If I hadn't walked into that bar...' A shadow of confusion moved across her face like a cloud. 'I still don't know why I did that—I just saw the bar and...'

'Maybe it was fate?'

Her feathery brows lifted in surprise. He was the last person that she had expected to hear talk about fate. 'I don't believe in fate. I slept with an incredibly sexy man. That wasn't fate—it was hormones!' And given the opportunity she suspected nine out of ten unattached females would have done the same. She would have thought that she was the one who wouldn't have been attracted to him, but apparently she was no different. But he was, she thought as her glance drifted across the carved, perfectly symmetrical lines of his bronzed face, a dreaminess drifting into her expression. He made her think of some warrior with a poet's soul—his mouth was definitely poetry. The dreaminess was swallowed up by a stab of hungry longing as she studied the sensual outline.

'Incredibly sexy...?'

She jumped guiltily and dodged the wicked gleam in his eyes and found herself staring again at his mouth. Once she had started it was hard to stop. She cleared her throat and forced the words past the achy occlusion that made speaking difficult. It felt like wading through syrup.

'Like I'm not telling you anything you don't already know.'

He grinned but didn't deny it, she noticed. The wicked grin made him look years younger and even more wildly attractive.

'She must have been very young, your mother, when she died. It was unexpected?'

She nodded. Her mother had been a very young sixty-four.

'She was in her forties when she had me. She'd been ill for a while.' The onset of the illness that had struck her mother down had been insidious, although not immediately life-threatening. But she had been living with the effects of the degenerative disease that would eventually kill her. 'I was angry.'

'Yes.' He knew about anger.

During his stays on the oncology ward Roman had seen that reaction to death, seen enough people suffering the effects of shock and grief that it seemed to him that it was sometimes worse for the healthy ones who had to stand by helpless as their loved ones suffered and sometimes lost their battles for life.

The point was he should have seen the signs. He could recognise now with the wisdom of hindsight that she had been displaying all of them that night in the bar.

Roman closed his eyes and groaned.

Izzy looked at him uncertainly and he looked very pale when he looked at her again. A moment later he swore in his native tongue.

'You were in shock.' And he'd been too busy wallowing in self-pity to notice. He suddenly froze, his dark eyes swivelling her way. 'You just said you'd never done it before.'

Izzy expelled a choky sigh. Hell, just when she thought she was safe.

'Well, I don't make a habit of picking up strange men in bars. One-night stands are not really my style.'

He studied her down-bent head with a frown before moving his head slowly from side to side in a firm negative motion. 'No, that wasn't what you meant.'

Shifting uneasily under his severe gaze, she walked across to the sofa and sat down. 'I wish you wouldn't tell me what I mean. I am quite capable of saying what I mean.'

Roman refused to be distracted. 'And capable of lying, it would seem.'

'So you think one-night stands are my style...' She gave a little laugh. 'Thanks a lot.'

'It was your first time.' Even as he said it he rejected the statement; he had not actively avoided taking a virgin to bed, but then neither did he avoid meteorites. They both existed but the chances of encountering one were pretty remote.

She was not laughing or at the very least looking amused by such a preposterous notion. Instead she refused to meet his gaze and gave a defensive shrug.

CHAPTER EIGHT

'It WAS a figure of speech.'

'A figure of speech as in you were a virgin.'

Roman's sarcasm made her flush and for a moment Izzy considered lying. But did it really matter if he knew the truth now? She thought not, so decided to come clean.

'My only time, actually.' She flashed him a warning glance and added fiercely, 'And don't ask me why because, to be honest, I don't know.'

She did have her suspicions, though, the most likely that being a twenty-year-old virgin had been a form of rebellion for her—not against parental control but against a total lack of parental control.

While other girls' parents gave them curfews and warned them of the dangers of teenage sex, her liberal mother had been telling her it was fine if she wanted to have boyfriends stay the night.

Izzy had always found such conversations excruciatingly embarrassing, but her mother had favoured what she called a frank and open exchange of views.

'You didn't act like a virgin.'

'How is a virgin meant to act, Roman?' She adopted

an expression of fake interest as she started to feel angry. 'In the strange world you live in.'

'I live in the real world. You're the one who...' He stopped and pinned her with an intense, almost accusing stare. 'You must have had boyfriends?' he persisted, remembering how incredibly tight she'd been and her sharp gasp of shock as he had thrust deeply into her...

'For a semester I was in love with one of my mother's research assistants,' she recalled with a reminiscent grin. 'Happy now?'

He swallowed...happy? Happy that he had taken her innocence and not even noticed!

'So you had a relationship with this—?' A relationship that stopped short of sex. As he remembered her cool hands on his body and her hot, sweet tongue...that did not seem likely at all.

'Simon. No, it turned out he was gay.' She could smile now at the memory of her big moment when she had finally worked up the courage to ask him out. He had been nice about it and quite kind, but eventually the story had reached her mother, who had found it extremely amusing.

Unable to maintain contact with his intense stare, Izzy looked away.

Roman tried to think past the static buzz in his head. He felt numb. A virgin! It seemed impossible. The innate sensuality she projected had been one of the things that had drawn him to her. She was the most passionate creature he had ever held; the need to possess her had been all-consuming and she had matched his hunger and desire every step of the way.

'Why didn't you tell me?'

He still couldn't get his head around it, but it had

to be true. There was no reason for her to lie. She had
seemed totally at ease with her body, completely uninhibited and endlessly fascinated by his body. The
question of her virginity had not even crossed his
mind—why would it? She had seemed almost to know
what he wanted before he had himself.

*Face it, Roman, she was the best sex you ever had
and she was a virgin.* The staggering thought kept hitting him and the shock was not getting any less with
each successive impact.

She turned her head, recognised the anger in his
tense stance and shook her head. That was a reaction
she had not anticipated. 'Why didn't you notice?' she
countered.

At the time Izzy had presumed that he would.

She'd thought her sheer cluelessness would alert
him and had desperately hoped it would not be a deal
breaker.

But amazingly she hadn't felt awkward at all, or embarrassed or shy, which was insane because previously
the idea of even being naked with a man had been something she didn't feel comfortable with. The entire intimacy thing had always been a problem for her, not
because she was prudish but because she was choosy.

She had thought about it afterwards a lot and wondered if perhaps the fact that it had been anonymous
sex, that he hadn't known her or had any preconceptions
about her, had allowed her to let go. For once she didn't
have to be the person everyone thought she was—nice,
calm, sensible Izzy—she could be who she wanted to
be. It had been the most liberating experience of her life.

Why hadn't he noticed? *Good question, Roman.* 'You
were hardly shy.'

Did he expect her to apologise?

Her steady blue stare brought a dull flush of colour to his high cheekbones. 'Obviously if I'd known I'd have—' He stopped and thought, *Would I really have run a mile? Would I really have resisted the temptation to be her first lover?*

She'd given him a gift and he'd not noticed.

She acted as though it had been nothing and for some reason that made him angrier than anything else.

'I could have hurt you.'

'You didn't.'

'And you have never slept with any man since Lily was born?'

She gave a laugh. 'You really think that I've had the spare time or energy to have an affair? Besides it's a small place, everyone knows everyone and you can't sneeze without it being in the public domain.' That was one aspect of living in a small community that she hadn't come to terms with yet.

'So until you do have the time I'm the only man you've ever slept with.'

And Roman had never forgotten the night.

He ran a hand across his face and shook his head, unable to believe his total lack of control. He had never surrendered himself so totally to passion before or since that night; the searing fire of lust had totally devoured him. He had literally torn off his clothes like a fumbling boy who couldn't wait.

Izzy looked past him, trying not to see the image of his sculpted bronzed body in her head as she banded her arm around her midriff in an unconsciously protective gesture. It did not protect her from the memory of the warm silken feel of his skin against hers at the first shocking intimacy of his touch.

'There's no need to make such a big thing of it. We had sex,' she said, struggling to sound amused. 'That doesn't give us some magical bond.'

'Maybe not magic, but we have a bond—we have Lily.'

As if in response to her name the sleeping baby stirred, raising her voice in a fretful whimper. Izzy was up in a bound and beside the carrier.

'Per l'amor di Dio!' he rasped under his breath as he watched her bend forward, providing him with a perfect view of her pert round bottom.

Izzy, who was unfastening Lily, who was wriggling like an eel to escape, lifted her head at the sound of his soft curse and, misinterpreting its cause, cautioned, 'Babies don't time their demands to suit you, Roman.'

The man needed a reality check. Maybe he would be less eager to be involved with Lily when he realised the demands that went with a small baby. 'For the first three months I was rarely dressed before midday.'

From where he was standing that did not seem a bad thing to Roman.

She shook her head to toss back a strand of hair that was tickling her nose as she lifted up Lily. 'I can't remember the last time I visited the hairdresser's.' When she got back home, Izzy decided, she would take up Michelle's suggestion they let Grandad babysit while they went for a spa day treat.

'You have beautiful hair.' He remembered it soft and lustrous spread out on the pillow as she had reached up for him and pulled him down.

Her eyes flew to his face where the raw hunger

stamped on his bronzed features made her heart thud. It was Lily's small foot landing a lucky and painful kick in her stomach that broke the sexual thrall that had rapidly sucked her into its sensual vortex.

Her laughter was tinged with a good dollop of breathless relief as she kissed the sole of the bare foot that had pulled her away from the brink of making a total fool of herself.

'Now, what have you done with that sock…eaten it?'

'It's there.' Roman bent to pick up the lost item.

'Thank you.' She held her hand palm up rather than risk touching his long brown fingers. He probably knew but by this point Izzy was past caring. 'She's always losing socks,' she said, tucking it in the pocket of her cardigan. As if picking up on the tension in the air, Lily began to squall irritably.

Roman regarded her red face with a concerned frown. 'Is she ill?'

'No, she's hungry.'

'How do you know?'

'It's generally a matter of elimination. Is there somewhere I could heat up her food? Where did I put the bag?' She looked around for the holdall.

'I've got it.' Roman's brows shot up as he picked up the bag with the pink handle and cheerful teddy-bear characters. '*Dio*, what have you got in here?'

Izzy gave a rundown. 'Food, drink, nappies, a change of clothes and some toys.' She reeled off the items that she rarely travelled anywhere without. 'Somewhere I can heat up…?'

'Yes, of course, I'll show you.' He held open the door for her to pass through in front of him. 'The kitchen is this way, I think.' He led the way through a door into a stone-flagged inner hall. 'And there are rooms prepared upstairs if you want to change her.'

Before Izzy could protest he added, 'It's too late now to make the journey back to Cumbria. I can't promise luxury but the place is perfectly habitable, just a little tired décor wise. I'm not sure if you'll want to do any structural remodelling but—'

Trotting a little to keep up with his long stride, Izzy stared up at him. 'Why do you persist in acting as though it's a done deal? Don't you understand the meaning of no?'

He pushed open a heavy door and nodded for her to go through before him. 'Depends on the context. So what do you think? Could you do something with it?'

She might hate cooking.

She might be a domestic goddess.

It seemed impossible that they could know so little about one another and yet they had made a child.

He stood back and watched her look around the room.

'A bit small?' he suggested. 'The original kitchen is on the lower ground floor used for storage now. It could be reinstated. I'd thought possibly knocking through, incorporating the smaller rooms and knocking out the wall replacing it with glass and putting in a south-facing terrace…?'

The ambitious suggestion drew a laugh from Izzy.

'This house has got to be listed?'

He nodded.

'Listed means you can't just knock down walls. Besides, this is a lovely room. Not that it's any of my business,' she tacked on quickly. 'Will you stop looking so smug? I'm not staying. And if you want to make yourself useful, watch Lily while I organise her food.' She placed the baby on the floor and held out her hand for the bag.

Roman took a wooden tractor from the top of the bag, then handed it to her. 'Are you always so bossy?'

'Does that mean the wedding's off?'

The tentative rapport immediately vanished in a big black hole of heavy tension.

'This isn't about scoring points.' His expression remained stern as he bent down and pushed the wooden toy across the ground to the baby, who immediately grabbed it and pushed it in her mouth.

'Is that safe?'

Izzy, still stinging from his reproach, glanced over. 'Fine. She's teething—everything goes in her mouth.'

Roman straightened up, leaned back against a counter and stood watching while Izzy moved around the room until, in the act of pulling a lid off a jar, she was unable to bear his silent scrutiny another second. She stopped and expelled a sigh through clenched teeth.

Straightening her slender shoulders, she put down the jar and turned to face him. 'So, all right, it's not a joke or about scoring points. What is it about?'

Her eyes were incredible, the deepest, purest blue he had ever seen.

She arched a delicate brow. 'Well?'

'This is about damage limitation.' And controlling his desire to touch her. He cleared his throat. 'It's about you admitting you can't do it all yourself. It's about me being allowed to take my share of the responsibilities. You don't like this house? Fine. I…we can find something you do like.'

'I like where I live.' He just kept missing the point.

'That cottage, there's not enough room to swing a cat there.'

'My cottage!' she exclaimed. 'You have never seen my cottage. You don't even know where I live!'

'I may not have had an invite but be real, Isabel. Of course I know where you live, and I'm assuming your house is not dissimilar in size to your neighbour's, who kindly did ask me in after I admired her dahlias.'

'You…you…how dare you? You wouldn't know a dahlia from a daisy.'

'Now there you go again, making snap judgements based on what?'

'I don't care if you have green fingers.' Actually his fingers were brown and long and sensitive. Hand pressed to her fluttering stomach, Izzy dragged her gaze upwards and finished angrily, 'I won't tolerate being spied on and manipulated.'

His languid air vanished. 'And I will not tolerate my child living in a house paid for by Michael Fitzgerald.' Michael Fitzgerald was the least of Roman's concerns. There was no man in Isabel's life right now, but how long would that situation continue? How long before some man wanted to move in and bring up his daughter?

Izzy was taken aback by the underlying venom in his tone. 'What have you got against Michael?'

'Nothing. I barely know the man,' Roman cut back, looking impatient. 'Other than the fact he has an excellent reputation as a horse breeder.'

'For the record, I rent the cottage, not Michael. He offered to help financially, but I refused.' She lifted her chin. 'I can pay my own way.' She bent and scooped up the baby.

'Did Michael ask who the father was?' If the roles

had been reversed he would have tracked down the man responsible and… But he was the reckless bastard responsible and it was his job to protect his own daughter.

Izzy shook her head. 'No.' She suspected that Michelle had a lot to do with this restraint.

'But he knows now.'

'Obviously Michelle told him.'

Izzy brought her lashes down in a protective sweep. Michael's response, she realised in retrospect, had initiated their first father and daughter dispute. She had found herself placed in the strange position of defending Roman.

He had eventually cooled down and had even apologised after Michelle had supplied a large dose of common sense, but the subject was still a sensitive one.

'But don't worry, it doesn't have to go any farther. They won't tell anyone else.' She gave a sudden laugh, her glance moving from Lily to Roman. 'They won't have to if anyone sees you together.'

'People are going to know, Isabel.'

She swallowed. 'I suppose so.'

He studied her face and felt his anger grow without knowing why. 'You look delighted by the prospect.'

'Are you telling me you are? That you don't care about people talking and speculating?' She curled up inside at the idea of being the butt of gossip again.

'I do not care about what people say about me.'

Exasperated, she rolled her eyes. 'I get the message, but could you lower it a bit? The testosterone levels are giving me a headache…and before you come over all huffy,' she said wagging her finger at him, 'remember you don't care what people think about you.'

His taut expression faded to one of reluctant amused admiration. 'Huffy? Is that even a word?'

'And here was me thinking your English was better than mine.'

'And I said think not say, smart little witch.'

'Oh, I'm sure people only say what you want to hear,' she observed, thinking that it would take a brave person to cross swords verbally or otherwise with this man.

'Not all people. Tell me, if our paths had not crossed what did you plan to tell Lily when she asked about her father?'

Izzy's narrow shoulders lifted. 'Truthfully I don't know.' Her eyes drifted to his mouth.

'You're blushing!' he accused suddenly.

Izzy wasn't about to tell him that her own thoughts were making her blush—thoughts about his mouth.

'It's warm in here.'

'You think?' he drawled, wondering why she was lying.

Izzy ignored the scepticism in his smile. 'I don't want to lie to her.'

He arched a brow. 'But you would.'

'Truth?' She gave a helpless shrug and paused, seemingly lost in her own thoughts until he prompted.

'Truth?'

Her blue eyes connected with his. 'I don't know. I mean, at what age do you say to your child, I don't actually know your father's name—he was a one-night stand who picked me up in a bar?'

'Actually, if we're being totally accurate, you picked me up.'

She flashed him an insincere smile. 'Well, thanks for that.'

He tipped his head. 'Any time.'

'But a child wants to feel they were conceived with…' She stopped and lowered her gaze, unable to say love and invite his cynical retort. 'Well, that they at least knew each other's name and it wasn't some quickie…'

The coarse description brought a flash of anger to his eyes. 'The point is that parents do not discuss their conception with the children, unless your mother was the exception. Did she feel the need to share the gory details?'

'She told me my dad was a test tube.'

This casual revelation caused his winged ebony brows to hit his hairline. 'What?'

Izzy, who was wiping a stray blob of banana from her daughter's curls, turned to face him. She held the box of wet wipes in one hand, the used wipe in the other hand as she tried to sweep the stray strands of hair from her face with her forearm. One stubborn culprit remained, tickling her nose.

'Let me.'

His eyes were dark and intense as he looked down into her upturned features. Izzy stood very still, not even breathing as he took the silky hank of hair in his long brown fingers, brushing her cheek and jaw as he tucked it carefully behind her ear.

He took for ever and every second was torture. Her insides were quivering, her outsides were burning and her skin was so sensitive that every light touch of his fingers felt like a burning brand.

Torture was not an exaggeration for the effort it took for her not to react to either the impulse to slap his hand away or the contrasting and equally strong impulse to grab it and rub her cheek into his palm.

She started breathing again as he retook his place propping up the counter. Tall, elegant and not even slightly affected, but why would he be? Only crazed women got turned on by someone tidying them up. *If he'd wiped the banana out of my hair I'd probably moan and scream, 'Take me!'* she thought with a grimace of self-disgust.

Dropping the soiled wipe in a waste bin, Izzy grunted a thanks and picked up the threads of her narrative.

'She told me my dad…well, that I didn't have one. I always believed that I was the product of artificial insemination.'

'Madre di Dios!' he exclaimed.

'It seemed normal to me.' Until she had mentioned it to her friends in school.

'So when did she tell you the truth?'

'She didn't. She left a letter for me to read after she died. She left one for Michael too.'

'And you had read that letter on the day we…' He inhaled and closed his eyes, breathing through clenched teeth. 'Of course you did.' He bit out a savage-sounding curse that drew Izzy's attention to his face.

His mouth was taut and his narrowed eyes were almost black. 'Are you mad with me?' she asked, her voice rising to an indignant squeak. 'Because I don't see why.'

'No, I am not mad with you.' He framed the words from between clenched teeth. 'I am mad with me.' He took a deep breath, making a visible effort to put a lid on his emotions before continuing, his voice a careful monotone as he delivered his opinion.

'I think that how Lily was conceived is irrelevant. It is how she is brought up that is important. Do you agree?'

She nodded warily. Where was he going with this? 'Of course.' What else could she say?

'She deserves to be brought up to know she is wanted, cared for emotionally and physically.'

When you said it that way it sounded so simple, but it wasn't and he knew it. Roman sketched a small self-mocking smile. An ultra-confident person, he had never been plagued with self-doubt, he thrived on challenges, but this fatherhood thing scared him.

'I don't know what kind of father I'll be,' he admitted.

Would he be a good father…? He found the idea of being responsible for another person incredibly daunting.

'But I know I won't neglect her or leave her alone. I won't let her get on the wrong train when she is ten and have to find her way from Brighton in the dark to—' He stopped abruptly, adding in a hard voice, 'The point is, the things parents do impact on a child… I don't want my child to pay the price for my mistakes.'

'Roman, were you that little boy?'

CHAPTER NINE

'MY PARENTS were in love.' Roman would not personally call their obsessive, symbiotic relationship love or even healthy, but his was not the generally held opinion. 'Their love did not stretch to a child. So, yes, I was that child.'

Izzy didn't know what to say. 'I'm sorry.'

She could tell from his body language that he was regretting giving even this meagre amount of personal information.

'I am going to be part of Lily's life and you can deal with it like an adult or…'

'Or?'

'I'm not the bad guy, Isabel. Don't make me one,' he said quietly. 'Look, maybe I shouldn't have tricked you into coming here, but you wouldn't talk to me, and the marriage thing—I scared you. I get that, but sometimes I say things without thinking them through.'

'You were rushing me, pushing. You wouldn't give me time to think.'

He dragged a hand through his hair and levered himself away from the counter. 'I'm not good at waiting.'

'You mean you're impatient?'

An expression she struggled to read flickered in his deep-set eyes before he shrugged his shoulders.

'I like to live in the here and now, not waiting for some tomorrow that might…' He stopped, leaving the sentence unfinished.

She understood the significance of that look now.

'But there is for you?' she said, suddenly needing reassurance on this point. Well, he was Lily's father. 'A tomorrow, you mean…a lot of tomorrows?' He looked the picture of lusty health but who knew?

At the time he had not discussed his illness with her because from his experience the moment anyone heard the word cancer they saw *it* and not him. It remained a subject that he avoided.

'Who knows? But I have every intention of being around to see Lily grow up.'

The knot of anxiety in her stomach relaxed as she released a tiny sigh of relief.

He stepped away from the door he'd opened and Izzy saw the interior of a pantry that was filled with baby equipment. 'I asked Gennaro to pick up a few things,' he said, pulling out a wooden high chair and setting it beside the large wooden table that was set in the centre of the room. 'Is this any good?'

'A few things!' she exclaimed, staring at the stacked shelves and noticing that the piles of nappies were in every size available. 'It looks like he bought the shop. Yes, that's great,' she admitted, depositing Lily in the chair.

She fastened the bib around Lily's neck and took the spoon from the bowl of baby food, handing it to Roman.

'You got to start somewhere.' *Please do not make*

me regret this. 'It's just a spoon, so don't start with the smug smile,' she warned.

Roman saw the blue plastic spoon for what it was: an olive branch and the first thawing in her attitude. Careful to keep his expression clear of the smugness she accused him of, he took it.

Fifteen minutes later the tension in the atmosphere had diminished considerably and the food in the bowl seemed to be evenly distributed between the baby, Roman and the floor.

'That is not as easy as it looks. Did she actually swallow any?'

'Enough,' Izzy murmured, taking the empty bowl and spoon and dropping them in the deep old-fashioned stone sink. She looked at him surreptitiously through her lashes as he rolled down his sleeves. Would any of his boardroom colleagues have recognised their elegant designer-suit-wearing boss?

She hardly recognised him herself.

Could she talk to this man without feeling overpowered?

Perhaps she should try?

'You do know that I was always perfectly willing to give you access to Lily... It never even entered my head not to, but when a man you don't know proposes...'

'I did not propose. *Dio,* if I had gone down on one knee and said you made me complete I could understand your reaction.'

The mockery in his tone stung. 'Maybe I want the one-knee approach...' She saw his expression and added hastily, 'But not from you, obviously.'

His ebony brows hit his hairline. 'Now that I didn't see coming... You're a romantic.'

He made it sound as if she had some embarrassing disease. 'I don't have a romantic bone in my body.'

'Good, then let's discuss this like two rational people.'

Presumably rational and romantic were two things that did not coexist in his eyes.

'I'm listening.'

'You said to me that this is not about me or how I feel, but about Lily, and you are right, but are you not willing to concede that Lily would be better off with two parents?'

'She has two parents. They don't have to have the same address. I am willing to discuss a plan so long as you don't stray into la-la land again. We have Lily in common and nothing else...'

If she did ever consider marriage he was everything the man she married wouldn't be. She knew that there were women who found controlling behaviour a turn-on, but she had never wanted to be dominated by a man and Roman Petrelli was the ultimate in male chauvinism.

'We have lust...a chemical reaction in common.'

She was unprepared for the comment and the breath left Izzy's lungs in one sibilant gasp, but before she could contest the statement, before she could stop the hot, lurid images playing in her head, he added drily, 'And there is a lot of historic precedent for basing marriage on just that, though the days when the only way a nice girl could get any was with a ring on her finger are long gone.'

'Lust?' The scorn she tried to inject into her voice just didn't come off.

He lifted a sardonic brow and laughed. 'Come off

it, *cara*. You're not suggesting that you don't want to rip my clothes off…' His heavy-lidded gaze slid down her body before he added, 'I can feel the heat coming off you from here.'

His husky rasp stroked her nerve endings into painful tingling life. 'You carry on thinking that if it makes you happy,' she recommended. 'But it doesn't matter what situation you manufacture where we can play happy families, I'm not playing along.'

'Tell me who had the best upbringing—your siblings or you?'

The comparison was unfair and he had to know it. 'I wasn't a deprived child. Ruth was a good friend. Look, marriage isn't for me but I accept that for some people who are in love… I suppose you don't believe in love?' she charged, annoyed by the sneer curving his lips as he listened.

'Oh, but I do. My own parents were as deeply in love from the moment they met until the day they died.'

'You make that sound like a bad thing,' she accused. 'I know you didn't have a happy childhood,' she said, recalling his earlier comments.

'I think that love, the all-consuming variety, can be selfish and destructive, but more relevantly does not make the people in love good people or, for that matter, good parents.'

Izzy fought off a stab of sympathy. 'Didn't you get on with your parents?' Her mother might not have been the warm, fluffy, hands-on type of parent, but Izzy had always known she was loved and valued.

'I barely knew them.'

It was his offhand tone as much as the statement that made Izzy blink in confusion before comprehension struck. For a moment empathy dampened her antagonism.

'Oh, I thought…' She half lifted her hand to clasp his arm, the physical gesture instinctive, but thought better of it, instead threading her thumbs in the belt loops of her jeans. 'I'm sorry. I didn't know they died when you were young.'

'My parents died six years ago when I was twenty-five, but I was always on the periphery of their lives.' It had seemed appropriate that they had died together when the cruise ship they were on struck a smaller vessel. The damage to the ship had been minor but in the subsequent confusion and hysteria several people had gone overboard, including his parents.

'The reason couples like your father and Michelle have a successful marriage is because they are both intelligent people who work at it. They create a stable environment in which to bring up their children.'

'They're in love.'

'In love?' His scorn was overt. 'What does that mean exactly? People fall in and out of love every day of the week. How many times have you seen some celebrity being interviewed waxing lyrical about their soul mate?'

'Is the sneer for celebrities or love?'

Nostrils flared in distaste, he spoke over her sarcastic interruption. 'The next week their acrimonious break-up is being reported everywhere.'

'We're not celebrities.' Although, she mused, her glance drifting from the strong symmetry of his bronzed features to his body, there were a lot of Hollywood stars who worked hard to get what Roman had and never reached that elevated level of jaw-dropping, sexy perfection. It was hard to believe that she had...

'But we are parents.'

Izzy started, her guilty eyes flying back to his face. 'I know that,' she gritted out. 'What I don't know is why you have this weird fixation with getting married. It's not rational.'

'And the idea that you fall in love with someone at twenty and still love them thirty years later is? Being in love does not make a good marriage or good parents.'

'So what are you saying exactly?'

'I'm saying that we can be married and be good parents, and not be in love. No!' he said, lifting a hand to still the protest that trembled on her tongue. 'I know your instinct is to shoot down my arguments in flames, but think for one moment. We have a child—'

'You keep saying that like it might have slipped my mind!'

'Do we not owe it to her to explore all possibilities? I am not suggesting we rush up the aisle—living in close proximity might reveal that we are totally incompatible—but I am suggesting living here for a period of time, long enough for me to get to know my daughter and for us to see how such an arrangement would work.'

'You're suggesting a trial...what...?' She couldn't bring herself to ask if he was expecting her to sleep with him.

He gave a smile as though he could read her mind. 'There are many rooms in this house. We can be as close or as far apart as we wish.'

'It's a mad idea.'

'And you can flex your creative muscles, tackle a

room at a time, make it as you would wish it if you lived here. Money no object.'

'Is that the carrot?'

'For some women the chance to spend some quality time with me would be the carrot, which brings us back to lust. That night we spent together still feels very much unfinished business to me.'

'No, it's totally finished for me...completely!' She illustrated how completely with a sharp sweeping motion of her hand.

He greeted her hot denial with a look of polite disbelief, which set Izzy's teeth on edge.

'As you wish. If you agree to give this a go, I will agree not to propose to you again until we have established we can live together without wanting to kill one another. For the record there is a dower house on the estate that, if the worst comes to the worst, I can sleep in. Such an arrangement, though not ideal, would be acceptable to me in the future. I know someone who has bought the house next door to his ex-wife so that he can see his children every day.'

'You would live in the dower house here?' She was startled by the offer.

'We can live wherever you choose.'

She was impressed; how could she not be? He was prepared to totally turn his life upside down, relocate—anything, it seemed, for his daughter. Considering this, what he was suggesting no longer seemed such a big ask.

'All right, I'll give it a go.'

Roman greeted her choice with a nod of his head, but inside he was punching the air in triumph.

CHAPTER TEN

Izzy spent a couple of hours exploring the warren of rooms. She had felt fewer qualms about leaving Lily with Roman than she had imagined she would. It was hard to walk around the historic building and not be excited by the, what had he called it... *potential*?

She smiled to herself. The place had that, all right.

The room that had been made up for her was pretty and south-facing. There was a brand-new cot and stacks of fresh linen in the adjoining dressing room and beyond that a bathroom. Opening another door, she found herself in a room that was a twin to her own. The folded clothes on the bed said that she was standing in Roman's room.

Cosy, she thought. *Umpteen rooms and he's next door?* Was she appalled by this obvious manoeuvring? No, she was excited. The discovery shook her a lot more than seeing his boxer shorts neatly stacked!

She had anticipated sharing some sort of romantic dinner with him so she was a bit thrown when even before she had put Lily to bed he explained that there were urgent things he needed to attend to in the library, which it seemed was to be his temporary office.

Having decided to repulse any advances he made, she was miffed not to be afforded the opportunity! If

this was part of a 'treat 'em mean keep 'em keen' strategy, it was working, because as she sat enjoying a lonely
microwave supper she thought of little but him.

She fell to sleep listening for the creak of floorboards
and woke some time later, her maternal sensors picking up Lily's cry.

'Darling, it's all right, Mummy's here.'

She stopped on the threshold. She wasn't the only
one who was here. Roman was standing over the cot,
winding up the mobile suspended over it. He turned
and mimed a hushing gesture. Lily's heavy eyelids were
already closing; her lashes lay blue black against her
rosy cheeks.

Izzy nodded, aware rather belatedly that she was
wearing only her nightdress. She smiled and tiptoed her
way back into her own room, her heart beating faster
because she knew he was following her.

She turned just as he was closing the adjoining door
carefully behind him.

He struggled to keep his eyes on her face. 'I'm glad
I saw you.' The semi-sheer ankle-length nightdress she
wore was rendered virtually transparent by the lamplight, revealing the curvaceous outline of her body and
the strategic dark areas… 'I meant to catch you before
you went up. I'm sorry I had to leave you on your first
night, but there were some contracts I had to sort. I don't
mean to bore you. Did you find everything all right?'

'Yes, thank you…fine.' He looked like the living
incarnation of everything that was male and raw and
powerful. He was the very opposite of her and things
inside her shifted and tightened as she stared at him.

He tipped his head, feeling the flare of attraction
between them so strongly that it made his blood burn.

This was only ever going to work if he let her dictate the pace, one false move on his part and… 'Right, then, I'll… Sleep well.'

'No.'

He turned back, a question in his eyes.

She stood there wanting him so much it hurt; every cell ached with the wanting. She wanted to feel his body hard and male, smell his skin and enjoy the tactile sensations of flesh on flesh. She wanted to tangle her fingers in his hair, taste…oh, taste…!

How long could she carry on resisting and why should she?

The escalating desires were consuming her, sapping her ability to think beyond these basic primal needs. She felt as if she were drawn towards him by some invisible cord that was reeling her in. She'd been fighting so hard, fighting not to admit how much she wanted him, and why not…? The time to be cautious had been two years ago; this was no leap in the dark.

Why not?

Uneasily aware that her defiance masked a desperate need that she didn't want to think about, she faltered. 'I…I don't want you to go…'

The broken plea had barely left her lips and he was at her side, framing her face in his big hands, kissing her.

He felt his control slipping away as her hand slid up his back and she whispered in his ear, 'I want to feel your skin.'

He pulled back only far enough to rip off his shirt and place her hands on his bare chest.

Eyes slumberous and passion-glazed, Izzy ran her hands over the planes and ridges of muscle on his torso and up over his broad shoulders. Need ached through her, sweet like honey, sharp like a knife. 'Your skin feels like silk.'

She ran her tongue across her lips and the action caused his eyes to darken. He pulled her into him, causing their bodies to collide. His open mouth covered hers, hot and moist, his firm lips moving with the same erotic, sensuous motion that his hips were against her lower body.

'Yes…oh, God,' she murmured against his mouth. She was spinning out of control and she loved it!

Still kissing her, he scooped her up in his arms and carried her across the room. When they reached the bed he placed her on her feet.

The febrile glow in his eyes made her dizzy as he caught hold of the bottom of her nightdress. She lifted her arms to help him and a moment later her nightdress hit the opposite wall.

He lifted her bodily onto the bed, kneeling over her prone form, and allowed his burning gaze to roam freely over her naked body.

Izzy experienced a moment's doubt; the last time he had seen her she had not had a child—her body had changed since then. Her hips were wider, her breasts fuller and softer; she had a woman's body now.

Would he like what he was seeing?

'You are so beautiful…more beautiful.' He had never wanted a woman like this in his life; it was the same as that night, only more so.

Izzy released the breath she had been holding and reached up and dragged him down, her hands deep in his dark hair as she pulled his mouth to her aching breasts. He took first one hardened nipple in his mouth and then the other, drawing a series of moans and gasps from Izzy as she writhed beneath him in a frenzy of desire.

She bit into his shoulder, sliding her arms around his back and arching as she tangled her fingers deeper into his hair, bringing his mouth to hers. She sank her tongue between his lips, wanting to taste him, wanting him to taste her.

She was gasping for breath and almost delirious with pleasure when he began to kiss a path down her throat. Her body was limp and pliant as he pulled her onto her side, looping one of her thighs across his hip as he kneaded her buttock, his fingers sinking into the soft springy flesh. He eased a finger along the damp cleft between her legs, drawing a low moan from her parted lips as he stroked her slowly and rhythmically.

He rolled her onto her back and she lay there looking at him with big passion-glazed eyes as he tore off his remaining clothes and returned to her.

'Don't close your eyes,' he insisted. 'I want you to watch.'

She did watch as his hands were on her body, touching her everywhere, lighting fires and massive conflagrations until she burned all over and deep inside, releasing all the loneliness and fear that had been hiding there.

Izzy was dimly aware of a voice that sounded as if it was coming from a long way off, a voice begging and pleading, realising with a sense of shock that it was hers when he whispered in her ear.

'I can't wait either, *cara*.'

She arched her body, lifting off the bed as he slid into her in one hard thrust. She clung to him, her face pressed into his shoulder, her arms wrapped around his sweat-slicked muscled back as he filled her again and again until she almost fainted with the sheer bliss of it.

She climbed so high it felt as if she were flying. Then as the vibrations that began deep inside her grew, she fell, losing a sense of self as her entire body shook in a series of shattering sensory explosions.

Later, when their sweat-slick bodies had cooled, he pulled her face from his shoulder and ran a finger down the thin pink line low on her abdomen.

'Tell me about that.'

'I had a long labour and things went wrong… I had a Caesarean.'

She saw his expression and touched his face with her hand. 'It was nothing major… I just wish I could have seen her when she was born.'

She had given birth alone and in pain and she was the one offering comfort.

'Now we both have our scars,' she teased, reaching down to touch those on his leg. 'They're from your illness…?' She had thought when she first saw them that they were from an accident.

'I had bone cancer. I was lucky it was picked up early when they X-rayed me after a climbing fall. Not pretty.'

'They're part of you,' she said, looking surprised.

'Lauren didn't think so. I don't blame her—any woman would have felt the same.'

Izzy raised herself up on one elbow, wondering if he defended the indefensible because he still loved her. 'You have a very low opinion of women.'

Roman looked at her fondly. 'Not everyone has your strong stomach.'

Not everyone had a man like Roman in their bed, including the shallow and stupid-sounding Lauren.

* * *

As Gennaro pulled into the outside lane of the motor-
way Roman closed his laptop.

'Are things all right?' Last night had been the first
time he had spent a night away from Izzy and Lily. He
had spent most of the time wondering what they were
doing. He wouldn't have gone at all if Izzy hadn't insisted.

Parenting was a steep learning curve. The time he
spent working he felt guilty he was neglecting his family and the time he spent with his family he felt guilty
he was neglecting work.

When he had discussed it with Izzy she had laughed
and said, 'Welcome to my world, big boy. Women have
been feeling that way for ever and a day!'

Izzy... The situation was working out better than he
could have hoped. There was just one development that
he had not expected. People said things in the throes of
passion they did not necessarily mean, but three times
now she had moaned, *'I love you!'* Roman was certain
that she was just babbling nonsense; she had to be. The
whole point of their relationship was to be together without falling in love...

'What's that?' Izzy asked, looking at the gift-wrapped
box.

'Open it and see.'

She flashed him a smile and unpicked the prettily
tied bows, resisting the impulse to tear them. She carefully unfolded the beautiful layers of tissue paper to reveal the item that lay beneath.

'It's beautiful!'

'How do you know? It's still in the box! It's a dress.'
He had given women gifts on many occasions, many

more expensive than this one, but he had never watched his gifts being opened before. Now he found himself feeling almost nervous, experiencing a desire for them to be pleased.

Taking hold of the fabric, she took it out, gasping as the beaded silk unfolded to reveal the most glamorous dress she had ever seen.

'It's beautiful.' Her wide eyes took in details of the low-waisted, heavily beaded, twenties-inspired dress. It was made of silver-grey silk; the tiny beads arranged in geometric patterns were silver and they winked and caught the light. 'Real golden age Hollywood,' she enthused.

'It is only a dress.'

It was nothing.

Conscious that through his sophisticated eyes her reaction might seem a little over the top, Izzy damped down the enthusiasm levels of her response as she pointed out sensibly, 'But I'll never wear it.' Holding the dress against her, she studied her reflection in the antique mirror she had recently installed on the opposite wall.

'Why not?' he asked. She reminded him of a child opening her presents on Christmas morning.

She arched a delicate brow. 'When did you last see me in anything that didn't involve jeans?'

She looked very good in jeans, he thought as his eyes slid to her tightly rounded derrière. Especially the pair she was wearing now, which clung in all the right places.

'You will have an opportunity tonight.'

'Tonight?'

'You have spent the last three weeks in some sort

of self-imposed exile.' As exiles went the one they had shared had not been a trial, but enough was enough. 'We are going out.'

'Is this you asking?'

'No, this is me being masterful, or, if you prefer, autocratic?' He grinned and she thought just how charming he was.

'It is all arranged. I have asked Chloe to babysit. You have no problem with that?'

Chloe was an art student who had been helping Izzy out with the sample boards.

'It seems to me that she is level-headed and responsible.'

'Yes, she is.' And Lily loved her.

'So tonight we will dress up and dine together.'

'But why? Do you want to check out my table manners or something?' she teased. 'Check out I'm not a social liability before you sign on the dotted line,' she added, only half joking now.

Wishing she had not introduced a reference to the subject that was always the elephant in the room, Izzy veiled her eyes, but not before her cheeks had grown self-consciously pink.

'I have had no opportunity to show you off and it is your birthday, isn't it?'

Her blue eyes widened as they flew to his face. 'How did you know?'

He thought of the report he had downloaded on his laptop. He did not imagine that its existence would endear him to her, so instead he turned the question back on her. 'I think the question should be why didn't you tell me?'

Izzy was conscious of a fizz of excitement. The idea

of dressing up and eating a meal with an incredibly handsome man was not totally awful. If you had fallen deeply, hopelessly in love with said man it did not detract from the idea of making yourself beautiful for him and seeing his eyes light up with, if not love, she'd settle for lust.

She was a realist and this relationship could work if only she could keep her damned tongue under control. Luckily the few times her feelings had got the better of her and she'd blurted out her true feelings for him he hadn't noticed, but she couldn't rely on her luck holding out. She had to keep her mouth shut.

'Where did you have in mind?' She held the dress out at arm's length, admiring the way the hand-sewn beadwork caught the light. It was beautiful, but awfully dressy for the local places she knew of.

'Edinburgh…actually just outside.'

Her jaw dropped. 'Edinburgh!'

'The Dornie.'

'Dornie!' Izzy was neither star-struck or a foodie, but everybody knew about the restaurant that had been opened the previous year. You needed to know someone just to get on the waiting list! It was apparently the place to be seen and she was assuming the food wasn't bad either.

'I have a jet on standby; we will be home before the witching hour if you wish. Do not look at me like this is everyday stuff for fairy godmothers.'

And billionaire playboys, except she had been forced to rethink many of her assumptions about him over the past few weeks, including the playboy reputation she had believed him to have. Izzy gave a wistful glance at the dress. 'Really?' The prospect of wearing something feminine was incredibly tempting.

'Would I lie to you?'

Izzy's smile faded. 'No,' she said slowly. 'I don't think you would.'

When had that happened?

She trusted him, which was no reason to cry, she thought, blinking back the hot tears she felt swimming in her eyes. She looked down and sniffed and when she lifted her head her blue eyes were guarded. It was just as well he hadn't been there when she had realised she had fallen in love with him.

That had been the day she had discovered her old sketchbook and had seen his face drawn on every page. It had hit her almost immediately that each likeness of him she had sketched had been drawn with love. Her sketchbook was a love story—an unrequited-love story. She had cried over the pages until they were soggy. She'd experienced love at first sight and she hadn't even known it!

'What time do we leave?'

There was a slight pause and when he replied she had the impression he had been on the brink of saying something else.

'Six-thirty…?'

Her mouth opened in a silent O of protest. 'I'll never manage that. Lily needs—'

'I will see to Lily. You go get ready.'

Tipping her head in acknowledgement of this suggestion she turned to leave, then, with her hand on the door handle, turned back. 'It's a lovely birthday present, thank you, Roman.'

'It is not your birthday present.' He watched her eyes

flicker wider, saw the question in them and smiled. 'I hope the dress fits.'

It did fit.

It couldn't have fitted better and, nibbling her full lower lip, Izzy viewed her reflection through narrowed eyes from several angles.

It was perfect. The only thing she would have changed were the freckles on the swell of her bust where the square-cut neckline of the bodice was not as modest as it had appeared. But the rest, she gave a little nod of approval. Below knee length the beaded panels of the drop-waisted skirt swirled outwards when she moved, falling against her legs with a sexy swish.

The question was would Roman be as impressed?

The jury was still out on that one. She walked into the room a little while later complete with a jewelled, flapper-style headband placed in her glossy chestnut hair, her figure elongated by a pair of elegant spiky heels. Roman simply stared at her for what felt like a century, then tilted his head and said, 'You look good.'

It was hard not to feel deflated by such an under-whelming reaction, but then she had a tendency to ex-pect too much when it came to their relationship.

Izzy felt impatient with herself. *Maybe,* she reflected grimly, *I ought to write 'He doesn't love you' a hundred times, then it might sink in.* Then she might stop laying herself open to this sort of disappointment.

When she had walked into the room Roman's vision had blurred. It had taken all his control not to grab her and take her right there. Ironic it had taken him some time to persuade her to wear the thing and now all he wanted to do was rip it off!

He had stood there like a statue struggling to control his rampant arousal, knowing that he couldn't even move without revealing his condition. His libido-whacked brain hadn't even been able to come up with something to cover up his lapse—he must have looked like a total idiot.

He wanted to cringe every time he thought about it. But why?

Expressing his desire for Izzy had never been a problem for him, and definitely not an embarrassment! But this wasn't just desire, it was… He shook his head, refusing to acknowledge the word hovering there just on the outer limits of his consciousness, telling himself instead that she was just getting under his skin. On the other hand she was the mother of his child and it was only natural that there was a degree of emotional attachment. It didn't mean…

Bringing this internal debate to an end with a muttered curse, he shook his head and walked across the room, filling a heavy leaded crystal glass with brandy and lifting it to his lips.

It meant nothing, he told himself, draining the glass.

CHAPTER ELEVEN

'I THINK I could get used to this,' Izzy admitted as they disembarked from the private jet and into the waiting limousine. She repressed the urge to pinch herself. It felt as though she were playing a part in a film, but this was real.

'I think people might think I'm someone important,' she confided as he slid into the seat beside her.

'You are someone important.'

Her heart started thudding. 'I am?'

'You're the mother of our child.'

She hid her disappointment behind a smile of dazzling brilliance. While she was proud of being Lily's mother, she would have liked to be important for herself, not because she was part of a package deal.

'You owe me.'

If her film had been a romantic comedy he would have said, 'because you are the woman I love,' but this wasn't a romantic comedy or even a film.

It was her life and by most people's standards it was pretty amazing, so she told herself to stop whining and enjoy.

'I owe you?'

'The first person to mention the subject.' Baby talk

by mutual agreement had been banned for the evening. 'And that was you.'

He lifted a concessionary finger and looked amused as he leaned back in his seat. Slipping the button on his dinner jacket, he shrugged and held up his hands in mock surrender. 'All right, you win.'

'So go on, give it up.' She held out her hand. 'What's my prize?'

Roman took her hand and placed it behind his neck. Leaning in close, he positioned his mouth over hers, catching her eyes with his as he whispered throatily, 'This.'

Her eyes closed as he kissed her with small tantalising, nipping kisses that tugged at her lip, touched the corner of her mouth before going deeper. His arms were like steel bands wrapped around her, drawing her closer as he kissed her with a passion that amounted to desperation, kissed her as though he would drain her life force.

When his head lifted they were both breathing hard. They stayed close, his nose pressed to the side of hers, his fingers curled around her chin, stroking down the curve of her cheek.

'Was that my birthday present?'

'Pay attention, *cara*. That was your prize. This,' he added, leaning back in his seat to search the pocket of his jacket, 'is your present.'

Izzy looked at the small velvet box he held in his hand. 'I don't wear jewellery.'

'I'd noticed. I'll admit it does make present buying more difficult.' Though in his opinion her perfect satin-soft skin needed no adornment. He felt the familiar heat flicker in his belly as his eyes slid down the smooth column of her marble-pale neck and down to the freckle-sprinkled slopes of her breasts.

The flicker became a flame.

'So it's not jewellery?'

'Open it and see,' he urged, frowning at her apparent reluctance. He had taken a lot of trouble planning this moment, but her reaction was the one thing he wasn't able to plan or, as it turned out, predict.

She took a deep breath and opened the box, her normally animated voice sounding oddly flat to his ears as she said, 'It's beautiful.'

Beautiful hardly did the ring justice. The central diamond was massive and surrounded by dozens of smaller gems arranged like petals around the glittering centrepiece.

Frustrated, he compared her almost childlike enthusiasm for the dress with the stiff formality of her forced smile.

'You expected something else?' He placed his thumb under her small round chin and tilted her face up to him. 'You don't like diamonds?'

'Diamonds are… Is this an engagement ring?'

She had to be the only woman in the world who would need to ask. 'That was the idea. You do not have to sit on your hand. I will not force it on your finger.'

With a self-conscious flush she pulled her left hand free. 'But you said we wouldn't talk about—'

'Marriage,' he completed when she choked on the word. 'I agreed to wait and see if the trial was working, to see if we could work together as a unit, as a family.' Up until this moment he had thought they were a perfect fit, and not just in bed where she continued to delight and amaze him. 'I had thought that we were.' He arched a sardonic brow. 'You think differently?'

'No…not really,' she admitted slowly. 'But it's early days.'

Her addendum drew an incredulous look. 'How long did you have in mind?' he asked sardonically. 'Twenty years and then we will review the situation? I am sorry, Isabel, I have been very patient. These weeks have not been…unpleasant?' he bit out sarcastically.

Her reluctance felt like a betrayal. Their relationship had always been about Lily, about being with her, but he did not just look forward to seeing his daughter at the end of a day. He looked forward to seeing Isabel and spending time with her too. The sex between them was sensational and he had assumed they were on the same page here. But her lukewarm reaction had felt like a slap in the face… Actually the blow landed somewhat lower. It wasn't as though he had expected her to clap her hands and jump up and down with enthusiasm— well, actually, yes, he had.

Her lashes swept downwards. 'No, you know they haven't been unpleasant. Of course they haven't.'

He gave a shrug and waited.

'Can't we just leave things as they are?' The expression on his taut face made her stop and swallow before continuing in a fake cheery voice. 'I mean, like they say, if it's not broke don't fix it,' she quoted.

'I do not give a damn what *they say*,' he ground out. 'It may come as something of a surprise to you, but there are some women who would not consider it such a terrible thing to be married to me.'

'Well, marry them, then—all of them, for all I care!' she flung back.

'They are not the mother of my child.'

No, and that encapsulated the problem. The only reason he wanted to marry her was for Lily. Was it so wrong of her to want more?

Wrong maybe, unrealistic definitely. *You're not going to get more, Izzy,* said the voice of practicality in her head. *You take what's on offer or walk away from the table.*

The stark choice made her shiver. Over the past few weeks she had experienced the sort of life she had never even known existed. It wasn't just the incredible sex—though the thought of never losing herself in the sheer joy and bliss of belonging to him made her grow cold. No, it was so many other things too. Just hearing his voice, watching his face as he watched Lily, his dry sense of humour.

It was all about love.

She took a deep breath and thought it was worth a try.

'You're not going to pretend you're in love with me?'

She lowered her lashes in a defensive sweep; his silence spoke volumes and Izzy was lanced with an intense pain.

'I love Lily.'

She nodded. 'I know.' Watching Roman fall under the spell of his little daughter had been like watching a tender love story unfold, one that on occasions had brought emotional tears to her eyes. She squared her slender shoulders and lifted her head.

'Are you asking me to say I love you, Izzy? Is that what you're asking? Because I've already told you that—'

Pride made her keep her eyes trained on his face

and not reveal by as much as a flicker how much his comment had mortified her. 'You don't do love. Yes, I know.' Izzy even managed a credible laugh as she hid the pain in her heart behind a practical façade.

'Relax, Roman, people say things in the heat of the...' Her eyes dropped as memories of the occasions when she had been unable to totally keep her feelings inside caused her rigid composure to slip.

'In bed,' he supplied bluntly.

'Let's leave bed out of one discussion.'

'It's the one place we have no discord.'

'You can't live in bed!' Struggling for composure, she lowered her voice to a dull monotone, adding woodenly, 'I know that you don't believe you'll ever—but what if you do fall in love with someone else, Roman? What happens then?' She thought that she could just about cope with the pain of loving him and knowing her love would never be returned, simply because she knew the pain of not being with him would be so much worse. But could she really bear to witness him falling in love with another woman and all the time wishing and wanting it to be her?

'It will not happen.'

His quiet certainty made her want to scream. 'All right then, if I fall in love.' She pulled back in her seat, shocked by the expression of black fury that surfaced in his eyes.

'I will make sure you don't.'

She did not read too much into that statement; she had challenged his male ego, that was all. She was his property.

'I know you think you can do anything.' And most of the time he was right. 'But you can't stop falling in love with someone.' *Ask the expert,* she thought dully. 'It just happens.'

'*Happens?* Things do not happen unless we allow them to and you will be too busy juggling the demands of our children with your work and—' He broke off mid-sentence, frowning fiercely and muttering something in his native tongue under his breath.

'Wait a moment.' The screen separating them from the driver swished silently down. 'Why are we stopped?' Roman rapped, realising that they were no longer moving, though he had no idea of how long they had been stationary.

The driver replied with a slightly embarrassed, 'We're here, sir.'

'We're not ready yet. Just keep on driving.'

'Yes, sir.'

Was he going to carry on driving round and round until she said yes?

'What is so funny?'

'You…me…us, I suppose. You said children?'

'Well, we managed it once and we weren't even trying. I see no reason why we shouldn't try again.' The sardonic humour in his voice was edged out by a harder tone as he admitted, 'I do not like to think of Lily as a lonely only child. So, yes, not immediately but—'

'Were you lonely?'

'Isabel, do not change the subject. Will you marry me?'

'You're the one who changes the subject every time I ask you anything about yourself.'

'I have told you more about myself than any other person on the planet.' He took her calf and pulled her foot into his lap. 'Very pretty,' he admitted, turning her foot to admire the thin-strapped high heels she wore. His fingers slid upwards over the curve of her calf. He felt the shiver that rippled through her body and smiled. 'You have a tendency to think too much about the past.'

'Better than ignoring it.' She broke off, closing her eyes and gasping as his fingers slid higher under the skirt of her dress. The rush of moist heat to the juncture of her thighs was instantaneous.

'Please, Roman, we're not alone…' she appealed, flashing a warning look towards the driver.

He flashed a predatory grin and withdrew his hand with a show of reluctance, but kept her foot in his lap. 'You like rules and conformity. I'd have said that marriage and you are a match made in heaven.'

'Are you saying I'm boring?' Helpless to evade his unblinking black stare, she dodged the question. 'I never saw myself married.'

'I never thought of myself as a father. Marriage will be a legal contract, nothing more. It will formalise what we have.'

'What do we have?' *Say love,* she willed him. *Say love.*

'We have Lily and the desire to make a home for her. We would not be going into this with any unrealistic expectations—that has to put us ahead of the game.'

For unrealistic expectations, she read love. The logic behind the confident pronouncement passed her by, but she was fully occupied in trying to fight the sudden desire to burst into tears.

'We will make it work for us because it's the best thing for Lily. You know it and I know it. Yes or no, Isabel?' He looked at her steadily, his normally expressive voice flat almost. The rigidity of his expression and the faint hint of colour along the sharp edge of his chiselled cheekbones were the only outward indication of the tension within.

Izzy sucked in a deep breath. Roman was not the shallow womaniser she had initially taken him for and he was a good father. He loved Lily—wasn't that enough? Ignoring the voice in her head that told her she was settling.

Yes, she was settling. She would never have a place in Roman's heart, but she could have a place in his life. They would be together, a family; it would be enough, she told herself. It would have to be, warned the voice in her head.

'Yes, I will marry you.'

For a moment his expression was unguarded. Then a moment later the blaze of male triumph was concealed by the dark mesh of his lashes.

Izzy felt a stirring of unease. He had got what he wanted, but for how long? What chance did such a one-sided marriage have? Pushing away the voice of doubt, she took the ring from its velvet bed and slid it onto her finger. 'It's very beautiful,' she said, holding out her hand for him to examine. She would have to have enough love for both of them.

'It's too big.' He had wanted it to be perfect.

'Not really…' The ring slipped around her finger and she shrugged. 'Well, maybe a little,' she conceded.

'We can get it adjusted. What are you doing?' he asked as she slipped it off.

The sharpness in his voice brought her head up. 'I can't wear it, Roman. I'll lose it.'

'You won't lose it.' He took her hand and pushed the ring back down her finger. 'It looks good on you,' he said, retaining the grip on her hand. Her fingers curled of their own volition around his.

Izzy felt her cheeks heat and her breathing quicken as their glances tangled and locked. The sexual tension that materialised from nowhere was so dense it had a texture and a taste of its own. Her eyelids felt heavy and her body, conditioned to respond to him, ached.

She swallowed and whispered an agonised. 'Oh, God!'

His dark, hawkish gaze riveted on Izzy's face and Roman expelled a long hissing sigh. 'Just hold that thought for later. In the meantime…' He gave a regretful sigh and, releasing her hand, leaned back in the seat.

'In the meantime?' she prompted.

'Are you hungry?' He saw her expression and gave a rumble of laughter. 'In a three-star Michelin sort of hungry?'

'I knew that…and, yes, I am.'

He dragged a hand across his face and wrenched his eyes off the pouting invitation of her luscious lips. 'Then let's go see if this place lives up to its reputation.'

The meal was, if anything, too much of a success and a bubbling Izzy spent the entire journey back babbling about the famous faces she'd spotted there.

'Why didn't you tell me you were friendly with Rob Fullwood? He's not as tall as he looks in films, but very good-looking. I think it's the eyes. Thank you, Gennaro,' she added, smiling at the burly Italian as he held the door wide for her to exit the four-wheel drive. She waited for Roman to walk around the car to meet her.

Roman gritted his teeth and glanced at his watch. He hoped this star-struck Izzy would vanish as quickly as she had appeared. One of the things he liked about

Izzy was that, unlike many women, she did not feel the need to fill every silence with words.

'I am not friendly with him. We have met, that is all.'

'You have more than met his girlfriend.'

The words she had been trying so hard not to say just slipped out, and there they were, impossible to take back.

Izzy veiled her gaze and began to walk quickly towards the front door. 'I hope Lily has been good for Chloe.'

Halfway up the steps Roman caught her up. He caught her arm and pulled her back to face him.

Izzy stared at her hand, twisting the ring around her finger as she gave a theatrical shiver. 'Goodness, it's quite cold, isn't it?'

'No. Is that why you've been so weird?'

Her head came up. 'Is what why…? I have not been weird.'

He arched a sardonic brow. 'Yes, I have slept with Connie Brady.'

She felt the stab of jealousy like a sword thrust. 'That's really none of my business.'

'You don't have to be jealous. We only lasted a week.'

'I only lasted a night,' she countered spikily.

'The two situations are not comparable.'

An image of the tall Nordic blonde model with the endless legs, hair extensions and false eyelashes came into her head. Most men had been intrigued by her, particularly her gravity-defying breasts. 'True, I have a baby and she has massive boobs!'

She was not aware that she was clutching her own boobs when his amused glance lingered there. She dropped her hands hastily and reminded herself of the old adage of quality being superior to quantity.

'You are jealous!'

Izzy narrowed her eyes and delivered a haughty look. 'I don't much like the idea of walking into a room filled with your ex-lovers and having them laugh about me behind my back. Don't...' she snapped as he laid his hands on her shoulders.

He ignored her.

'I think the chances of you being in a room filled with my exes is unlikely, but, that aside, they will not be laughing at you when you are my wife. They will be envying you.'

A bubble of laughter emerged from her aching throat. 'Do you know how arrogant that sounds?'

'Yes, but it made you laugh so who cares?' He hooked a thumb under her chin and turned her face up to him. 'While the women will be envying you the men will be envying me. You put all those women in the shade tonight.' His glance slid down the slender length of her shapely body. 'I have wanted to kiss you all night and all you have done is witter on like a star-struck teenager. *Madre di Dio!*'

'What?'

'I have just realised that one day Lily will be a teenager.'

His horrified expression drew another laugh from Izzy.

'But seriously, Isabel, you do not have to be jealous. I have had lovers in the past, but once we are married I will respect my vows.'

Izzy nodded and expelled a sigh, allowing the jealous poison to drain away with the trapped air… A tiny portion lingered stubbornly.

She was ready to believe that the casual lovers he had had over the years meant nothing, but Roman had been engaged once before to Lauren. Lauren, the beautiful blonde who had dumped him. Theirs had not been a casual relationship; he had been going to marry her, not for practical reasons, but for love.

She touched the ring on her finger and looked up at him and felt something twist hard in her chest. He was so beautiful. She had ruined the entire evening by being eaten up with jealousy, but there was still some evening to enjoy.

'That kiss you were talking about…?'

She shivered as he framed her face between his big hands. The kiss was deep with a passion that sent a shiver of pleasure through her body and without a word he picked her up.

In the bedroom they stood facing each other and in the moonlight they undressed slowly, punctuating the slow striptease with murmurs and moans of pleasure and deep, languid, drowning kisses that made Izzy's lips tingle and her insides melt.

She closed her eyes as he removed the last item of her clothing, her panties, pressing a kiss to the curls at the juncture of her thighs as she stepped out of them.

Kneeling, he curved his hands around the taut curve of her rounded bottom, kissing his way up her belly. He stood up, slowly running his hands up her body to cup and caress the creamy swells of her aching breasts.

As he kissed her breasts, running his tongue across the engorged rosy peaks, Izzy's fingers closed over the hot, silky shaft of his erection, drawing a raw groan from his throat.

They both stumbled to the bed, falling on it in a tangle of limbs.

His hands shook as he parted her legs, but Izzy was shaking too hard herself to notice. The mixture of raw passion and tenderness in his face brought tears to her eyes in response to emotions she had no words to express.

A keening cry was wrenched from her dry throat as he slid fully into her, burying himself. The primal connection was stronger than she had ever felt it before as they moved together, straining towards the final explosion of mind-numbing pleasure.

When Roman finally rolled off her, she was relaxed in every cell of her body and she curled up against him and fell asleep.

Surely he could not make love like that without loving her a little, was her last wistful thought.

The next day Roman left early to attend a charity auction he had committed to months earlier.

'I would get out of it if I could,' he said, sitting on the bed to kiss her goodbye. A few minutes later he was back.

Izzy looked up at him drowsily. 'What's wrong?'

'Come with me.'

She blinked, startled. 'You mean to the charity auction?'

He nodded. 'Why not? I can wait.'

Fully awake now, Izzy gave a twisted smile. 'I'd love to, but I've already arranged to go shopping to the paint wholesaler's and Chloe is coming with me. She's a great sounding board and we're dropping Lily off for a play date with—'

'Fine. It was just a thought.'

She thought she saw something in his face that suggested her response had not pleased him, but when she had rubbed her bleary eyes it was not there… Maybe she had imagined it.

'Enjoy your day and I hope Lily enjoys her play date.'

Lily didn't, as it turned out, as she was a bit out of sorts when she woke that morning. Izzy cancelled her play date and her trip to the wholesaler's.

By lunchtime Lily's out of sorts had become something a lot more worrying. Lily was crying inconsolably, thrashing around in her cot red-faced. Izzy took her temperature and the reading on the strip was so high that she took it again.

The reading was a degree higher.

Should she bundle Lily in the car and drive to the local emergency department or should she ring for an ambulance? Having been in the habit of making decisions for herself for most of her life, it struck her forcibly how much her mindset had changed when she found herself wishing that Roman were here to share the responsibility with.

After a few minutes she no longer cared if she came across as an overanxious mother and dialled the emergency number.

Rocking Lily in her arms, as the baby had gone scarily quiet, she tried to ring Roman, but kept getting put straight through to his messaging service. She decided not to leave an alarming message for him when there was a chance this was a false alarm and took the decision to wait until she could speak directly to him.

There were several times during the ambulance journey that she regretted this decision and would have given anything to know that Roman was on his way or even waiting for her at the hospital.

The doctors in the accident department were attentive and quietly efficient, which was comforting; what they had to say was not.

'It looks very much like Lily has appendicitis. We need to operate.'

'But she's a baby… No, that can't be right.' Fear tightened like an icy stone in her chest, panic clawing its way into her brain. She struggled to keep it at bay.

She had to stay in control; Lily needed her. She made herself take a deep breath and tried to lower her tension-hunched shoulders… *I want Roman…no, I can do this myself.*

'I realise this is alarming, but we will look after Lily for you and—'

'Of course, I'm sorry… When will you…?'

'Immediately.'

Lily's dark lashes fluttered against her cheeks and her eyes were filled with fear as she stared at the medic. 'That's not good, is it?'

'If you could sign the consent for us?'

Izzy sniffed and wiped a shaky hand across her face. 'Of course, she's just so little and…of course.'

Her hand continued to shake so hard she doubted her signature was legible. Everything happened very quickly and Izzy still wasn't sure whether to read good or bad things into this, but one minute she was sitting next to Lily's cot and the next she was walking along a seemingly endless corridor beside a cheery porter who wheeled Lily's cot to the entrance of the operating theatre.

Everyone was very kind but when she had to say goodbye to Lily she couldn't hold back the tears, as much as she tried. Back on the ward they promised that they would let her know the moment Lily was out of surgery and offered her a cup of tea.

Unable to stomach the idea of swallowing anything, she refused. Pacing the small cubicle, she dialled Roman. On the fourth time the phone was picked up.

She felt weak with relief until a voice she did not recognise said, 'This is Roman Petrelli's phone.'

A female voice.

'Who is this?'

There was a pause the other end, then a small laugh.

'Who is this? I want to speak to Roman.'

'Don't we all, darling?' the female voiced drawled.

Before she could respond Izzy heard a very familiar voice in the background. She didn't catch all of what Roman said; actually just one word—Lauren.

It was enough.

'Am I speaking to Lauren St James?'

'Yes, Roman is here now—'

'It doesn't matter—you can give him a message.'

'Sure, but—'

'Tell him his daughter is in surgery and that he can go to hell and stay there and I never want to hear, speak to or see him again!'

Having delivered her message, she sat on the plastic chair wanting to cry, but there were no tears. She felt cold and empty inside.

She hated him.

* * *

Later Roman had no memory of the drive from the city to the hospital; he just knew he made it in record time.

When he saw her face he immediately thought the worst.

His eyes went to the empty cot and Roman felt as though someone had reached into his chest and ripped out a vital organ. His lovely little girl… He couldn't bear life without his daughter, either of the women in his life—they were his heart. His haunted glance slid to Isabel. How had he been so stupid?

He had let himself love Lily, but he had been too weak and too scared to allow himself to admit that his heart held two women—mother and daughter, the two for ever inextricably linked.

And now one was gone…his baby. He breathed through the pain—his pain could wait. Right now Isabel needed him.

She looked like a broken doll, so pale and fragile, so vulnerable. It was enough to rouse the protective instincts of even a hardened professional.

But he was not a professional; he was the man who loved her. The man who had spent the last weeks avoiding facing this knowledge because basically he was a coward, he concluded contemptuously. A woman had rejected him once, a shallow woman who had little to recommend her but a pretty face and a family tree that stretched back into the mists of time, and for that reason he had decided to exclude the possibility of love from his life with all the logic and self-preservation instincts of a wounded animal.

He'd not been licking his wounds, he'd been nursing his bruised ego.

'Isabel.' The blazing blue eyes that lifted to him were not tear-filled, they were hate-filled. *'Tesoro mio.'*

'Do not speak to me. Do not touch me!' she shrieked shrilly, glaring at his outstretched hand as though it were a striking snake. 'You are not wanted here.'

'Well, tough, because I am here.' He looked at the empty cot and swallowed again. His eyes misted as he thought of Lily, the ache in his chest so intense that it felt like a steel band tightening like a vice around his ribcage. 'I should have been here for you.' His hands tightened into white-knuckled fists at his sides as he asked in a pain-filled whisper. 'When she…did she suffer?'

Izzy was blind to his suffering. 'Of course she suffered. Her appendix was about to burst, they said.'

'Appendix…burst…' His relief was cautious, the relief of a man who had lost something precious and was being offered it back. If he was given this second chance he would not waste it. 'You mean she is not…our little Lily is alive.'

The break in his deep voice brought her eyes to his face where strain drew the skin tight across his perfect bones, deepening the lines that radiated from his mouth and fanned out from around his eyes. Izzy gripped her lip between her teeth and fought against a tide of empathy. This was not about shared pain—she was alone.

'She's in recovery now,' Izzy said, watching as the colour slowly seeped back into his face and the awful grey receded. 'You thought she was dead?' She hated him but not enough to wish that on him. She wound her hands together to stop herself reaching out for him.

He nodded and swallowed.

'I didn't say…'

'I got your message.' Lauren had taken some delight in relaying it word for word—not that Lauren had the power to hurt him. 'But when I saw you looking so...'

'Needy and pathetic?' she charged acidly.

'Broken, I jumped to the conclusion.'

Izzy had paled at the description that was so close to how she did feel. She felt as though she had been shattered into a thousand pieces.

'Well, you were wrong so you can go.' She stuck out her chin and added, 'We don't need you!' Then proceeded to spoil the effect by bursting into tears.

In a heartbeat he was at her side, drawing her into the protective circle of his arms. She stood there sobbing, her head against his heart, knowing all the time she felt warm and protected in his arms that it was a lie.

He stroked her hair. 'I know what you think but you're wrong.'

Izzy lifted her tear-stained face and tried to pull away.

'No, you will listen. You will not continue to torture yourself and me with your imaginings. Lauren and I were seated at the same table at the charity auction.'

'Just a coincidence, I suppose.'

'I would hardly plan to meet another woman and then invite you to the same event, would I? Think about it.'

Izzy did and the first chink of doubt appeared in her betrayal scenario.

'She had your phone...'

He grimaced as he recalled the sequence of events that had led to this. 'I left my phone on the table. You know how I am with my phone.'

She nodded warily. For an organised man Roman managed to lose his phone more times a day than she could count. She had teased him about it, especially as often it was right under his nose.

'I was not at the table when it rang. I was with Lauren's husband, being fleeced for raffle tickets. I think it is likely I have won a balloon flight over the Masai Mara. How do you feel about balloon flights, *cara*?'

How do you feel about me?

'Lauren is married?'

He nodded.

Was it possible? A slow flush ran up under her skin until her face was burning.

'I blame myself. I knew you thought that I still had feelings for Lauren and I let you think it, because while you thought I was in love with her I wouldn't have to admit even to myself...*especially* to myself, that I had fallen in love with you.' He gave an uncomfortable shrug. 'I was so determined not to have my pride trampled over again that I refused to acknowledge what I was feeling. I was scared to admit that my fate, my happiness, depended on another human being—you. I let you think it was all about Lily, but it was always all about love.' He took her hand and raised it to his lips. 'You hold me in your hand, *cara*. I hope you will allow me into your heart.'

She stared at him in utter amazement, his smoky voice sending shivers down her spine.

'Roman, you've always been there. I think there was always an emptiness inside me that only you could fill.'

He kissed her then with a tenderness and passion that brought tears of emotion to her eyes.

He drew back a little and framed her face with one big hand. 'When I think of you all alone trying to cope with this... But of course you did cope alone—you are a remarkable woman and a perfect mother. I know you don't need me, *cara*, but will you have me? I know I have proposed before but this time is different.'

'I know,' she said, looking at him with eyes that were bright as stars. 'And I do need you. I have loved you so much and not being able to say it has been…hell!'

They kissed until the sound of a phone ringing in the main ward brought them back to earth.

Roman took her hand and pushed her into a chair, then dropped down into a squat at her side. Holding her hands between his, he said, 'Now tell me what happened and how our baby is. I wish so much that I had been there for you both. In the future I will always be there for you—you do know that.'

The anxiety and sincerity in his face brought a lump to her throat. 'Of course, you couldn't have known.'

'So tell me.'

She did and the sharing had a cleansing effect. She was finishing relating the tale and Roman was mopping her tears when the door opened and a cot was wheeled in.

'Here she is,' said the pretty nurse. 'Now, don't you worry about the drip—that's just until she starts taking fluids. Doctor will be along shortly but there are no problems. Everything is going to be fine.'

Izzy looked from her baby to her future husband and nodded. 'Yes, I do believe it is,' she said.

And even if it wasn't, she would always have Roman there to support her through the bad times and, of course, laugh with her through the good times.

'I wish I'd been here,' Roman said for the umpteenth time as he gazed into the cot.

Izzy went and took his hand. 'You're here now. That's what matters.'

She couldn't ask for anything more.

EPILOGUE

'AND it all began here,' Emma said with a sigh as she dropped to her knees to straighten the hem of Izzy's dress.

Izzy smiled and thought, *Actually, it all began in a crowded bar,* but she didn't correct her sister.

'It's so romantic and so quick too—three months.'

'No so quick,' Izzy murmured, glancing at her daughter, who looked as pretty as a picture in pink and was clutching a satin cushion in her chubby fingers.

'Watch your veil…' Michelle moved in to twitch the gauzy short antique lace that had belonged to her own grandmother. 'So pretty, darling,' Michelle said with a misty smile. 'You look truly glowing, and don't worry—I'll give Lily the ring at the very last minute.'

'Wing!' Lily said, her face wreathing in an expectant smile.

'Yes, darling…rings.' Izzy smiled. It had been decided that their daughter would deliver the wedding rings and the toddler had been given ample training in her role, though taking into account her tendency to try and eat the rings it had also been decided that she would be given the rings by Michelle at the crucial moment.

'Emma, remember—do not stoop when you go up the aisle.'

'Yes, Mum,' her willowy daughter responded to this maternal directive with a long-suffering sigh, adding as her mother vanished into the church with Lily, 'Do you know how many times a day she says that to me?'

She encountered Izzy's dreamy stare and grinned.

'You're not listening to a word I'm saying, are you?'

'No,' Izzy admitted. She wasn't nervous, she was just happy; she doubted people ever got to feel this happy.

Emma laughed. 'You look so soppy and I don't blame you. If I was going to get married to a hunk like Roman I would be on another planet too, but for goodness' sake don't cry,' she instructed firmly. 'Rachel looked terrible when her mascara ran. On half the photos she looks like a panda,' she continued with her usual exuberance. 'But you look much prettier than Rachel did,' she added loyally. 'A pity you didn't choose that big dress with the proper long train. Not,' she added quickly, 'that that doesn't look nice.'

'Thank you.' Izzy gave a serene smile and smoothed down the dress she had picked in preference to the elaborate creation her sister had considered the ultimate in romance. A simple strapless, ankle-length cream silk, it clung to her curves, revealing a suggestion of cleavage, emphasising her pert bottom and making her waist look tiny, managing to be both sexy and demure.

Izzy had fallen in love with it the moment she had seen it.

The same way she had fallen in love with her gorgeous husband the moment she had seen him.

And he had fallen in love with her. It still didn't seem real sometimes, but it was, and Izzy had contractual evidence. No one else knew they had already married at a civil ceremony a week after Lily had been discharged from hospital. It had just been the three of them with a cleaner and a passer-by as witnesses. Roman had said they had wasted long enough and he wasn't prepared to waste another second.

It had not been romantic like today, in a traditional way with the pretty village church decked in clouds of white gypsophila and red roses and the beautiful dress and the speeches to come, but for Izzy it had been the most perfect day of her life when Roman had stood there, this strong, proud man with the glint of tears in his beautiful eyes, and said he would love her for ever.

She didn't need the window dressing; she just needed the man she loved and their baby girl. Not that she didn't intend to enjoy every second of this day. There was no way she was going to rob her family, Michael in particular, of the wedding they craved, and his chance to walk his daughter up the aisle.

'Ready, darling?'

Izzy smiled at her father, who had been striding nervously up and down the path outside the church, and took the arm he proffered. 'I am.'

The only thing she remembered about the service afterwards was the laugh that had rippled through the church when Lily had stolen the show when she delivered the rings, and Roman's face when he had turned and looked at her.

The incandescent love and pride in his face had brought the tears she had vowed not to shed; thank heaven for waterproof mascara!

Falling into the wedding car later in a cloud of confetti, she sank back into the seat and waved through the window at the crowds of well-wishers. When the car drew off, she turned and found Roman watching her. Her tummy did the crazy flip lurch it always did when she saw him; he was so handsome, and especially today in his beautifully tailored morning suit.

'What are you looking at?'

'The most beautiful woman in the world…and you're mine…' He took her hand and raised it to his lips, still holding her eyes with his. 'My woman.'

His smoky voice sent delicious shivers down Izzy's spine.

'You know,' he mused, stroking her cheek with one brown finger, 'I will never get tired of saying that.'

She caught his wrist and pressed a kiss to his palm. 'And I won't get tired of hearing it,' she promised, looking at him through the dark screen of her lashes.

Roman's free hand came up to cup her face. 'Your skin is so soft. You must remember to put on plenty of sun screen—apparently we are promised a very hot September.'

Izzy smiled. They were spending their honeymoon at Roman's villa at Lake Como.

'What is that secretive little cat's-got-the-cream smile for?' he wanted to know.

'I got you.'

Izzy broke away, breathless from the passionate kiss, some time later as the car arrived at the hotel where the reception was being held.

'Ready?' he asked, watching with a smile as she desperately tried to straighten her veil.

Ready for the rest of my life with you, Izzy thought, and nodded. At the last moment before they emerged

into the September sunshine and their waiting guests,
she caught his wrist.

'Is something wrong, *cara*?' Roman asked, picking
up on her tension.

'Not wrong,' she admitted. 'Pretty right, actually. I
didn't mean to tell you now, but…'

'The tension is killing me here, *cara*.'

'You know that appointment you planned to make to
check that Lily was not a one-off—that you can… Well,
don't bother, because it looks like you can.'

'You mean…?' Roman swallowed, his eyes going to
her trim middle. 'You are…'

She nodded. 'I did the test last night.' The night
Michelle had insisted she didn't spend with the groom.
'It's been killing me not telling you. I wanted to blurt it
out right there in the church. You're happy?'

'Happy!' he exclaimed, pulling her into his arms. 'I
am the luckiest man in the world!'

The ripple of applause and laughter given by the
waiting guests caused Izzy to draw back, pressing her
hand against his breastbone to lever herself off his lean
body.

'Roman, people are watching.'

'Shall I tell them to go away?'

'Roman, you can't tell guests to go away.'

His wicked grin flashed. 'Watch me,' he said.

Izzy did.

* * * * *

GILDED SECRETS
MAUREEN CHILD

Maureen Child is a California native who loves to travel. Every chance they get, she and her husband are taking off on another research trip. The author of more than sixty books, Maureen loves a happy ending and still swears that she has the best job in the world. She lives in Southern California with her husband, two children and a golden retriever with delusions of grandeur. Visit Maureen's website at maureenchild.com.

To the five talented, amazing women I was lucky
enough to work with on this set of stories.
Thanks to you all for making the
work so much fun!

One

Vance Waverly stood outside the auction house that bore his name and stared up at the impressive facade. The old building had had a face-lift or two over the past 150 years, but the heart of it remained. A structure dedicated to showcasing the beautiful, the historical, the unique.

He smiled to himself, letting his gaze slide across the "lucky" seven stories. At street level, twin cypress trees, trained into spirals, stood silent sentinel at the doorway. Windowpanes glittered in the early-summer light. Black, wrought-iron railings framed a second-story balcony. Gray stone gave the building its aura of dignity and the wide, arched window above the double front doors was etched with a single word—*Waverly*.

A glimmer of pride rose up inside Vance as he stared at the world his great-great uncle, Windham Waverly, had created. The long-dead man had ensured his own version of immortality by leaving behind the auction house that carried an illustrious reputation around the world.

And Vance was one of the last remaining Waverlys. So he had a proprietary interest in seeing that the auction house remained at the top of its game. As a senior board member, he made certain that he was involved in everything from the layout of the catalog to hunting down pieces worthy of being auctioned at Waverly's. This place was more his home than his luxury condo overlooking the Hudson River. The condo was where he slept.

Waverly's was where he lived.

"Yo, buddy!" a voice shouted from behind him. "You gonna be there all day or what?"

Vance turned to see a FedEx driver, packages stacked on the dolly he was balancing, waiting impatiently behind him. Vance stepped out of the way and let the man pass.

Before slipping into Waverly's, the driver muttered, "People think they own the damn sidewalks."

"Gotta love New York," Vance muttered.

"Morning."

Vance glanced to his right and watched as his half brother walked up to meet him. Rarely in New York, Roark had flown in for a meeting with some of his contacts. He was as tall as Vance, over six feet, with brown hair and green eyes. Not much of a family resemblance, but then, the brothers only shared a father. And until five years ago, when their father, Edward Waverly, died, Vance hadn't even known Roark existed.

In those five years, they had built up a solid friendship, and Vance was grateful—even though Roark insisted on keeping their family ties a secret. Roark still wasn't convinced that Edward Waverly had actually been his father. But the connection was enough to keep him at Waverly's. There was no proof beyond the letter Edward had left with his will. It was enough for Vance, but he could respect his brother's wishes.

"Thanks for meeting me," Vance said with a nod.

"Better be important," Roark said, falling into step beside Vance as they walked past Waverly's toward a small café on the corner. "Late night and I'm not officially awake yet."

He was wearing dark glasses against the sunlight, a worn brown leather jacket, T-shirt, jeans and boots. For a second, Vance envied his brother. He'd rather be in jeans himself, but his suit and tie were what was expected at Waverly's. And Vance always did the right thing.

"Yeah," he said as they claimed an outside table beneath a cheerfully striped umbrella. "It's important. Or it could be."

"Intriguing." Roark turned his coffee cup over at the same time Vance did and they both waited for the waitress to fill the cups and take their orders before speaking again. "So tell me."

Vance cupped the heavy porcelain mug between his palms and studied the black surface of his coffee for a long minute while he gathered his thoughts. He wasn't a man who usually paid attention to gossip or rumor. He had no patience for those who did, either. But when it concerned Waverly's, he couldn't take a chance.

"Have you heard any talk about Ann?"

"Ann Richardson?" Roark asked. "Our CEO?"

"Yes, that Ann," Vance muttered. Seriously, how many Anns did they know?

Roark pulled his sunglasses off and set them onto the table. He took a quick look around, at the people passing on the tree-lined sidewalk, at the other customers sitting at tables. "What kind of talk?"

"Specifically? About her and Dalton Rothschild. You know, the head of Rothschild auction house? Our main competitor?"

Roark just stared at him for a beat or two, then shook his head. "No way."

"I don't want to believe it, either," Vance admitted.

The CEO of Waverly's, Ann Richardson was brilliant at her job. Smart, capable, she had worked her way up to the top position in the firm, becoming the youngest person ever—male or female—to head an auction house of its size and scope.

Roark sat back in his chair and shook his head firmly. "What have you heard?"

"Tracy called me last night to give me a heads-up about a column that's appearing in today's *Post*."

"Tracy." Roark frowned, then nodded. "Tracy Bennett. The reporter you dated last year."

"Yeah. She says the 'story' breaks today."

"What story?"

"That Ann had an affair with Dalton."

"Ann's too smart to fall for Dalton's line of BS." Roark dismissed the idea out of hand.

Vance would like to. But in his experience, people made stupid decisions all the time. They usually blamed "love" for those bad choices, but the truth was, love was just the excuse to do whatever the hell they wanted to do. Love was a fable sold by greeting card companies and bridal fairs.

"I agree," he said. "But if there is something between them—"

Roark whistled. "What can we do about any of it?"

"Not much. I'll talk to Ann to let her know about this article that's coming out."

"And?"

"And," Vance said, gaze fixed on his brother, "I want you to keep your eyes and ears open. I trust Ann, but I damn sure don't trust Dalton. Dalton's always wanted Waverly's out of the way. If he can't buy us out, he'll try a takeover—or try to bury us." Vance took a sip of his coffee and narrowed his gaze on Roark. "We're not going to let that happen."

"Good morning, Mr. Waverly. I've got your coffee and the week's agenda ready for you. Oh! And the invitation to Senator Crane's garden party arrived by messenger late yesterday after you'd left."

Vance stopped in the doorway to his office and stared at his new assistant. Charlotte Potter was petite and curvy, with long, wavy blond hair restrained by a ponytail at the base of her neck. She had vivid blue eyes, full lips on a mouth that was rarely quiet and she seemed to be in constant motion.

He'd hired her as a favor to a retiring board member who had developed a fondness for her when she'd been his assistant. But Charlotte had only been with Vance a week now and he knew it wasn't going to work out.

She was too young, too pretty and too… She turned away to bend down and open the bottom drawer of the wood-grain file cabinet and he shook his head. Vance's gaze locked on the curve of her behind in the sleek black slacks she wore. Charlotte was too *everything*.

When she stood up, producing a thick, linen envelope for him, he told himself that he should simply pawn her services off on someone else in the company. He couldn't exactly fire her for being a distraction, but he sure as hell resented it.

Politically incorrect or not, Vance preferred his assistants to be either matronly or male.

His former assistant, Claire, had retired at sixty-five. She was cool, unflappable and notoriously anal about her workspace. There had never been so much as a pen out of place on her desk. Vance had felt confident that Claire was on top of everything.

Charlotte, on the other hand… He scowled at the ficus tree in the corner, the ferns on the shelf closest to the window and the deep-purple African violets on the corner of her desk. There were framed photos taking up space on her desk as well, though he hadn't looked at them too closely; he hadn't taken the time to do much more than notice the clutter.

Her pens were kept in a mug shaped like a New York Jets football helmet and there was a dish of M&M's beside her phone. Clearly, he never should have done that favor. *No good deed goes unpunished,* his father had often said. Turned out, the old man was right.

Vance didn't want distractions in the office under the best of circumstances. And now, with possible trouble looming with Rothschild, he wanted it even less—and if that made him a damn chauvinist, so be it.

As one of the last Waverlys associated with the auction house, Vance liked keeping his business hours devoted to business. And a pretty woman was not conducive to concentration.

"Thanks, Charlotte," he said, heading for his office. "Hold my calls until after the board meeting."

"I will. Oh, and call me Charlie," she said brightly.

Vance stopped, looked back over his shoulder at her and was nearly blinded by her brilliant smile. She went back to her desk and began flipping through the stack of mail. The long sweep of her hair fell over one shoulder and lay across her breast. Something inside him fisted uncomfortably. He hated to admit it, even to himself, but the woman was impossible to ignore.

Scowling to himself, he leaned one shoulder against the doorjamb and sipped at the coffee she'd given him. Watching her, he realized she was humming again as she had all last week. Off-key humming. Tone-deaf off-key.

He shook his head wearily. He had calls to make to Waverly's London office, to check on upcoming auctions there. A corner of his mind was still working over the rumors about

Ann and what that could mean to the auction house. And he was in no mood for the board meeting scheduled for that afternoon.

Charlotte straightened up, turned around and gasped, slapping one hand to her chest as if to hold her heart in place. Then she laughed shortly and shook her head. "You scared me for a second. I thought you had gone to your office."

He should have. Instead, he'd been "distracted." Not good. Frowning at his own wayward thoughts, he asked, "Did you have a chance to type up the agenda for today's meeting? I want to make some new notes before I meet with the board."

"Of course." She walked to her desk and plucked a file folder from a stack of similar ones. She handed it to him. "Along with the meeting agenda, I printed out the list you made of the private collections coming up for bid in the next few weeks."

He opened the folder, noting the neatly presented agenda with his handwritten notes now added in bold typeface. There were a few pages behind the first and he idly flipped through them, stopping at the last one. "What's this?"

"Oh." She smiled. "The next catalog layout looked a little crowded, so I adjusted a couple of the pictures and…"

He glanced at the work she'd done and had to admit it looked much better than it had before. The Ming Dynasty vases were each spotlighted now against a softly lit background, rather than lumped into a section that buried their distinctive beauty.

"I know I shouldn't have, but—"

"You did a good job," he said, closing the folder and looking up into her soft blue eyes.

"Really?" She gave him a bright smile. "Thank you. That's great. I was a little nervous about taking that on myself, I can tell you. It's just that this job is very important to me and I want to do it well."

An unfamiliar twinge of guilt poked at Vance as he read the eagerness in her gaze. She fairly vibrated with the thrill of her new job. Which only made him feel worse for regretting taking her on in the first place.

So maybe he'd give this a shot. All he had to do was stop noticing Charlotte as a woman.

But one quick look up and down her petite, curvy figure shut down *that* idea.

The phone rang and she reached for it. "Vance Waverly's office."

Her voice was low, seductive. Or maybe that was just his impression, he chided himself.

"Please hold," she said and hit the button on her phone. When she turned to him, Charlotte said, "It's Derek Stone, calling from the London office."

"Oh, good." Grateful for the excuse to leave Charlotte and get back to work, Vance took the folder and stepped into his office. "Put him through, please, Charlotte. And after this call, hold all the others."

"Absolutely, Mr. Waverly," she said.

Vance closed the door then strode across the room to his desk, barely noticing the thud of his footsteps against the gleaming wooden floor. Paintings by undiscovered artists hung alongside a couple of old masters on the ivory walls. A long couch hugged one wall, with a low-slung table and two chairs opposite it. A wall of windows stood behind his desk, offering a view of Madison Avenue and the always-busy city of Manhattan.

Reaching for his phone, he turned his back on the view, dropped into his chair and said, "Derek. Good to talk to you."

Completely drained, Charlie blew out a relieved breath and practically crawled back to her desk. The bright, cheerful smile on her face felt brittle enough to crack and she hoped to heaven that Vance Waverly hadn't sensed just how nervous she was around him.

"Does he really have to *smell* so good?" she muttered as she fell into her chair and propped her elbows on the desk. Cupping her face in her palms, she told herself to get a grip.

Her hormones didn't listen, sadly, and continued their happy little dance of excitement. This happened every time she got close to Vance Waverly and it was damn humiliating. How could she be so attracted to a boss who terrified half the people in this building?

But there it was. He was tall and broad-shouldered with dark brown hair that always looked a little tousled. His brown eyes had flecks of gold in them and his mouth almost never curved in a smile. He was all business and she had the distinct feeling that he was watching her closely, looking for any excuse he could find to fire her.

Which she was not going to allow to happen.

This job was the most important thing she had going for her. Well, she thought, sliding a glance at the photo of the smiling toddler on her desk, the *second* most important thing. But professionally, it was no contest. Working for Vance Waverly, a *senior* board member, was the chance of a lifetime and she wasn't going to lose it.

Taking a breath, Charlie nodded and sat up straight. She glanced at the photo of her son, Jake, again, and reminded herself that she might have been hired as a favor to an old friend, but she had the qualifications to do this job brilliantly. She was going to stay positive and upbeat and cheerful if it killed her.

When her phone rang, she grabbed it quickly. "Vance Waverly's office."

"How's it going?" a familiar, feminine voice asked in a rush.

Charlie shot a quick look at the closed door to her boss's

office as if to make sure he was locked away and oblivious to this phone call. "So far so good," she said.

"What did he think of your ideas for the catalog layout?"

"You were right, Katie," she said, imagining her friend down in Accounting grinning in response. Charlie had worked on the new layout for the catalog in secret, indulging herself with how she would have done things. Katie was the one who suggested she actually show her ideas to Vance. "He said I did a good job."

"See? Told you." Katie was typing as she talked; Charlie heard her fingers tapping wildly against the keys. "I knew he'd like what you did. He's a smart guy. He's bound to notice that you're doing a terrific job."

"In the last week, mostly he's just been watching me, as if he's waiting for me to screw up," Charlie told her, with another glance at her baby son's smiling face.

"Maybe he's just watching you because you're gorgeous."

"I don't think so." Though that thought sent a skittering of something delicious whipping through her. Instantly, though, she poured metaphorical ice water on those feelings. She wasn't here for a *date*. She was here to build a better life for her and her son. And this new job with the lovely raise was a big part of her grand plan. All she had to do was convince her new boss that she was indispensable.

"Have you looked in the mirror lately?" Katie countered. "Trust me, if I was playing for the other team, even I would hit on you."

Charlie laughed at the very idea. Katie was juggling so many men she hardly had a moment to herself. But the truth was, Katie had a point. Most people looked at Charlie—blond hair, big blue eyes and boobs any Barbie doll would be proud of, and immediately came to the conclusion that she didn't have a brain in her head. She'd spent most of her life proving people wrong.

The one time she had gone with her heart instead of her head...

"He's not like that," Charlie said with another look at his closed door.

"Honey, all men are 'like that.'"

Charlie ignored that and lowered her voice. "I know he only hired me as a favor to Quentin."

"So what? Who cares *why* he hired you, Charlie?" The sounds of typing stopped abruptly and Katie's voice came across the phone loud and clear. "It doesn't matter how you got there. The point is, the job is yours now. And you're already proving that you're perfect for it."

"Thanks," Charlie said. "Now, I'm going to do some perfect filing. Talk to you later."

When she hung up, Charlie was still smiling.

Two

Two hours later, Vance crumpled the newspaper and tossed it aside. Fury rose up inside him but he quickly reined it in. Just as Tracy had promised, the story about a possible affair between Ann Richardson and Dalton Rothschild was on page twenty-six. For a second, Vance told himself that since the so-called story was buried in a small column on a page filled with ads, it might get ignored.

But the chances of that were actually slim to none. There was nothing people liked better than the makings of a good scandal and this one would be talked about for weeks. It wasn't just the rumors of an affair, but the possibility of collusion that had him worried. He hoped to hell there was nothing to it, because if there was, they were looking at official investigations, charges—possibly even the destruction of Waverly's.

He snatched up his phone, punched in a number and waited

for it to be answered. When it was, he snapped, "Dammit, Tracy."

"Vance, not my fault," the woman on the other end said matter-of-factly. "My editor got a tip and we acted on it. At least I gave you a heads-up."

"Yeah, for all the good that does me." Tracy had called him late last night. Not much of a warning system, and he had a feeling she had only done it because she wanted to give him a little extra time to stew over it.

He stood up and turned to stare out at the city streets. Manhattan was sweltering under a vicious summer sun. Tourists strolled along Madison Avenue, getting buffeted by the quicker-moving locals who had places to go and didn't want to linger in the heat.

"Is there any proof of this story?"

"You know I can't answer that."

"Fine. But if you have any other 'tips' let me know before you go to print, will you?"

"No promises," she snapped. Then she asked, "Sound familiar?" just before she hung up.

Vance winced, knowing full well she shouldn't be telling him a damn thing. A year ago, Tracy had been in his bed for a couple of months and when he'd told her it was over, he had reminded her that he'd gone into the affair warning her of "no promises."

It was the same warning he gave every woman who entered his life. He wasn't looking for long-term. He'd seen what his mother's and older sister's deaths had done to his father. Hell, it had crippled the man, leaving him a broken, empty shell. If love was that powerful, then Vance wanted nothing to do with it. As for having a family of his own? He'd never even been tempted. So, since he had zero interest in finding a wife, for God's sake, why bother pretending anything different? Wasn't it better to be honest with a woman up front?

He shook his head to rid himself of those thoughts, since they really had nothing to do with the current situation anyway.

Setting the phone back in its cradle, Vance stuffed his hands into his pockets and shook his head. Waverly's was all he had and damn if he'd lose it. His family had built this place and, as one of the last Waverlys still standing, he would do whatever was necessary to save it.

Turning, he buzzed the intercom. "Charlie, would you come in here, please?"

A second or two later, his door opened and she was standing in the doorway. Her long blond hair hung over one shoulder and her wide blue eyes were fixed on him. Once again, Vance felt that punch of something hot hit his system and he was forced to deliberately quash it.

"Is there a problem?"

"You could say that," Vance muttered and waved her inside. He pointed at the couch on the far wall and said, "Have a seat."

She did and he noticed the wary expression on her face.

"Relax," he said, sitting down on the opposite end of the couch. "I'm not firing you."

She let out a breath and gave him a smile. "Good to know. What can I do for you, then?"

Bracing his forearms on his knees, Vance looked into her eyes and said, "You can tell me everything you've heard lately about Ann Richardson."

"Excuse me?"

"If there's been talk, I want to know about it," he told her flatly. "You must have heard about the article in the paper."

Her eyes shifted away from him for a second before returning to meet his stare. "The phone's been ringing for the last half hour with people wanting to talk to you."

"Perfect," he muttered. "Who?"

"I've got a stack of messages on my desk, but mainly, it's the other board members and then there were a couple of reporters. Also, a cable business network wants an interview."

He fell back against the sofa cushion and shook his head again. "This is going to get much worse before it's over." He had to talk to Ann. Figure out what was going on and the best way to mount a defense. His gaze speared into Charlie's.

"I know people are talking about this here in the company. What have you heard?"

She frowned at him. "I don't listen to gossip."

"Ordinarily, a good thing. Right now, I need to know what people in the building are saying."

She took a long, slow breath and looked as if she were having an internal argument with herself on whether or not to answer him. Briefly, Vance considered making that request an order, but discounted that notion. He didn't want to make her defensive and careful about what she said. He needed as much information as he could get.

She bit into her bottom lip and finally blurted out, "People are worried. They're afraid Waverly's will be shut down, that they're going to lose their jobs. Frankly, I'm a little worried, too. The article mentioned possible collusion—"

"Yeah, I know it did," he muttered.

"What does Ms. Richardson say?"

Vance scowled. "I haven't spoken to her about it yet. I got a tip about the article coming out today, but not in time to do anything about it. I expect it will be a topic of conversation during the board meeting, though."

"What do you think is going on?" she asked and he realized that by asking her opinion on what was happening in Waverly's, he'd opened a door between them.

A week ago, she would have been too skittish, too nervous to ask him that. Now, though, things had apparently changed. Oddly, he didn't mind. She was a good listener and it was nice to be able to talk this out with someone who knew what was going on, yet didn't have a major stake in the outcome.

"I don't know," he admitted and that cost him. Vance didn't like not having the answers. He wasn't accustomed to being in the dark. He preferred being on top of any given situation. Knowing the answers before the questions were asked. In this case, though, all he had to go on were his gut instincts. "I like Ann. She's always struck me as a sensible, honest woman. She's been good for Waverly's…"

"But?"

One corner of his mouth lifted. Not just a good listener, but insightful, too, hearing the hesitation in his voice.

"But the truth is, I don't know her very well." He leaned back against the couch. "No one here does. She does her job, but keeps to herself."

"There's a lot of that going around," she murmured.

Cocking his head, he asked, "What's that supposed to mean?"

She stiffened. "Sorry. I didn't mean— I only meant that you— Well, you're pretty much a loner, too, and… Oh, just fire me and get it over with."

For the first time in longer than he cared to admit, Vance laughed. He saw the surprise on her face and knew it was echoed on his own features. For a week, he'd been regretting hiring Charlotte Potter. Right at that moment, he couldn't remember why. She was smart, competent and she made him laugh.

If only she didn't smell so good.

"As I said," he told her, "I'm not going to fire you."

Still, irritated by his own thoughts, by the flicker of something hot bristling inside him, Vance shut it all down. He pushed up from the couch and purposely made his voice brisk and businesslike. Back on firm footing, boss to assistant. "If you do hear anything, I want you to tell me immediately."

Charlie slowly rose to her feet and lifted her chin in a defiant tilt. "I won't spy on my friends."

She went up another notch in his estimation. One thing Vance could admire was loyalty. "I'm not asking you to spy," he pointed out. "Just to listen."

"I can do that."

"Good." He opened the closet door, pulled out his suit coat and slipped it on. "I'm leaving for the board meeting now." He checked the gold watch on his left wrist. He'd be late if he didn't leave right away, and Vance Waverly was never late for *anything*.

"I should be back by four—have those condition reports on the Ming vases ready for me when I get back."

"Yes, sir."

He heard her sharp reply, and for a second, regretted the fact that she was doing much as he was—shifting back into business mode. Then the regret dropped away. Better this way. Easier. And far more logical. He didn't look back as he stalked from his office, headed for the boardroom and the meeting that would no doubt shake up a few things at Waverly's.

Charlie let out a breath she hadn't even been aware she was holding. For a few brief moments, she and Vance had actually been talking like…friends. She'd had a chance at a tiny peek at the man behind the cool facade that usually shrouded him.

And that one peek had completely intrigued her and made her want more. So not a good thing, Charlie told herself firmly. Wanting more with Vance Waverly made as much sense as wanting to spend the afternoon in Paris. And had as much chance of happening.

Nope. He was boss. She was assistant. And never the twain would meet or mingle or anything else for that matter. Frowning to herself, Charlie walked back to her desk. She had been completely off men for more than two years. Hadn't been attracted to one. Hadn't been so much as tempted by the *thought* of romance. Ever since she had made the giant mistake of trusting the *wrong* man.

But now, for the first time in way too long, she had felt that little tingle of…appreciation? Interest?

"And just like before," she muttered in disgust, "you picked exactly the wrong man." Wrong for different reasons, of course, but still…

No, she wouldn't jeopardize her job, her newfound security, for a passing flirtation. No good could come of that. So Charlie reined in her hormones and then tied them down nice and tight. She didn't need to be indulging in any fantasies about her boss, for heaven's sake. What she needed to be doing was impressing the hell out of him—as she'd spent the past week doing—so she could keep this job.

Every step up the ladder was a good one. Charlie had plans. She wouldn't always be an assistant. She was going to keep learning the business, eventually get her master's in art history and then get a job as curator or an art specialist there at the house. Just as Ann Richardson, their CEO, had done when she was starting out. The higher Charlie climbed the proverbial ladder, the better the life she could provide for herself and her son.

Jake was what mattered, she reminded herself sternly. Her baby boy was counting on her and she wasn't going to let him down.

With that thought firmly in mind, Charlie dismissed all her earlier notions about Vance Waverly and got back to work. Picking up a file folder from the edge of her desk, she headed for the jewelry salesroom on the second floor. She had the provenances for several pieces to deliver.

Plush carpet muffled her steps as she walked down the long halls toward the elevator. Throughout the floor, she heard typing and quiet phone conversations. It was a rarified atmosphere up on the seventh floor. Here was where the officers of Waverly's worked, made the decisions that kept the auction house one of the top of its kind in the world. And here she would make her mark, she told herself as she stepped into the elevator and punched the button for the second floor.

The doors slid shut on a whisper and the subtle strains of classical music sighed out around her. She caught her reflection in the polished brass doors and smiled. When the doors opened again, she walked along gleaming wood floors, listening idly to the click of her own heels tapping out a fast beat.

The first two floors of the venerable old building were devoted to the salesrooms. Each of them was different. Each of them beautiful in its own way.

Polished oak floorboards stretched for what seemed like miles. Paintings and sculptures lined the walls and huge vases filled with fresh flowers created a subtle scent that permeated the air.

The hush of this floor was almost churchlike, and why not? Here was where the treasures of the world came to be admired, and then sold to live again with someone new. Charlie walked to the far room and stepped through the wide, double doorway.

"Charlie!" A male voice called her name and she turned.

Justin Dawes was walking toward her. Justin was the head of the precious-gem department at Waverly's. About forty, he was balding, far too thin and his kind blue eyes were always narrowed in a squint. He had told her once it was the curse of his profession. Too many hours looking through jeweler's loupes at the stones he loved so much.

Today Justin looked a little harried and less than his urbane self. His tie was loosened and the sleeves of his white dress shirt were rolled up to the elbow. His suit coat had been abandoned and thin wisps of brown hair stood straight up at the crown of his head.

"You have the provenances?"

"Right here," she said and handed over the file.

"Good. That's great." He flipped through them, then shot her a look. "They've been verified?"

"Over and over again," she said, smiling. "Justin, you checked all the stones yourself, remember? Even before the provenances came through. Don't worry. Everything's good."

"It's an important collection," he told her, glancing back into the room where an auction would be held in two days. "Want to take a look?"

"I really do."

He took her arm and guided her into the center of the room.

Lighting was everything in an auction house, and Waverly's spared no expense in seeing things done right. Around the circumference of the huge, oak-paneled room, glass cases stood beneath spotlights that shone down on the fabulous items inside those cases. Those lights made the precious gems glitter and shine like fallen stars—or pieces of a rainbow.

Charlie couldn't stop the sigh of appreciation. They turned in a slow circle, admiring the whole setup before Justin said, "Come look at this one piece. It's amazing."

"Oh, my," she whispered as she followed Justin toward a single display case. Beneath the glass lay a swell of black velvet and on that velvet was a necklace unlike anything she'd ever seen before.

Gold wire, as thin and fragile as a single strand of hair, dripped with rubies and diamonds. The stones themselves were wrapped in the gold thread, then left to dangle like dreams from the slender chain that made up the base of the piece. The rubies shone like fresh blood and the diamonds were…

"It's beautiful."

"Isn't it?" Justin stared at the stones like a man in love. "Worn by the queen of Cadria more than a hundred years ago. It was crafted especially for her—some say, by Fabergé himself." He sighed a little. "Of course, we can't prove that, because even Cadria's royal family today doesn't know for sure. A shame, really. Wouldn't that have looked impressive in the provenance? But still, stunning."

Charlie shook her head as she looked at the necklace. She wanted to touch it but was terrified to breathe too close to it. "It's amazing, Justin. But why is the king of Cadria auctioning off so many of the royal jewels?"

"Ah," he said with a wink, "the current king is honoring his grandmother by establishing a charity in her name, and the proceeds from this sale are going directly to that. Plus, he thinks the publicity from this sale will spur more donors to support his grandmother's charity."

"Still seems a shame to get rid of something that belongs to your whole family."

"Oh, don't worry about royals, sweetie," Justin told her. "They have more jewelry and shiny stuff than they know what to do with. These pieces probably won't even be missed."

"I would miss a necklace like that," she said softly. "I'd be too scared of breaking or losing the darn thing to actually *wear* it, but I would miss it."

"You've got a soft heart, Charlie," Justin told her with a grin. "Which means you'll love the legend of the necklace."

"A legend?"

"Oh, yes. All the best stones come with a legend. Apparently, the then-king had this crafted especially for his bride as a wedding present. It's said the rubies are charmed somehow and hold the secret to a long and happy marriage."

Charlie looked over at him and smiled as her heart twisted in her chest. What would that be like, she wondered, to be loved so much? She thought of the queen who had worn it and the king who had clearly adored her and thought that sometimes, real life was even better than fairy tales. "That's lovely."

Justin winked at her. "Yeah. And it should really push up the price on the necklace, too. Nothing a bidder likes more than a little history added to a piece."

She laughed. Couldn't help it. "You're shameless."

"Guilty as charged," he admitted with a grin.

Charlie reached out one hand toward the glass enclosure, then stopped before touching it. Her fingers curled into her palm.

"It's okay. Alarms are turned off for the moment. Here, let me show you." Justin lifted the glass case off the tall wooden base and allowed the necklace the freedom to shine.

"Even prettier," she said on a sigh. Though it was so far out of her range of possibilities it might as well have been on Mars, Charlie couldn't help the tickle of avarice that made her want to snatch it up.

"You want to pet it?" he asked, laughing.

"Pet it, try it on, wear it home and sing it to sleep," Charlie admitted, deliberately putting her hands behind her back to keep herself from giving in to the urge to touch those glittering stones that shone so warmly under the lights.

"Can't blame you," Justin said. "And with your coloring, it would look gorgeous on you."

She thought so, too. In fact, Charlie could almost feel the cool glide of the gold against her skin and the icy feel of each stone settling into place around her neck. Oh, it would be wonderful as well as terrifying to own something that looked so…magical. Then she imagined the expression on Vance Waverly's handsome face as he draped that priceless necklace around her throat and— Okay. *Stop it!*

Clearing her mind of thoughts that had no business being there she said, "Yes, well. When I marry a rich prince, I'll be sure to tell him what kind of necklace to have made for me."

Justin laughed. "There you go. I like a woman with a plan."

He set the glass cover back into place and Charlie let her gaze slide around the room. Tomorrow, this room would be filled with rows of straight-backed, velvet-tufted chairs. A podium would be centered at the end of the room and the sound system would be hooked up. The day after that, this room would be bustling with bidders from all over the world, each of them hoping to take home a small piece of the long-dead queen's collection.

Charlie had already signed on to work the auction in whatever capacity she was needed, but she wouldn't be envying the buyers. Justin was right, she thought. Charlie *did* have a plan. But it didn't include diamonds and rubies. It entailed working her way to the very top of the auction world and being able to buy a house with a yard for her son to play in. Before he was too old to be interested in playing.

Charlie Potter wasn't the kind of woman men draped in diamonds, and that was okay with her. These pieces were lovely to look at, but the truth was, she'd be too afraid of losing them to ever enjoy owning them.

She had nothing in common with the kind of people who could come in here and walk out with a queen's jewelry. Which meant, she reminded her hormones, that she had nothing in common with Vance Waverly. That a few minutes of relaxed conversation wasn't the go-ahead for her to get all dreamy-eyed over him. Besides, she told herself, it was important to pause and remember what had happened the last time she had let her heart take control of her mind.

Three

She took a deep breath, forced a bright smile and said, "You've done an amazing job, Justin."

"Thanks." He swept the room with an experienced eye. "I think so, too. Should be a hell of an auction. You'll be working it, right?"

"Oh, I'll be here."

"Thought you would." He gave her a knowing wink.

In the two years she'd been at Waverly's, she had spent as much time working the actual sales as possible. Her love of auctions had started in college when her roommate had dragged her to a small auction of movie memorabilia. That was all it had taken.

The fast-paced bidding, the treasures from the past and the excited atmosphere sparked by the people attending had all come together to energize Charlie in a way she'd never experienced before. She had loved the whole thing. Every moment. She had watched the bidders, studied the auctioneer and thrilled to the quick pace of items bought and sold. She'd felt a stirring of excitement she had never known and that was enough to set her on the path that had eventually led her to Manhattan and her entry-level job at Waverly's.

She'd learned everything she could about the auction world and studied both this house and the other stately auction houses. She had wanted to be part of something amazing and every time she walked into this wonderful old building, she felt as if she'd accomplished her dream. At least, the first part of it.

Charlie made a point of working the auctions here, to support Waverly's, to help where she could and to continue to learn the ins and outs of a business that seemed to change daily. From the first moment she had stepped inside Waverly's, she had known that she'd found where she belonged. And the feeling had only intensified since that day.

"You know me," she said quietly, her gaze sliding across the familiar, the exciting. "Wouldn't miss it."

"Excellent. We'll need as many hands as possible behind the scenes."

"Sure." Thankfully, the day-care facility at Waverly's was open during all the auctions so that employees could leave their children somewhere safe while they worked. Jake did love being with all of his little friends and… She checked her watch. "I've gotta go, Justin. Thanks for the grand tour."

"No problem," he said, already opening the file she'd brought him to study the provenances. "See you Saturday."

"Right." She turned and walked out of the luscious display of jewels that were the stuff of dreams. Taking the elevator up two floors, she eagerly left behind dreams for a chance to see her reality.

"I'm not going to dignify these unfounded rumors with a response," Ann Richardson said softly, her gaze sweeping the board members gathered around the long, cherrywood conference table. "And I hope I can count on all of you for your support."

People shifted uncomfortably in their seats, but Vance held perfectly still, his gaze fixed on the woman facing them down with the air of a young queen. Tall and willowy, Ann had her ice-blond hair styled into a perfect, curled-under style that ended at her jawline. Her blue eyes were sharp as she met the stares of the other board members. She wore one of her elegantly tailored business suits—this one black with gray pinstripes—and her chin was lifted at a defiant angle. She looked proud and strong as she silently dared anyone to contradict her.

Vance had always admired Ann Richardson, but never more so than right now. With the article in the newspaper, the entire city would be whispering about her, speculating about her. But it seemed that she had chosen a path to take— steely indifference—and he had to applaud it. If she fought the charges with a vehement argument, it would only spur on the talk. She couldn't admit they were true—even if they were. The only road she could take was the "no comment" route. By doing it here first, with the board, she would be able to gauge how well it would go over elsewhere.

The board members looked shaken and worried and he knew they were all thinking about the possible ramifications of this situation. If it wasn't cleared up soon, rumor would become suspicion and suspicion would become fact. Whether or not she was guilty of anything, Ann's career and reputa- tion could very well be destroyed—along with Waverly's.

Seconds ticked past and the quiet in the room was deafen- ing. Here on the seventh floor, the boardroom was a study in understated elegance. The walls were a pale beige, the crown molding a stark white. Old masters hung on the walls and a twisted brass sculpture of Atlas balancing the world on his shoulders stood in one corner.

Vance held his peace, since he wanted to hear everyone else's reactions before he spoke. He knew he wouldn't have to wait long. It took about ten seconds.

"It's outrageous is what it is," George Cromwell sputtered first.

"These innuendoes are baseless," Ann insisted, her voice calm. "I would never put Waverly's at risk, and I hope you all know that."

"Yes, Ann," George Cromwell said from his seat at the end of the table. "I'm sure we all appreciate your devotion to the company, but this article clearly states that we have a problem."

Vance saw the flinch Ann couldn't quite disguise. But since he was the youngest member of the board, he was betting no one else noticed.

"The article is nothing more than rumor and supposition."

"But it's smoke," George insisted. "And people will assume that where there is smoke, there is fire."

Vance rolled his eyes and shook his head. If there was a cliché, George would find it. At seventy-five, he was long past the age of retiring, but the old fox had no intention of giving up his seat on the board. He liked the power. Liked being able to have a say in things. And right now, it looked as though he was enjoying putting Ann through the wringer.

"How can we take your word for this, when there was clearly enough evidence for this reporter to write his story?"

"Since when does a reporter need to back up a story?" she asked haughtily. "There's more fiction in the daily papers than you'll find at the nearest bookstore and you all know it."

Good point, Vance thought, still regarding their CEO warily. He wished he knew Ann better, but he didn't. She seemed like a warm, congenial enough person, but she'd made a point of keeping people at a distance, refusing to make friends—and now that strategy just might bite her in the ass.

"People believe what they read," George intoned darkly.

"George, do hush up." Edwina Burrows spoke up from the end of the table.

"You know I'm right about this," the man countered hotly.

As the two older people shot verbal darts at each other, Vance watched Ann. Her mouth worked as if she were grinding her teeth and Vance couldn't really blame her. It had to be hard, standing in front of this bunch, defending yourself against what was at this point merely rumor.

Finally, she turned to him and asked, "Vance? What about you? As the last remaining Waverly on the board, I value your opinion. Do you believe me?"

He studied her for a long minute. Vance knew that now the others were waiting to hear what he had to say. And he knew that whatever he said would swing sentiment either for or against Ann. His first responsibility was to the company and the thousands of people both here and abroad who depended on Waverly's for their very livelihoods.

But he also owed Ann his support. She'd stepped into the role of CEO and done a hell of a job. She was smart and capable and had never given him any reason to doubt her motives or her loyalties to the house.

He wasn't convinced that she was telling the complete truth, though. Like it or not, George had a point. That reporter had picked up on *some* tidbit of gossip as the basis for the story. But even if there was something between Ann and Dalton, Vance still didn't believe she would sell out Waverly's.

He'd like to have all the information before he took a stand one way or the other, but that wasn't going to happen. What it came down to for Vance was this: Did he trust his gut instincts or not? Bottom line? He *always* went with his instincts. So he took a chance.

"I believe you," he said loudly enough that no one could miss it.

He saw her shoulders relax just a bit in silent relief and he knew he'd done the right thing to support her publicly. But he wasn't finished.

"That said," Vance continued, looking directly into Ann's blue eyes, "if this reporter continues to throw mud at Waverly's, we'll all need to be prepared."

His silent message to her was, *If I'm wrong about you, you had better have a good backup plan—because if it means saving Waverly's, you're gone.*

She gave him a small, tight nod and Vance was pretty sure she understood.

"You're right," Ann said aloud. Shifting her gaze back to the rest of the board, she continued by saying, "Dalton Rothschild is not to be trusted. If he thinks there's a chink in our armor, he will make a move."

"Such as?" Edwina asked.

Ann gritted her teeth. "A hostile takeover wouldn't be out of the question."

Vance listened to the outraged shouts and furious whispers that rolled through the room and wondered why none of them had considered that possibility before. He certainly had. The implications of what this might mean were staggering. Rothschild knew that if he tried to simply buy out Waverly's he would hit a stone wall. But if he thought to take it over by means of destroying the auction house first, then scooping up what was left, that was something else.

Ruin the house's reputation, and then buy them out when the business was trashed.

Not a bad plan, Vance thought with icy calm. But one that would fail. He'd see to it himself. Gaze fixed on Ann, he watched as she waited for the tumult around the table to die down. When it didn't happen fast enough, she rapped her knuckles against the cherrywood table as if she were a teacher trying to restrain a room full of kids. But it worked. When it was quiet, she spoke up again, cool and collected.

"I need you all to be on guard at all times. Keep an eye on our employees. If Dalton means business, he could be wooing an insider into spilling our secrets. We can't take anything for granted right now. Waverly's needs us—all of us—to be on our toes."

Vance scowled at the thought. He didn't like the idea that there might be a spy among them at Waverly's. He'd known most of the people he worked with for years. A lot of them had watched him grow up. Looking at them now with suspicious eyes went against the grain. Besides, he couldn't help asking himself *why* someone would betray Waverly's. The house had always been a good place to work. The company took care of the employees. Hell, there was even a day-care center on the fourth floor so that mothers didn't have to worry about their children while they were at work.

Children.

An image popped into his mind. The framed photo on Charlie's desk. That of a small boy, grinning up at the camera, displaying two impossibly tiny teeth. Unease washed through him as the board meeting went on around him.

For a brief moment, he wondered if he should be suspicious of Charlie.

Ordinarily, he wouldn't even have to listen to the voices rising and falling in the room to know what they were saying. The only two female board members, Veronica Jameson and Edwina Burrows—grande dames of society, each well into her seventies—were extremely protective of Ann. Maybe it was the whole "woman power" thing, but those two were always Ann's most vociferous supporters.

"I'm sure you'll know best how to handle this, Ann," Veronica said, her thin voice chirping like a hungry bird's.

"Thank you. I appreciate that."

"I'm sure you do," Simon West carped in apparent frustration.

"I realize what a difficult situation this is," Ann said, her voice briefly carrying over the rest. "But if we band together, I'm sure we'll—"

"Band together? Against what? Some ephemeral danger? Or against you?" Simon, a shrunken, wizened man of about a hundred, slammed the tip of his cane against the tabletop to get everyone's attention. Even Vance let go of his thoughts long enough to stare at the older man.

Simon had been at Waverly's for as long as anyone could remember. There were some who insisted he was there at the dedication of the building 150 years ago. Vance smiled to himself at the thought.

Simon was furious and looked as if he were about to have a stroke. His eyes bugged out, his cheeks were splotches of red and spittle gathered at the corners of his mouth as he shouted, "Nothing like this happened before we allowed a *woman* to be in charge!"

"Oh, for God's sake," Vance muttered. Sometimes the old guard was so old they forgot they were living in a shiny new world where women didn't stay at home unless that's where they wanted to be.

"That's not helpful, Simon," Ann muttered, and Vance had to give her points for patience. If it was him, he'd have grabbed the cane away and tossed it into the corner.

Then he rolled his eyes as Veronica and Edwina charged into the fray in defense of their CEO.

He glanced across the table at the empty chair. Vance's uncle, Rutherford Waverly, should be sitting there. As the most senior member of the board, he should have been at every meeting. And right now, Vance would have liked to get his uncle's take on all of this. But Rutherford had hated

Waverly's and everything about it ever since he and Vance's father, Edward, had had a falling-out decades ago. Vance himself had hardly spoken to the other man in years.

But right now, he could have used a cooler head. An unbiased opinion.

"Whether or not we like what's happening," Ann declared, effectively silencing the last of the grumblers around the table by keeping her voice low and calm, forcing them to quiet down long enough to hear her. "The situation is here and we have to deal with it. If Dalton Rothschild is preparing for a takeover, all of us have to watching for any signs of treachery or betrayal. As much as I hate to say it, one of our people may be spying for the enemy."

Once again, the image of his new assistant popped into his mind. What did he really know about her?

The fourth floor was part of Waverly's and yet, so wildly different from the rest of the venerable auction house it could have been on another planet. Every other floor in the building was sedate, lovely, elegant.

Here, though, it was all primary colors and the scent of crayons and cookies and milk. The rest of the building was usually couched in what felt like a cathedral-like hush. But here, there was laughter, giggles that bubbled up to the high ceilings and fell back down like a rain of daisies.

Every time Charlie stepped onto this floor, she felt a wave of gratitude to Waverly's for taking such good care of its employees. If she had to pay for day care on her own, she wouldn't have been able to save enough money to move into the two-bedroom apartment where she and Jake now lived. Not to mention the fact that she would have spent every minute of every workday worried about her son's safety and happiness. Was he being fed or played with or hugged when he fell down?

At Waverly's she didn't have to worry about any of that. This space was completely childproof and safe. The women hired to work here had been vetted by HR and licensed by the State of New York in child care and early childhood development. Each child here was cared for and looked after and the nominal fee she paid every month was more than worth it.

She walked past the room that was set up with tables and chairs and two computer stations where older kids would come in after school and do their homework while they waited for the workday to end. She peeked into the nap room, furnished with a half-dozen cribs and two comfy rocking chairs, then slipped past quietly to stand in the doorway of the toddler play area.

Here again, there were bright colors on the walls and murals of fairy gardens and rainbows to enchant the kids. There were baby walkers for the infants, stuffed animals and games for the toddlers. There were shelves filled with books for the older kids and dozens of play rugs and pillows covering the wood floor.

An excited squeal greeted her, and Charlie reacted instantly. With a rush of love swamping her, she hurried across the floor to pick up her son and cuddle him close. He smelled like shampoo and bananas. She smiled when his little arms came around her neck and he dug his face into the curve of her neck. "Mamamamamama…"

It thrilled her to hear the babble of sound that defined the essence of who she was now. The old Charlie had faded away the moment she'd learned she was pregnant. The woman who had had vague, hazy dreams of success and flashy cars and beautiful homes had become a *mother*. Her dreams now were filled with plans for her son. With ways to ensure his happiness. With hopes for the future she could provide for him.

As she held that warm little body close to her, she told herself that Jake would never wonder if he was wanted. Would never be afraid.

Pushing all else but her baby aside, she looked into the dark blue eyes he had inherited from the father he'd never known. "Are you being a good boy?"

Jake grinned and her heart melted.

"He's a terrific boy and you know it," Linda Morrow said, coming up behind her. "Sweetest baby ever."

"I think so," Charlie agreed and gave Jake a quick kiss before setting him down on the rug again. When he screwed up his face to cry, she handed him a ball and he laughed in response. Nothing upset Jake for long.

"I was downstairs checking out the salesroom for Saturday's auction and couldn't resist stopping by to see him."

"Oh, I get it," Linda said, her gaze constantly shifting to take in the ten or so children scattered around the room and the other two women in charge of them. "That's the beauty of working at a place like this. Being able to see your child during the day, reassure yourself..."

"Am I that obvious?"

"All good moms are," Linda told her with a wink. "You know your baby's safe here, but your heart insists on seeing for yourself once in a while."

"Wish it was more often," she said wistfully as she watched Jake crawl in a mad rush toward a giant, purple, plush teddy bear. In a perfect world, she'd be a stay-at-home mom with a dozen kids. She'd always wanted a big family. But since she had to work, she was grateful that she'd found a job doing something that she loved. Being part of something as fast-paced and exciting as the world of high-end auctions was a dream come true. Except for the not having enough time for her son thing.

"Jake took a step this morning all on his own."

"He *did?*" Charlie's heart gave a sharp, painful twist. She hadn't been there to see that first step. She'd missed it and that memory was now Linda's. The sting of that knowledge cut deep, but she quickly reassured herself that stolen moments didn't make up a lifetime and that she would have years of memories of Jake's "firsts" to take out and relive again when she was a doddering old woman.

"It was only the one step," Linda was saying, "then he got this incredibly surprised look on his face and dropped like a stone." She smiled. "But he's getting it, and pretty soon he'll be running everywhere."

"He will, won't he? God, it's all going by so fast."

Charlie watched her son go up on his knees, lift his arms, then fall forward onto the stuffed teddy bear with a wild giggle. His first step, then running. Then he'd be in school and then graduating and then college and marriage and a family and— Charlie laughed at her own thoughts. He was barely thirteen months old and she had him practically retired.

Plenty of time to build memories, she told herself. "I've got to get back to work," she said and reluctantly turned for the door. She stopped, though, and asked, "Did he eat the watermelon chunks I sent with him today?"

"No, but he scarfed down the banana," Linda told her.

One thing wasn't changing. Jake would eat nothing but bananas if given half a chance.

"Okay, then." She looked at her son one more time, as if to remind herself just what she was working for, then left the playroom behind.

Back at her desk, Charlie got caught up on Vance's mail, the requests for authentication from the fine arts division and the incoming provenances on the next auction to be held, the Ming Dynasty porcelain.

She skimmed each one on her computer screen before sending them to the printer. It was fascinating to read about artists who had lived and died centuries ago. Who had created such beautiful, fragile things that had survived through the years.

What must it have been like to create such a long-lasting legacy? Had they expected their art to survive all this time? Or had they thought only of making a vase worthy enough of purchase so they could feed their families? No one would ever know, but Charlie loved imagining the lives of those long-dead artists and wondered what they'd make of seeing their treasures here, in a modern auction house.

While the laser printer hummed along, a ding sounded, alerting Charlie to an incoming email. She switched over to the mail program, clicked on the header INFORMATION REQUIRED and then froze.

Her gaze locked on the screen, her heart stopped. Breath was trapped in her lungs.

And fear rose up to take a bite out of her soul.

Four

Vance left the boardroom, still considering everything Ann had said. He wanted to believe that there was nothing between her and Dalton Rothschild. He also *wanted* to believe that there was no hostile takeover in the works. The thought of any of Waverly's employees secretly working for the enemy was a hard one to take.

But worse was the thought that had been circling in his mind like some twisted tornado. No matter how he tried to dislodge the thoughts, they kept coming back.

If he was going to suspect an employee of betraying the house, then he had to take a good, hard look at Charlotte Potter. Relatively new to the company. New to the position of his assistant, which would give her access to all kinds of sensitive information about Waverly's.

He stalked down the long hallway toward his office and the scowl on his face was fierce enough to have others scatter with one look at him. A path was cleared for him and Vance barely noticed. His mind was racing. Was Charlie a spy? Or was she as innocent as she looked?

Vance stopped dead and paid no attention to the people forced to walk around him. If there was something going on here, he had to find out what it was.

Charlie's gaze locked on the few simple lines of type.

I know who you really are. Forward to this address all of V. Waverly's files for the last five years of business or risk facing charges of being an unfit mother.

"Unfit?" Her stomach churning, Charlie lifted one hand to her mouth as the tidy little world she'd built around herself crumbled.

Fear was roaring inside her and it was hard to breathe. She wasn't an unfit mother. She loved her son and she would fight anyone who said differently. But while her fear and fury pumped hot through her veins, a voice in her mind whispered, *The past is there, Charlie. You can't change it. Can't hide it. If someone finds out...*

"Someone has. But who?" She heard the icy dread in her voice as chills snaked along her spine. This couldn't be happening. It just wasn't possible. No one in New York knew anything about her—where she'd grown up, who her family was. Except for...

Realization dropped on her like rocks rolling down the side of a mountain. All thunder and fury, crashing into her system and leaving her shaken, as she realized that the only person who knew about her past was Jake's father. A man she hadn't seen since she'd told him she was pregnant.

A man, she had found out when she'd started looking for him, who didn't even exist.

God, she'd been such an idiot. So young and stupid and trusting. Fresh off the bus from a small town upstate, she'd taken her entry-level job at Waverly's and felt...sophisticated.

She had been a walking cliché. Young woman arrives in big city, doesn't know anyone. Gets overwhelmed by the possibilities of a world far wider than she'd ever known before.

She found a tiny apartment in Queens. Rode the subway every day into Manhattan. She had felt like part of the bustling, exciting city and, looking back, she could see what easy prey she had been for the man who had romanced her.

In a blink, she saw it all again. Felt the rush when she'd dropped her phone and a tall, handsome man had picked it up for her. She'd taken one look into those smiling brown eyes and had lost every ounce of common sense her grandmother had spent years instilling in her.

"He hadn't even had to work that hard," she whispered, ashamed to admit even now how susceptible she had been to the flattery. To the attention.

He had swept her off her feet, and in a few short weeks had her in his bed and convinced that it was true love. Charlie had had stars in her eyes, thinking that an important architect like Blaine Andersen wanted to be with no one but her. He'd told her that it was his great-grandfather who had designed the Waverly building. He'd been doting and kind—stopping by her office to bring her flowers and candy—helping her find her BlackBerry both times she had lost it. He was the fairytale prince and Charlie had believed in him.

Until she'd told him she was pregnant and he'd disappeared. Until she'd tried to find him and discovered that there *was* no Blaine Andersen. That the Andersen who had long ago designed the Waverly building had never had children. That she had swallowed a tangle of lies in her pathetic need to be loved. Accepted.

All those thoughts and more raced through her mind in seconds, leaving her shaken, but still furious. This had to be Blaine. He was the only one she'd told about her past. The only one she'd trusted with that information.

"Well, he's not going to make a fool of me twice," Charlie muttered and set her fingers on the keyboard.

Hitting Reply, she typed in, *Who are you?*

The answer came in an instant. *Doesn't matter. I know you. And I will see you lose your baby.*

Fresh fear erupted. Just seeing those words on the screen twisted her heart and sent what felt like a lead ball dropping into the pit of her stomach. Whoever it was had included a link in the email. Dreading what she was going to find, she clicked on it.

An old newspaper article flashed onto the screen. A story about her father and how he'd died. Quickly, she shut it all down, as if afraid that article might somehow etch itself onto her computer screen and remain there like a stain for anyone to read.

Clenching her hands together, she squeezed until her knuckles went white. She didn't know what to do. If she had to go to court and fight for her son, she would lose. She knew that. Charlie didn't have the kind of money it would take to hire a shark of a lawyer. Besides, what could she say? She couldn't even name Jake's father. She had no idea what the guy's real name was. And if the court looked into her past—where she was from, who her family was...

"Oh, God."

"Problem?"

She jumped and spun around. Vance Waverly was standing in the doorway. Did she *look* as guilty as she felt? Could he see the panic in her eyes? How long had he been there? What had he seen? What had he heard?

He took a step into the room and he seemed to fill the space. The man was so tall, so broad-shouldered, and his eyes were sharp enough to see inside a woman's soul. She hoped to heaven he wasn't looking that deeply at the moment.

"No," she blurted out when she could find her voice again. "No problem."

The lie came easily, though it tasted bitter. She didn't want to lie to him. She didn't want to live a life where lying was *necessary*. But what choice did she have?

"Good," he said, still watching her. "Do you have the paperwork on the Ming vases ready?"

"Yes, I'll bring it right in."

"You're sure everything is fine?" He was studying her and his brown eyes narrowed thoughtfully.

Get a grip, Charlie. She couldn't let him know how shaken she was. Or that someone, somewhere, was trying to blackmail her. She couldn't risk anyone finding out anything about her—at least, not until she'd found a way out of this mess. She'd think of something. All she needed was time. Just a little bit of time.

Charlie took a short, sharp breath and nodded. "Absolutely. I'll just get those papers for you."

When he walked into his office, her bravado dropped away. What was she going to do? If she sent the files to whoever was threatening her, she could lose her job. If she didn't send them, she could lose her *son*. But if she sent the files and got caught, she'd go to jail and lose her son anyway.

Tears burned at the backs of her eyes, but she fought them back. She wouldn't cry. She wasn't the naive young thing she had been when Jake's father had conned her. She was older. Wiser. She'd been burned and learned her lesson. And now she wasn't just protecting herself. She was a mother. And no one was going to take her son from her.

No one.

For the next few days, Vance kept an eye on his new assistant. Granted, he didn't know her well, but even he could see the change in her. She was jumpy. Nervous. She opened her email as if she were half expecting the computer to explode.

"Something's going on with her," he said.

"So," Roark urged him, "find out what it is."

"What a great idea. Wonder why I didn't think of that?"

Oblivious to the sarcasm, Roark shrugged. He shifted his gaze to pedestrians rushing up and down Fifth Avenue. Summer was here and the sun was making sure everyone knew it. The sky was clear blue, the heat was blistering and the biggest sellers from the street cart vendors were icy bottles of water.

Under a wide umbrella, Vance still felt the heat. His suit coat was stifling, but he'd insisted on eating at the sidewalk café so he and his brother could talk without risk of being overheard. The cacophony of sound outside provided enough white noise that no one would be able to listen in on their conversation.

"Just yesterday, I walked into my office and Charlie was at my desk. When I came into the room, she was so startled she looked ready to faint."

Roark grinned. "Doesn't necessarily mean anything. You can be a scary guy."

Vance frowned. He wasn't scary. Was he? Now that he thought about it, most people did tend to scuttle out of his way when he walked through a room. Was that it? Was Charlie just nervous being around him?

He shook his head. "No, that's not it. She didn't look scared. She looked guilty."

Blowing out a breath, Roark turned to his brother, pushed his sunglasses to the top of his head and said, "If you really want to know what's going on, romance it out of her."

"What?"

"A little dinner. A little dancing. A little wine…" He shrugged again. "Fastest way to get to the bottom of it."

"And unethical," Vance retorted.

"So's spying on your employer."

Vance shook his head. "I can't *date* my assistant."

"No rules against it."

"There are sexual harassment lawsuits."

Roark laughed. "I didn't say sleep with her."

No, but that's exactly where Vance's mind had gone with absolutely no help. He'd been thinking about Charlie Potter for days and it wasn't *all* about suspicion.

That hair of hers had become something of a fixation for him. He wanted to push his fingers through that long, thick mass of blond waves and feel the cool slide of it against his skin. And then there was the scent of her—something light and floral that seemed to cling to the air in the office even when she wasn't in the room. The sound of her voice, the way her legs looked in those mile-high heels she wore… Yeah, she was on his mind way too much lately.

Shutting the mental door on those images, he said, "And if I find out she *is* guilty?"

"Then you fire her. Or," Roark mused, "use her to give disinformation to Rothschild."

"Use her and lose her—that's what you're saying?" Roark hadn't even been raised as a Waverly and he had their sensibilities. Maybe it was in the blood. Hell, their own father—after recovering from the loss of his wife and daughter—had gone through women so quickly, there had practically been a revolving door on the Waverly house.

Vance had grown up in a love vacuum. His father had never again risked his heart and Vance had learned to do this same. Roark had been raised by a single mother, so maybe he hadn't seen any evidence of love, either. Which just gave the brothers even more in common, Vance thought.

"Look," Roark said, "if she's guilty, you don't owe her anything. If she's innocent, you don't have to do a damn thing. It's a win-win."

"I'll think about it." As if he'd been thinking about anything else lately anyway.

"Good. Let me know how it goes." Roark put his sunglasses back on and dragged his brown leather jacket off the
back of the seat. Pulling it on, he added, "I'm out of here in
the morning. Got a flight to Dubai tonight and still have a
few things to do before I go."

"Dubai?" Vance smiled. His younger half brother was a
master at turning up valuable items to sell at Waverly's auctions. The downside? He was hardly ever in New York. He'd
been around the globe so many times, he was on his third
passport—he just kept filling them up with stamps.

"Yeah," Roark said with a quick grin. "Got a lead on something amazing. I pull this off and Rothschild's is out of luck.
We'll be so far on top, they'll never be able to touch us."

"What is it?" Intrigued, Vance looked at him and waited.

"A surprise," Roark said. "It'll be worth the wait. Trust
me."

He did. Funny, though they hadn't grown up together,
Vance felt closer to Roark than to anyone else he'd ever
known. He looked at Roark and saw the family resemblance
and wished to hell their father had told him about Roark years
earlier. And wished Edward Waverly had sought out his second son himself before he'd died.

Roark was raised by a single mother who had refused to
name his father. By the time Vance had found him and told
him exactly who he was, Roark was his own man and un-
willing to accept the truth as easily as Vance had. He wanted
proof and who could blame him, really? But all Vance had
was a note, written by their late father, and for Roark, that
simply wasn't enough.

Still, they were building a relationship and whether the
younger man admitted it or not, they were family.

Vance threw down cash for the bill and walked out with

his brother. Taxi horns blared, an ambulance wailed in the distance and the scent of cooking hot dogs drifted on a sullen breeze.

"Take care of yourself," Vance said.

"Always do," Roark assured him, then slapped Vance on the shoulder. "I'll be back soon enough. And I've got the satellite phone on me all the time. If you need me, call."

"Yeah. I will." Vance watched Roark walk away until he was swallowed up by the crowds.

His brother, the rogue treasure hunter, was off on a quest. And Vance was about to start a quest of his own. *Romancing the assistant.* He frowned to himself as he joined a crowd of pedestrians to cross the street. He had a feeling that Roark's job was going to be a hell of a lot less interesting than his own.

By that weekend, Charlie was at the end of her rope. She'd tied a knot and dug her fingernails in tight, but the rope was fraying and any second now she was going to—

"Lot 32," the auctioneer called out.

She jumped, startled out of her thoughts. She'd had so much adrenaline shooting through her system this week she could probably fly to the moon and back on her own power.

Charlie took a breath, told herself to concentrate and carried a teak tray bearing a diamond-and-sapphire-studded tiara into the salesroom. Steering her thoughts away from the blackmailer now stalking her with daily, ever-more-threatening emails, she focused solely on the task at hand. She couldn't afford to trip and fall and drop the tray, sending that tiara spiraling off to crash against a wall or something.

Oh, God. Just the thought of *that* made her stiffen up and slow her steps. The auctioneer turned to fix her with a glare as if to say, *Get a move on, already.*

She ignored him and stopped beside the podium, holding

the tray at a slight angle that afforded the audience a nice view of the tiara.

Items too big or too fragile to be carried into the auction were displayed on a sixty-inch flat screen behind the auctioneer. But it was more traditional to carry lots like the tiara into the auction room so everyone could see the items up close.

Of course, the bidders had already had a chance to study the sale items. There had been a reception before the auction where the über-rich and celebrities could sip champagne and decide what they wanted to buy.

But as Charlie stood in front of the audience now, dressed in her tidy black suit, she felt everyone stir as if leaning in toward her for a better look at the tiara. And who could blame them? Under the lights, every single diamond sparkled like an individual star. The sapphires were so dark they looked almost black until the light hit them just right and they revealed a hue of blue so rich and deep it was like looking into the heart of the ocean.

Any other day, Charlie would be loving this. She would smile at the crowd as she walked down the center aisle so that people could take a closer look. She would move smoothly, slowly, proud to be a part of the Waverly's tradition.

Today it was all she could do to remain upright.

She should have called in sick and skipped today's auction. But she needed the extra money the overtime would bring her. And, more than that, she didn't want her world disrupted. Didn't want to be afraid, so she was pretending she wasn't. Didn't want to lose what she'd begun to build here, so she clung to that frayed and tired rope with everything she had.

"We'll start the bidding at $35,000…."

The auctioneer went into his patter and Charlie zoned out again. She kept one corner of her mind on the task at hand, of course, walking to the front of the room once again and turning, holding the tray so that the lights caught the gems in just the right way.

But the other part of her mind was racing. Desperate to find a solution to her problem. Every day, she opened her email with fear and trepidation. And every day, her blackmailer was a little more curt. A little more dangerous. She hadn't written back to him since that first day, hoping that he would think that she wasn't getting his emails.

But even as she hoped and wished for it, she knew that wasn't going to happen.

Whoever was emailing her wanted information and wasn't going to go away until he or she got it. Which left Charlie exactly where?

Jail or out of a job? Losing her son?

Her heartbeat skittered in her chest and she felt a little faint. So she swallowed hard, locked her knees and held on. The bids came fast and furious. Red paddles lifted and lowered. Nods of the head. A wave of a hand. A cough. A phone ringing as anonymous bidders made their play for the stunning tiara. There was excitement, magic all around her, and Charlie didn't feel any of it. Finally, beside her, the slam of the gavel made her jump.

"Sold for $75,000."

That was Charlie's signal to return the tiara to the holding room where its new owner would pick it up after the sale.

Justin took the tiara from her as soon as she returned. "Thanks, sweetie. You've got time to sit down or something. I'll need you again to take in lots 41 and 46."

She forced a smile. "I'll be here."

"Hey." Justin frowned at her. "You okay?"

God, was she that easy to read? How could she ever be a spy and sneak something out from under Vance Waverly's nose if Justin—a man who barely looked up from the treasures he was in charge of— noticed right away that she wasn't herself?

"I'm fine. Just a little hungry, I guess. Haven't really eaten in a while. Didn't have breakfast."

"Well, go get something, honey." He gave her an absent-minded pat on the arm. "We've got snacks set up for everyone in the break room."

"Okay, I will."

But Justin had already moved on. "Sam, put red velvet under the onyx rings. If you use black, who's gonna see them?"

While the rest of the auction team bustled around in an organized manner, Charlie slipped off for some quiet. Some time to herself so she could think.

Trouble was, she'd been "thinking" for days about this problem and didn't have a solution. Couldn't figure out how to handle it. Didn't know who to talk to about it, because no one here knew who she had been before coming to Manhattan. And that was how she wanted it to stay.

Charlie dropped into a chair beside the table loaded with sandwiches, cookies and cupcakes and idly picked up a snickerdoodle. She broke a corner of the cinnamon cookie off, popped it into her mouth and chewed—even though it tasted like sawdust.

Upstairs, Jake was playing in the day-care center. Her little boy was safe and happy. She had to keep him that way. But to do that, she would have to steal information from the people who trusted her to do her job. She was torn in two.

"Nothing's that bad," a deep voice said from the doorway.

She turned her head to see Vance Waverly standing there watching her. Her stomach did a quick pitch and roll and a hum of something hot and delicious swept through her. In the business suits he usually wore, Vance was too hot for words. Today, though, he was wearing black jeans, a white long-sleeved shirt and black boots, scuffed from long use. He looked not only hot…but dangerous. And so sexy her mouth went dry and she choked on the rest of the snickerdoodle.

Coughing, gasping, she thumped her chest with the flat of her hand as her eyes watered and she fought for air.

He came over, handed her a bottle of water and waited while she took a sip and the coughing eased off. Finally, when she was quiet, he smiled. And oh, that smile was absolutely devastating. Probably a good thing he didn't do it often. No woman would be immune to a smile from Vance Waverly.

"Don't think I've ever caused a woman to choke to death before."

She frowned at herself. "You surprised me."

"Clearly." He tipped his head to one side. "You okay now?"

"Yeah." She held the bottle of water in both hands. "Fine."

"Good." He pulled out a chair and sat down beside her. Propping one booted foot on a knee, he leaned back to study her. "So what has you so jumpy?"

"Nothing," she lied, and looked into his brown eyes with their irresistible gold flecks. He had beautiful eyes, with long lashes and a steady stare that seemed to be peeling her open, layer by layer. Well, that wasn't a happy thought. "I'm just tired. My son didn't sleep last night, which means that neither of us does."

"Couldn't your husband help take care of him?"

She flushed. "I'm not married. It's just Jake and me."

"Must be hard."

"I won't argue with that, but I wouldn't change anything if I could, either." In fact, she couldn't imagine a world without Jake in it.

"Lucky boy," he mused, still watching her.

"So, what are you doing here?"

"I work here," he said, one corner of his mouth lifting.

Brilliant, Charlie. Just brilliant. "Yes, but you usually don't come to the auctions."

He shrugged. "I wanted to see you."

"You see me every day." Nerves plucked at her insides and Charlie fought to keep from showing them.

"Yeah, but this way's different," he said. "We're not in the office. We're more like…friends."

She laughed and took a sip of her water. "Friends?"

"Something wrong with that?"

Oh, if he only knew. They weren't friends. Friends didn't make friends feel all hot and flustered and nervous. Friends didn't inspire dreams that had her waking up in the middle of the night, reaching out for him. And friends most certainly didn't spy on each other or have the power to fire each other for that matter.

"I guess not," she said because she could hardly repeat everything that had just raced through her mind.

"Good. Because I'd like to take my 'friend' out to dinner tonight."

"What?"

Five

Vance had never been big on surprises.

They usually didn't work well for either the surpriser or the surprisee. He liked knowing what was coming, how he would handle it and exactly how any given situation would play out.

His brother, Roark, was the exact opposite. Roark lived his life on the road, on the edge. He had a place to stay in town, but was hardly ever there. He didn't like plans and lived for the rush of the new.

Vance couldn't imagine living like that. More than one woman in his life had suggested that he "loosen up." Let go of his schedule long enough to enjoy himself more. But he enjoyed himself plenty and his relentlessly-adhered-to agenda kept everything straight.

So no one was more astonished than he when he blurted out that invitation to dinner. Although, judging by the expression on Charlie's face, she was running a close second in the shock department.

He'd come here today not only to support Waverly's, but to keep an eye on Charlie. See what she did, who she talked to. He hadn't actually planned to ask her to dinner. Vance was well aware that having any kind of relationship with his assistant was problematic at best and a disaster in the making at worst.

But everything Roark had said kept resonating with him. Getting to know Charlie outside the office was one sure way to dig deeper. To find out all he could about her and discover if she was a spy or as innocent as she seemed.

"Dinner?" Her voice rose. "With you?"

He rolled his eyes. "No, with Justin."

She laughed a little. "I don't think Justin's wife would appreciate that."

"I don't have a wife to care…" His gaze dropped to her left hand and the absence of a ring. "And you're not married, either, so what's the problem?"

She curled her fingers into her palms and folded her hands on her lap. "You're my *boss*."

"So if I say it's okay, it should be."

"I don't know," she said, gaze shifting as if to make sure they were still alone in the break room.

"It's just dinner, Charlie," he said, not even sure why he was trying so hard to convince her. Maybe it was simply because he wasn't used to women turning him down. He was more accustomed to women flinging themselves at him. Charlotte Potter was different. "You have to eat."

She blew out a breath, unfolded her hands and tapped one finger nervously against the tabletop. "I appreciate it, but I've got Jake upstairs in day care and—"

"We can take him with us." He could hardly believe he'd said that. Spending time with a baby hadn't been part of the plan. Hell, he couldn't remember the last time he'd even *seen* a baby. But he'd sensed a refusal coming and damn if he was going to give up that easily. He could deal. How hard could it be?

She laughed shortly. "You want to have dinner with a baby in tow? *You?*"

Just a second ago, he'd been doubting his own sanity for the same reason, but somehow hearing her laugh at the very idea was insulting. "I haven't eaten a child in at least a decade," he said solemnly. "I think your son will be safe."

A smile was still curving the corners of her mouth. "He will, but will you survive?"

"It's *dinner,* Charlie. I think I can handle it."

"Mr. Waverly…"

"Vance," he corrected.

She looked horrified, and Vance felt a rush of irritation.

"I don't think I can call you that."

He scowled at her. She wasn't making this easy. He'd never had to work this hard to get a woman to spend time with him in his life. He had fully expected her to accept his invitation with a pleased smile and a gracious thank-you. Should have known, he told himself, that Charlie Potter wouldn't do the expected.

"I'm the boss," he reminded her again, "so if I say you can, it's okay."

"All right then, *Vance.*" She shook her head a little as if to dispel the weirdness of the moment. "As I said, I do appreciate it, but I just can't imagine you spending time with a baby."

Irritation sparked inside him. He wasn't a damn monster. So what if he was never around children? What difference did that make? Millions of people dealt with babies every day. Besides, he was Vance Waverly. There was *nothing* he couldn't handle. "Rumor has it, I was actually a child once myself."

"Do they make suits that small?"

He cocked his head and studied her. "Are you teasing me?"

"A little bit," she admitted.

Vance couldn't remember the last time that had happened. More surprising was the fact that he was sort of enjoying himself. Something else he hadn't planned on.

"That's fine." His gaze locked with hers, he said softly, "I can take it."

"Mr. Waverly—*Vance*," she corrected herself before he could. "I don't know what's going on, but…"

She was going to turn him down and, dammit, he wasn't going to let her. He told himself he was doing this for Waverly's, but the truth was more complicated than that. And he didn't want to examine that any further.

Leaning forward, he braced his forearms on his knees and looked into her eyes. "Charlie, it's just dinner. When you're finished here, we'll get your son and go get something to eat."

Narrowing her eyes on him, she said, "That sounds a lot like an order."

"Does it have to be?"

She thought about that for a moment, then nodded. "It might make it easier on me."

He blew out a breath and fought down a fresh stirring of irritation. "I'm only talking about dinner, for God's sake, not taking you to Bali for a sex-filled weekend—"

That thought stopped him cold then heated him up as his mind filled with some truly amazing images. Charlie naked, her skin glowing in the moonlight, her long, blond hair spread across a pillow. Her eyes looking up at him, her arms— He shifted uncomfortably in his chair and realized that she was speaking.

"Uh," she said, nervously, "okay then. Dinner. Sure. Um, it'll be an hour at least before I can leave, though."

"Fine," he muttered, wondering where in the hell those thoughts and images had come from. And he couldn't help wondering if the same kind of imagery had filled her mind, too.

"Charlie!" Justin's voice came from the other room. "I need you in here!"

"Coming." She sounded grateful as she answered Justin and that told Vance all he needed to know. Her mind had taken the same kind of imaginative trip his had. It seemed she was recovering a lot quicker than Vance, though.

She jumped to her feet and looked down at him. "Are you going out to watch the auction?"

Gritting his teeth against the pain in his groin, he said tightly, "Yeah. I'll be out there in a minute. You go ahead."

She looked at him oddly, but shrugged. "I'll see you later."

"Vance," he prompted.

"Vance," she said softly.

Nodding, he watched her go, his gaze dropping to the curve of her behind in the narrow black skirt she was wearing. And then farther down to those black heels that made her legs look so long and slender and—

Stop watching her or you'll never be able to get out of here, he told himself and turned to reach for a damn cupcake.

The auction picked up speed as some of the more fabulous pieces were brought out. On any other day, Charlie would have been enjoying herself immensely. But how could she keep her mind on business when she had a threat hanging over her head? Worry was constantly plucking at the edges of her mind.

But if she was going to be honest with herself, not even her would-be blackmailer had her as rattled as Vance Waverly did. *Sex-filled weekend in Bali?*

As soon as he'd blurted out those words in a flash of frustration, her mind had taken her on the quickest imaginary trip in the history of the world. Instantly, she'd seen the two of them—Vance and her—on a beach, beneath the moon, leaning into each other. His arms came around her and his hands on her naked skin were as hot as the passion burning in his eyes.

In one split second, she had gone from thinking of Vance Waverly as *boss* to imagining him as lover. What had stunned her was just how easy that shift in thinking had been. She had absolutely no trouble at all imagining him in her bed and that meant she was in some seriously deep water.

Her heart kicked hard in her chest and her mouth was dry, just remembering the flash of something hot and dangerous that shone in his eyes so briefly as their gazes met.

What was she supposed to be feeling? How was she supposed to act? And why was he being so nice all of a sudden? So…interested in her?

Taking her *and* Jake to dinner? Most men ran for the hills the moment they found out a woman was a single mother. And Vance—how weird and yet exciting was it to think of him as *Vance*—didn't strike her as the kind of man who was fond of children, either. So why?

"Sold for $47,000," the auctioneer intoned and Charlie gratefully came up out of her confusing thoughts. She was up next and she needed to keep her mind on what she was doing.

She looked down at the porcelain display stand that held the necklace Justin had shown her earlier in the week. The porcelain resembled a woman's neck, showcasing the necklace far better than having it lie flat on a bed of velvet ever could. Charlie hated having to carry the necklace into the room because she was terrified of dropping it. But she slapped a smile on her face and stepped out into the salesroom.

"Now, we have the last item up for bid and by far the star of this collection. The queen of Cadria's diamond-and-ruby necklace. As you can see," the auctioneer said, "the detail is astonishing."

A close-up picture of the necklace was displayed on the

wide flat screen behind the podium and a sigh of appreciation rose up from the women in the room.

Charlie could understand that sentiment completely. The jewels themselves were beautiful, even though Justin had pointed out that the antique cuts of the diamonds and rubies actually lowered the price. Which made no sense to her at all, but since she wasn't going to be buying it...

As she walked down the center aisle, the auctioneer said, "This magnificent necklace was a wedding present to the former queen of Cadria. Legend promises a happy marriage to the woman who wears this beauty. Please check your programs for the total carat weight. Bidding starts at $150,000."

Charlie staggered a little at that, but caught herself quickly. Cradling the display stand even more carefully, she continued down the center aisle, pausing occasionally to allow the attendees to get a better look. In the last row, she spotted Vance, sitting alone, his gaze locked, not on the necklace, but on *her*.

Instantly, she remembered that imaginary beach in Bali and the feel of his hands on her and everything inside Charlie quickened. Her heartbeat jumped into a gallop and something delicious stirred inside her. She wasn't used to men looking at her with such...hunger. But it was unmistakable and Charlie told herself that going to dinner with Vance might just be opening a door that would be better left closed.

The heat in his eyes raised her temperature enough that she felt warm all over and she knew that whether it was a smart move or not, she would be opening that door. His eyes burned and his features were cool and dispassionate as he met her gaze. No one looking at him would have guessed what he was thinking, but Charlie knew.

She gave him a small smile that wasn't returned before she headed up the center aisle to take her place beside the podium. The bidding was fierce, but she had zoned out, so she really didn't notice much more than the flash of an upraised paddle or the wave of a hand.

She didn't hear a thing, beyond the buzzing in her own ears and the pounding thrum of her own heart. How had her life taken such a gigantic turn in the space of a week or so? Not only was she being blackmailed, but she was having seriously erotic daydreams about a man who had terrified her just a few days ago.

Maybe she was having a breakdown. That would explain a lot.

Drawing her mind away from thoughts that were churning too fast to be examined, she looked down at the necklace and found herself hoping that it went to someone who would appreciate it for its beauty not just for the investment it represented. Something that beautiful deserved to be worn. Touched.

"Thank you, ladies and gentlemen," the auctioneer announced. "This concludes our auction today and Waverly's would like to extend our thanks for your patronage. There is a champagne reception in the main salon, should you care to linger. And to those of you fortunate enough to have won the pieces you wanted, we will conclude our business in the anteroom. Thank you all again."

A sedate round of applause broke out and Charlie came up from her thoughts to realize that her mind had been so busy, she hadn't even heard the winning bid. Turning for the anteroom, she carefully carried the necklace back inside.

Her turn as a would-be Cinderella was over and it was time to let go of the royal jewels and go back to her pumpkin-filled life.

"That was amazing," Justin cooed as she handed him the queen's necklace.

The whole day had been amazing as far as Charlie was concerned. "What was the final selling price?"

"You didn't hear?"

She shook her head. "I must have zoned out."

Justin just stared at her as if he couldn't understand how anyone could *not* pay attention to something as important as diamonds and rubies. "The final came in as a phone bid." He paused to frown. "I hate phone bids. I like to *know* who bought one of our pieces."

Charlie smiled, because Justin really was very proprietary when it came to the jewels in his care.

"Anyway," he said airily, "the necklace finally went for three seventy-five."

Charlie blinked at him in astonishment. *"Three hundred seventy-five thousand dollars?"*

Justin's eyebrows wiggled and his squinty eyes sparkled with glee. "I said it was an amazing piece, didn't I?"

She looked down at the necklace, with its antique jewels shining up at her, and took a long, slow breath. "I'm so glad I didn't hear that when I was still holding it."

"Thanks for your help tonight, hon." Justin set the porcelain stand down onto the pedestal waiting for it.

Whoever the lucky bidder was would be paying for the necklace right now. Then it would be wrapped up to be sent from Waverly's. She didn't even want to imagine how someone would get such an expensive item safely home. Did you hire armed guards? But that was so not her problem.

"You know I love working the auctions, Justin." She checked her wristwatch. "I'd better get moving, though. Still have to pick up Jake."

"Sure, sure."

"You ready?"

Vance's deep voice sounded out from the doorway behind her and Charlie felt a small, involuntary sizzle of reaction shoot through her veins. She so didn't want to feel that. Had no business sizzling over her boss. Yet, somehow, her body wasn't getting that message.

"Yes," she said, turning to face him.

"Ready for what?" Justin asked in a suspiciously innocent tone.

Oh, damn. Charlie loved Justin, she really did, but the man wouldn't know how to keep a secret if someone stapled his lips shut. Surely Vance knew that. So why had he spoken up unless he didn't care if people knew they were going to dinner? And if he didn't care, was this more of a business thing than a date? But if it was a business thing, would she be calling him Vance? Would he have really said that about sex and Bali?

And why couldn't she stop thinking about it?

Vance didn't say anything and Justin was waiting, shifting his far-too-interested gaze back and forth between the two of them.

Finally, Charlie said, "Vance—I mean Mr. Waverly—is giving Jake and I a ride home."

"Hmmm…"

"First to dinner, then a ride home," Vance clarified.

Charlie groaned inwardly.

"I see," Justin said, his eyes shining so brightly now it was a wonder they weren't giving off actual sparks. "Well, then, don't let me hold you up any longer."

When the older man winked at her, Charlie sighed. Damage done. Justin's romantic heart and love of gossip would take care of alerting the building to whatever was or wasn't going on between her and Vance.

She picked up her purse from a nearby chair and slipped the strap over her shoulder. Looking up at her boss, she said, "We might as well go."

As soon as they were out of earshot, Charlie glanced at

Vance. "You do realize that by tomorrow, everyone at Waverly's will know that we went to dinner together."

"Yeah," he said. "I've known Justin a long time."

"So why did you say anything in front of him?"

"You wanted to keep our dinner date a secret?"

"Not a secret," she countered as they stepped into the elevator for the short trip to the fourth-floor day-care center. "But—"

One eyebrow lifted. "Is there a problem?"

"Shouldn't there be?" she asked, unsure what she should be thinking now. He was her boss, and now her date. He didn't seem to care who knew, but she felt odd about the whole situation. He was making her feel things she didn't want yet certainly enjoyed. Then there was the fact that his family had *founded* Waverly's and now there was a blackmailer trying to make her betray not only him but the auction house she loved.

Could her life get any more complicated?

"I think," Vance said, taking her hand in his, "you're thinking too much."

Her palm to his, heat swamped her. When he drew her out of the elevator and led her down the hall to where Jake waited, Charlie knew she was in really big trouble.

The worst part?

She didn't care.

Vance was in hell.

He could tell because of the screaming.

When he had invited Charlie out to dinner, he'd had in mind a nice steak place. Not too elegant, not too casual. Just a nice in-between, with good service and a quiet atmosphere so they could talk. So he could try to discover if she was an enemy or not.

He had *not* planned on a zoo-themed diner where chil-

dren outnumbered adults and the specialty of the house was
macaroni and cheese.

"You look uncomfortable."

"What?" He shouted to be heard over the screaming three-
year-old in the booth behind him.

"I said, you look like you're miserable and wishing that
you were anywhere but here."

"No, you didn't."

"Okay, I just *thought* most of that, but you do look miserable."

She didn't, Vance noticed. Her son was in a high chair
pulled up to their table. Vance didn't know much about babies—happily—but this one seemed good-looking and far
better behaved than the little tyrants running all over the
restaurant.

"It's just a little loud."

"Is it?" She shrugged and shredded a piece of chicken onto
her son's tray table. "I didn't notice."

"Really?" He leaned forward, and frowned when his elbow
came down in a spill of soda. "I didn't realize you were deaf."

She laughed and something inside Vance fisted so tightly,
he could hardly breathe. When she smiled, she was beautiful.
When she laughed, she was incomparable. Her whole face lit
up, her eyes shone and the laugh itself was not one of those
quiet, restrained society titters; this was full-throated laughter that had him grinning in response.

"I'm so sorry, Vance. This is just killing you, isn't it?"

Suddenly, it didn't seem so bad after all. "Doesn't bother
me a bit."

"Other than making you wear the expression of a man who
would like to chew off his own foot to escape."

He frowned. "That's not what I'm feeling."

"Then you should smile to reassure me."

He did and she said, "You really should do that more often. You're far less intimidating when you smile."

"Maybe I like being intimidating."

"Well, you are really good at it," she said, then leaned over and kissed her son's forehead. The little boy grinned and kicked his feet before grabbing a tiny fistful of shredded chicken.

Vance glanced around the diner—he refused to think of the place as a restaurant. The servers were dressed in animal-print uniforms, as zebras, lions, tigers. There were other employees over by the play area dressed in wild animal costumes and they were being besieged by an army of toddlers. Vance couldn't even fathom a worse job.

But he was here with Charlie and she was happy and relaxed, so he decided to make the best of the situation. While she had her guard down, he would gather as much information as he could. And by the end of the night, he would know if she was an enemy—or a potential lover.

Six

Vance leaned in toward her so he wouldn't have to raise his voice above a roar. "So what did you think of the auction?"

Her gaze snapped to his and excitement shone in her blue eyes. "It was wonderful. It is every time, but today, seeing the royal jewels? Knowing that I was touching something worn by a queen more than a hundred years ago? Wonderful, if terrifying."

"Terrifying?"

"Did you hear what that necklace sold for?" She shook her head and laughed. "I was terrified I'd drop it or accidentally twist the gold wire or gouge out a stone or something…."

His mouth quirked. "A busy imagination."

"Oh, incredibly busy. I'll probably drive Jake crazy as he grows up. If he gets a cold, in my head it escalates in seconds to pneumonia, then an oxygen tent and my donating a lung or something." She paused, took a breath and said wryly, "Now that you know I'm nuts, feel free to run."

"I'm not going anywhere."

"You're not, are you?" She tipped her head to one side to look at him and a cascade of blond hair swung down by her shoulder like a slice of sunlight. "I wonder why."

He wondered that, too. She wasn't the kind of woman who usually drew him in and, yet, she fascinated him enough that he was willing to put up with complete bedlam just to sit across the table from her.

"Anyway," she said, returning to his earlier question, "I love the auctions. Being part of the excitement, even in a small way."

Vance nodded. "I understand that completely. My father took me to my first auction when I was ten. It was sports memorabilia. Baseball cards, Babe Ruth's glove, Ted Williams's favorite bat, that kind of thing." She was smiling at him, silently encouraging him to go on.

So he did. "Even at ten, I felt that rush you were talking about. Seeing those things from the past getting a new shot at being appreciated…"

"Exactly." Absentmindedly, she reached out and patted his hand in solidarity. "Like the jewelry today. Justin says the collection was most likely kept locked away in Cadria, in a vault or a crown jewels room—who knows? But today, the pieces were in the light again. Being admired. People were buying them so they could be worn again. Dazzle again." She sighed.

"Liked the jewelry, did you?"

"What woman wouldn't? Especially that necklace. But it wasn't just the stones themselves, it was the romance of it. A wedding present from a king to his queen. The legend of happily-ever-after attached to it. The diamonds and rubies themselves were just part of the whole." She shook her head, still awestruck. "Amazing."

Behind Vance, the crazed three-year-old was shouting about cake and his parents were quietly telling him to use his inside voice. Vance wasn't sure the kid *had* an inside voice and if he did, whether it would be heard in the cacophony of sound.

Keeping his voice as low as he could and still be heard, he leaned toward Charlie and caught her gaze with his.

"How'd you get interested in auctions? I mean, I was born into it. What's your reason?"

The waitress showed up with two coffees and a small dish of fresh fruit. As Charlie cut the pieces of cantaloupe, watermelon and grapes into even tinier pieces for her son, she started talking.

"In college I went to a few auctions with friends." She lifted her gaze to his. "Nothing like the ones we hold at Waverly's, of course. These were more country auctions, selling crates of mystery goods or farm equipment, some furniture and antiques. But the *feeling* was the same, if you know what I mean. The sense of anticipation—people hoping to find something special. Maybe buying a painting for a dollar and discovering an old master under an ugly dog playing poker—"

He laughed.

Charlie shrugged and said, "It was everything. The auctioneer, the crowds, the bidding. I loved all of it. So when my grandmother died—"

"Your grandmother?"

She stopped and he read hesitation in her eyes as she bit at her bottom lip. He knew she hadn't meant to say that and his curiosity was piqued.

"My grandmother raised me," she said briefly then hurried on. "Anyway, when she died, I packed up and moved to New York. Two years ago, I got a job at Waverly's. I started out in HR, but worked my way up, and now I work for the boss."

He laughed. "One of the bosses, anyway."

"Why did you take us to dinner?" Charlie asked suddenly. She smoothed wisps of light brown hair off her son's forehead and said, "I can't imagine you've been dying to have dinner with a bunch of screaming kids." Her eyes widened as she looked past him. "Oops."

Vance felt someone watching him and slowly turned his head to meet the three-year-old screamer's big, dark eyes. The boy was hanging over the back of the bench seat, watching him intently. Vance stared right back at him. When the boy stuck out his tongue, Charlie laughed and Vance winced.

"Trevor!" the boy's mother snapped, and dragged him back down to his seat. "Sorry," she murmured.

Shaking his head, Vance turned back to Charlie. "Clearly the evil Boss Stare doesn't work on kids," he muttered, then looked into her eyes. "You're enjoying this, aren't you?"

"Would it be wrong to say yes?"

"Yes, it would."

Soberly, she nodded. "Then no, I don't like it at all. It's absolutely terrible how you're suffering."

He gave her a rueful smile. He couldn't even remember the last time he'd been teased. Usually people—women—were wary around him. They spoke softly and moved slowly, as if he were a live grenade about to go off. Not Charlie. And while he never wanted to see this diner again, he was actually having a good time.

Something he hadn't expected. He'd only thought about how to get her talking. To spilling secrets, if she had any. But if she had those secrets, they were still her own. Which meant that he'd be spending more time with her.

A plan he didn't have a problem with.

When her son rubbed at his eyes with tiny fists, Charlie said, "I have to get him home to bed."

"It's barely eight."

Tipping her head to look at him, she said, "Babies go to bed earlier than we do."

"Oh, right." Idiot. He signaled the waitress for the bill and took care of it while Charlie cleaned up her son. Once they were ready, he stood up and Charlie lifted the little boy from the high chair.

Instantly, Jake held out both pudgy arms to Vance.

Vance stared at the boy for a long moment. The baby's hair was practically standing on end. There was a food stain on his *I love Mommy* T-shirt. And his dark blue eyes were fixed on Vance as if he were Santa and the Easter Bunny rolled into one. He'd never been around babies much and hadn't really missed the experience. Until tonight, Vance would have said he had zero interest in kids altogether.

But this baby seemed…different, somehow. Certainly quieter than the other kids in the diner. It was younger, softer and it had a dimple in its left cheek, just like its mother.

"Jake…" Charlie was clearly surprised by her son's move and, frankly, so was Vance. But who was he to argue? He reached for the boy, tucked him against his chest and headed for the front door, Charlie trailing behind.

The baby laid his head down on Vance's shoulder and, despite his best efforts, something inside Vance melted.

"I cannot believe I had to hear this from *Justin!* Did you lose your phone again?"

"No," Charlie said, laughing. "I haven't lost my phone in almost two years, thanks. And I was going to tell you but—"

"You were too busy dating your boss?"

Charlie had a feeling that Katie's stunned expression was probably an echo of her own. Heck, she had *lived* through last night and she was still feeling the shock. After dinner the night before, Vance had hailed a cab to take Jake and her home. The surprise was when Vance had joined them for the trip.

Jake had fallen asleep on the way home, cuddled comfortably against Vance's broad chest. Though she'd offered to take the baby from him, Vance had held the boy all the way to her apartment. And for a moment or two, Charlie had actually been envious of her son.

Being with Vance in the quiet of the cab had been…nice. They talked as the city whizzed past in a stream of subdued noise and neon color and when they were finally at the small apartment she called home, Vance had walked her to her door, handed Jake to her and said good-night.

"I can't believe this," Katie was saying in an awed, hushed tone. "You do know the whole building's talking about this."

"Thank you, Justin," Charlie said on a sigh.

"Well, even if he hadn't told, you never could have kept this a secret for long. You have to know that."

"I suppose so." She frowned and said, "I don't think Vance even cares if people know."

"Vance?" Katie repeated that one word in a dumbfounded tone. "You call him *Vance?*"

"'Mr. Waverly' seemed a little formal for a date."

Her friend shook her head slowly. "A date. With your boss."

"Are you getting past that anytime soon?"

"I don't think so," Katie admitted, then shifted on the stone bench to look at her. "Did he kiss you?"

Charlie's mind slipped back to the night before. When her apartment door was open and the light from inside was slanted across Vance's face as he looked down at her. There had been a sort of expectant hush hanging in the air between them. He bent down, she leaned in toward him and for one heart-stopping moment, she was just a breath away from being kissed. But then Jake woke up with a cry and the cab driver honked impatiently and the moment was gone. Probably for the best. She was sure that was a date Vance would never want repeated, so why indulge in any more fantasies?

"No."

"Well, that sucks." Frowning, the tiny redhead with bright

green eyes grumbled, "And how did I miss all this excitement?"

Charlie shook her head and grinned at her friend. Katie lived in an apartment upstairs from her and most mornings they rode the subway into work together. In fact, it was Katie who had helped Charlie get the apartment in her building. "You weren't home last night for me to tell and this morning you came in early, so we didn't get a chance to talk on the train."

"All true. Still. Dating your boss. It's sort of sexy, unless," she added with a shudder, "it's *my* boss."

"I think Vance was just being nice."

"Uh-huh. He took you and Jake to dinner, then brought you all the way home to Queens just to be nice. Sure, I buy that."

Frowning, Charlie took a sip of her iced tea and studied the faces of the people hurrying down Fifth Avenue. They often brought their lunch out here to sit and watch the city go by. It was hot, steamy and the lunchtime lines at the food carts were busy. Even in the summer heat, it was nice to get out of the building for a while and rejoin humanity.

Especially now, when Charlie was doing everything she could to avoid thinking about her blackmailer. She'd received another email threat just that morning and the message was burned into her brain.

No more stalling, it had said. *Get those files or risk losing your son.*

She was running out of time and was no closer to knowing what to do about it. She couldn't steal files. And she couldn't not steal them. Lose her job, lose her son. It was a vicious circle with no way of winning.

"Katie," she said abruptly, turning her head to look at her friend, "have you heard anything about Rothschild's lately?"

"Like what?"

"Anything."

Katie shrugged. "A couple of people are talking about that article in the paper. You know, the bit about Ms. Richardson and Dalton Rothschild. Did they or didn't they? But I mean, who cares? If they did, it's not as if she would have handed him the keys to Waverly's, you know?"

Charlie chewed at her bottom lip. "But it doesn't look good."

"True, but Ms. Richardson is devoted to Waverly's. She wouldn't put the auction house at risk." A long pause. "Would she?"

The problem was, Charlie didn't know. And neither did Vance apparently or he wouldn't have asked her to listen for gossip at the house. She worried. It wasn't a coincidence that the article had appeared in the paper the very same day she'd received that first threatening email. Whoever was behind her current trouble was no doubt also the source of that article.

What did that tell her? A lot of nothing, really.

"Hey," Katie said, nudging Charlie with her shoulder. "Don't take it so personally. These big companies are always having some kind of trouble. They'll work it out."

"You're not worried?"

"The only thing I'm worried about is finishing the audit of last quarter's books before my boss decides to have a stroke on my desk."

Charlie smiled, but it was halfhearted. Thankfully, Katie didn't seem to notice. She'd give anything to be as uninterested in what was happening as her friend apparently was.

"I've got to get back to work," Katie said abruptly after a check of her phone for the time. "I'll meet you for the subway ride home...unless you get a better offer."

"Not much chance of that," Charlie said. "I'll see you later."

She still had twenty minutes before she had to return to work and she was in no hurry to face her computer and the email program that had her so spooked. So she'd just finish her tea, and then stop by the day-care center to see Jake on her way back upstairs.

"Waiting for someone?" Vance's voice came from behind her.

"Were you watching me?" she asked, turning to look up at him.

"Watching sounds so stalkerlike," he said as he sat down on the stone bench beside her. He laid one arm along the back of the bench and stretched out his legs, crossing his feet at the ankles. "I prefer...admiring."

Charlie shook her head. She'd seen so many different sides of Vance in the last week or so, she could hardly keep them all straight. He was ruthless in business, didn't tolerate stupidity in the workplace and was gentle with her son. He laughed when she teased him and gave her looks that set fire to her insides. Now he was sprawled on a stone bench in the hot sun as if he had all the time in the world when she knew he was a workaholic.

"I saw your friend go back to work, so thought I'd join you," he said, tipping his face up to the brilliant blue sky and the blistering sun. "Nice day."

"It's hot."

He tilted his head to look at her. "Yeah, but nice anyway. What's wrong, Charlie?"

"Nothing's wrong."

"You seem a little on edge."

"No, just thinking."

"About?"

"Lots of things."

"Want to narrow that down any?" he asked.

"Not really." She wouldn't have known where to begin. Besides, it wasn't as if she could tell him she was being blackmailed. And she couldn't very well tell him that whatever thoughts weren't being taken up by the mystery threats were devoted to *him*. God, could this get any more complicated?

He straightened up, but kept that one arm along the bench, almost close enough to touch Charlie. She had the strangest impulse to lean back into him. But she didn't do it. "Your friend. She works at Waverly's?"

"Yeah," Charlie told him, taking a sip of her tea. "She's in Accounting."

He nodded. "Has she said anything about the situation with Rothschild's?"

"She doesn't know anything," Charlie said on a sigh. "And she's not really worried about it, either. She thinks it'll all work itself out."

He laughed shortly but there was no humor in the sound. "I wish she was right. Truth is, we have no idea what Dalton is up to."

"Ms. Richardson hasn't said anything more?"

"No." He frowned and looked out at the bustle of Fifth Avenue. Charlie followed his gaze and thought how odd it was that the world could go on so blithely while she was tied up in so many knots. Brilliant splashes of color sprouted from the flowers spilling from cement planters. Car horns blared, a siren wailed in the distance and a dog walker herded six dogs of varying sizes along the sidewalk.

"I had a good time last night," he said quietly.

She laughed, keeping her gaze on the street because it was so much safer than staring into his gold-flecked brown eyes. "No, you didn't."

He reached out, cupped her chin and turned her face to his. Then he grinned at her and the flash in his eyes took her breath away. The man was absolutely devastating when he smiled and put his heart into it.

"Crazy," he said as he released her. "But I really did. Not

that I'm in any hurry to go back to the Zoo Diner. Appropriate name for it, by the way. But I had a good time with you."

God, it would be so easy to let herself fall for him when
he was like this. Just the touch of his hand on her skin made
her yearn for more. The soft smile on his face had her wanting to kiss that delectably curved mouth. He was the most
dangerous man she had ever known.

"Vance, what're you doing?"

"What do you mean?"

She shifted on the stone bench and felt the sun-warmed
heat of it soak into her. Looking into his eyes, she asked,
"This. With me. Why are you being…nice?"

One eyebrow went up. She had already noticed that he did
that when something caught him off guard.

"I have to have a reason for being nice?"

"It's just—" She took a breath and blew it out. "You're
acting like you're interested in me and I'm not sure why. Or
what you expect."

He reached over, took her hand and held it for a second or
two. Long enough to get her pulse pounding and her heart
rate jumping into high gear. Then he gave her hand a squeeze
before letting go and said, "I like you. Is that so strange?"

"I guess not." Though silently she was saying, *Yes, it is
strange. I'm your assistant. I'm not rich. I have a baby. I'm
not the kind of woman you usually spend time with, so what's
going on?* She had seen enough photos of him in the society
pages of the newspapers to know that most of the women in
his life had trust funds, rich ex-husbands or both. So why,
she asked herself again, was he coming on to her?

"Good." He stood up, checked his watch and said, "Lunch
is over and I hear your boss is a real bastard about work
hours."

"Yeah." She stood up, too. "You wouldn't believe the stories about him."

He stopped. "There are stories?"

"Millions of 'em," she quipped. "But I don't gossip."

"I'll keep that in mind."

There was something here, she thought. Just under their words. A feeling. A sense of something that wasn't being said. Attraction yes, but that wasn't all and it felt…off. He trusted her and she wasn't going to do anything to ruin that. But at the same time, she had a threat hanging over her head that jeopardized everything in her life.

Suddenly, Charlie wanted to tell him all of it. To ask for help. But she was too afraid of what he might think. What he might do. She couldn't lose her job. She couldn't lose her son.

So, instead, torn with confusion and indecision, she settled for losing her mind.

"I'll see you at the office," she said and tossed her iced tea cup into the nearest trash can.

Then she walked alone down Fifth, part of the crowd, but separate. And she felt the heat of his gaze follow her.

"This is starting to become a habit," Charlie said when she opened her front door to Vance three nights later. He smiled at her and Charlie's heart did a slow flip and curl. The man was just…overpowering. Even now, when he was wearing blue jeans, a short-sleeved red shirt and a pair of boots, he exuded power and a sensual heat that should have been illegal.

Every evening since the first night he had brought her home, Vance had appeared at her door, and they'd gone for long walks with Jake. Sometimes they window-shopped, sometimes they stopped for cookies and a latte. Most of the time, they just took turns pushing Jake's stroller and…talking.

And Charlie was getting *way* too used to it.

Vance leaned against the doorjamb and grinned at her. "Are you complaining?" he asked, then half turned. "Because I could leave…"

"No," she said quickly. She wasn't sure what was going on between her and her boss, but whatever it was, she liked it. Probably too much. "Not complaining."

"Good." His eyes fixed on her and Charlie's heartbeat quickened. Then he squatted down to eye level with the toddler in his stroller. "So, Jake, where to tonight?"

The tiny boy squealed with delight and shouted "Ba! Ba!"

Vance looked up at Charlie. "He says a night at the ballet would be clichéd. He'd prefer a stroll through the park."

"Well, then," Charlie said, laughing, "by all means."

Vance maneuvered the stroller out the front door and down the short set of steps to the grass. Charlie pulled the door closed behind her and locked it. Then she paused to take a quick look up and down her street. She loved it here.

Her apartment building had once been a grand old house, built to look like a Tudor-style English manor. Years ago, it had been converted into four apartments. She had the ground-floor apartment on the right side and her friend Katie was just upstairs. Charlie never would have been able to afford an apartment in this area ordinarily, but the owner was an elderly woman currently living in England and she had a soft spot for babies, so she'd made Charlie an excellent deal.

The streets in Forest Hills, Queens, were narrow and decked with trees that looked as though they'd been there for centuries. Her neighbors were quiet but friendly and Manhattan was just a train ride away. But here, New York moved more slowly and Charlie could almost convince herself that she was living in a small town again. It was a perfect place to raise Jake. She looked at Vance smiling at her son and thought, at the moment, *everything* was perfect.

"Where are you guys going tonight?" a woman's voice called out and shattered the quiet.

Charlie sighed, turned and looked up. Katie was hanging out her living room window, grinning down at them. She had probably been haunting her window just waiting for Vance to show up. Charlie couldn't really blame her. This was all so odd, so out of the ordinary...

"To the park," Vance answered, then picked up the stuffed dog Jake had tossed.

"Have a good time," Katie said, a teasing tone in her voice. Then she gave Charlie a knowing wink before darting back into her apartment. No doubt, Katie would be turning up with a bottle of wine and a dozen questions later tonight. Charlie only wished she had a few answers for her.

Charlie turned to Vance. "You realize that Katie has told everyone at Waverly's about your coming to see me every night."

He shrugged. "Do you care?"

She should, Charlie knew. Getting involved with Vance Waverly was probably a huge mistake. But looking into his eyes, she knew she couldn't regret a moment of this—whatever it was. Every evening, when the light was just slipping away, he showed up to spend time with her and Jake. And every evening, she told herself not to expect him. Not to look for him. But she did anyway and when she saw him, her heart got a little more involved. How could it not? He was so good with Jake. And so much fun to talk to. And when he took her hand in his, she felt...*treasured*.

Silly.

"No," she said firmly, "I don't care."

"Good." He smiled at her as if she'd given him the perfect answer. "So let's go."

They walked a few blocks east and the world changed perceptibly. As lovely as her street was and as much as she loved it, Charlie always felt a little twinge of...not envy, exactly, just a bit wistful when she walked through Forest Hills Gardens. Exclusive mansions sprawled behind wide, manicured lawns and what looked like private forests.

"I haven't been in this neighborhood since I was a kid," Vance mused.

"You lived here?" Charlie couldn't imagine living in a more beautiful spot. She could practically *see* Jake growing up on these gorgeous streets, riding his bike up and down circular driveways, climbing the majestic trees. Of course, that was a completely unrealistic daydream—but what was the point of having ordinary dreams?

"No, a friend of my father's did," Vance said. "We used to visit him a lot. Funny, I haven't thought of this place in years. But it's really nice, isn't it? And close to the city."

"It's perfect is what it is," Charlie said, with a little sigh of pleasure.

"Yeah?" He stopped pushing the stroller and looked at her. "If you had to pick, which house would you buy?"

She took a deep breath and smiled. "It wouldn't be easy to choose, but I do have a favorite," she admitted, because she had played this little game with herself every time she took Jake for a walk down there. There were brick mansions and bungalow styles. There was even a home with a red Spanish tile roof. But the house she loved had stood out for her from the beginning. Hooking her arm through his, she gave Vance a tug and said, "Come on. It's a little farther down."

Halfway down the block, she stopped. Giving his arm a squeeze, she said, "That's my house. Well," she added with a half shrug, "the owners don't know it, of course."

She always found the chance to walk past the house she considered her dream home. It was like an English cottage only bigger. It was three stories high with sloped roofs and dark red shutters on the windows. There were brilliant splashes of pink and yellow flowers crouched around the long porch, and the wide double front doors were arched, like a storybook castle.

"It's beautiful," Vance said.

"It really is," she agreed, and met his gaze only to find him staring at *her* not the house. "All it needs is a porch swing."

"You'd like a swing?"

"Oh, yes. That would be nice," she mused, staring at the house for another long moment. "Sitting outside, watching the sun go down, saying hi to your neighbors…" Her voice trailed off as she turned her head to look up at him.

A soft, warm wind raced down the street. From a few houses down came the rhythmic thumping of a basketball, and a dog barked just because he wanted to be heard. The light in the sky was easing into twilight and Jake was in his stroller, laughing and talking to himself.

It was a perfect moment.

Vance leaned toward her. Charlie went up on her toes, her gaze drifting from his eyes to his mouth and back again. Her heartbeat was pounding and the world around her seemed to take a breath and hold it in anticipation.

His mouth was just an inch from hers when Jake tossed his stuffed animal and then howled in frustration. The baby's shout broke the spell growing between Charlie and Vance and she could only be grateful for it.

Infatuation was one thing. Allowing herself to make a fool of herself over a man she would never be able to have was something else entirely.

Quickly, she picked up the stuffed dog, handed it back to Jake and told Vance, "We should get Jake home."

"I suppose it is getting late," Vance murmured.

She flashed him a glance, then looked away quickly. It was already too late, Charlie thought. Her heart was involved whether she wanted to admit it or not.

A week later, Vance was wound too tight and seriously on edge. The only one he *hadn't* lost his temper with was Charlie. Which was ironic, considering that *she* was the one who had his insides tied into knots that only got tighter with every passing second.

The woman was getting to him and that had not been in the plan. Every damn day around her, his blood ran hotter, his mind clouded a little further and the idea of *having* her dug claws of need ever deeper into him.

Add to that the fact that he knew damn well she was lying to him about something. They'd spent nearly every night together. Oh, not in bed. More's the pity, he told himself. But at dinner, taking Jake for walks or just sitting around her small, tidy apartment in Queens.

Hell, he was going to *Queens* for her. What was next? Brooklyn? At the thought, he jumped up from his desk chair and stared down onto the tree-lined street below Waverly's.

Charlie was antsy. Nervous. And getting worse every day. She checked through the daily mail as if afraid of what she might find. She jumped when he entered a room and just yesterday, one of the security guards reported that Charlie had been in the records room, where all the old files and reports were kept. Why the hell would she be down there? And why hadn't she told him? What was she hiding?

His gut told him something was off with Charlie. Another part of his anatomy told him he shouldn't care. His mind was stuck somewhere in the middle.

When the office intercom buzzed, he stabbed at the button, focusing all his frustration on it. "What is it?"

"Jeez," Charlie said. "Bite my head off."

He rubbed one hand across his face and shook his head even as he smiled to himself. It hadn't taken long for Charlie to feel at ease in the boss-assistant relationship. "Sorry. A lot on my mind. What is it?"

"Security's on line 2 for you," she said a little breathlessly.

"Right." He didn't think about the fact that she sounded

nervous. Instead, he punched a button on his phone and said, "Waverly."

"Mr. Waverly, this is Carl in Security. You asked us to let you know if anything out of the ordinary happened."

"Yeah?" Hell, he'd had the whole place on alert for the past couple of weeks in hopes that they might catch whoever might be trying to sell them out to Rothschild's. Now that they had something, though, Vance wasn't entirely sure he wanted to hear what was coming.

Carl said, "We had the IT department keeping a tight lock-down on sensitive areas—in general, setting up their version of alarms. They alerted us to the fact that someone in your office was trying to access secure files this morning. And it wasn't from your computer."

This morning, when Vance had been at a meeting with a potential client. When Charlie was alone in the office.

"What files?" He shot a look at the closed door separating him from Charlie. Was she worried, knowing that he was talking to Security?

"Apparently," Carl told him, "they were older records on minor auctions. According to the IT guys, this person didn't get to anything important. A new firewall's going up as we speak so everything's secure." Carl paused and asked, "Is there anything you'd like us to handle?"

"No." His brain was racing and anger was beginning to churn inside. He needed to take care of this himself. He needed to look Charlie in the eye when he confronted her, because only then would he know for sure if she was being honest. Her face gave away everything she was thinking, feeling; he'd already learned that much about her. And hell, for all he knew, it hadn't been her. She might have been in another part of the building and someone else had slipped in to use her computer just to incriminate her.

He wasn't going to assume she was guilty of anything.

Not yet, anyway. But he didn't like it. He didn't like the notion that Charlie was a traitor.

"I'll take care of it," he told Carl and hung up a second later. All he had to do now was figure out how.

Seven

Charlie hated this. Hated feeling on edge all the time. Hated the sense of guilt that seemed to cling to the edges of her mind constantly these days.

Vance was being so nice. And she was lying to him. Every time she spoke to him, she lied. Her grandmother had always insisted, *It's a lie, Charlie, if you know something and you don't say so. Same as if you were spinning tales yourself.* And Gran had been right. Charlie knew something dangerous and she wasn't saying anything about it because of her need to protect herself. And her son.

Which made her a liar.

And now Vance was talking to Security. Was it about her? Had someone seen something? Was she being watched by someone besides her blackmailer? Oh, God.

Charlie opened up her email program and clicked Reply on the latest threat she'd received only that morning. When that threat had come in, she'd actually tried to open up the older record files this morning, but she hadn't gotten far before she had shut everything down. She couldn't do it. Not to Waverly's. Not to Vance.

Now she typed in a quick note to whoever was threatening her, asking for more time. Even as she hit Send, she knew it wasn't going to help. This wasn't going to go away until she either betrayed Vance and Waverly's or took Jake and ran.

But where would she run? She had no family now. No one. The only people she knew in the world were here, in the city. She had a little savings, but not enough to set herself and Jake up anywhere else. She sat back in her chair, letting her fears rise up until they nearly choked her. When the light on line 2 went out, she shivered. Vance had finished speaking to Security. What was next? Would she be arrested? Fired?

"Gran, I really wish you were still here. I'd run home so fast…"

And just whispering those words made her ashamed. Running away wasn't the answer and she knew it. She had to face this. Tell Vance the truth and hope to heaven he believed her when she swore she would never sell out Waverly's.

Oh, God.

Fear still jumped in the pit of her stomach, but somehow, it was easier knowing that at least she'd made a decision. She knew what she had to do. All she needed was the courage to get it done. Because she knew that once she told him about her past, about where she'd come from, he wouldn't want anything more to do with her. And oh, she would miss him. But first—

She buzzed his office and waited for his gruff reply. "Yes?"

"Vance, I'm taking a break. I'll be back in fifteen minutes."

"Sure. Fine."

He sounded as stern and unyielding as he ever had and she wondered again how a man as ruthless as he was in business could be so different when it was just the two of them. She headed out of the office for the elevator. Before she spoke to Vance, she needed a few minutes with her son.

When she got to the fourth floor, Jake was sleeping.

Charlie slipped into the nap room, walked up to the only occupied crib and stared down at her son. Curled up on his side, Jake had one fist pressed to his mouth and the other curled into his soft, brown hair. His sock-clad feet were drawn up tight and his tiny sighs arrowed straight into her heart.

Scooping him up, Charlie cradled him against her and patted his back until he settled again. She sat in one of the rocking chairs in the shadowy half light and looked down at him through tear-filled eyes. She and her baby boy were alone in the darkened room and his warmth eased some of the chill snaking through her. Smoothing one hand over his hair, Charlie bent close enough to kiss his forehead.

"I'm so sorry, sweetie," she whispered. "I tried, really. I wanted to give you so much and now I don't know what to do."

The baby slept on and Charlie relished the solid, warm weight of him close to her heart. No matter what else was wrong with her life, she had Jake. And she wouldn't let him down. She would give him a safe, warm world to grow up in.

"I'll fix it somehow, baby boy. Everything is going to be all right." Was she trying to soothe her son or reassure herself? She didn't know and wasn't sure it mattered.

Tears rolled down her cheeks and she let them fall. Here in the dark, who would see?

"Why're you crying?"

She stopped rocking, lifted her gaze to the doorway and met Vance Waverly's steady stare. He was tall, gorgeous and, right now, she could see that his eyes, even in the shadows, were glinting with carefully banked fury.

"It's nothing," she said, because what else could she possibly say?

"You're sitting by yourself, holding your sleeping son in the dark and crying. That's not nothing." He pushed away from the doorjamb and locked his gaze on her. Even in the shadows, she felt the power of that cool stare. "I have to know something. Are you a spy, Charlie?"

"I'm not a spy," she said, patting her son's behind gently, keeping her voice as quiet as she could. Her tears still rained down her face and as Vance entered the room, she tried wiping them away.

Here it was then. She wasn't going to get the opportunity to confess. To go to him and tell him everything. Instead, he'd found her out and now he was looking at her as if he didn't know her at all. But then, she thought sadly, he really didn't.

He squatted down in front of her and locked his gaze with hers. "What's going on, Charlie? What is it you're trying so hard not to tell me?"

"Believe it or not, I was going to tell you," she said softly as Jake murmured in his sleep. "I just needed to see my son first. Sort of center myself, then I was coming to you."

Vance nodded. "I do believe you. But I'm here now. So talk to me."

Still meeting his angry eyes, she shook her head. "I don't even know where to start."

"How about you put Jake back in his bed and you and I take a walk?"

She took a breath and let it out on a heavy sigh. The time for stalling was over. And oddly, the heavy ball in the pit of her stomach that had been her constant companion for almost two weeks was already dissolving. Living with lies wasn't easy. Telling the truth wouldn't be easy, either. But at least she'd be able to breathe again.

Charlie stood up, settled Jake back down again, then turned to look up at Vance. Lifting her chin, she whispered, "It's a long story."

* * *

He took her to the park. Central Park on a bright summer day was filled with locals and tourists and was far enough away from Waverly's that whatever they said would stay between them. They stayed clear of the lakes and the swimming pool, skirted the carousel and the zoo. He bought them each a bottle of water from a waffle vendor, then steered her toward a wooden bench beside a walking path through the trees.

Vance sat down beside her on the bench beneath an ancient willow. The tree's branches hung low, its feathery leaves grudgingly waving in the desultory breeze. The scent of flowers and burned coffee from a nearby food cart filled the air as they sat in the dappled shade.

Of course, Vance had followed her when she'd left her desk to take that "break." Angry and suspicious, he'd felt like a third-rate private detective, slinking along in her wake as she made her way through Waverly's. He'd had no idea what he might discover, but he certainly hadn't expected to find her crying over her sleeping son. As her boss, he was wary, suspicious. As the man who…cared for her, he was worried.

"Start talking," he said, when she made no move to say anything. "I want it all, Charlie."

She laughed shortly, broke the seal on her water bottle and took a long drink. When she had neatly screwed the cap back on, she lifted her gaze and looked out over the park. Two women pushing strollers laughed and chatted. A young man threw a Frisbee for a golden retriever and somewhere in the distance, a siren sounded.

"I don't even know where to begin," she admitted, crossing her legs demurely.

"Then start with this." He waited until she looked at him. "Were you the one trying to access Waverly records this morning?"

Her pale blue eyes went wide in shock. "Oh, God."

"I'll take that as a yes," he muttered darkly and took a drink of his own water. "Security told me that the IT department had found someone hacking into the records. I really hoped it wasn't you."

Dammit. He would have been willing to bet money that she was innocent. He didn't like feeling as though he'd been played. Was she that good an actress? Could she really pretend to be an innocent and pull it off so completely? His gaze fixed on her, he tried to balance this new information with the woman he had come to know the past couple of weeks and couldn't do it. Who was the real Charlie?

But even as he thought that, he remembered her alone in the dark with her son and the tears coursing down her face. She hadn't known he was there. Hadn't known she'd been caught. So the tears were real. Now all he had to do was find out what else was.

"I couldn't do it," she said after a long moment of silence. "I tried. Went to the records file, but I closed it again right away. I couldn't steal from Waverly's. From *you*."

"Glad to hear it," Vance said and meant it. His suspicions were dissolving. A real thief wouldn't have changed her mind. She would have scoped out all the information she could glean and then disappear. But the frustration chewing at him was still fierce. He believed she hadn't wanted to steal from him. But she'd come close.

"Now how about you tell me *why* you tried it in the first place?" He heard the tightly leashed anger in his voice and didn't bother to disguise it. "What's got you so jumpy? So worried that you were thinking about stealing, even though you didn't want to?"

She started talking then and the words rushed over themselves as if they'd been banked up too long and couldn't wait to get out into the light of day. Vance listened without interrupting, though it cost him to keep his growing fury trapped inside. His grip on the water bottle tightened to the point where he half expected to crush the plastic container and be doused in icy water. And maybe that would have been a good thing. It might have gone a ways toward cooling off the fire of the rage pumping through his body.

When she finally finished talking, Vance couldn't sit still a second longer. He jumped to his feet, paced off a step or two, and turned back to look at her. The hot wind teased the ends of her hair and sent leaf-painted shadows dancing across her face.

She stared up at him. "You're angry."

"Good call," he said tightly. He tossed his nearly full bottle of water into a nearby trash can with such force it was like the crash of a gong.

It didn't help any. Frustrated and furious, he shoved both hands through his hair. "Dammit, Charlie."

"I wasn't going to do it," she said firmly, and stood up, grabbing his arm to force him to look at her. "You have to know that. I wasn't going to sell Waverly's out. To anyone. I wouldn't do that to the house. Or to you."

He snorted in disgust. "You think that's why I'm mad?"

"Isn't it?"

Vance looked down at her misery-filled eyes, and got mad all over again. "God, you must think I'm a real bastard."

"No, I don't," she argued.

"Then why didn't you tell me you were in trouble?" His demand was short, sharp and to the point. He couldn't believe this. Any of it. He'd been suspecting her of betrayal when all the time— "You've been threatened by some creep and you didn't say anything? Why the hell not?"

The wounded expression on her face faded and was replaced by grim resolution. "Because it was *my* problem."

"That's not an answer, Charlie," he said, voice thick with

the fury nearly choking him. "You've been scared for two weeks and never said a damn word."

"What was I supposed to say?" she argued. "If I had told you that I was being blackmailed, what could you have done? You'd have assumed that I was going to betray you."

One short, sharp bark of laughter shot from his throat. "That's great, thanks. Good to know the high opinion you have of me."

Stunned, she tilted her head and looked at him. "You're saying you would have believed me?"

"I believe you *now*," he pointed out, irritated beyond belief that she thought so little of him. "The minute you finally told me what was going on, I believed you."

"I had no way of knowing that. And besides, I didn't need help. Or, I did," she corrected, muttering now as her words came faster. "Okay, I did need help but I didn't *want* to need help, you know? I'm a big girl. I can take care of myself and Jake and— God, I've made a mess of this."

"Everybody needs help sometimes," he told her, and realized that most of his anger was draining away. At least now he knew what was going on. Knew that she was being threatened and he could do something about it.

"You don't," she charged, and didn't look happy about it.

"Wrong," he said. "I need your help right now, to make sense of all this. You with me?"

She nodded and took another drink of water.

"So, someone you don't know threatened you with losing your son unless you stole my files for the last five years?"

"Yes." She huffed out a breath. Her pale blue eyes were red-rimmed from crying, but they were dry now. As if she had decided she'd spilled enough tears and now she was gathering her strength for whatever she might need. "I got the first email the day that article about Ms. Richardson was in the paper."

"Probably not a coincidence," he said wryly.

"That's what I thought," she agreed.

"The question is, why did this person think they could get Jake taken away from you?" He watched her. "I've seen you with him. Been at your apartment. You're a good mother, providing a good home."

"Thanks," she said, a half smile curving one corner of her mouth briefly.

"There's more going on here, Charlie. You haven't told me everything." The air was hot and still as the wind suddenly died away. The sounds of summer at the park were in the distance and in the lacy shade it felt as if they were alone in the world. "Tell me the rest, Charlie. Let me help."

She tugged at the end of her long, blond ponytail, twisting the ends around her fingers in a nervous gesture. "I wish you could. Help, I mean. But you can't help with this, Vance. Things are what they are. They can't be changed."

"Try me," he said, steel in his tone. He'd never admit that there was something he couldn't fix. Couldn't set right. "You might be surprised at what I can manage."

"Not even Vance Waverly can change the past."

He stiffened at the words because he knew she was right—about that, at least. Vance was a take-charge guy. If something needed doing, he did it. In his world, things ran the way they were supposed to. Now. Of course, that wasn't always the case.

If he could have changed the past, he'd have done it by now. He'd have saved his mother and sister from the car wreck that had killed them. He'd have somehow convinced his father to find Roark earlier so Vance could have known his brother before they were adults. Yeah, there was a hell of a lot he'd go back and change if he could. But if the past couldn't be changed, then at least its impact on the present could be.

"If you don't tell me, then for damn sure I can't help," he reasoned. "So what've you got to lose?"

"A lot," she said so quietly he almost missed it. Then she looked at him again and he saw emotions crowding her eyes, so many he couldn't separate them all. Whatever she was keeping locked away was tearing at her. And that ripped at him in turn.

"What's this guy got on you, Charlie? What is it you're so desperate to keep secret?"

She took a breath and blew it out. "Remember how I told you my grandmother raised me?"

"Yeah?" He led her back to the bench and sat down beside her.

"I didn't tell you why." She shook her head and a sad smile curved her mouth for a split second before disappearing again. "When I was five, my father robbed a grocery store."

Vance hadn't expected that. Her features were a mask of shame and humiliation, but he didn't say anything because he was pretty sure there was more coming.

"He died in a chase with the police. Drove his car into a tree."

"Charlie…"

"My mother left soon after that. I never saw her again." She tore at the label on the water bottle, ripping one long strip off carefully, as if it were the most important thing in the world. "After that, my mother's mom took me in and raised me."

She lifted her gaze to stare out over the park again, deliberately keeping her gaze from his. "You know the old saying about 'the wrong side of the tracks'? Well, that was us. Me. When Gran died, I left and came here and never told anyone where I was from."

Vance felt for her. She'd had it tough and she'd come through to make something of her life. But none of this was enough to make for good blackmail.

"Come on, Charlie. There's got to be more," he said. "This isn't blackmail material."

She nearly choked on a swig of water. She half turned to fire a look at him. "Didn't you hear me? My father was a thief. He died being chased by the police. My mother ran off and disappeared. Not exactly a picture-perfect background."

"Not exactly your fault, either. You said you were *five*."

"Easy for you to say," she said, shaking her head and blinking back—thank God—a fresh sheen of tears. "You have no idea what it was like. Everyone in town gossiping about us. You couldn't understand. How could you?"

"Thanks for the faith," he muttered. "You're not the only one people gossip about. Seen the newspapers? People are always talking about the Waverlys."

"Yes, poor you," she said, sarcasm dripping off every word. "How horrible to be followed to all your fancy dinners and be made to pose for pictures. Very intrusive."

One eyebrow lifted. "Good to know you've got a temper. And a snide side, too."

She frowned at him. "You're only the second person I've ever told about myself. I would think you could understand how embarrassing this is for me."

"I get that you're embarrassed," he said. "I just don't get why. So you grew up poor. Who the hell cares?"

"You don't understand," she said, shaking her head more in temper than misery and Vance was glad to see it.

"Fine. I don't understand. Now give me the rest of it."

"Not much left," she said primly, scooting away from him on the bench. "I put myself through college and when Gran died, I moved to New York."

He moved in closer. "And Jake's father?"

She pushed up from the bench and put a stranglehold on her water bottle. "Why not? Let's just spill the last of the humiliation and get it over with." She whirled around to face him and the look in her eyes had Vance standing to walk toward her.

But she held up one hand, palm out to keep him at bay. "Don't be nice to me right now, okay? I'm hanging on by a thread here."

"Okay, then finish it."

"I met Jake's father right after I was hired at Waverly's." She dropped her water bottle into the trash and crossed her arms over her chest. Scraping her hands up and down her forearms as if to ward off a bone-deep chill, she started talking again. "His name was Blaine Andersen—at least that's what he told me."

Vance didn't say anything. He had a feeling he knew where this was going and nothing he could say would help the situation any.

"He was sweet and funny," she mused. "We went for walks in the park and to movies. He brought me flowers. He even replaced my BlackBerry when I lost mine. He said he loved me and—"

"You loved him back." Strange, but those words had a bitter taste to them.

"I thought I did," she corrected. "When I found out I was pregnant, I went to tell him, but he was gone." She shook her head as she remembered. "Familiar story, right? Small-town girl comes to the city and gets taken advantage of. God, I felt so stupid. I even went to the Andersen Architectural firm that he told me was his family's. They'd never heard of him."

"Charlie—"

"It's okay," she said quickly, interrupting him. "Doesn't matter anymore. I got Jake out of it and he's everything to me."

Vance gave her a grin, as he thought about the tiny boy who had already wormed his way into Vance's heart. One more complication that he hadn't planned on. "He's a great kid."

"Yeah." She smiled back and it was her first real smile

since this started. Vance was glad to see it, even if it did look a little trembly around the edges. "He really is."

"So is that it? All your deep, dark secrets?"

"Well, I didn't tell you about my wild addiction to chocolate-dipped strawberries, but other than that, yes. That's it." She sighed and added, "Feels like fifty pounds have fallen off my shoulders."

"Not surprising. Why'd you keep it to yourself, Charlie?" His voice was quiet. "Why didn't you come to me?"

"I'm used to taking care of myself, Vance," she told him with another deep sigh. "And I didn't think you'd believe me."

"Yeah, well," he said, "I do."

When she looked up at him, with hope shining in her eyes, he felt like a damn knight in shining armor, which he really wasn't. Hell, half the people in Manhattan would be willing to swear that he was a villain, not a hero. But he certainly enjoyed seeing her look at him like that.

"So I'm not fired?" she asked.

"You will be if you ever hold out on me again." He dropped one arm around her shoulders and pulled her in close. "Charlie, you don't have to be alone in this."

"I don't know how to be anything else."

"Then it's time to learn," he muttered. Drawing her up against him, he wrapped both arms around her and held on. She fit—that's all he could think of. Fit as if she were made to slide in next to him. As if she were the missing piece to his puzzle.

He closed his eyes and shut down that particular thought. He already knew he wanted her more than anything. Now that he knew she'd been terrorized, he felt bad for her. That's all this was, he told himself.

Need and sympathy. Nothing more. And he'd do well to remember that.

"I don't like your being scared," he said softly.

"Me, neither." She tipped her head back to look up at him and he was relieved to see that her eyes were clear. No more tears, no more shadows. She looked, he thought, too damn good.

When she went up on her toes and tilted her head to one side, everything in him tightened. But as much as he wanted her, he had to say, "Charlie, you don't owe me anything."

"This isn't about owing," she told him, dropping her gaze to his mouth before looking into his eyes again. "This is about wanting."

He skimmed his hands up her body until he was cupping her face between his palms. Smiling, he whispered, "Wanting is something completely different."

"Show me."

He did. His mouth came down on hers and his heart nearly slammed through his chest. The taste of her filled him, the need for her was raw heat pumping through his bloodstream and when she parted her lips for him, he took a deeper taste and lost himself in it.

It was her soft sigh that brought him up out of a kiss he wanted to linger over for days. But when he did his lingering, they'd be alone. In a bed. Not in the middle of a damn park.

Reluctantly, he broke off the kiss and lifted his head to look down at her. Her eyes were glassy and her mouth full and ripe. It took everything he had not to kiss her again.

"We're going back to the office, Charlie, and you're going to show me every email this guy's sent you."

"Okay." Nodding, she pulled in a deep breath. "Then what?"

"Then," he said with a fierce smile, "we fight back."

Eight

"He kissed you," Katie blurted out the moment Charlie walked into her friend's office and sat down.

She probably shouldn't have gone down to Accounting to see Katie, but Charlie hadn't wanted to be alone at the moment, either. Practically the instant she and Vance had returned to Waverly's, Ann Richardson had asked to see him.

He hadn't been happy about it, but he'd had to leave before Charlie could show him the emails. Before they could decide what to do next. Still, he'd kissed her again, hard and fast, then promised they would straighten it all out when he returned. But she hadn't been able to simply sit alone and stew, so she'd come to see her best friend. Who apparently was either psychic or had X-ray vision.

"Do you have radar or something?" she asked.

"Don't need it," Katie told her. "You're all dazzle-eyed and your lips are puffy. That's not even counting the fact that you're practically glowing. So spill." Katie grinned wickedly and rubbed her palms together in eager anticipation. "I want every detail. Spare nothing. He said hi, you said hi, he grabbed you up in his oh-so-manly arms and planted one on you and—"

"*I* kissed *him*," Charlie said, cutting her friend off mid-sentence.

"Seriously?" Astonished, Katie stared at her openmouthed for a heartbeat or two. Then she slapped one hand to her chest and said in an overly dramatic voice, "I'm so proud. I think I'm having a moment here."

"Very funny."

"Well, come on," Katie teased. "You haven't been interested in anyone since…"

"I know." Charlie winced. Katie knew the whole story of Jake's father and how Charlie had been so completely conned by the first smooth-talking, good-looking guy she came across. Katie had been after Charlie for the past year to move on, find someone nice. Take a chance again. Now that Charlie finally had, Katie was ready to take a bow.

"Boy, when you step back into the dating pool, you go straight for the deep end, don't you?"

"Seems that way. But, honestly, I don't remember jumping in. One minute we were talking and the next—" Charlie could hardly believe it herself. Her body was still buzzing from the sensations aroused by that kiss. She could still feel Vance's mouth on hers, the soft brush of his breath on her cheek, and the strength in his hands as he held her.

"I don't even know what made me do it," she confessed, then instantly said, "Oh, that's not true. Of course I know. He's been so nice. So un-alpha-top-dog the last couple of weeks."

"I *like* alpha guys," Katie argued.

"Oh, he's still alpha," Charlie assured her. The man just charged ahead, sure he could fix whatever was wrong. He didn't take no for an answer and had supreme faith in his own abilities. Hard to argue with that kind of confidence.

She hadn't told Katie about the blackmail threats or why she'd been so worried and distracted lately, so she didn't bring up just how supportive Vance had been about that.

Katie sighed and cupped her chin in her hands. "And he kissed you back?"

"Oh, yes."

"Then why is your happy-little-world glow slowly fading?" Straightening up, Katie folded her arms on her desk and frowned. "Honestly, Charlie, cut yourself a break, will you? You're allowed to kiss a gorgeous guy and actually *enjoy* it."

"Am I?" Charlie stood up and walked to the narrow window next to Katie's desk. Not much of a view, but she could at least see the sky. "I'm a mom. It isn't only *me* I have to worry about. If I make a mistake with a guy, it impacts Jake, too."

Katie swiveled her desk chair around. "And Vance is a mistake?"

Her friend's voice was quiet, but the question rang out loud and clear. The problem was, Charlie didn't know the answer. If she went by how she was *feeling*, then, no, Vance was so not a mistake. But if she let reality into the hazy thoughts clouding her mind, then the answer was a big *oh, yes*. Walking into a relationship with Vance Waverly was just asking for future misery and pain.

He knew the truth about her now. Knew her background. Knew that she'd been foolish enough to be seduced by a man whose real name she didn't even *know*. She'd confessed to being blackmailed and the auction house his family had founded was threatened.

They couldn't be more different. Their worlds were so far apart they were in opposing galaxies.

"You're going to talk yourself out of this, aren't you?" Katie asked on a sigh.

Charlie looked over her shoulder at her friend. "Out of what? A kiss? Come on, Katie—me and Vance Waverly? That wouldn't even make a good *book*. No one would believe it was possible, even as fiction."

"You don't read the right books," Katie muttered, then stood up to join Charlie at the window. "You're thinking too much. I get it. After Jake's father, you were burned bad and I really understand why you're being so cautious. But, Charlie, if you don't open yourself to possibilities, you'll never have anything in your life."

"I've got Jake," she argued stubbornly.

"You do." Katie shook her head slowly. "But Jake's going to grow up eventually. He'll go out and get a life and you'll be alone."

Charlie choked out a laugh. "I think I've got a few years before I have to think about getting a cat to keep me company."

"Okay, you're right about that," she admitted. "But my point is, if you don't start living a little now, by the time you think you're finally ready? It'll be too late."

Maybe she had a point. And maybe Charlie just *wanted* Katie to have a point. She was falling again. Just as fast and hard as she had for Jake's father.

That relationship had turned out to be nothing more than smoke and mirrors. Could she really risk more pain? Then, remembering that kiss and how the warm summer breeze had wrapped itself around the two of them under the shade of that willow, she asked herself if she could really walk away.

Kendra Darling guarded Ann Richardson's office like a well-dressed, charming dragon. Her hazel eyes were sharp behind tortoiseshell glasses and her shoulder-length, straight red hair was pulled back in a no-nonsense gold clip at the nape of her neck. She smiled as Vance approached. No one got past Kendra if they weren't expected. Not even a senior board member.

"Mr. Waverly," Kendra said with a brief nod, "Ms. Richardson is expecting you."

"Thanks." He walked past her desk, then paused for a quick look back. Kendra had been here for several years, he reminded himself. Who would know their secrets better? Then he discounted the notion entirely. After all, he'd suspected Charlie and there hadn't been anything to it. And Kendra was loyal to the bone. For all he knew, the traitor— if there was one—could be one of the old guard. He took a moment to imagine George, Simon or one of the society ladies on the board sending threatening emails to Charlie. Or stealing information and passing it on to Dalton.

"Is there something else, Mr. Waverly?"

He met Kendra's inquiring gaze and shook his head. "No, everything's fine. Thanks."

Vance dismissed his imaginings as wildly improbable. It was going to take time to find whoever was trying to sink Waverly's. It wouldn't be easy and it wouldn't be pleasant. But he *would* uncover what was happening here.

Opening the door, he stepped inside.

Ann Richardson's icy-cool exterior was nowhere to be seen. She was pacing her office in brisk strides, all the while staring down at a sheaf of papers she held in her hands. A smile curved her mouth and even from across the room, Vance could see the gleam of excitement glittering in her eyes when she looked up as he walked in.

"Vance! Good. Have you talked to Roark?"

"Two days ago, why?" She'd brought him here to talk about his brother?

"Then you don't know. Even better. I want to see your reaction. See if it's anything like mine."

He didn't have time for games. He needed to get back to

Charlie. Look at the emails from her blackmailer. *Kiss her again.* Scowling at the wayward thought, he focused on Ann. Confusion settled down in him and he didn't like it. "What're you talking about, Ann?"

"This." She walked to him and held out the papers. He took them and swiftly scanned the few lines of text before concentrating on the pictures.

"Is this what I think it is?" he asked, lifting his gaze to hers.

"If you're thinking it's the Rayas collection, including the Gold Heart statue," she whispered almost reverently, "then yes. It is."

"But it's been missing for more than a hundred years," Vance murmured, gaze dragging up and down the photo of the statue.

"Roark found it," Ann told him, with barely restrained glee. "Honestly, your brother can be hard to deal with and even harder to keep track of, but he makes some truly miraculous finds for the house."

Miraculous. Exactly what tracking down this piece of art was. Stunned, Vance stared down at the photo of the famed statue. Everyone who lived and worked in the fine art world knew the story of the lost statue from the Middle Eastern kingdom of Rayas.

One of only three in existence, each of the statues was a woman, two feet high, her heart etched and inlaid in gold. The pedestal the female figure stood on was an inch-thick block of pure gold and stamped with a unique seal. Legend said that centuries ago, the king of Rayas commissioned three Gold Heart statues, one for each of his daughters, to bring them luck in love.

The daughters were lucky, as were all the generations to follow—as long as the statues remained in their respective palaces. One of the three matching works belonged to the

family of Sheikh Raif Khouri, another still graced the palace
of the original family to inherit it. And about a century ago,
the third statue went missing—presumed to have been either
stolen—or sold by a member of the family. Either way, without the statue in the palace, that branch of the family met with
heartache, disaster and eventually died out altogether. Which
made a man put a little more faith in the strength of a legend.

But for this Gold Heart to suddenly turn up as part of the
collection was damn irregular. Where had it come from?
How had his brother found it? And why hadn't he told Vance?

They'd spoken only two days ago, so he must have had
a line on the statue then. Why wouldn't he have mentioned
it? Frowning now, Vance asked, "Roark sent these photos
to you?"

"Just got them this morning by fax." She grabbed the top
paper back and skimmed over the full-color picture. "Gorgeous. Just gorgeous. And Waverly's has it."

This was huge. Vance stared down at the paper she'd left
him with and examined photos of three of the other items
that would be included in the auction. He felt a satisfied,
proud smile crease his face. Roark had done it. He'd secured
the most sought-after auction items in the world at a time
when Waverly's really needed the good press. It was a gift,
he thought. A damn timely one.

"Where's the statue itself?" he asked.

Ann looked up at him and blinked as if she had to refo-
cus her mind. And who could blame her? Things had been
tense and ugly here for a couple of weeks and this news could
change everything. For Ann as well as for the house.

"He locked it in his overseas vault. It's safe until he can
bring it back home. But he's authenticated it, Vance. There's
no mistake. This *is* the missing Gold Heart."

He nodded.

"I want to announce this to the press," Ann said. "But

before I do, I wanted your take on it. We can't afford any mistakes about this. Once the Gold Heart acquisition is announced, we're putting Waverly's reputation on the line."

Vance knew what she was talking about. If it turned out that the statue was a copy or something even worse, it would shatter the house. They were already under siege and couldn't afford any more bad press.

Looking at Ann, he said, "You know as well as I do that Roark knows his stuff. No one else on this planet has his kind of instincts—or his knowledge of antiquities. If he says it's real, then it is."

His brother had the unerring ability to locate treasures that others either overlooked or missed completely. Roark had an encyclopedic knowledge of the weird and the unique. He had managed to acquire collections for the house that no one else would have been able to procure.

She let out a relieved sigh. "That's exactly how I felt about it. I just needed that feeling verified. God, Vance. Do you know what this will mean for Waverly's?"

"I do. It's an amazing find and right when we need it the most."

Ann sent him a quick look. "It's been rough, I know. But this will turn things around."

"Undoubtedly," he agreed. "But why the hell did Roark leave something this valuable overseas? Why not bring it home right away?"

Ann waved that question aside, but said simply, "He didn't have time. After his stop in the Middle East, he was on his way to the Amazon, for some top secret meeting with another one of his contacts. If he'd taken the time to bring the Rayas treasures home, he might have lost out on the next acquisition."

Vance still didn't like it. The Gold Heart was legendary. Collectors all over the world had been looking for this missing statue for more than a century. Leaving it in a vault, no matter how safe, was taking a risk. "When will he be back?"

"I'm not sure," Ann said, still smiling down at the photo she held in her hand. "He said he might run into some trouble with his latest quest."

"Trouble? What kind of trouble?"

"He didn't say."

His brother didn't say much, dammit. If he was expecting trouble, then Vance wanted to know about it. "Well, what the hell is he after in the Amazon?"

"He didn't tell me that, either." Lifting her gaze to his, Ann said, "Roark doesn't exactly keep us in the loop when he's on one of his trips. You know that yourself, Vance. And you just admitted that no one is better than Roark at what he does."

"Yeah," he muttered. "Doesn't mean I like it."

"Forget about everything else for a second, Vance. Don't you see what this means for us? At auction, the Gold Heart could bring in as much as 200 *million*. Maybe more. And that's not even taking into account the rest of the collection, which is pretty extraordinary."

"I know, Ann." Still, he had a bad feeling. Maybe it was the fact that he'd been steeped in a morass of suspicion for the past couple of weeks. But his internal alarms were ringing. Oh, not about the statue. As he'd told Ann, he had no doubts about its authenticity. If Roark gave his approval, that was good enough for Vance. But why now? Didn't it seem just a little bit coincidental that the one thing that could pull Waverly's out of this mess just happened to show up at the perfect time?

"It isn't just the sale itself that will do a world of good for us. With all that's going on right now," Ann was saying, "this is just the big news we needed. The fact that Waverly's acquired this statue to sell at auction is the kind of cachet you can't buy.

"We'll be above reproach and no rumors will be able to touch us. Any of us. This will push all speculation out of the paper. When word of this gets out, no one will be talking about anything beyond the fact that Waverly's is the top auction house in the world. Let's see Dalton try to pull something now." She whispered that last part and Vance shot her a look.

Was there more to the rumors about Ann and Dalton than she was saying? She'd denied it all to the board, but that didn't mean she was telling the truth. Of course she would lie to save her ass—the question was, would she sell out Waverly's to do it?

He didn't think so, but the woman was clearly on the raw edge of emotional meltdown. Her usually cool, dispassionate gaze was fired with an excitement he hadn't seen in her before.

Maybe it wasn't only Charlie dealing with threats from an unknown source. Maybe Ann was doing battle with a few demons of her own.

"That's all of them?"

Charlie turned her head to look at Vance. He was crouched beside her office chair, studying the emails she'd pulled up on her computer screen. The heat of his body, so close to hers, went straight to her head and clouded all rational thought. It was a wonder she remembered to breathe.

He glanced at her and must have seen something in her expression because his brown eyes darkened and those gold flecks seemed to shine more brightly. "You keep looking at me that way and we're not going to get anything done."

"Sorry," she said and unbelievably enough felt a *blush* burst onto her cheeks. At least, she assumed she was blushing. Her face felt hot and she was mortified. *Idiot,* she told herself firmly. *He's trying to help you. The least you could do is remain coherent.* "Yes, that's all the emails. Well, except for the one I got this morning."

"You got another one?" His tone was as sharp as a knife. "Pull it up."

She hadn't wanted to show him this one, which was just stupid, since she'd told him everything else. But this email was darker. Scarier. Heck, she didn't want to read it again herself. But she clicked on the message and when it popped open, her gaze went right to the bold-faced type.

No more stalling. Give me what I want or you lose the kid. I know where you live. I know your secrets. I'm through screwing around with you. Contact me by five p.m. tomorrow.

"Son of a bitch," Vance muttered through gritted teeth. "Have you answered him?"

"Yes," she said. "Right after the first threat came in, I tried to make him tell me who he was. Naturally, he wouldn't. And when I got this note this morning, I sent him an email trying to stall for time. I didn't hear back from him. But I don't know what to do. I can't steal from Waverly's and if I tell him that, I might lose my son—"

"You won't lose Jake."

"I can't risk it," Charlie said and even the distraction of having Vance's face so close to hers wasn't enough to ease the panic inside her. "I have to do something."

He nodded, his gaze fixed again on the email. "He knows where you live."

"Yeah, I saw that." She rubbed her hands up and down her forearms in an attempt to ease back the chill snaking through her. It didn't help. It was creepy enough to get emails. To know that he could show up at her apartment was downright terrifying. "It's scary to think he's watching me."

"Yeah, well, he's *done* watching you."

"I don't know how I can stop him."

"I do," Vance said, his voice low and dark. "You and Jake are moving in with me for a while."

Charlie just stared at him. *Impossible,* her mind was shouting. *Woo-hoo,* her body screamed. And somewhere in the middle Charlie tried to make sense of what he'd just said. But nothing came to her.

"I can't let you do that." She shook her head firmly, coming down on the side of reason instead of listening to her body's urging.

"You're not *letting* me do anything," he told her. "Decision's made."

"Excuse me?" Her spine went as stiff as a poker and her chin lifted. Locking her gaze on his, she didn't back down an inch from the steel she saw shining in his eyes. "I don't take orders from you—" She caught herself and thought about that for a second, then amended, "Well, all right, I do, since you're my boss, but you can't order me to do this."

An impatient sigh shot from his throat. "Charlie, do you want Jake to be safe?"

"Of course I do. What a ridiculous question."

"Then you're moving in with me, because this guy—" he stabbed one finger at the computer screen "—knows where you live. That means neither you *nor* Jake is safe."

She didn't want to be Vance Waverly's good deed for the year. Didn't want to be so pathetic that she needed a big, strong man to come riding to her rescue, for pity's sake. Then she silently admitted that she also didn't want to go home alone and worry about some nameless, faceless threat. She could stay with Katie, but her friend's apartment was smaller than Charlie's and she didn't want to risk endangering Katie, either.

Should she do it? Should she risk moving in with her boss? Even to keep her son safe, was it the smart thing to do? She looked into Vance's eyes and read the grim determination there. *Mistake,* she told herself. This was probably a huge mistake. But try as she might, she couldn't think of a logical reason to say no.

Nine

Vance insisted that they take part of the afternoon off and move her and Jake into his condo. With the baby at Waverly's day-care facility, Charlie got them both settled at Vance's place.

Her first look at his home was enough to convince her that this was a bad idea. She could have plopped her entire apartment into just the living room of Vance's penthouse and still have room left over. One entire length of the condo was a wall of tinted glass overlooking the Hudson River. Pleasure crafts and bright yellow kayaks, looking like fallen crayons, floated on the deep-blue water, and Charlie could only guess that the view of city lights at night would be stupendous.

The great room had been decorated by an expert so that it was starkly beautiful and about as kid-friendly as a set of steak knives. There were black leather chairs and couches gathered into a conversation area and another set of matching pieces in front of a now-empty hearth. Black lacquered tables stood on tile floors dotted with what looked like expensive rugs. Lamps that looked more like modern art than anything else were staggered around the room.

"See," he said, spreading his arms wide, "plenty of room."

"For me and an army," she whispered as she followed Vance down a hallway that led to three bedrooms. She glanced in at the master suite as they passed, and her heart did a quick jolt when she saw his bed, huge and inviting, with a dark blue duvet and a mountain of pillows stacked against a black headboard.

"You really like black, don't you?" she commented.

He looked down at her and shrugged. "It goes with everything. Or so the decorator told me."

"Right," she said, nodding. "Decorator."

Just one more way that they were different. Even if she could have afforded a professional, Charlie never would have paid someone to furnish *her* home. The place that would be both haven and refuge. She would want to put her own stamp on this place. For example, she thought, in the great room, she would have had overstuffed furniture, less expensive but softer rugs and tables you could put your feet up on without having a bottle of Windex handy to wipe off the smudges. And she would have brought color into the place—blues, greens, even a sunshiny yellow. Anything to relieve the black and white and gray monochrome feel.

Oh, boy. Stop it, she told herself. *This isn't your home. You're not staying. You're a guest and probably a short-lived one, so just smile and be nice.*

Vance opened the door to a guest room and Charlie was actually relieved to see pale blue walls, dark blue chairs drawn up in front of another fireplace and a bed done in pale blue and green. It was so different from the rest of the place, she could hardly believe it. "It's lovely."

"You sound surprised."

"Well, it's not what I was expecting." She'd been thinking, of course, more black. "Thank you."

"You're welcome. The bathroom's through here," he said, showing her a palatial space with sky-blue tile, white sinks and tubs with what looked like teak wraparounds. The back half of the bathroom was a glassed-in shower space that looked big enough for—*all kinds of things,* she thought before she ruthlessly shut down that thought.

Like the rest of his home, the bathroom was stylish and elegant and intimidating.

"There's a connecting room through the bathroom and it should work great for Jake. I can have a crib up here in an hour."

"You don't have to do that," she said, glancing around the third bedroom, another study in blues and greens. Apparently, his decorator had run out of ideas when it came to the guest rooms. "In fact, Vance, you don't have to do any of this. Jake and I will be fine."

"Yeah, you will," he agreed. *"Here."*

He laid both hands on her shoulders and she felt the heat of his hands sliding through her system. Seductive. That's what he was. God, how had she ever believed he was cold and closed-off? In the past two weeks, he'd shown her more care and more attention than she could ever remember receiving from anyone.

Now, he'd even opened his home to her. Why? She had told him the truth about who she was. He had to know that whatever it was that sizzled between them when they were close couldn't last. Wasn't real. Wasn't anything that should even have gotten started. So why hadn't he turned his back on her?

He said he believed that she wasn't trying to undermine Waverly's. So was it something a lot simpler? Was he simply planning on using her for sex and then firing her later? *No.* She refused to believe that. Vance Waverly wasn't that kind of man. He was being kind, and she wasn't going to second-guess that. But oh, it probably hadn't been a good idea to move in here, however temporarily.

"This guy knows where you live, Charlie," Vance said as if he were reading her mind and knew that she was regretting the decision to come here. "What if he gets tired of email and wants to make a personal visit. Then what?"

She actually shivered at the thought. "I know, but I feel guilty. You've already been so nice, Vance…."

"Dammit, Charlie, you don't have to go this alone." He pulled her in to him until she had to tip her head back to look into his eyes. "I'm not being *nice*. I want you here where I know you and your son are safe. You can see I've got the room. What's the problem?"

She reached up and laid her hands on his. "Vance, I appreciate it, I do. But you've never lived with a baby and I just don't think you know what you're getting into."

"Let me worry about that, okay? Let me *help*."

His features were tight, his eyes blazing as he looked down at her, practically *willing* her to agree. And though she knew she might one day come to regret this decision, Charlie knew she would be staying.

"Okay," she said softly, admitting at least to herself that there was nowhere else she wanted to be.

"Good. Now," he said, taking her hand, "drop your stuff. I'll show you around."

The tour of the rest of the condo had Charlie shaking her head in amazement. Vance's house was lush and beautiful and she would never be comfortable there. Even the kitchen was set up more for a professional chef. It was like a model home. Meant to intrigue buyers and seduce them with clean lines and elegant furnishings.

But it wasn't homey. It wasn't comforting.

In fact, the only thing it had that appealed to her was Vance.

"I don't want you to worry about bringing Jake out here to the garden," he was saying now. "It's perfectly safe for him."

She stepped through the sliding-glass doors from the great room to a rooftop terrace oasis and gasped. They were at least thirty stories high and the views were incredible—as long as she didn't look straight down. Potted plants and summer flowers burst from dozens of containers along the wall. A glass-topped table and chairs were set up at one side of the terrace and several lounge chairs, covered in white fabric, were gathered around one of those outdoor portable fire pits.

"No worries on the fire pit, either. It's gas and it's not as if Jake could turn it on."

"Oh, I don't think Jake needs to be out here," she said, moving closer to the wall so she could take one very brief glance all the way down to the street below. Her head swam and she closed her eyes. "Yeah. He'll be fine inside."

Vance laughed. "Charlie, it's perfectly safe."

"It's a long drop."

"And we're surrounded by a three-foot-high stone wall that is then topped by four feet of Plexiglas. There's no way he could fall."

Just the thought of that made her stomach sink. "I'm sure it's safe, but we won't be here that long anyway."

Vance was at her side in an instant. He grabbed her upper arms and pulled her in close. Looking down into her eyes, he said, "Stop doing that. Stop talking about leaving."

"I'm not," she argued, even though a small voice in her head was urging her to do just that. Pull away before it was too late. Before her heart was even more engaged than it was already.

Before she did something so stupid as to fall in love with Vance Waverly.

"Yeah, you are." He laughed shortly. "Mentally, you've got one foot out the door already and you've been in the house maybe ten minutes. So stop it, Charlie. You're here now. With me. And I'm not letting you go."

She should have argued with him. Should have told him that she came and went as she pleased. That he didn't have the right to order her around or make demands or anything else outside of her job at Waverly's.

But she didn't say any of that. Instead, she gave in to what her heart and body were demanding she do. Charlie simply leaned into him and whispered, "Good."

He grinned, fast and sharp, then bent his head to hers and, once more, Charlie was swept up in the rush of sensation that only Vance could cause. Every cell in her body sparkled into life. Every square inch of her skin buzzed in anticipation of more, and deep inside her, something opened, as if it had been waiting for just this moment. She was seriously afraid that it was her heart.

He pulled her closer still, hands running up and down her back, molding her body to his, caressing her until she moaned and pressed herself into him. Good. It felt so good to have him hold her, touch her. It felt...*right*.

Her fingers raked through his hair and skimmed across the back of his neck. He wasn't wearing his suit coat, so she felt the strength of his shoulders beneath the soft fabric of his shirt. And she wanted to feel more.

The sun shone down on them. A breeze dove over the top of the Plexiglas wall and stirred the flowers until their scent was overwhelming, drowning Charlie's senses as completely as Vance was taking over her body.

"I feel as if I've been waiting *years* for this," he admitted.

Charlie knew just what he meant. His hands swept up and down her back, caressing, exploring. And every touch was fire. Magic. Her skin felt flushed and sensitive. As if she'd been waiting for his touch to come suddenly, almost painfully, alive.

He kissed her again, like a man starved for what she alone could give him. Their tongues met, tangled together in a frantic exchange of passion. Desperation, need, fueled every move, sighs lifted into the air and seconds ticked into minutes.

Charlie's heart was pounding so hard she could hardly breathe and she didn't care. All she cared about was the next touch, the next kiss, the next sweep of his tongue against hers.

Her mind splintered and all thoughts dissolved. Her body roared into life, hungering as it never had before. Her blood raced and desire was nearly strangling her. This was so much more than she'd expected. So much *bigger* than anything she'd ever felt before.

"You've been driving me crazy for days, Charlie," Vance murmured when he tore his mouth from hers. "I can't stop thinking about you."

She laughed, feeling a rush of pure, feminine power at his confession. Reaching up, she pulled at his dark red tie, loosening the knot, then slid it free of his collar. "How? What have I been doing?"

"Your hair," he admitted, tearing off the clip she wore so her long hair spilled down around her shoulders and lifted in the wind. "I've been wanting to see your hair down since that first day I saw you. It was worth the wait."

She shook her hair back from her face and looked into his eyes. "My hair's been making you crazy?"

"And those shoes you wear," he said, undoing the buttons of the simple white blouse she wore tucked into the waistband of a slim-fitting gray skirt.

Confused, she said, "My shoes?"

"God, yes," he said, pausing to take a look down at the plain, black pumps. "What they do to your legs should be illegal."

"Really?" she asked, ridiculously pleased.

"Really." He shook his head and gave her a quick grin. "I'm thinking of having them bronzed."

She laughed, delighted, and felt suddenly more carefree, more *alive* than she'd felt in years.

"Sure, you can laugh. I'm the one suffering, watching you walk across the office...." He shook his head again in memory, then he finished unbuttoning her shirt and pulled the tail of it free of her skirt. He swept the edges of the material back to expose the lacy bra covering her generous breasts.

He took a quick breath and exhaled just as fast. "You're amazing."

Her fingers worked at the buttons on his shirt, too, her skin heating not just from his compliment, but from the intensity of his gaze, as well. She felt it as she would a touch. He looked at her with such...hunger, such need, that she swore she could feel actual flames licking at her insides.

Charlie wanted to see him, too. Wanted to run her fingers over his skin and feel the warmth of his flesh beneath hers. He stood still under her touch and once his shirt was unbuttoned, she laid her palms flat on his broad chest and smoothed her fingers through the thatch of dark hair dusting his skin. He hissed in a breath and she knew he was as susceptible to her touch as she was to his.

"Can't wait another minute, Charlie. We've already waited long enough. I've got to have you."

"Yes, Vance. Oh, yes," she said. This, she told herself, had been inevitable. From the first moment she had walked into his office as his new assistant. They had always been headed directly to this moment.

She felt beautiful and desired and *so* ready.

Charlie lifted her hands to the front clasp of her bra—then stopped and looked around. Broad daylight. Outside. Okay, maybe no one could see them but for passing planes and the occasional bird, but... "Maybe *inside* would be better."

"What?" He looked around much as she had. "Oh. Yeah." He choked out a laugh. "I actually forgot where we were. What do you do to me, woman? I'm *always* on top of things. Never lose focus. But with you—" He huffed out an exasperated breath and reached for her. Bending, he hooked one arm behind her knees and the other around her back and lifted her right off her feet.

"Vance!" She wrapped her arms around his neck and held on. Laughing up into his eyes, she said, "I can walk, you know."

"Yeah," he said with a shrug, "but this way, I get to keep my hands on you."

"Can't argue with that," she said as he headed back inside.

His legs were long and his pace was brisk. He carried her through the penthouse into the master bedroom so quickly, it was only seconds before Charlie dropped onto his bed and lay there, looking up at him.

Nerves jangled inside her, but she quieted them. If this was a mistake, then she was going into it with her eyes wide open. Even if she regretted being with Vance one day, in this moment, she was reveling in it.

Shaking his head slowly, he let his gaze wander over her thoroughly. "I can't tell you how many nights I imagined you lying here just like this."

Charlie smiled. She liked knowing that she'd been in his thoughts as much as he had been in hers. "In your dreams I was fully clothed?"

One corner of his mouth tipped up briefly, but it wasn't humor shining in his eyes, it was *hunger*. For *her*.

"Nope," he said. "All you were wearing were those shoes and a satisfied smile."

A curl of something wickedly exciting started in the pit of

Charlie's stomach and spread like a wildfire, rushing through her veins, making her skin feel tight and hot. She'd never felt anything like this before and she was suddenly eager to feel so much more.

Keeping her eyes on his, she wiggled out of her skirt and kicked it off. His eyes flashed as she sat up to take off her shirt and toss it to the floor, too. Then she was wearing only her white lace bra, matching panties and the shoes he seemed to have such a fondness for.

"Well, don't stop now," he said, voice sounding strangled.

Muted sunlight slanted in through the glass wall behind him, throwing his features into shadow as he stood so still, watching her. But even in the dim light, his eyes blazed with such ferocity, it took her breath away.

With him watching her like a starving man eyeing a feast, Charlie slowly unhooked her bra, then slid it off her shoulders, baring her breasts to him. As the cool air in the room kissed her heated skin, she felt ripples of gooseflesh course over her body. But it wasn't just the air. It was Vance's gaze that gave her chills. She was both embarrassed by her nudity—hello, she had had a baby and wasn't quite as toned as she used to be—and excited, an interesting combination that had her heart throttling into high gear and turning every breath into a hard-won battle.

She lay exposed to his gaze but for the panties she still wore. But when she hooked her fingers under the elastic band, he stopped her.

"No, don't," he said, his voice still that low thrum of need and hunger that filled her with so many different sensations she couldn't even sort them all out. "Let me."

While she watched breathlessly, he tore off his clothes. She couldn't take her eyes off him. Even in the backlight of the sun, he was amazing. His chest was broad and muscled, his legs were long and lean and his— She swallowed hard and lifted her gaze to his.

"No more waiting, Charlie," he murmured and she nodded, lifting her arms up to him.

Like him, she was done waiting. She wanted to feel. Wanted to be held and touched. By Vance.

He joined her on the bed and his heated skin was a counterpoint to the cool silk of the duvet sliding against her. Cupping her breasts in his palms, his thumbs and forefingers tweaked her rigid, so-sensitive nipples, until a moan ripped from her throat.

Then his hands shifted, moving over her body with an expert's touch. As if he were playing her, he coaxed a symphony of sighs and groans from her. He explored every curve, every valley; he slid one hand down the length of her, across her abdomen, down to the narrow elastic band riding low on her hips.

Charlie sucked in a gulp of air. "Vance…"

Dipping his hand beneath that tiny swatch of lace covering the juncture of her thighs, he cupped her heat in his palm, making her twist and writhe beneath him as she ached for more.

"Please," she whispered and didn't care that she sounded desperate. She *was* desperate. For his touch. For the orgasm she felt couched inside, ready to crash down on her body and splinter her into shards of trembling release. "Vance, *please*…"

He turned his head and looked down into her eyes. Smiling now, he whispered, "Not yet, Charlie. I'm gonna make you want me as badly as I want you."

"I do," she swore, rocking her hips into his hand as he held her. The heat of his palm pressed to her core was agonizing, thrilling. And not nearly enough.

"Not yet," he whispered, "but soon."

Then he dipped his head to take one pebbled nipple into his mouth. His lips and tongue tortured her with exquisite care. He lavished attention on first one nipple, then the other, until he had her twisting wildly beneath him while holding his head to her, making her half afraid he would stop.

He suckled her, drawing deep at her breasts, and Charlie whimpered with the sexual need that grew and grew until it was all-encompassing. Vance's mouth on her breasts. Vance's hand at her core. Vance's breath dusting her skin.

A sensual haze dropped over her vision, blurring him, the room, even the slant of sunlight that now looked like a simple wash of gold across everything. She didn't need to see, she told herself. All she needed was *him*. All she cared about now was the next touch. The next stroke. The next pull at her breasts.

"Time to lose these," Vance murmured as he lifted his head to claim a quick, hard kiss. Then he flicked his wrist and the elastic band on her panties snapped.

"Good," Charlie said, swallowing past the knot in her throat. She parted her thighs for him and he caressed her heat, drawing a sigh from her as she whispered, "That's good."

"About to get better," he promised.

Sliding first one finger then two into her depths, he stroked her, inside and out, until she was trembling, quivering, from head to toe. She clutched at him—arms, shoulders, back. She dragged her nails down his skin, loving the feel of him beneath her hands. His thumb moved over the most sensitive spot at her center and Charlie jolted at the lightninglike sensations that shot through her.

Wild now, hungry beyond the telling of it, she rocked her hips like crazy, trying to take him deeper, higher, and she groaned because it still wasn't enough. She needed to feel his thick, hard body pushing within. Charlie felt her climax building and coiling inside her and she yearned for it, ached for it.

"More, more," she whispered, voice broken on a gasp.

"Want it, Charlie. Want it more than your next breath," he said softly, lifting his head to watch her face.

Her gaze caught with his, she managed to choke out, "I *do*. Want it. Want *you*. Always have." She shook her head from side to side on the cool silk and licked her lips as he pushed her closer, higher, faster. "Always wanted you. Now have to have you. No more waiting, Vance." Her gaze pinned his. "Now."

"Now." He lifted his hand from her core and she nearly wept with the loss of him.

But in seconds, he shifted on the bed, tore off what was left of her panties and tossed the ruined scrap of lace over his shoulder. He ran his palms up and down the length of her legs and smiled when he glanced at the high heels she still wore.

Charlie managed a short laugh in spite of what she was feeling. "Your fantasy?"

"Not until you're wearing that satisfied smile."

She wiggled her hips and parted her thighs even farther. "I'm ready when you are," she said.

"Almost." He reached for the bedside table, yanked open the drawer and grabbed a condom.

"I didn't think. I—" Charlie was grateful. She'd been so caught up in the sensual delights, she hadn't given a single thought to protection.

"Only one of us had to," he told her as he tore open the foil square, then sheathed himself.

He knelt between her thighs, scooped his hands under her behind and lifted her slightly off the mattress. She looked up into his eyes and saw a need that matched her own. She had never known anything like this before. Hadn't realized that sex could be so…*much*. Always before, it had been…nice. Pleasant. But there was nothing "pleasant" about sex with Vance. This was raw, powerful, all-consuming *need*. If she didn't feel him inside her soon, Charlie knew she would lose what was left of her mind.

And as that last coherent thought twisted through her brain, Vance pushed himself inside her in one hard stroke.

He was big and thick and oh, so good. Charlie gasped, then groaned his name as she lifted her hips into him, taking him even deeper until he filled her so completely, so totally, she couldn't imagine ever being without him inside her again. It was as if she had been waiting her whole life for this moment. For this man. She felt it. Knew it deep in her soul.

He moved in her and her body tightened around his, her inner muscles clenching and releasing as he led her into a dance as old as time. Her back arched, her hips rocked furiously as she rode the crashing wave of pleasure he induced.

He set the rhythm and she matched it. He touched her, she stroked her hands up and down his chest, his abdomen. He lifted her legs and set them on his shoulders, allowing him to go deeper, higher within her.

Charlie gasped at each invasion and nearly wept at each retreat. Passion exploded between them and as her climax peaked, sending her shrieking into a world filled with light and color, she heard him shout her name just before she felt him follow.

And as their bodies reached completion, they clung to each other like shipwreck survivors huddled on the shore.

Moments later, Vance whispered, "It's those shoes, Charlie. Never get rid of those shoes."

And she laughed, delighted.

Ten

In the kitchen twenty minutes later, Vance rustled up some cold Chardonnay, crackers and some cheese. As he took down two wineglasses, he paused for a moment and thought about the woman waiting for him in his bedroom.

Slapping both hands to the granite counter, he let himself remember the incredible feeling of being deep inside Charlie's body and how he'd had the momentary thought that he'd like to stay that way forever. Almost instantly, he'd instinctively pulled back from that word.

He didn't *do* forever. What he did was weeks. Maybe months, tops. Forever was for people too dumb to know that lust wasn't love. Desire wasn't lasting and passion cooled off just as fast as it burned.

Reluctantly, he scraped both hands across his face, then pushed them through his hair. He glanced across the room at the view through his windows and told himself to get a grip. What he had with Charlie was damn good, but that's *all* it was.

All this self-exploration only went to prove that he'd waited too long between women. It had been more than three months since he'd stopped seeing Sharon—Karen—something.

Scowling now, he realized he not only couldn't remember her name, he couldn't remember anything else about her, either. While Charlie, on the other hand, was indelibly etched into his mind. If he never saw her again, he'd still recall everything about her. *Never see her again.* Okay, he didn't like that thought, either. But that was only natural, he assured himself. At the beginning of an affair, which this most certainly was going to be, everything was brighter, hotter, better than anything that had come before.

Wasn't it?

A silent voice inside him argued that Charlie was different from *any* woman he'd been with. What he'd just shared with her had shaken him right down to his bones and he didn't even want to try to figure out what that might mean.

Instead, he grabbed the tray of snacks and the glasses in one hand and the bottle of wine with the other and headed back to the bedroom. Just outside the doorway, he muttered, "Keep it simple, stupid."

Charlie was sitting up in the bed, waiting for him, and everything in Vance stilled for a long second or two. The woman was stunning and just looking at her made him want her all over again. Scowling, he told himself it meant nothing. But a voice in the back of his mind whispered something else entirely.

"Are you arguing with yourself?"

He blinked, looked at her and asked, "What?"

"You had this look on your face, like you were having a silent battle."

"Well, I'm not," he lied, disconcerted to discover he was

so easy for her to read. Hell, his opponents in business had long told him that he had the best poker face in the world. That nothing he didn't want to reveal showed up on his expression. But Charlie took one look at him and knew what he was thinking.

Yeah. Disconcerting.

He walked naked across the room, set the tray of crackers and cheese on the bedside table, then poured each of them a glass of wine. Just like in his fantasies, her long, blond hair was spread across the dark blue duvet like spun gold and he couldn't resist touching it. It was smooth and soft and smelled, he thought, of peaches. The woman was edible, head to toe.

She took a sip of her wine and said, "That's good, thank you."

He gulped at his own wine, hoping to ease the knot of need that was now lodged in his throat. Everything about her called to him. The way she licked a drop of wine from her lips. The way she shook her hair back over her shoulder. The way she reached one hand out to cup his cheek, sending lines of heat shooting through his body.

"I'm suddenly not very thirsty," he admitted. "You?"

"Not very," she agreed, handing him her glass so he could set both of them down on the table beside the bed.

Her fingers caressed his cheek and he caught her hand in his. "Think you can read my thoughts?" he asked quietly. "What am I thinking now?"

"If you're thinking what I think you're thinking," she murmured, "I'm thinking it, too."

"Good to know," he said and dropped his head to claim a kiss. The first taste of her exploded in his mouth and rocketed through him. Just like the first time he had kissed her, in the shade of a willow tree, he felt that pitch and roll in his stomach and a weird sort of ache in his chest. But he didn't want to consider what any of it might mean.

For now, all he wanted, needed, was Charlie. The feel of her, the hot silk of her body surrounding him when he entered her. Everything else in the damn world could just wait its turn.

He loved the feel of her soft hands sliding over his skin, the heat of her touch, kindling the fire inside him into something wild and uncontrollable. He caressed her, she responded, she ran her fingernails along his back and he shivered.

This woman got to him on levels he hadn't even known he possessed. She invaded his body, his soul, his mind and, he suspected, his heart. And that was something that no one had ever managed to do.

He shook his head, deliberately dismissing his own thoughts. He wanted nothing interfering with this moment. He was hard and tight and ready for her again and couldn't wait to get back inside her. Where he belonged, a voice inside whispered. Where he most wanted to be. He grabbed another condom and sheathed himself quickly.

Shifting, he sat up, and dragged her with him. She came willingly and when his back was braced against the headboard, he lifted her up to straddle him.

She whipped her long hair back from her face, but it slid forward again, lying in blond ribbons across her full, truly amazing breasts. Her nipples peeked through the golden strands like hidden treasures waiting to be discovered.

With her hands on his shoulders, she went up on her knees, and slowly took him inside, inch by glorious inch. His hands at her hips, he guided her down as his eyes locked with hers. He saw the flash of wonder, of want burning in those pale blue depths, and lost himself there. In the heat they built together. In the need that had them both by the throat.

Why was that need even more desperate now? Shouldn't it have been assuaged by their first joining? Shouldn't he be feeling satisfied instead of hungrier for her than ever?

"You're killing me," he muttered when she was fully seated on him and his body was locked within hers.

"I was thinking the same thing about you," she admitted and ground her hips against him, dragging a groan from each of them.

"I wanted to take this time slow," Vance told her after a long minute when he fought for control. "But I don't think so."

"Who needs slow?" she asked, then let out a *"Whoop!"* when he moved fast and tossed her onto her back, keeping his body joined with hers.

"There's lots of time for slow," he told her, voice low and scratchy. *"Later."*

"Right. Later." She lifted her legs, hooked them around his hips and pulled him in deeper, higher. "Right now, I just need. Need…"

"Me, too." He buried his face in the curve of her neck, shut down his racing mind and gave himself up to instinct. The raw, pure hunger roaring through him demanding to be sated.

His hips moved like pistons. He took her fast, hard and completely. He heard her sighs and they fed his desire. He felt her body shiver as her climax jolted through her. She screamed his name as her body trembled and, moments later, he shouted victoriously as his body exploded into the heat of her, leaving him locked in her arms—and he didn't let her go.

"Weird afternoon," Charlie whispered to herself an hour later as she sat at her desk, going over Vance's mail.

She'd been in his bed. Held his body in hers. And now they were back at Waverly's as if nothing had happened.

But it had, she reminded herself with an inner smile. She just didn't know what that meant for either of them.

One corner of her mind asked if it really had to mean something. Wasn't it enough for now to simply enjoy what she had while she had it? And though that was good advice, she would never be able to follow it. Charlie never had been the girl to accept "for now."

She'd always been more the home-and-hearth type rather than the use-'em-and-lose-'em kind of girl. So where did that leave her, exactly?

Living with her boss. Sleeping with him.

And worrying about what happened next.

For whatever reason, Vance was being kind and very protective of her and her son, and Charlie was grateful. But she knew that soon enough, he was bound to move on to one of the empty-headed beauties he usually dated. And that was just depressing.

Her desk phone buzzed and she picked up. "Yes?"

Vance's voice came across loud and clear, "Come in here, Charlie. I've got an idea."

She walked into his office and paused for a second to enjoy the view. He sat behind his desk like a king. Power emanated from him and when he smiled, everything inside her drew up into tight knots.

Oh, God. It had happened. She'd gone and done it.

She was in love with Vance Waverly.

And doomed to misery because he would never return that feeling. How could he? He knew the whole sordid truth about her now. Where she was from, what kind of family she had had. They were night and day, light and dark, power and powerlessness.

Heart aching, she forced a smile onto her face and prayed he couldn't see what it was costing her. If all she had left was her pride, then she was going to cling to it.

"What kind of idea?" she asked, taking one of the chairs in front of his desk.

He leaned back in his chair and looked at her. "I want you to email that bastard who's been hounding you and tell him you want to meet."

"What?" Fear closed her throat as she stared at him. "Why?"

"Because I want to find out who he is. That way we'll know who's behind all this." He stood up, came around the desk and took the chair next to hers.

Charlie stared into his eyes and saw the gleam of anticipation there. "I don't know."

"I do. You can do this, Charlie." He reached over and picked up her hands from her lap. Holding them in his, he met her gaze and reminded her, "We already figured out this isn't a coincidence. Your first threatening note arriving the same day as the article on Ann and Dalton showing up in the paper? No way. Whoever's behind the threats to you has to be involved in whatever's being planned for Waverly's."

"But, Vance…"

"I'll be there. Well," he hedged, "not *with* you, but close by. I swear I'll never you out of my sight. You'll be safe, Charlie, but I think this is our best chance of stopping this guy."

She didn't like any of it. The thought of meeting someone who had been threatening her was terrifying, and she wasn't ashamed to admit it. Charlie understood why Vance wanted to do this, but her *son* was at risk. "What if he sees you? What if he makes good on his threats and tries to take Jake from me?" Shaking her head, she tried to pull her hands free of his, but he held on even tighter.

"That won't happen."

"You can't guarantee that."

"No," he agreed.

Charlie bit her lip. "Why can't we just call the police?"

"Because the press would be alerted. I'm sorry, Charlie. Waverly's can't risk that."

"No, of course not. I don't want this in the papers, either," she said with a shudder.

"But I can arrange for a member of Waverly's security

staff to be in the area. I'll be there, too. You won't be in any danger, Charlie. And I promise you that you won't lose Jake. If it came to it, I'd hire the best attorney in the city to fight for you. You won't lose your son, Charlie. You just have to trust me. Can you do that?"

Everything in her wanted to hide in a dark hole and pull the hole in after her. She thought of Jake, safe in the playroom downstairs, and her heart shivered at the thought of losing that little boy. But if she didn't do this, if she didn't find the courage to try to stop the threats, then she'd always be hiding. Always be afraid. And she didn't want to live like that.

"Okay," she said, before she could change her mind. "Okay, I'll do it."

He let go of her hands, reached for her and cupped the back of her head. Pulling her in close, he kissed her, hard and fast, sending jolts of white-hot sensation shooting through the chill in her blood. "Atta girl. It'll work. You'll see. Now, he wanted you to contact him by five tomorrow, right?"

"Yes." There was that tight ball of dread in the pit of her stomach again. Was it wrong that she was starting to get used to it?

"Then we'll wait until 4:45. You'll email him telling him you want to meet." Vance squeezed her hands again when she chewed at her bottom lip. "You'll say that you're not going to give him anything until you've talked in person."

"What if he refuses?" She was pretty sure her mystery blackmailer was going to do just that.

"He won't. He can't afford to. If you call his bluff, he'll have to bend," Vance assured her. "You're his only access to Waverly's files as far as we know. So he's going to have to do it your way or get nothing."

"Maybe."

"Charlie," Vance insisted, his gaze locked with hers, "the

only reason his threats have worked at all is because he knows he scared you. Now you're not scared anymore."

"I'm not?"

"Why would you be?" he countered. "You've got *me* now."

Did she? She looked into his eyes and wondered if she did have him, how long would that last? Until this threat was over? Until Waverly's was secure?

Until he got tired of her in bed?

"I hope you're right," she said, still unconvinced.

"I'm always right, remember?" He gave her a wide smile and her heartbeat fluttered in response.

Oh, God, she was an idiot. A first-class idiot. How could she have fallen in love? Hadn't she sworn off the elusive feeling when Jake's father disappeared? Hadn't she told herself never to trust another man? Never to risk the kind of pain she'd felt when she'd first discovered she'd been had?

But this was different, she told herself. Vance was real. He hadn't lied to her. Hadn't tried to seduce her purposely for his own reasons. Falling in love was her mistake and she would pay for it, no doubt. Because what she felt for Vance was as real as he was.

And now she knew that what she had thought was love before, hadn't been. What she had experienced with Jake's father wasn't even a shadow of what she felt now. *This* was real love. *This* was what she had dreamed of all her life.

And losing it was going to kill her.

Maybe it was the sex.

Maybe it was having Charlie in his house. Vance couldn't be sure, but whatever the reason, his legendary impatience had roared to the surface. He didn't like the idea of a threat hanging over Charlie's head. He didn't like her being scared, and he'd be damned if he was going to stand for it. That's when he'd come up with his brilliant plan to face the black-mailer down.

He knew it was the right thing to do. He also knew that Charlie was worried about it.

She was on edge. One glance at her moving around his kitchen told him that. Vance already knew her well enough to notice the tightness in her shoulders, the deliberate squaring of her jaw. As if she were *willing* herself to hold it together.

He admired strength, and Charlie had plenty of it. She'd had a bad situation growing up, but she'd fought through that, too, and built a life for herself. She loved her son and her determination to protect him touched something in Vance. In fact, he was spending way too much time thinking warm thoughts about Charlie Potter.

Looking across the great room to the galley-style kitchen, he watched as Charlie made dinner. Chicken parmesan, she had said, and he had to admit, it smelled great. Usually, he ordered something from a nearby restaurant or nuked something frozen.

It was...odd, having her and Jake in the house, but it also wasn't making him nuts. And that worried him.

He'd never brought a woman here before.

His home was *his* place. He didn't share. When he was with a woman, they went to her place or an upscale hotel. This condo overlooking the river had been inviolate.

Until Charlie.

Hell, he mused, there was a lot going on lately that he could say "until Charlie" about. Going to a diner, taking walks with a baby, leaving work early, having wild, crazy-making sex in the middle of the day. All that was under the heading "until Charlie."

"Babababa!"

Vance's thoughts stopped when the baby pounded little fists against his leg to get his attention.

"What's a 'ba'?" he asked, throwing a glance at the woman across the room from him.

"Ball," Charlie answered, then added, "I brought his favorite. It's in his room."

"Babababa!"

The baby's eyes were wide and his bottom lip was trembling. A couple of weeks ago, Vance would have hit the front door running. He couldn't imagine why. Now, he scooped up the baby, then carried him down the hall to his temporary room.

The crib had arrived and was already standing ready for the baby to sleep in. The dresser was filled with baby clothes and a box of diapers stood on a low table.

"Babababa!" Jake laid his head down on Vance's shoulder and patted one small hand against his chest.

"Almost got it, little man," Vance told him, giving him a pat on the back in reassurance. He found the bright red ball on the closet floor. Setting the baby down, he rolled him the ball and Vance smiled when the baby chortled with glee. Lifting the rubber ball, he swung his left arm wide and flung it back at Vance.

"What a throw!" Vance said with a grin. "And a southpaw. You're going to be in demand on a Little League team, kid. A left-handed pitcher can name his own terms."

"Bababa!"

Still smiling, Vance rolled him the ball and Jake tossed it again, happy with the game. Vance looked into those dark blue eyes and felt something clutch at his heart. This baby had gotten to him as easily as the boy's mother had. Between the two of them, Vance didn't know up from down. All he knew for sure was that, for the first time in his life, he *wasn't* looking for the nearest exit.

In fact, weirdly enough, he was enjoying this. The baby.

Charlie. The sounds of life and laughter in his normally quiet home.

He frowned and told himself he should probably be worried.

Vance didn't have to hear Charlie's approach. He actually felt her watching him. He turned his gaze to the open doorway where she stood, one shoulder leaning against the doorjamb. Her hair was in one long, thick braid hanging over her right shoulder. She was barefoot and her scarlet-painted toes peeked out from beneath the hem of faded jeans that hugged her legs like a familiar lover. Over the jeans, she wore a T-shirt that read *Skip the Movie, Read a Book*.

"Did I tell you I like your shirt?" He especially liked the way the clingy red fabric outlined her breasts.

She looked down and laughed shortly. "Thanks."

Then he realized her eyes looked shadowed. "Is there a problem?"

"I got an email."

Everything in him went on red alert. The baby tossed his ball and it rolled right past Vance unheeded. "What'd he say?"

"You were right," Charlie reluctantly told him. "He's agreed to meet with me."

"Excellent. Did you tell him where?"

"Yes. He'll be at the Coffee Spot tomorrow at four."

Nodding, Vance said, "It's almost over, Charlie."

"Is it?"

Jake crawled up onto Vance's lap and he automatically wrapped one arm around the tiny boy's middle. Holding on to the sturdy weight of her son on his lap, Vance looked into Charlie's eyes and thought about what he'd just said. *Almost over*. When they had this wrapped up and the blackmailer stopped, Charlie would be leaving. She and Jake would go back to their lives and he would be here, in the quiet.

That's when it occurred to Vance that things might just be sliding out of his control.

Eleven

"So you decided to take my advice and seduce it out of her?"

That sounded a lot colder when Roark said it aloud than it had in Vance's mind. But yeah, the upshot was, that's exactly what he'd set out to do. It had all started so simply. A dinner date. Then walks and talks and before he had known it, he had been as seduced as she was.

Sex had been the next logical step.

Seduction might have been the plan at the beginning, but it had morphed into something else. Something that felt a hell of a lot more permanent than he had ever considered.

Scraping one hand across his face in irritation, Vance frowned at the phone in his hand, and muttered, "Yeah, all right? I did."

"And you sound really pleased about that," his brother shot back with a laugh.

"It's...complicated."

"Uh-oh. Sounds bad."

"Could be," Vance admitted, hating the fact that he didn't *know* where this thing with Charlie was going. Ordinarily, he'd say enjoy it then move on. Just like always. But he didn't *want* to move on. Plus, the thought of Charlie moving on to some other guy made him want to hit something. Breakable.

"Okay, leaving that aside for now, what've you found out?" Roark asked.

His brother's voice rose and fell like applause at a bad play. The connection was terrible.

"Where the hell are you that your satellite phone is having a bad day?"

Roark snorted a laugh that came through loud and clear. "In the middle of the jungle."

"Still in the Amazon?" Vance stood up and looked out his office window at the Manhattan view. Summer was making the streets practically steam, but he had a feeling the heat and humidity were much worse where Roark was.

"Yeah, almost done, though, so should be able to jet back soon. But we were talking about your assistant, remember?"

Like he could forget.

He had expected that sex with Charlie, finally satisfying that staggering need he'd felt for her, would take the edge off. Would, in a way, be liberating. Allow him to take a step back and look at the situation through clear eyes. Instead, sex with Charlie had just pulled him in deeper. Made him think dangerous thoughts. Made him want—

"So, she's not the spy?"

"No." Grateful to have his mind pushed off its traitorous track, he shook his head and studied the street scene below. Office workers striding up and down the sidewalk with purposeful steps. A kid on a skateboard was holding on to his dog's leash for a fast ride and Vance smiled as a woman in heels had to jump out of the kid's way.

"You're sure?"

"Yeah, I'm sure." In a few short sentences, Vance brought his brother up-to-date on the whole blackmail situation—and his plans to end it.

"Well, damn, that's intriguing. Who the hell is this guy?"

"That's what I'm going to find out this afternoon."

"How? The street around the coffee shop will be jammed at four in the afternoon. If this guy sees you with Charlie, he won't make contact."

"I've got that figured out, too," Vance said, turning his back on the world to sit at his desk again. He filled Roark in on the plan.

"Sounds good. Lemme know how it goes."

"I will," Vance said, then finally brought up the real reason he had called his brother. "About the Gold Heart statue…"

"What about it?"

"How'd you find it? Where's it been all these years? Ann's letting the world know about it and people are really talking. This auction's going to be the biggest thing we've ever handled."

"I can't get into it right now, Vance," Roark said, his voice fading. "Just trust me, it's all good."

"Wait a minute!" Vance called into the phone and heard nothing in reply. Either his brother had just hung up on him, or the connection had abruptly died.

He did trust Roark. But Waverly's had a lot riding on the upcoming auction of the Rayas collection. They couldn't afford for anything to go wrong.

Anything could go wrong. Vance wore black jeans, a black T-shirt and boots. Nothing against any of his suits, but if he had to sprint to Charlie's side he wanted to be able to move fast and sure.

As it was, he didn't like any of this. Yeah, it had been

his idea, but now that it was happening, he really hated the thought of Charlie being out there on her own.

He stood half-hidden behind the edge of a building on Fifth Avenue. A shoe store, he thought, but didn't really care. What he cared about was that he had a direct line of sight to Charlie, standing in front of the Coffee Spot. It was a popular enough coffee shop that the crowds were moving in and out constantly. Hard to keep an eye on her, but it would also be hard for the blackmailer to try anything dangerous. She was safe, surrounded by hundreds of strangers.

The summer sun was brutal in late afternoon, blasting down out of a clear blue sky. Traffic was piled up as always, and hordes of pedestrians leaped off the curbs and crossed the street whenever the hell they wanted to. Red lights meant nothing to New Yorkers.

Scowling, he lifted his binoculars and focused on Charlie's face. She looked worried. And his insides twisted in response. He wasn't sure how he'd developed this protective streak, but when it came to her and her son, it was ramped up beyond anything he'd ever felt before.

Charlie glanced around, let her gaze slide slowly over where she knew he was hiding and a small smile curved her mouth. Good. He didn't want her scared. He wanted this to be over. And if he couldn't be right beside her, then at least she felt better knowing he was close. It also helped to have one of the Waverly security guards in plainclothes, standing nearby.

When the man approached, Vance almost didn't notice him for a second. He looked so nondescript. Ugly brown suit, bad black wig and ridiculously oversize glasses. Vance focused the binoculars on his new target and wished to hell he could read lips when the man started talking to Charlie.

Twenty minutes later, she was sitting across a table from Vance recounting what had happened.

"Everything went wrong," Charlie complained over a latte and a doughnut.

"Not everything," Vance argued with a frown. "You met him. Up close and personal."

"And didn't recognize him," she pointed out. Taking a sip of her latte, she held the cup between both palms to ease the chill she still felt. He even had a weird voice. Like he was disguising it, too.

It had been scary, meeting the man who had been threatening her for weeks. But she also felt good about at last doing something proactive instead of simply hiding beneath her desk hoping it would all go away. Plus, knowing that Vance was just across the street with a pair of binoculars had helped a little. Now that the disastrous meeting was over, she and Vance were sitting in the Coffee Spot, comparing notes.

"Tell me again what he said."

She shook her head and broke off a piece of her glazed doughnut. Rather than eating it, though, she crumbled it until it was doughnut dust on her plate. All around them, people talked or laughed, the espresso machine hissed and steamed and the clatter of plates and cups played background noise.

"He was furious that I wanted to meet," Charlie said, remembering the man's deep, scratchy voice and the rage that had driven him. "Really angry. I think I've stalled him as long as I can. He said he was through fooling around and that if I didn't hand over the files by this weekend, he would go to Social Services and file a complaint about me."

Grimly, Vance clenched his jaw tight enough to grind his teeth into powder. "I was sure one of us would recognize the bastard." He took a drink of his coffee. "I can't believe he wore that stupid disguise."

"It was creepy. And not so stupid," she added, "since it worked and kept both of us from knowing who he was."

Frowning, she admitted, "He did seem familiar, though. Something about him…"

"With that outfit he was wearing, it was no wonder neither of us recognized him," Vance grumbled. "The glasses alone made his eyes almost impossible to see."

True. The ultramagnified lenses had blurred and distorted the guy's green eyes completely, and you could usually tell a lot about someone from his eyes. The only really distinctive thing about him was the bright red scar that ran from his forehead down to the left side of his jaw. The whole time they'd talked, Charlie's gaze had fixed on that scar to the point of ignoring everything else.

"The scar—"

"Fake," Vance muttered.

"What? Why?" she asked. "Why a scar?"

"To keep you from noticing anything else," he explained. "And it worked. On me, too. I was too far away to be sure, but for a minute or two, I could have sworn I'd seen the guy before." Disgusted, he blew out a breath. "The way he moved, stood. There was something there, as you said, *familiar.* Then he turned and all I saw was that scar. Smart, really, to use that to distract us. Plus, he disappeared into the lunch crowd so fast, our security guy missed him completely."

Disappointment welled inside her and tangled up with the anxiety that seemed to be such a part of her these days. "So we're no closer to knowing who he is."

"Not yet."

"So Jake is still at risk." Now fear rose up and swamped her disappointment.

His gaze snapped to hers. "My gut tells me this isn't really about *you.* Remember, all this started the day the newspaper article was published. I think this is about Waverly's."

"But they're using Jake as leverage."

"I told you, I won't let anything happen to your son."

Charlie nodded, but couldn't keep the ache in her chest from showing in her eyes. Vance would do all he could—she believed that. But the truth was, she'd hoped that this would be over today. Instead, they were right back where they started.

The next few days were hectic at Waverly's.

There were provenances to clear, appraisals to collect and a presale exhibition to arrange. With another, although smaller, less celebrated auction to take place in two weeks, Waverly's would put the items to be included on public display after the weekend.

Open to everyone, the presale exhibition usually garnered a lot of good press and, right now, Waverly's could use all it could get. Of course, most people only wanted to talk about the Gold Heart statue.

The papers were full of speculation. Every day someone was coming out with a new theory on where the Gold Heart had been all these years and how Waverly's had managed to get hold of it.

"I don't have an answer for them," Ann said as she paced the interior of Vance's office. "Roark didn't have time to explain how he came to lay claim to the statue on our behalf. At first, the media was just frenzied about the statue. Now, they're looking for details and I've got nothing."

"Just leave it alone, Ann," Vance suggested. "The press is good for the house and when we auction off the statue, it's going to solidify our reputation and quiet any more rumors."

"I hope you're right," she said wryly.

"I'm always right," he quipped, thinking that he had said just that to Charlie a few days ago, after their unsuccessful attempt to stop her blackmailer.

"You haven't heard anything else?" Ann walked to his desk and leaned over, planting both hands on the edge. "No more rumors about a possible hostile takeover by Dalton?"

"Nothing. You?"

"No, everything's gotten quiet and that worries me," she admitted. Pushing up from the desk, she folded her arms over her chest and added, "I've got Kendra looking into it, trying to feel people out, see if anything pops, but so far, nothing." She frowned slightly. "Plus, have you noticed, there's been no response from Rothschild's about our acquiring the Gold Heart. Doesn't that seem odd to you?"

"Excuse me, Mr. Waverly."

A voice spoke up from the open doorway and Vance winced. Hell, his mind had been so scattered lately, he hadn't even shut the door when Ann showed up to talk. Anyone could have been listening to their conversation. But with Charlie out at lunch with her friend Katie, he'd left the door open purposely to be able to keep an eye on the outer office.

Vance looked at the mailroom kid. Teddy. That was his name. Couldn't have been more than twenty-two, with bright red hair, green eyes and so many freckles he looked as if he'd been spattered with brown paint.

"Come on in, Teddy."

"Sorry to interrupt, but your assistant's not at her desk and I've got the mail here and—" He stopped nervously. "Ms. Richardson," he said and just barely resisted bowing.

Ann was gracious, as always. She gave the kid a smile and said, "It's okay, Teddy. We've all got our jobs to do, don't we?"

"Yes, ma'am," he answered, leaving his pushcart at the door and carrying a stack of mail to Vance. Once he'd handed it over, Teddy hurried out again.

When he was gone, Ann turned back to Vance and repeated, "Dalton being so quiet about our good fortune. Doesn't it worry you?"

"It does," he said, glancing briefly at the stack of mail and the one oversize manila envelope beneath all the others. Then he stood up to walk around to the front of his desk. Leaning back onto it, he continued, "It's not like Dalton to be so circumspect. I fully expected him to at least question the authenticity of the statue. Do something to take the shine off the good press we've been getting lately."

"Exactly," Ann said. "He's up to something. I just know it."

"Then all we can do is wait for him to make a move," he said, not liking that one bit. He hated waiting. Hated feeling as if his hands were tied. And he really hated not being able to ease Charlie's mind about these threats that were still hanging over her head.

Just a day away from the blackmailer's weekend deadline, Vance was no closer to discovering the man's identity. Though the sense of familiarity had been bugging him for days.

Who the hell was that guy?

"I'm not very patient, I'm afraid," Ann said, with a quick glance at her wristwatch.

"No, neither am I. But I don't think we have a choice this time."

"Which only makes it harder," Ann said, giving him a rueful smile. "Thanks for listening to me, Vance. I've got to run to make my meeting with the heads of publicity. They want to show me what they've come up with so far on the Gold Heart auction."

"Already?" Impressive, he thought, since the auction wouldn't be held for months yet.

"This is the biggest auction we've—*anyone's*—ever done," Ann said simply. "We're going to see to it that this is the most talked about event of the year."

"Sounds like a plan," he said, then turned back to his desk when she'd gone.

There was so much going on at Waverly's these days, there was a damn near *tangible* thread of anxiety slipping through the whole house. And everyone was feeling it.

He sat down and picked through the mail, setting most

of it aside for Charlie to deal with when she got back from lunch. But the thick manila envelope got his attention. There was his name in big block letters. No return address. Heavy. Vance balanced it on his palms and finally flipped it over, undid the clasp and slid the contents onto his desk.

There was no note.

Only pictures.

Dozens of them. Full color and black-and-white and they were all of the same man. Vance tensed as he flipped through them quickly. Every photo showed the same man wearing a different disguise. There was enough about the shape of his head, the way he stood, the way he squinted into the light, that all seemed familiar, again and again, despite the ways he was trying to hide his real identity. In some, he wore colored contacts, others, those magnifying glasses Vance had seen him in. In every photo, he wore wigs, sometimes a scar, sometimes an eye patch, always something to distract the viewer. But it was always the same man.

Charlie's blackmailer.

"Who the hell took these?" Vance muttered as he found a shot of the mystery man talking to Charlie outside the Coffee Spot the day of their scheduled meet. Vance had been there. He hadn't seen anyone pointing a camera, although, he'd been too busy focusing on Charlie to have noticed. He continued looking through the photos until he came to the last one.

Then he dropped the others and studied the photo of a good-looking man with wide, dark blue eyes. He tapped the photo with his finger as a flare of satisfaction shot through him.

"Dammit," he whispered in satisfaction, "I *knew* you were familiar." He knew this guy. Had known him for years.

Henry Boyle, one of two assistants to Dalton Rothschild, CEO of Rothschild's auction house. "You son of a bitch. I've got you now. And whatever you and Dalton are planning—not going to work."

He studied that photo for a long minute or two, reveling in the pleasure he felt at the knowledge that he could tell Charlie her problems were over. Now that he knew who was behind all this, he was going to the police. They'd have Henry arrested before end of business.

Then, as he continued to look at the photo, something else dawned on him. Something that he should have guessed. Who the hell else would have known all Charlie's secrets? Who else would have known what to threaten her with?

"I know those eyes of yours, too, you bastard," he said to the man in the picture. "I see them every day, in your son."

Charlie's blackmailer was Jake's father.

It wasn't easy to tell her. And once it was done, all he could do was listen as she poured out her fury.

"How could he do that to me? To his son?" she raged, prowling the confines of his office as if it were a cage she couldn't escape. "What kind of man treats people like that?"

"A bad one," Vance offered.

"'Bad'?" she repeated, staring at him openmouthed. "He's more than bad. He's…evil. Disgusting. Appalling. He was using me to take Waverly's down!"

"Yeah," Vance said, "he was."

If he had needed more proof that Charlie was in no way involved in any of it—which he didn't—seeing her like this would have convinced him.

"And he's my son's father!" She stopped at that and turned wide eyes on Vance.

"What?" he asked, going to her, holding her.

"Jake. Oh, my poor baby. What can I possibly tell him about his father?"

He heard the pain in her voice and speaking only to that, said, "Tell him you loved him."

"I thought I did, yes." Her gaze shot to his. "And what does that say about me? What kind of judge of character am I that I could make a child with a man who could do something so hideous?"

Vance pulled her in tightly to him and closed his eyes as she wrapped her arms around his waist and held on. He didn't like acknowledging that she had cared for the bastard. That some other man had had a shot with Charlie and then was fool enough to waste it. "It says you have a generous heart. It says you don't look for the bad in people."

"And that I'm an idiot. Don't forget that part," she muttered, her face buried in his chest.

He laughed a little and cupped her head in his palms, tipping her back so that he could look into her eyes. "You're the smartest woman I know, Charlie. This isn't about you. It's about Henry Boyle and the mistakes he made."

"But—"

"But nothing," Vance told her, willing her to believe him as his heart broke at the sheen of furious tears in her eyes. "He was stupid enough to walk away from you and your son. He's the idiot. Never forget that."

Her lips twisted into a half smile. "You're being nice to me again."

"I shouldn't be?"

"You should be furious. Because of me, Waverly's might have been ruined."

"It wasn't."

"Could have been," she argued.

"Could-haves don't count," he said with a smile. "Besides, look at it this way. You started this scared to death, but you stood up to him. You fought back and you won."

"You're just trying to make me feel better."

"Is it working?"

"Yeah," she said softly, "it is." She laid her head down on his chest again and sighed heavily. "It's over, isn't it? Jake's safe."

"Yeah." He wrapped his arms around her and held her as tightly to him as he could. "It's over. Jake's safe. And so are you."

"Thank you." Her whisper was almost lost, but Vance heard it and whispered a "thanks" of his own to whoever it was who had sent those photos.

A couple of hours later, calls had been made, charges filed and it was all over but for the last act.

"You're sure you want to be here for this?" Vance kept one arm around Charlie's shoulders, holding her tight to his side.

They stood outside Rothschild's auction house in the late-afternoon sun. A police patrol car was parked at the curb and people passing on the sidewalk were slowing down to see what was happening.

"I'm sure," she said, lifting her chin and stiffening her spine. "I want to see him arrested. I want to *know* that it's over. Really."

He understood that, though he would have kept her away if he could. Hell, just remembering the shocked, stunned expression on her face when he'd told her what he'd discovered had been enough to level him. But then he remembered how quickly she had shifted from shock to fury and his admiration for her soared.

No one would ever keep Charlie down. She had too much strength. Henry Boyle should have recognized that.

Vance came up out of his thoughts at the outraged shout.

"You can't arrest me! You have no proof of anything!"

Still holding on to Charlie's shoulders, Vance turned to watch as two police officers—one man, one woman—walked

Henry Boyle out of Rothschild's. The man was shouting and pulling at the officers, trying to get away, but with his hands cuffed in front of him, it wouldn't be easy. A crowd was gathering on the sidewalk, but the traffic in the street was still a steady stream of movement and color.

Charlie stiffened against him when Henry's wild gaze landed on her and he screamed in impotent rage.

"You stupid *bitch!* This is all your fault! All you had to do was give me the damn files!"

Vance's fury was growing to match Boyle's but he stood his ground and tugged Charlie half-behind him to protect her from the enraged man getting closer.

"Bitch! Stupid!"

"Come on now," the male officer said as he reached down to open the squad car door. "Enough of that. Let's go. You'll get your say eventually."

"Screw that!" Henry yanked free of the man's grip, head-butted the female officer, and when she staggered backward, pulled free of her as well. With a last, frantic look at Charlie, Henry sprinted for freedom, pushing through the onlookers, rushing for the street.

He dodged a hybrid car and a yellow cab. Brakes squealed. People shouted. Horns blared. He was almost clear when he ran straight into the path of a city bus unable to stop in time.

Charlie choked out a cry as she turned her face into Vance's chest. And as the street erupted into shocked screams, he held her there, sparing her from seeing what had become of Henry Boyle.

Twelve

Three nights later, Vance found Charlie on the terrace in the moonlight. Even in his too-big T-shirt that she'd been wearing to sleep in, she looked like a pagan goddess, standing in front of a bank of flowers with the star-filled sky and moon above her.

That wonderful hair of hers hung loose to the middle of her back and the breeze sliding over the Plexiglas wall lifted long blond strands into a dance around her head.

Her gaze was locked on the river, with the city reflected on the water in brilliant, wavering slashes of light and color. She was so still, so quiet, so entranced at staring out at the view, she wasn't even aware of him. So Vance had time to get control of the raging emotions rushing through him. Just minutes ago, he'd awakened, reached out for her in their bed and found her gone. For one heart-stopping second, fear had closed his throat before he'd realized that she'd probably gotten up to check on Jake. So he had, too. He'd found the baby sleeping peacefully, curled up into a ball—but Vance had had to search out the baby's mother.

Finding her here, in the moonlit darkness, shifted something elemental inside him. It was bigger, deeper than anything he had ever known.

Was this love?

God, he hadn't even mentally jerked back from that word. Which just went to prove how far gone he was. His whole life, he'd never seen love last. People in his family didn't stay married. His parents had split up when he was just a kid. Even his friends fell in and out of "love" with regularity, so it was never something Vance had had any faith in.

It was a word he'd never used with a woman because he didn't want to say what he didn't—couldn't—feel.

But now, with Charlie… All right, he was the first to admit that he didn't know jack about love. But he *did* know that this woman and her child had carved a place for themselves in his heart. That was saying something, wasn't it?

She turned her head to smile at him and his breath caught in his lungs. Her eyes shone and the curve of her mouth was irresistible to him. Everything about her was. And with that thought came the realization that he was in so deep now, he didn't think he'd ever find his way out.

"What're you doing out here?" He stepped through the sliding-glass door onto the tiled floor of the terrace.

"I woke up," she said with a shrug. "I checked on Jake, then it was such a nice night, I came out here to do some thinking."

"Always dangerous when a clever woman starts thinking," he said, walking toward her. He came up behind her, wrapped his arms around her middle and let her lean back into him.

Since the end of the threat against her, Charlie had been… thoughtful. She was sad about Henry's death, but relieved that her son was safe. But there was more she wasn't saying, Vance knew. And that bothered him more than he wanted to admit.

She laid her hands on his arms and her head against his chest. And Vance felt...complete.

"Want to tell me what you've been thinking about?"

Her fingers stroked the skin of his arms with a gentle touch. "That it's time Jake and I went home."

He took a breath and held it. He wasn't even sure his heart was still beating. "Home? Why?"

She turned in his arms then and looked up at him, shaking her hair back from her face. "Because we don't belong here, Vance. You've been wonderful. Helped us when we needed it. Helped *me*. But this was never supposed to be permanent, right?"

No, no one had said anything about permanent. But they hadn't put a time limit on it, either. Frowning, he swallowed hard and instead of answering her question, asked one of his own. "What's the rush? You've been happy here. Jake and I get along great—"

"You do," she said wistfully. "But I have to go back to my life, Vance." She took a moment and looked around the terrace, the view and even the sky above. "As beautiful as all of this is, it isn't my home."

"It could be."

"Vance—"

"I'm just saying." Hell, he didn't know what he was saying. All he knew was that her talking about leaving had blown a hole through his insides. Even his heartbeat was ragged. "Stay a while, at least. Let's enjoy each other without the threat of doom hanging over our heads."

She smiled sadly. "That won't change anything."

"Why does it have to?" He let her go, took a step or two away, then turned back to face her again. "Do we have to classify this—whatever it is—between us? Why can't we just go on the way we have been?"

"Because it's not just me, Vance." She didn't sound angry. Just sad. "I have to think about Jake, too."

"I am thinking about Jake," he argued and didn't care for the sound of desperation in his voice. "He's happy here. He likes his room. He likes me."

"Too much," she said and those two words jabbed at him.

"What's that supposed to mean?"

"It means he's getting more aware every day. It means I heard him say 'Dada' this morning when you were feeding him his oatmeal."

Yeah, Vance thought, remembering the little boy's delight at mastering another word. Remembering also how happy he'd been when the boy reached out for him and said that word.

"If I don't leave, he'll start believing you are his father and then taking him away later will just hurt him that much more."

"Why now?" Vance demanded, rubbing one hand against the ache that was dead center in his chest. "Why all of a sudden the talk of leaving?"

She pushed her hair back with one hand as the wind tossed it across her eyes. "It's not all of a sudden. Ever since Henry… died, I've known I had to leave. You have, too, Vance. You just don't want to admit it."

"Ah," he said tightly, "now you're a mind reader."

"Nothing so fabulous," she countered. "But I recognize reality when it's right in front of me."

Vance's brain was racing even as his heart seemed to be slowing down into a sluggish rhythm. She was wrong. He hadn't even considered Charlie and Jake leaving. He'd gotten used to having them there. To tripping on the baby's toys in the darkness. To the smell of oatmeal in the morning and, mostly, to the feel of Charlie, nestled in his arms every night.

He hadn't been thinking beyond getting rid of the threat to her. Now he could see that freeing Charlie meant— freeing Charlie.

Without a reason to stay, of course she would want to take her son back to their apartment. So all of them could get back to their lives. No more watching baseball games with Jake on his lap. No more glasses of wine with Charlie before dinner. No more laughter. No more anything. He would have his privacy again. The quiet of an empty penthouse. He'd see Charlie at work and this—whatever it was—between them would eventually shrivel and die.

That was what should happen, wasn't it? He'd never meant for any of this to last. He'd only begun this thing to save Waverly's, right? He looked at her now and felt everything in him go cold and still. Life without her sounded bleak. How the hell was he supposed to give her up?

"Vance?"

Flowers scented the warm air. They were high enough above the city lights that the stars were clear in the black sky. And the moonlight—God, she was made for moonlight— poured down over her like magic.

He didn't want to talk. Didn't want to think. He wanted to *feel* what he only felt with Charlie. He wanted to lose himself in her. And wasn't that a sort of answer to her question?

He crossed the terrace to her, grabbed her hard and pulled her tight against him.

"No more talking," he muttered, "and no leaving. Not yet. Okay?"

Charlie looked up at him and nodded. "Not yet. Okay."

A stay of execution was all he could think of before he claimed her mouth in a soul-searing kiss that left him staggered and hungry for all of her.

In seconds, he had the hem of her nightshirt lifted, scraping it up along her luscious body, and then off and over her head. Moonlight kissed her skin and then he was doing the same. Lavishing attention on every square inch of her body, he turned her, laid her down on the cushioned chaise nearby and in the darkness heard her gasp of pleasure. "Vance—"

As his mouth covered the very heart of her and he felt her tremble, he thought, *This is what matters.* Before shutting his mind down and reveling in the glory of Charlie, he told himself that what they shared together wasn't just important. It was everything.

Ann Richardson presided over the board meeting at Waverly's the following morning. Standing at the head of the conference table, she looked at each member of the board for a moment or two before finally settling her gaze on Vance.

"Thanks to Vance," she said with a regal nod of her head, "we managed to stop at least one threat against Waverly's."

"Never could trust a Rothschild," George muttered darkly and Veronica shushed him.

"Dalton's issued a press release denying any knowledge of what Henry Boyle was up to," Vance put in, giving George a quick look.

The old man snorted. "Dalton knows *everything* that goes on in his house. You can take that to the bank. Dalton's got *two* assistants. Henry was one of 'em. You really believe that fool came up with this plan on his own? I don't think so."

"Neither do I," Vance agreed. Dalton was no doubt behind the attempt at gaining information. But they'd have a hell of a time trying to prove it. He looked over at Ann, who nodded again. "I think all of us are on the same page there, George. But the bottom line is that Dalton's denied it and the police have found nothing tying him to Henry's plan."

"Your assistant doesn't know anything more?" Edwina's voice sounded soft, concerned.

"No, she doesn't," Vance said. "She's simply relieved that the threat is over."

"As are we all," Simon piped up from his seat, slapping one arthritic hand against the table for emphasis.

"The problem," Ann put in, silencing everyone with her cool voice, "is that we can't be sure the threat is over." She waved away George's objections before he could start speaking again. "Yes, of course, this particular incident is over. But that doesn't mean that Dalton Rothschild will quit trying to take us down. We all have to remain alert. Aware of what's going on in the house." She looked at each of them in turn again. "We can't trust anyone," she said softly.

Vance knew she was right, but he was glad he and Charlie had already passed through their test of fire. He knew he could trust her with his life. Now if he could just bring himself to trust her with his heart…

"We have to stay together on this," Ann was saying. "A team. To protect Waverly's."

"Of course, dear," Veronica said, softly applauding Ann's words. "You know you have our full support. Isn't that right, George?"

The older man nodded grudgingly. "Yes, yes. We're all a team. Rah, rah. Can we stop talking about Dalton Rothschild now? You're giving me indigestion."

Vance smothered a laugh and Ann rolled her eyes. "Very well," she said, "if we've finished with the Rothschild portion of the meeting, I have an announcement to make."

"Better news I hope, dear," Edwina said.

"Much better." Ann gave them all a wide smile. "You all know Macy Tarlington?"

George harrumphed. "Knew her mother," he said with a knowing wink. "Tina Tarlington. Now *that* was a woman. Hell of an actress, too."

"Her daughter hasn't done as well, has she?" Veronica asked no one in particular.

"Hell, no," George said. "Not a shadow of Tina."

Tina Tarlington had been a rare beauty who'd died recently at the relatively young age of sixty-two. Famous all over the world, Tina was as much known for her three marriages and her collection of diamonds as she was for her acting skills.

Vance gave Ann a shrewd look. "You got it?"

"I got it," she said and practically crowed with delight. Then, to the rest of the board, she said, "I've convinced Macy Tarlington, after much wining and dining, to allow Waverly's to conduct her late mother's estate sale. Tina's jewelry collection alone will make the sale a not-to-be-missed event."

Vance only half listened to the congratulations and the rife speculation on what might be included in Tina's collection of mementos. Smiling to himself, he took his first easy breath in a couple of weeks.

The threat to Charlie was gone. It looked like Waverly's was going to be safe and retain its well-earned reputation. The only thing left to do, he thought, was decide what he wanted and then to go after it. Charlie's face swam up into his mind and everything in him jolted with excitement. Just thinking about her had his pulse pounding and his body tightening. She was what he needed. What he had *always* needed.

The answer was so simple. His heart had known from the beginning. It was only his brain that had refused to see the truth.

He loved Charlie Potter.

And he was never letting her go.

Charlie waited outside the boardroom for Vance to be free. She had a sheaf of papers requiring his signature and Justin had been haranguing her on the phone about them for the past half hour. Once Vance had signed them, she'd take them downstairs so Justin's heart palpitations could stop.

Standing against the wall, she shifted from one foot to the other, uncomfortable standing too long in the high heels

Vance liked so much. She smiled to herself as she remembered their first time making love when he'd insisted that she never get rid of them.

Silly, she knew. But he made her happy. Enough that she was postponing the inevitable by staying with him a few more days. She didn't want to leave, but what choice did she have? She couldn't love a man who didn't love her back. There was no future in that. For any of them.

Her head tipped back against the wall and she stared up at the ceiling. How would she ever live without him? How could she continue to work for him knowing that what they had shared so briefly was over? She wouldn't be able to and she knew it. The only sane thing to do would be to quit her job.

Then she would have lost everything.

Frowning now, she straightened up when the boardroom door opened. She heard George Cromwell speaking, his gruff voice unmistakable.

"That was a good job you did, Vance. Catching the black-mailer."

"Yeah, thanks. I'm glad it worked out."

Her stomach dipped and rolled in reaction to Vance's voice, and she nearly sighed at the hopeless case she'd become.

"I heard the rumors about you and that cute assistant of yours. Clever of you, romancing her so you could get to the bottom of it so fast."

Vance stepped out of the boardroom and saw her. He stopped dead and though he didn't say anything, guilt was stamped so cleanly on his features, he didn't *have* to speak.

Charlie felt as though she'd been slapped. Was that all she had been? A tool used to capture Henry? Had none of it been true? Ever? Reeling from the implications of George's statement, and the fact that Vance hadn't denied it, she hurried down the hall, away from the boardroom, away from the man shouting her name.

"What the—" George muttered as Vance took off after her at a dead run.

Charlie beat him to the office and turned to slam the door on him, but Vance was too quick. He slapped one hand against the door and hit it hard enough that it smacked against the wall.

"Don't you even speak to me," she warned, and threw the papers needing his signature at him. They fluttered like over-size snowflakes to the floor.

Hurt, humiliation and good old-fashioned temper were steering her course now. She felt as if she were going to ex-plode from the pressure building inside.

"Charlie, dammit," he said, slamming the door closed so no one could overhear them, "hear me out at least."

"No. There's nothing you can say to me now that I want to hear. That's it. I quit." And to think only moments ago, she'd been dreading that decision. Now there was no other choice.

She hurried across the room to her desk and bent down to yank open the bottom drawer. She grabbed her purse, kicked the drawer shut and stood up.

He was right in front of her. His dark hair falling over his forehead. His brown eyes, with those gold flecks, were churning with emotion and his jaw was so tight, she saw the muscles there twitching.

"No way are you quitting."

"You can't stop me."

"Watch me." He grabbed her and held her in place, though she squirmed and wriggled and tried to break free. Finally, in desperation, Charlie drew her right foot back and kicked him in the shins.

He yelped, and that was satisfying, but he didn't let her go, and that was infuriating.

"Dammit, will you just hold still for a second and listen to me?"

"Why should I?" she shouted. "I heard what George said to you and more importantly what you *didn't* say back."

"I didn't have a chance to say anything. I saw you there and then you were running—"

"What would you have said, Vance?" She threw the words at him as a challenge. "Would you have denied it? Could you?"

He didn't say anything, but the flicker of regret on his features said plenty.

Pain lanced through her. "I wondered, you know, why you were being nice to me. Remember, I even asked you. You didn't answer me, but then how could you?" She shook her head in disgust. "Not easy to say, 'I'm seducing your secrets out of you, Charlie—that okay with you?'"

"All right, fine," he grumbled. "That was how it started. I think. Hell, I don't even know for sure anymore."

"Right."

"I'm telling you the truth, Charlie." He let her go, shoved both hands through his hair and said, "Ever since you walked in here, I haven't been able to think straight. At first I thought it was your hair distracting me. Or maybe those damn shoes." He shook his head again as if trying to understand all this himself.

"But it wasn't any one thing at all. It was just you, Charlie. Your laughter. Your eagerness to learn. Your love of... everything." He choked out a laugh. "You sneaked up on me. And yeah, I thought it would be a good idea, to take you out a couple times, romance you a little. See if I could figure out if you were a spy or not."

"Romance me. At the Zoo Diner?"

"See?" He threw both hands high and let them drop to his sides again. His expression was baffled. "See what you do to me? I sat in the middle of that toddler hell and actually had a good time. I didn't expect that. Didn't expect *you*. What you did to me. How you made me feel. How you made everything better."

Charlie wished she could believe him, but how could she? How could she ever trust him again? She felt the sting of tears in her eyes, but blinked them back. "You were using me. Just as Henry did."

"No," he said firmly.

"Yes," she said. "But I'm done being used. By you. By anyone. I quit, Mr. Waverly. I'll be by this weekend to pick up Jake's and my things."

"Charlie—"

She walked past him, head held high. He didn't follow and that was good. Because Charlie didn't know if she had the strength to walk away from him twice.

Vance shut himself up in his condo and didn't speak to anyone. He didn't go to work. Didn't return his brother's calls and refused to give a flying damn about Waverly's or anything else.

His house was so quiet, it was driving him crazy. He stood in the doorway of Jake's room and looked at the empty crib, feeling a similar emptiness in his own chest. The room still smelled like baby and Jake's toys were still scattered across the floor. He bent down and picked up the red rubber ball and idly tossed it from hand to hand.

Then he wandered across the hall to the master bedroom. The room he hadn't been able to sleep in since Charlie left. How the hell could he? She'd stamped herself all over the room. The T-shirt she slept in. Her hairbrush on the bathroom counter. Her slippers on the floor beside the bed. Her pillow that smelled like peaches.

The damn woman was everywhere but where she belonged.

He tossed the ball to the floor, stalked down the hall to the living room and out onto the terrace. He didn't look at the chaise because recalling that particular memory at the moment might just finish him off. Instead, he stared at the river and mentally went over the plan that had begun forming when Charlie called that morning to say she would be at his place at one o'clock to pick up her things.

"I know what I want now," he said, squinting into the sunlight dancing on the surface of the river. "And what I want, I *get*."

He'd given Charlie two days to cool down. But when she showed up there at one to pack up her stuff, they were going to talk. Well, he was going to talk and she was going to listen. If he had to tie her to a chair.

The doorbell rang an hour later and Vance cursed. He wasn't completely set up yet. He needed five more minutes. It figured the woman would show up early.

He walked barefoot across the room, his worn jeans dropping low along his hips, his bare chest warm from being out on the terrace collecting every damn flower he owned.

Yanking the door open, he stared down at her and he felt that hard, solid jolt of lust and what he recognized now as... *love*. She looked so damn small. Her hair was in a long braid hanging down the center of her back. She wore a bright blue blouse that did amazing things for her eyes and her khaki shorts stopped midthigh. Her sandals had daisies on the toes and her nails were painted a rich crimson.

Everything about her made him want to gather her up and hold on so tight she'd never get free. But first, she had to listen.

"I won't bother you for long, Vance," she said, stepping past him into the great room. "I'm just going to throw our things into the boxes we used when we came here—you still have them, don't you?"

"If I said no would it stop you?"

"No," she said sadly as she turned and headed for the bedrooms.

"Where's Jake, Charlie?" He stopped her with one hand on her arm and that simple touch sent a bolt of heat dancing throughout his body. He'd been so cold without her that the heat was staggering. God, how could he have been so stupid to have waited so long to see the truth? How could he have risked this? Risked *her?*

She looked down at his hand on her arm, then lifted her gaze to his. "With Katie. Don't, Vance. Don't make it harder on both of us. Just let me pack up, okay?"

He let her go and followed her down the hall to the master bedroom. She opened the door and stopped dead on the threshold.

Exactly the kind of response he'd been hoping for.

He'd dragged every one of those pots of flowers in from the terrace. His bedroom looked like a tropical garden. The blue duvet on the bed had been sprinkled with rose petals and there was a bottle of champagne chilling in a silver bucket on the bedside table. The drapes were drawn and candles lit and soft jazz poured from the stereo.

"What is this?"

"*This* is seduction, Charlie," he said, satisfaction plain in his tone.

"Vance…"

He turned her around, hands first on her shoulders, then sliding up to cup her face. His thumbs stroked across her cheekbones and caught a single tear that rolled from her eye. "Just listen to me, okay? Give me that?"

She swallowed hard, and nodded.

Encouraged, he took her hand and drew her into the bedroom, seating her on the edge of the bed. She perched there uneasily, as if ready to bolt. He'd have only one chance to get this right. Or his entire life was screwed.

No pressure, as Roark would have said.

He took a breath and blew it out, scraped one hand across

his face and finally forced himself to meet her eyes. "You were right. I did start out to romance you for all the wrong reasons."

She frowned.

"But that changed so fast, Charlie." He laughed at himself. "Sitting in that godawful diner, listening to the howls of all of those kids and looking into your smiling eyes, I started falling."

"Vance…"

"No more lies, Charlie," he said, stepping up close to her. He cupped her cheek in his palm briefly before backing away again, because he knew he had to have a clear head to do this right. And touching Charlie fogged up his brain like nothing else. "I didn't know what was happening and when I finally figured it out, I told myself it *wasn't* happening. Because that was easier than risking what I felt for you.

"See, I didn't know what the hell love was, Charlie. Until you."

She gasped a little and folded her hands together in her lap, squeezing until the knuckles went white.

"I've never even used the word before, so how could I believe what I was feeling was real?" He reached up and shoved one hand through his hair, then looked around the room at what he'd made of it. "From the first minute you walked into my office, I felt…different. You woke me up, Charlie. Made me see the world around me. Made me realize everything I'd been missing."

"Vance," she said softly.

"No, don't talk yet," he ordered, stabbing one finger in the air at her. "You said everything you had to say the other day in the office and I don't blame you. I was a jerk and you were hurt. But I never was using you, Charlie. Don't think that. Even when I didn't consciously know it, I loved you."

She sucked in a gulp of air and another tear coursed along her cheek. Vance's heart fisted in his chest.

"Don't cry. I can't take it when you cry." He walked up to her again, pulled her up off the bed and looked down into her eyes. "I love you so much." He tucked a loose strand of hair behind her ear and said it again. "I love you. Believe me, Charlie. I will always love you."

"I do," she whispered, her mouth curving in that delectable smile that turned Vance's insides to mush.

He grinned and let loose a relieved sigh. "Now there's a phrase I want you to get comfortable with."

"What?"

"*I do*. Two words I'm going to want you to repeat as soon as I find a judge to marry us."

"Marry?" She stared up at him, dumbfounded. "You want to *marry* me?"

"What did you think this was all about?" he asked, laughing. "Think I dragged all these damn flowers in here to ask you to go steady or something? Think I've got champagne chilled because we're going to shack up?"

"I—I—"

"I never thought I'd see this," he said with another quick grin. "She's speechless."

"Sort of. Vance, remember, I'm a package deal."

"And I want the whole package," he told her as his heart thudded painfully in his chest. "You and Jake. If you'll let me, I'll adopt him. I already feel like he's mine."

"Adopt—" Her mouth dropped open and she slapped one hand to it.

"And I want more kids, Charlie. At least three or four."

"Four—"

"I bought your house."

"You *what?*"

"That house you love in Forest Hills Gardens? I bought it."

"How? When? Why?"

He grinned. "Three excellent questions. Let's just say

I went over there last night and made them an offer they couldn't refuse. The house is ours, Charlie. We can move in next month. All you have to do is say yes."

"You bought the house?" She was stunned, blinking as if she half expected to find herself in a dream with someone waking her up any moment.

"Charlie, I want to give you and Jake everything. I want us to be a family. I want to say *I love you* every day for the rest of my life."

"I can't believe you bought that house."

"You loved it."

"Yes, but…"

"Charlie," he said, his voice an urgent whisper as he fought for the thing he had wanted most in his life, "it's just a building. Until you say yes and live in it with me, it's just bricks and mortar and stone and— You're the heart, Charlie. The heart of me. The heart of that house. Without you, we're both incomplete."

"I do love you so much, Vance," she finally whispered as if she said it too loudly, it would shatter the moment.

"Say it again," he urged, pulling her closer.

"I love you. I *love* you."

He bent his forehead to hers. "God, that sounds good."

She laughed shortly and looked around at the wonder he'd created just for her. "Vance, I can't believe you did all this…."

"Hey!" He stopped, kissed her hard and fast. "There's one more thing. Almost forgot. If you hadn't been early, I'd have had it here. Can't believe I left out this part. Amazing. Woman, you completely destroy my mind whenever I'm near you." He pushed her onto the bed again, took a step and said, "Stay right there. I'll only be gone a minute."

She laughed and the wonderful sound of it followed him down the hall into the great room. He swung the painting over the hearth out of the way, opened the vault hidden behind it and reached inside for the surprise he'd left to the end, just in case he needed it.

Then he was back in the bedroom and holding out a flat, black velvet case to her. "I got this for you. I didn't know it at the time. I had my representative call in and buy it. For an investment. But I think, even my subconscious realized that it was meant for you. And for me."

"What?" She tipped open the box, gasped and said, "Oh my God! The queen of Cadria's necklace?" She lifted her gaze to his. "Are you crazy?"

He laughed and dropped onto the bed beside her. "Only for you, Charlie. That necklace promises a long and happy marriage. And that's what I want. With you."

"You *are* crazy," Charlie whispered as she dragged the tip of one finger across a ruby surface. Then she carefully closed the box and looked into Vance's eyes. "And I love you being this crazy."

"Show me," he said.

And she did.

Three days later at Waverly's…

"Ms. Richardson?" Kendra said into the intercom. "There's a call for you on line 3."

"Who is it?"

"He claims to be Sheikh Raif Khouri of Rayas. He says to tell you it's about the Gold Heart statue."

Ann felt a cold chill snake along her spine. Slowly, she reached for the phone with the same enthusiasm she would have shown for grabbing a live cobra.

When she punched into the line, she said smoothly, "Hello, this is Ann Richardson."

"Ah, Ms. Richardson, thank you for taking my call."

"Not at all. How can I help you?" Her mouth was dry

and her stomach was doing twists and spins. Nerves jangled through every part of her body, but she kept her voice steady.

"I believe I am the one who can help you."

"In what way?"

There was a long pause and then the man on the other end of the line sighed before saying, "It is about the Gold Heart statue. What I have to say may save you and your company a great deal of embarrassment."

"I don't understand. Is there a problem?"

"I would think so," he told her, voice clipped with just an undercurrent of anger and suspicion. "The statue you have in your possession is either stolen—or a fake."

The bottom dropped out of Ann's world. This couldn't be true. The press surrounding the acquisition of the statue had been global. Everyone in the world knew that Waverly's had the Gold Heart. If they were found to have obtained it illegally—or, worse yet, to have been trying to palm off a fake as the real thing...

"That's ridiculous," Ann said, standing up since she couldn't sit still another minute. "My experts tell me the statue is genuine. And as for it being stolen—"

"Two of the three statues in existence are now missing," Sheikh Raif interrupted. "One was stolen over a hundred years ago—"

"And that is the one we have."

"So you say. But since that statue has been missing for a hundred years, it seems unlikely that Waverly's would have found it, don't you think?"

Ann didn't say anything.

"The other Gold Heart," he continued, "was stolen just weeks ago from the palace. This is the statue I believe you have now. If so, I must insist on its return to Rayas. Immediately."

Ann dropped back into her desk chair, completely exhausted. She couldn't seem to catch her breath and her heart was beating so fast that she was surprised it hadn't simply flown out of her chest.

This was a nightmare.

Roark had sworn the statue was legitimate, so she knew it wasn't a fake. Could he really have found the long-missing statue, even though it had eluded discovery for more than a century? Or had he somehow been given a stolen artifact?

"Ms. Richardson?"

"Yes, I'm here," she said.

"I'm afraid we have a problem that we must solve. To-gether."

Oh, this was a problem, she thought as she listened to the sheikh telling her exactly what his country expected of her and Waverly's.

She had to get hold of Roark. Had to know if the statue was real and how he'd come by it. She needed the provenance to be clear and unmistakable.

Otherwise, the scandal that would break would be Waverly's undoing. And all that she had worked for her entire adult life would come crashing down around her.

* * * * *

AN INCONVENIENT
AFFAIR

CATHERINE MANN

USA TODAY bestselling author **Catherine Mann** lives on a sunny Florida beach with her flyboy husband and their four children. With more than forty books in print in over twenty countries, she has also celebrated wins for both a RITA® Award and a Booksellers' Best Award. Catherine enjoys chatting with readers online—thanks to the wonders of the internet, which allows her to network with her laptop by the water!

Contact Catherine through her website, www.catherinemann.com, find her on Facebook and Twitter (@CatherineMann1), or reach her by snail mail at P.O. Box 6065, Navarre, FL 32566, USA.

To my stellar editor, Stacy Boyd!
Thank you for the wonderful brainstorming
session that gave birth to The Alpha
Brotherhood.
It's a joy working with you.

Prologue

North Carolina Military Prep
17 years ago

They'd shaved his head and sent him to a reform school.

Could life suck any worse? Probably. Since he was only fifteen, he had years under the system's thumb to find out.

Hanging around in the doorway to the barracks, Troy Donavan scanned the room for his rack. The dozen bunk beds were half-full of guys with heads shaved as buzz-short as his—another victory for dear old dad, getting rid of his son's long hair. God forbid anyone embarrass the almighty Dr. Donavan. Although, catching the illustrious doc's son breaking into the Department of Defense's computer system did take public embarrassment to a whole new level.

Now he'd been shuttled off to this "jail," politely disguised as a military boarding preparatory program in the hills of North Carolina, as per his plea agreement with the judge back home in Virginia. A judge his father had bought off. Troy clenched his hand around his duffel as he resisted the urge to put his fist through a window just to get some air.

Damn it, he was proud of what he'd done. He didn't want it swept under the rug, and he didn't want to be hidden like some bad secret. If the decision had been left up to him, he would have gone to juvie, or prison even. But for his mom, he'd taken the deal. He would finish high school in this uptight place, but if he kept his grades up and his nose clean until he turned twenty-one, he could have his life back.

He just had to survive living here without his head exploding.

Bunk by bunk, he walked to the last row where he found *Donavan, T. E.* printed on a label attached to the foot of the bed. He slung his duffel bag of boring crap onto the empty bottom bed.

A foot in a spit-shined shoe swung off the top bunk, lazing. "So you're the Robin Hood Hacker." A sarcastic voice drifted down. "Welcome to hell."

Great. "Thanks, and don't call me that."

He hated the whole Robin Hood Hacker headline that had blazed through the news when the story first broke. It made what he did sound like a kid's fairy tale. Which was probably more of his dad's influence, downplaying how his teenage son had exposed corrupt crap that the government had been covering up.

"Don't call you that…or what?" asked the smart-ass on the top bunk with a tag that read: *Hughes, C. T.* "You'll steal my identity and wreck my credit, computer boy?"

Troy rocked back on his heels to check the top bunk and make sure he didn't have the spawn of Satan sleeping above him. If so, the devil wore glasses and read the *Wall Street Journal*.

"Apparently you don't know who I am." With a snap of the page, Hughes ducked back behind his paper. "Loser."

Loser?

Screw that. Troy was a freakin' genius, straight As, already aced the ACT and SAT. Not that his parents seemed to notice or give a damn. His older brother was the real loser—smoking weed, failing out of his second college, knocking up cheerleaders. But their old man considered those forgivable offenses. Problems one's money could easily sweep under the rug.

Getting caught using illegal means to expose corrupt DOD contractors and a couple of congressmen was a little tougher to hide. Therefore, *Troy* had committed the unforgivable crime—making mommy and daddy look bad in front of their friends. Which had been his intent at the start, a lame attempt to get his parents' attention. But once he'd realized what he'd stumbled into—the graft, the bribes, the corruption—the puzzle solver inside him hadn't been able to stop until he'd uncovered it all.

No matter how you looked at it, he hadn't been some Robin Hood do-gooder, damn it.

He yanked open his duffel bag full of uniforms and underwear, trying to keep his eyes off the small mirror on his locker. His shaved head might reflect the light and blind him. And since rumor had it half the guys here had also struck deals, he needed to watch his back and recon until he figured out what each of them had done to land here.

If only he had his computer. He wasn't so good at face-to-face reads. The court-appointed shrink that evaluated him for trial said he had trouble connecting with people and lost himself in the cyberworld as a replacement. The Freud wannabe had been right.

And now he was stuck in a freaking barracks full of people. Definitely his idea of hell.

He hadn't even been able to access a computer to research the criminal losers stuck here with him. Thanks to the judge, he was limited to supervised use of the internet for schoolwork only—in spite of the fact he could handle the academics with his eyes closed.

Boring.

He dropped down to sit beside his bag. There had to be a way out of this place. The swinging foot slowed and a hand slid down.

Mr. Wall Street Journal held a portable video game.

It wasn't a computer, but thank God it was electronic. Something to calm the part of him that was totally freaking over being unplugged. Troy didn't even have to think twice. He palmed the game and kicked back in his bunk. Mr. Wall Street Hughes stayed quiet, no gloating. The guy might actually be legit. No agenda.

For now, Troy had found a way through the monotony. Not just because of the video game. But because there was someone else not all wrapped up tight in the rules.

Maybe his fellow juvie refugees might turn out to be not so bad after all. And if he was wrong—his thumbs flew across the keyboard, blasting through to the next level—at least he had a distraction from his first day in hell.

One

Present Day

Hillary Wright seriously needed a distraction during her flight from D.C. to Chicago. But not if it meant sitting behind a newlywed couple intent on joining the Mile High Club.

Her cheeks puffed with a big blast of recycled air as she dropped into her window seat and made fast work of hooking up the headset. She would have preferred to watch a movie or even sitcom reruns, but that would mean keeping her eyes open with the risk of seeing the duo in front of her making out under a blanket. She just wanted to get to Chicago, where she could finally put the worst mistake of her life behind her.

Hillary switched from the best of Kenny G before it put her to sleep, clicking through the stations until she settled on a Broadway channel piping in "The Sound of

Music." Passengers pushed down the aisle, a family with a baby and a toddler, then a handful of businessmen and women, all moving past her to the cheap seats where she usually sat. But not today. Today, her first-class seat had been purchased for her by the CIA. And how crazy was that? Until this month, her knowledge of the CIA only came from television shows. Now she had to help them in order to clear her name and stay out of jail.

A moan drifted from the brand-new Mrs. Somebody in front of her.

Oh God, Hillary sagged back into her seat, covering her eyes with her arm. She was so nervous she couldn't even enjoy her first visit to Chicago. She'd dreamed about getting out of her small Vermont hometown. Her job as an event planner in D.C. had seemed like a godsend at first. She met the exciting people she would have only read about in the news otherwise—politicians, movie stars, even royalty.

She'd been starstruck by her wealthy boyfriend's lifestyle. Stupidly so. Until she allowed herself to be blinded to Barry's real intentions in managing philanthropic donations, his lack of a moral compass.

Now she had to dig herself out from under the mess she'd made of her life by trusting the wrong guy, by believing his do-gooder act of tricking rich associates into donating large sums of money to bogus charities, then funneling the money overseas into a Swiss bank account. She'd proven herself to be every bit the gullible, small-town girl she'd wanted to leave behind.

As of today, her blinders were off.

A flash of skin and pink bra showed between the seats.

She squeezed her eyes shut and lost herself in the do-re-mi refrain even as people bumped past. *Focus. Will away the nerves. Get through the weekend.*

She would identify her scumbag ex-boyfriend's crooked banking acquaintance at the Chicago shindig. Give her official statement to Interpol so they could stop the international money-laundering scheme. Then she could have her life back and save her job.

Once she was back in her boss's good graces, she would again be throwing the kinds of parties she'd wanted to oversee when she'd first become an event planner. Her career would skyrocket with her parties featured in the social section of all major newspapers. Her loser ex would read about her in tabloid magazines in prison and realize how she'd moved on, baby. Maybe she would even appear in some of those photos looking so damn hot Barry would suffer in his celibate cell.

The jackass.

She pinched the bridge of her nose against the welling of tears.

A tap on her shoulder forced her out of her silly self-pity. She tugged off an earbud and looked over at a…suit. A dark blue suit, with a Hugo Boss tie and a vintage tie clip.

"Excuse me, ma'am. You're in my seat."

A low voice, nice, and not cranky-sounding like some travelers could be. His face was shadowed, the sunlight streaking through the small window behind him. She could just make out his dark brown hair, which was long enough to brush his ears and the top of his collar. From the Patek Philippe watch to his edgy Caraceni suit—all name brands she wouldn't have heard of, much less recognized, before her work with high-end D.C. clients.

And she *was* in his seat.

Wincing, she pretended to look at her ticket even though she already knew what it read. God, she hated the aisle and she'd prayed she would luck out and have an empty next to her. "I'm sorry. You're right."

"You know what?" He rested a hand on the back of the empty seat. "If you prefer the window, that's cool by me. I'll sit here instead."

"I don't want to take advantage." Take advantage? The cheesy double entendre made her wince. A moan from the lovebirds a row ahead only made it worse.

"No worries." He stowed his briefcase in the overhead before sidling in to sit down.

Then he turned to her, the light above bringing him fully into focus— And holy cows on her hometown Vermont farm, he was *hot*. Angular. But with long lashes that kept drawing her gaze back to his green eyes. He was probably in his early thirties, gauging from the creases when he smiled with the open kind of grin that made him more approachable.

She tilted her head to the side, studying him more closely. He looked familiar, but she couldn't quite place him.... She shook off the feeling. She'd met so many people at the parties she'd planned in D.C. They could have crossed paths at any number of places. Although, she must have seen him from a distance, because if they'd met up close, she definitely wouldn't have forgotten him.

His seat belt clicked as the plane began taxiing. "You don't like flying."

"Why do you say that?"

"You want the window seat, but have the shade closed. You've already plugged into the radio. And you've got the armrest in a death grip."

Handsome and observant. Hmm...

Better to claim fear of flying than to go into the whole embarrassing mess she'd made of her life. "Busted. You caught me." She nodded toward the row in front of her just as one of the seats reclined providing too clear a view of a man's hand sliding into the woman's waistband. "And the lovebirds up there aren't making things any more comfortable."

His smile faded into a scowl. "I'll call for the flight attendant."

He reached for the button overhead. She touched his wrist. Static snapped. At least she hoped it was just static and not a spark of attraction.

Clearing her throat, she folded her arms over her chest, tucking her hands away. "No need. The flight attendant's in the middle of her in-flight brief—" she lowered her voice "—and giving us the death glare for talking."

He leaned toward her conspiratorially. "Or I can kick the back of their seat until they realize they're not invisible—and that they're being damned inconsiderate."

Except now that he was so close, she didn't notice them. Her gaze locked on the glinting green eyes staring at her with undisguised, unrepentant interest.

A salve to her ego. And an excellent distraction. "I guess we can live and let live."

"We can."

"Although, honestly, it doesn't seem fair the flight attendant isn't giving the evil eye to the handsy twosome."

"Maybe they're celebrating their anniversary."

She snorted.

"Cynic?"

"And you're trying to tell me you're a true believer in flowery romance?" She took in his expensive suit, his dimpled smile and his easy charm. "No offense, truly, but you seem more like a player to me."

A second after the words left her mouth, she worried she might have been rude.

He just laughed softly and flattened a hand to his chest.

"You think the worst of me. I'm hurt to the core," he said with overplayed drama.

Her snort turned into a laugh. Shaking her head, she kept on laughing, tension uncurling inside. Her laughter faded as she felt the weight of his gaze on her.

He pointed to the window. "We're airborne now. You can open the shade and relax."

Relax? His words confused her for a second and then she remembered her excuse for nerves. And then remembered the real reason for her nerves. Her ex-boyfriend. Barry the Bastard Bum. Who she was hoping to help put in prison once she identified his accomplice in Chicago—if she didn't get offed by the bad guy first.

She thumbed her silver seat belt buckle. "Thank you for the help…"

"Troy." He extended his hand. "My name is Troy, from Virginia."

"I'm Hillary, from D.C." Prepping herself for the static this time, she wrapped her fingers around his, shaking once. And, yep. *Snap. Snap.* Heat tingled up her arm in spite of all those good intentions to keep all guys at bay. But then what was wrong with simply being attracted to another person?

Her ex had taken so much from her, and yes, turned a farm-fresh girl like her into a cynic, making her doubt everyone around her. Until she now questioned the motives of a guy who just wanted to indulge in a little harmless flirtation on a plane.

Damn it, there was nothing bad about chatting with this guy during the flight. He had helped her through her nerves about identifying Barry's accomplice at the fundraiser this weekend. A very slippery accomplice who had a way of avoiding cameras. Very few people had ever seen him. She'd only seen him twice, once by showing up at

Barry's condo unannounced and another time at Barry's office. Would the man remember her? Her nerves doubled.

She desperately needed to take full advantage of the distraction this man beside her offered. Talking to Troy beat the hell out of getting sloshed off the drink cart, especially since she didn't even drink.

"So, Troy, what's taking you to Chicago?"

Troy had recognized Hillary Wright the minute he'd stepped on the plane. She looked just like her Interpol file photo, right down to the freckles on her nose and the natural sun streaks through her red hair.

The photo hadn't, however, shown anything below the neck—a regrettable oversight because she was…hot. Leggy with curves and an unadorned innocence that normally wasn't his type. But then when had he ever given a crap about walking the expected path?

That's why he'd shown up here, on her flight, rather than following the plan laid out by the CIA operatives, who were working in conjunction with the American branch of Interpol. To see what she was like in an unguarded moment.

Lucky for him that window seat was empty so he'd been able to wrangle his way in beside her. It had been too easy, and she was totally unsuspecting. She might as well have "fresh off the farm" tattooed across her freckled nose.

A sexy uptipped nose he wouldn't mind kissing as he worked his way around to her ear. He'd expected pretty from her picture, but he hadn't been prepared for the undefinable energy that radiated off her. It was as damn near tangible as her innocence.

This plane on the way to Chicago was the last place she should be. More so, that viper's nest gala this weekend was *absolutely* the last place she should be.

Damn, damn, damn the "powers that be" for making her a part of some crazy power play. He could have accomplished the identification in Chicago without her, but they'd insisted on having her backup confirmation. It was obvious to him now that she was too naive to brush elbows with the sharks at that gala—a bunch of crooks using a fundraiser to cover up their international money laundering.

"Troy? Hello?" Hillary waved her hand in front of his face, her nails chewed to the quick. "What takes you to Chicago?"

"Business trip." Truth. "I'm in computers." More truth. Enough for now. She would see him again soon enough after they landed and when she learned who he really was... Well, she would likely change, close up or suck up. People judged him based on either his past or his money. "What takes *you* to Chicago?" he asked, even though he already knew.

"A fundraiser gala. I'm an event planner and, uhm, my boss is sending me to check out a chef at this weekend retreat."

She was a really crummy liar. Even if he didn't already know her real reason for going to Chicago, he would have sensed something was off in her story.

"A chef... In Chicago... And you work in D.C. You work for lobbyists?"

"I specialize in fundraisers for charities, not campaigns. I didn't plan the one in Chicago. I'm just, uh, scoping out competition. It's a pretty big deal, kicking off Friday night, running all the way to Sunday afternoon with parties and—" She paused self-consciously. "I'm babbling. You don't need the agenda."

"You specialize in polishing the halos of the rich and famous." He smiled on the outside.

Her lips pursed tightly. "Think what you want. I don't need your approval."

A sentiment he applauded. So why was he yanking her chain? Because she looked so damn pretty with righteous indignation sparking from her eyes.

That kind of "in your face" mentality was rare. But it also could land a person in trouble.

He knew too well. It had taken all his self-control to buckle down and meet the judge's requirements when he'd been sentenced at fifteen. Although, he'd found more than he expected at the military school. He'd found friends and a new code to live by. He'd learned how to play by the rules. He'd slowly gotten back computer access and started a video games company that had him rolling in more money than his pedigreed, doctor old man had ever brought home—three times over.

But the access had come with a price. His every move had been monitored by the FBI. They seemed to sense that the taste of megapower he'd felt delving into the DOD would be addictive. Irresistibly so. At twenty-one, he'd been approached with an enticing offer. If he ever wanted a chance at that high again, he would need to loan his "skills" to the American branch of Interpol on occasion.

He'd chafed at the idea at twenty-one. By thirty-two, he'd come to begrudgingly accept that he had to play by a few of their rules, and he'd even found a rush in being a sort of "on call" guy to assist in major international sting operations. He was committed to the job, as he'd proven every time they'd tapped him for a new assignment.

Over time, they also began utilizing him for more than computer help. His wealth gave him access to high-power circles. When Interpol needed a contact on the inside quickly, they used him—and other freelance agents like him. For the most part, he still provided behind-the-scenes computer advice. He was only called upon for something out in the open like this about once a year, so as not to overuse his cover.

Some of that caution would have been nice now, rather than recklessly including Hillary Wright in this joint operation being run by the CIA and Interpol. She wouldn't be able to carry off the charade this weekend. She couldn't blend in.

He'd known it the second he read her profile, even if they'd missed it. God only knew why they called him a genius and then refused to listen to him. So he'd arranged to meet her on this flight to confirm his suspicions. He was never wrong. He would stick by her side all weekend and make sure she didn't blow the whole operation.

Granted, that wouldn't be a hardship, sticking near her for the weekend.

For the first time in years he wasn't bored. Something about this woman intrigued him, and there weren't many puzzles in life for him. So he would stay right here for the rest of the flight and play this through. When she found out his full name—his public, infamous identity—she would pull away. She would likely never know his real reason for being part of this sting, and someone like Hillary Wright wouldn't go for a guy with the reputation of Troy Donavan, especially so soon after getting her fingers burned in the relationship department.

Not that he would let that affect his decision to stick by her. She needed him to get through this weekend, whether she knew it or not.

A flight attendant ducked to ask, "Could I get either of you a complimentary beverage? Wine? A mixed drink?"

Hillary's smile froze, the lightheartedness fading from

her face with the one simple request. The mention of alcohol stirred painful memories. "No, thank you.

Troy shook his head. "I'm good. Thanks." He turned back to Hillary. "Are you sure you don't want a glass of wine or something? A lot of folks drink to get over the fear."

She inched away from the wall and sat upright self-consciously. "I don't drink."

"Ever?"

She refused to risk ending up like her mother, in and out of alcohol rehabs every other year while her father continued to hold out hope that this time, the program would stick. It never did.

There was nothing for her at home. D.C. was her chance at a real life. She couldn't let anything risk ruining this opportunity. Not a drink. Not some charming guy, either.

"Never," she answered. "I never drink."

"There's a story there." He toyed with his platinum cuff links.

"There is." And honest to God, the bay rum scent of him was intoxicating enough.

"But you're not sharing."

"Not with a total stranger." She was an expert at keeping family secrets, of sweeping up the mess so they would look normal to the outside world. Planning high-profile galas for the D.C. elite was a piece of cake after keeping up appearances as a teenager.

She might look like a naive farm girl, but life had already done its fair share to leave her jaded. Which might be why she found herself questioning the ease of her past hour with Troy.

Nothing about him was what she'd expected once he'd first flashed that bad-boy grin in her direction. They'd spent the entire flight just…talking. They'd discussed favorite artists and foods. Found they both liked jazz music and hokey horror movies. He was surprisingly well-read, could quote Shakespeare and had a sharp sense of humor. There was interest in his eyes, but his words stayed light all the way to the start of the plane's descent.

His eyes narrowed at her silence. "Is something wrong?"

"You're not hitting on me," she blurted out.

He blinked in surprise just once before that wicked slow smile spread across his face. "Do you want me to?"

"Actually, I'm having fun just like this."

She sat back and waited for him to stop grinning when he realized she wasn't coming on to him. Was she? She never went for this kind of guy, hair too long and a couple of tiny scars on his face like he was always getting into some kind of trouble. A line through one eyebrow. Another on his chin. And yet another on his forehead that played peekaboo when his hair shifted.

But then Barry had been Mr. Buttoned-Up, clean-cut and respectful. Except it had all been a cover for a deceitful nature.

Troy stared deeper into her eyes. "You don't get to have fun often, do you?"

Who had time for fun? She'd worked hard these past three years building a new life for herself, far away from a gossipy small town that knew her as the daughter of a drunk mother. Barry had tarnished her reputation with his shady dealings—stealing scholarship money for God's sake. And unless she proved otherwise, people would always think she was involved, as well. They wouldn't trust her.

Her boss wouldn't trust her.

She picked at the hem of her skirt. "Why would you say I'm a wet blanket?"

"Not a wet blanket. Just a workaholic. The portfolio under your seat is stuffed with official-looking papers, rather than a book or magazine. The chewed-down nails on your otherwise beautiful hands—sure shout stress."

She'd tried balancing her career and a relationship. That hadn't gone very well for her. Thank you very much, Barry, for being a white-collar crook—and not even all that good of an embezzler, given how easily he'd been caught. She'd been so busy with her job that she'd completely missed the signs that he'd been using her to get close to her clients—and sucker them in.

"Troy, I'm simply devoted to my career." Which would be wrecked if she didn't make sure everyone knew she was a hundred percent against what Barry had done. Her boss would fire her and no one else would hire her since the clients would never trust her. "Aren't you?"

What exactly did he do in computers? She was just beginning to realize that they'd talked all about her and not so much about him and the flight was already almost over.

"Work rocks—as do vacations. So if you were taking this plane trip for pleasure, no work worries and you could pick up any connecting flight when we touch down—where would you go?"

"Overseas." She answered fast before realizing that again, he'd turned the conversation away from himself.

"That's a broad choice," he said as the ground grew larger and larger, downtown Chicago coming into focus.

"I would close my eyes and pick, some place far away." Far, far away from the Windy City gala.

"Ah, the old escape idea. I get that, totally. When I was in boarding school, I made plans for places to live and visit, places without fences."

Boarding school? Interesting and so far removed from her childhood riding the ancient bus with cracked leather seats each morning with all the friends from her neighborhood.

She settled deeper into her seat. "Isn't that the whole point of a vacation? To do something that is totally the opposite of your daily routine. Like open spaces being different from the walls of your old boarding school."

"You have a point." His smile went tight for a flash before his face cleared. "Where are you from originally—so I can get a sense of your daily routine when I'm choosing our great escape?"

Our? "Theoretically of course."

"Theoretically? Nu-uh. You're wrecking the fantasy."

"Right, sorry about that." His magnetism had a way of drawing her into this fantasy. No harm in that. "I'm from Vermont, a tiny town nobody's heard of. Coming to D.C. was a big enough change for me—and now I'm going to Chicago."

"But you don't look happy about it."

She forced herself not to flinch. He was too perceptive. Time to put some distance between them, let him show himself to be a jerk so she could move on. "I'm scared of flying, remember? And this is where you're supposed to ask me for my phone number."

"Would you give it to me if I did?"

"No," she said, almost believing what she was saying. "I'm not in a good place to date anyone right now. So you can stop trying to charm me."

"Can't a guy be nice without wanting something other than engaging conversation?"

She couldn't help but smile. "Did you really just say that?"

He slumped back in his seat, respect glinting in his eyes. "Okay, you're right. I would like to ask for your phone number—because I am single, in case you were wondering—but since you've made it clear you're not open to my advances, I'll satisfy my broken heart and soothe my wounded ego with the pleasure of your company for a little while longer."

God, he was good. Funny and charming, so confident he didn't think twice about making a joke at his own expense. "Do you practice lines like that or are you just really good at improvisation?"

"You're a smart woman. I'm confident you'll figure it out."

She liked him. Damn it. "You're funny."

"And you are enchanting. It was my pleasure to sit next to you on the flight."

They'd landed? She looked around as if waking up from a nap to find more time had passed than she realized. Passengers were sliding from their seats. The aircraft had stopped.

Troy stood, hauling her simple black roll bag from the overhead. "Yours?"

"How did you know?"

He tapped the little dairy cow name tag attached to the handle. "Vermont. Highest cows to people ratio in the country."

"Right you are." She stood, stopping beside him. Close beside him. All the other passengers crowded the aisle until her breasts brushed his chest.

His rock-hard chest. That suit covered one hundred percent honed man, whipcord lean. The bay rum scent of him wrapping around her completely now, rather than just teasing—tempting—her senses.

But still, he didn't touch her or hit on her or act in the least bit skeezy. "Have a great visit in the Windy City."

She chewed her bottom lip, resisting the overwhelming urge to tug his silk tie.

The flight attendant spoke over the loudspeaker. "If you could please return to your seats. We have a slight delay before we can disembark at the gate."

Hillary pulled away quickly, ducking into her seat so fast she almost hit her head. Troy reclaimed his seat slowly while the flight attendant opened the hatch. The yawning opening revealed the long metal stairs that had been rolled up outside. Confused, Hillary yanked up her window shade. They'd stopped just shy of the terminal. A large black SUV with some kind of official insignia on the door waited a few feet away. Two men wearing black suits and sunglasses jogged up the stairs and entered the plane.

The first one nodded to the flight attendant. "Thank you, ma'am. We'll be quick with our business."

The identical duo angled sideways.

Her stomach tumbled over itself. Was there a problem? In spite of what she'd told Troy, she hadn't been freaked out about flying, but now she felt that lie come back to bite her as fears fluttered inside her. How long before she knew what was wr—

Not long at all, apparently.

The dark-suited men stopped beside her row. "Troy Donavan?"

Troy Donavan?

Her stomach lurched faster than a major turbulence plunge. Oh God, she recognized that name. She waited for him to deny it...even though she already knew he wouldn't.

"Yes, that's me. Is there a problem, gentlemen?"

Troy Donavan.

He'd confirmed it. He was far from a nice guy, far from some computer geek just passing time on a commuter flight. His reputation for partying hard and living on the edge made it into the social pages on a regular basis.

"Mr. Donavan, would you step out of your seat, please?"

Troy shot an apologetic look her way before he angled out to stand in front of the two men. "We could have met up at the gate like regular folks."

The older man, the guy who seemed in charge, shook his head. "It's better this way. We don't want to keep Colonel Salvatore waiting."

"Of course. Can't inconvenience the colonel." Muscles bunched in Troy's arms, his hands fisting at his sides.

What the hell was going on?

The "men in black" retrieved Troy's Italian leather briefcase and placed a streamlined linen fedora on his head, the same look that had been featured in countless articles. If she'd seen him in his signature hat, she would have recognized him in a heartbeat.

He was infamous in D.C. for having hacked the Department of Defense's computer system seventeen years ago. She'd been all of ten at the time but he'd become an icon. From then on, any computer hacking was called "pulling a Donavan." He'd made it into pop culture lexicons. He'd become a folk legend for the way he'd leaked information that exposed graft and weaknesses within the system. Some argued he'd merely stepped in where authorities and politicians should have. But there was no denying he'd broken major laws. If he'd been an adult, he would have spent his life in jail.

After a slap-on-the-wrist sentence in some military school, he'd been free to make billions and live out his life in a totally decadent swirl of travel and conspicuous consumption. And she'd fallen for his lying charm. She'd even liked him. She hadn't learned a damn thing from Barry.

She bit her lip against the disappointment in herself. She was here to put the past behind her—not complicate her future. She pressed her back against the body of the plane, unable to get far enough away from the man who'd charmed the good sense right out of her.

Troy reached for his briefcase, but the younger man took a step back.

The older of the two men held out...*handcuffs*.

Cocking an eyebrow, Troy said, "Are these really needed?"

"I'm afraid they are." *Click. Click.* "Troy Donavan, you're under arrest."

Two

"Were the handcuffs necessary?" Holding up his shackled hands, Troy sprawled in the backseat of the armored SUV as they powered away from the airport. The duo that had arrested him sat in the front. His mentor and former military school headmaster—Colonel John Salvatore—sat beside him with a smirk on his face.

As always, he wore a gray suit and red tie, no variation, same thing every day as if wearing a uniform even though he'd long ago left the army.

"Yes, Troy, actually they are required, as per the demands of the grand dame throwing this gala. She's determined to have a bachelor auction like one she read about in a romance novel and she thought, given your checkered past, the handcuffs would generate buzz. And honest to God, the photos in the paper will only help your image, and therefore our purposes, as well."

It was always about their purposes. Their agreement.

He'd struck a deal with Colonel Salvatore at twenty-one years old, once his official sentence was complete. Salvatore had been the headmaster of that military reform school—and more. Apparently he helped recruit freelancers for Interpol who could assist with difficult assignments—such as using Troy's computer skills and later utilizing his access to high-power circles. Other graduates of the military school had been recruited, as well, people who could use their overprivileged existence to quickly move in high-profile circles. For these freelancers, no setup was needed for a cover story, a huge time and money saver for the government.

A person might be called on once. Or once a year. Maybe more. Salvatore offered things no one else in Troy's life had ever given him. A real chance to atone.

He may not have felt guilty at fifteen, but over time he'd come to realize the repercussions of what he'd done were far-reaching. His big DOD computer exposé as a teen had inadvertently exposed two undercover operatives. And even though they hadn't died, their careers had been cut short, their usefulness in the field ruined.

He should have taken his information to the authorities rather than giving it to the press. He'd been full of ego and the need to piss off his father. He knew better now, and had the opportunity to make up for what he'd cost the government and those two agents.

And yeah, he still enjoyed the rush of flying close to the flame while doing it.

Troy worked his hands inside the cuffs. "You could have waited. There was no need to freak out Hillary Wright. I would think you'd want her calm."

Her horrified, disillusioned blue eyes were burned in his memory as deeply as the sound of her laugh and the genuine warmth of her smile.

Sighing, Salvatore swiped a hand over his closely shorn head. "If you'd been on the private jet like you were supposed to be none of this would have happened. Stop caring what Hillary Wright thinks of you. She'll be out of your life by Monday. Your time will be your own soon enough and, with luck, I won't need to call on you again for a long while."

The years stretched ahead in monotony. His company all but ran itself now. The past eleven months since he'd been called upon had been boring as hell.

His mind zipped back to Hillary and how he would see her for the rest of the weekend—how she would see him. "A bachelor auction, huh? That grand dame can't expect me to strut down some catwalk."

"When did *you* start worrying about appearances?"

"When did *you* start using innocents like Hillary?" he snapped back, unsettled by the protective surge pumping through him. At least he would have a chance to explain to her some of what had happened on the plane. He could claim the event swore him to secrecy about the handcuffing gig, even if he wasn't authorized to tell her about his role with Interpol. "I thought your gig was to, uh, collaborate with the fallen."

"My 'gig' is to mentor people with potential. Always has been."

"Mentor. Jailer."

Salvatore smirked. "Someone's grouchy."

Troy rattled his cuffs as they drove deeper into the skyscraper-filled city. "Could you just take the cuffs off?"

He hated being confined and Salvatore knew that, damn it. Although looking at the cuffs now, other uses scrolled through his head, sexy fantasies of using them with Hillary. Maybe he would lock his wrist to hers, and take it from there.

"The mistress of ceremonies has the key."

"You're joking." He had to be. "That's hours away."

"When have I ever had a sense of humor?"

"Valid point." Troy's hands fell in his lap. He might as well settle in for the scenic ride through downtown Chicago. He would be free, eventually, and then he would check on Hillary. For now, he was stuck with Salvatore.

The colonel was one eccentric dude.

Sure, Salvatore was the Interpol handler for the group of freelancers whose lifestyles gave them a speedy entrée into a high-profile circle when fast action was needed. But it must blow to be an overgrown babysitter for Troy at some shindig hosted by a local grand dame at a downtown hotel. Tonight's gala kicked off a whole weekend of partying for the rich and famous, under the pretense of charity work.

And apparently Salvatore wasn't just here for Troy, but helping the CIA by being here for Hillary, too.

"Colonel, I am curious, though, why do we need Hillary for this? How much does she know?"

The more Troy learned about her, the more of an edge he would have over her the next time he saw her.

"She's here to identify contacts of her former boyfriend. And because we and the CIA need to be sure she's truly as innocent as she seems."

Was his protectiveness misplaced? Could he have so misread her? Either way, it didn't dim how damn badly he wanted to peel her power suit off with his teeth. "This is really just to test her?"

The colonel waved aside Troy's indignation. "Speaking of Hillary Wright. Your little stunt—switching from the private jet to her flight? Not cool. I had to cancel lunch with an ambassador to get here in time."

"You're breaking my heart."

Sighing, Salvatore shook his head. "How the hell did you even get on that plane?"

"Really?" Troy cocked an eyebrow. "Do you even have to ask *me*, the guy who broke through the school's supposedly impenetrable computer firewalls in order to hack your bank account and send flowers to the Latin teacher on your behalf?"

A laugh rumbled in the old guy's chest. "As I recall, that trick didn't go so well for you since she and I were quietly seeing each other and I'd already sent her flowers. She figured out fast who pulled that off."

"But the flowers I chose were better—Casablanca lilies, if I recall."

"And I learned from that. Same way you should accept you can learn from others once in a while." Salvatore and the teacher had eventually married—and divorced. The man's laughter faded into a scowl. "The internet is not your personal plaything."

Troy held up his cuffed wrists. "These give me hives *and* flashbacks."

Salvatore's eyes narrowed. "I don't know why I put up with you."

"Because I'll get the job done. I always do. I'll find our mystery guy either in person or through the hotel's security system. I will make sure this time that he doesn't get away with hiding from the cameras. We will track his accounts and nail the bastard." He'd only caught a glimpse of the guy once, a month ago shortly before they'd taken down Barry Curtis. If only they'd caught both men then… "But now, as far as I'm concerned, my job also includes making sure Hillary Wright stays safe in that pool of piranhas posing as scions of society."

"As long as you don't make a spectacle of yourself or her, I can live with that. Keep it low-key for once."

"Okay, deal," he agreed, perhaps a bit too quickly because Salvatore's eyes narrowed suspiciously. Time for a diversion. "One last thing, though."

"You're pushy today."

"Look in my briefcase. I brought John Junior—" Salvatore's only kid "—a copy of Alpha Realms IV. He'll have a month's head start mastering it before it hits the market."

"Bribery's a crime." But Salvatore still reached for the Italian leather case. "What's the favor?"

"It's just a gift for your son from my software company. No strings attached."

"What's the favor?" he repeated.

"I don't agree with your pulling Hillary Wright into this. She's too naive and uninformed. After the party tonight, I want her sent home to D.C. Scrap keeping her around for the weekend."

Troy would figure out a way to contact her in D.C., without all the hidden agenda crap. But make no mistake, he would see her again.

"She's not so innocent if she was involved with Barry Curtis." The colonel slid the video game into his black briefcase. "She'll prove herself this weekend—or not."

"Guilty of bad judgment, that's all." Troy was sure of that. What he didn't know—something that bothered him even more—was if Hillary still had feelings for the creep.

God, why did he feel such a connection to a woman he'd only just met? Maybe because she possessed an innocence he'd never had.

"Are you so sure about her?" The leather seats creaked as Salvatore shifted back into place.

Troy was certain he couldn't let her go into a ballroom full of crooks alone. "I'm sticking with her tonight and putting her on a plane in the morning."

Salvatore patted his briefcase. "You should really keep

me happy if you want me to put in a good word with your brother's parole officer."

Troy looked up sharply. Pulling in his brother was dirty pool, even for Salvatore.

"I'm not an enabler." His brother, Devon, had more than a drug problem. He'd blown through his trust fund and had been sent to jail for dealing to feed his cocaine addiction. Troy forced himself to say blandly, "Do whatever you want with him."

"Tough love or sibling rivalry?"

Anger pulsed—at Salvatore for jabbing at old wounds. "You'd better tell the driver to move this along so I can get out of these handcuffs before I have to take a leak. Otherwise you'll have to help."

"Bathroom humor is beneath you, Donavan."

"I wasn't joking." He pinned Salvatore with an impassive look as the SUV stopped in front of the towering hotel.

Salvatore reached for the door handle as the driver opened Troy's side. "Time to rock and roll."

Standing in the elevator in the Chicago hotel, Hillary smoothed her sweaty palms down the length of her simple black dress. Strapless and floor length, it was her favorite. She'd brought it, along with her good luck charm clipped to her clutch purse, to bolster her and steady her nerves. It wasn't working. Her hands went nervously to her hair, which was straight with a simple crystal clasp sweeping back one side.

She'd been nervous enough about this weekend from the moment she'd been asked to come to Chicago, but at least she'd had a plan. She'd thought she had her head on straight—and then she'd fallen right into flirting with a notorious guy seconds away from handcuffs. The experience had thrown her. Right now, she wasn't sure of much of anything.

There'd been a time, as a little girl, when she'd dreamed of staying in a five-star hotel like this one, in a big city, with all the glitz included. As a kid, after she'd finished her chores on the dairy farm, she'd hidden in her room, away from her drunken mother. For hours and hours, Hillary had played on the internet, escaping into another world. Researching other places and other ways to live. Clean places. Pretty, even.

With tables full of food.

She'd spent a lot of time thinking about the cuisine, learning recipes, planning meals and parties to fill her solitary world. Even if only in her imagination.

Once she'd turned eighteen, she scrounged together enough college loans to get a degree in hospitality and economics. Three years ago, she'd landed with a major D.C. corporation that contracted out events planners. Someday, she hoped to start her own company. Be in charge of her own business. She refused to live her life as the scared little country girl she'd once been, hiding in her room, too afraid to slip out and grab a mushy apple from behind mom's beer.

The elevator doors slid open and she smiled her thanks to the attendant before stepping out into the wide hall, sconces lighting the way into the glittering ballroom. Nerves ate at her stomach like battery acid. She just had to get through this weekend. She'd make the proper identifications, which would help confirm her innocence. Or at least get her off the hook, even if they still didn't believe she'd known nothing about what Barry had in mind for those supposed college scholarships.

Forging ahead, she passed her invitation to the tuxedoed man protecting the elite fundraising bash from party crashers. Media cameras flashed. Even with spots in front of her eyes, she already recognized at least two movie stars, an opera singer and three politicians. This party rivaled anything she'd seen or planned—and her standards were top-notch. The ballroom glittered with refracted lights from the crystal chandeliers. Columns and crown molding were gilded; plush carpets held red-and-brass swirls.

A harpist and a violinist played—for now—but from the looks of the instruments set up throughout the room, the music would obviously be staggered. The stage was set for a string quartet. A grand piano filled a corner, with a 1940s-era mic in place alongside.

The dance—at two thousand dollars a head—was slated to fund scholarships. But then that was the root of Barry's scam—collecting money for scholarships, most of which were never awarded, then funneling the cash out of the country into a Swiss bank account.

Bile rose in her throat. She thumbed the charm clipped to her bag, rubbing the tiny silver cow pin like a talisman, a reminder of where she'd come from and all she intended to accomplish.

Men wore tuxedos or military uniforms, the women were in long dresses and dripping jewels that would have funded endless numbers of scholarships. Well, everyone wore formal attire except for the gentleman in a gray suit with a red tie. Her contact.

Colonel Salvatore.

She'd been introduced to him by her lawyer. Apparently, the colonel worked for international authorities. The CIA had promised he would ensure her safety and oversee her cooperation while she was in Chicago. Only one more weekend and she could put this all behind her.

The colonel stepped up beside her and offered his arm.

"Miss Wright, you're here early. I would have escorted you down if I'd known you were ready."

"I couldn't wait any longer to get this evening under way." She tucked her hand into the crook of his arm. "I hope you understand."

"Of course." He started into the ballroom, moving toward the seating section with a runway thrust into the middle.

She recalled there being some mention of an auction of items donated by the elite from around the globe.

More money laundering? Couldn't anyone or anything be genuine anymore? Was everything tainted with greed and agendas?

Salvatore gestured her toward a seat reserved with his name and "guest". They took their places five rows back, not conspicuously in the front. She was also in the perfect spot to see both of the screens panning shots of the guests while a matriarch of Chicago high society took the stage to emcee the auction. Of course Colonel Salvatore had planned everything.

Hillary forced herself to focus on studying each face on the screen, on searching for the two familiar individuals who Barry had claimed were his "silent partners"—not that Barry was talking to authorities now that he'd lawyered up.

But then when had she ever been able to count on a man? Her father certainly hadn't done anything to stop her mother from drinking or to protect Hillary and her sister. He'd buried himself in working in the fields, and as long as she worked alongside him, she was safe.

The hard work of her childhood had taught her to work hard as an adult. Life was just hard. Plain and simple. She was still trying to keep herself safe so her efforts could finally pay off.

As bid after bid went by for posh vacations, jewelry and even private concerts, her thoughts raced back to Troy Donavan and that hour of lighthearted banter on the plane. For a short snap, life had felt fun and uncomplicated.

Yet, it had all been a lie. She couldn't have bantered with a more complicated person. Troy was a perfect example of the cold, hard truth. Everyone wanted something from someone else. People didn't do things exclusively out of the goodness of their hearts. There was always a payoff of some sort expected. The sooner she accepted that and quit believing otherwise, the happier she would be.

Madame Emcee moved closer to the microphone, her gold taffeta dress smooshed against the podium. "And now, before we move on to dancing the night away, we have one final auction left for the evening, one not on your programs." She swept a bejeweled hand toward the large flat screens. "If you'll turn your attention to our video feed, you'll see media footage you may have caught earlier."

Troy Donavan's face filled the screen.

Oh. God.

Hillary clenched her hands around her handbag, the silver charm cutting into her palm. She glanced quickly at the colonel to see if he'd noticed her panic. But her escort simply sat with his arms folded, watching along with everyone else.

In full color, high-definition, the whole runway scenario played out again in front of her. Troy, walking off the plane in handcuffs, wearing that quirky, undeniably sexy hat. Troy, escorted into some official-looking SUV. Hillary had been so rushed getting checked in and ready for the kickoff gala, she hadn't even turned on the television in her room.

Madame Emcee continued, "But what does that have to do with us tonight? Prepare yourself."

The lights shut off. The ballroom went pitch-black. Gasps rippled. A woman squeaked.

After a squeal of microphone feedback, the emcee continued, "For our final bid of the night, we have for you..."

A spotlight illuminated a circle on stage.

Troy Donavan stood in the middle, wearing a tuxedo now instead of his suit, but still cuffed with his hands in front of him. A white silk scarf gave him the same quirky air he'd had on the plane. Her eyes took in the whole man. How could she not? He'd been hot in a suit—in a tuxedo, he stole the air from the room.

"Yes," Madame continued, her fat diamond earrings sparkling disco ball refractions all around her face. "Troy Donavan has offered himself as a date for the weekend. But first, someone must 'bid' him out of our custody in an auction. He's been a bad, bad boy, ladies. You'll want to handle with caution and by no means, let this computer whiz get his hands on your software."

Laughter echoed up into the rafters from everyone— except Hillary. She sat stunned; her hands gripped the sides of her seat so tightly her fingers went numb. The whole arrest had been a gag, a publicity stunt for this party. She'd spent the entire afternoon thinking of him in a jail cell—and yes, sad over that in spite of her anger.

Now she was just mad. He had to have known what she thought in those last minutes on the airplane and he'd said nothing to reassure her. He didn't even bother to lean down and whisper "Sorry" in her ear.

She should be relieved he wasn't in trouble, and she was. But she couldn't forget. He was still the Robin Hood Hacker.

Still playing games.

The bidding began—and of course it soared. Half the women and a couple of men were falling all over themselves to win a weekend with him. The war continued, shouts growing louder and escalating to over seventy thousand dollars. The ruckus continued until just three bidders remained.

Winning at the moment was a woman wearing skintight silver and chunky sapphires, with a sheen of plastic surgery to her stretched skin.

Not far behind, a college-aged student who'd begged Daddy for more money twice already.

And coolly chiming in occasionally, a sedate woman in a simple black sheath.

College girl dropped out after her daddy shook his head at the auctioneer and drew his hand across his throat in the universal "cut off" signal. Still the bidding rose another ten thousand dollars, money that would go to underprivileged schoolkids who needed scholarships. This was all in fun, right?

Yet, the way these people tossed around money in games left her...unsettled. Why not just write a check, plus cancel the event and donate that amount, too? Of course if they did that, she would be out of a job.

Who was she to stand in judgment of others? Of Troy?

As much as she wanted to look away from his cocky smile, which had so charmed her earlier, she couldn't. The way she stayed glued to the bidding upset her. A lot.

She found herself rooting for the one less likely to entice him. Not that she really knew anything about him. But a part of her sensed—or hoped—Ms. Plastic Surgery with her wedding ring wouldn't be at all alluring to Troy. And if she was, then how much easier it would be to wipe him from her mind.

But the sedate woman in the black dress? She could have been Hillary's cousin. And that gave her pause. If that woman won and if she was his type, then that meant he could have been genuine on the airplane when he flirted....

As fast as "going, going, gone" echoed through the room, Ms. Sedate had a date with Troy Donavan for the weekend, won by an eighty-nine-thousand-dollar bid. And gauging from his huge "cat ate the canary smile" he was happy with the results.

The depth of Hillary's disappointment was ridiculous, damn it. She'd spoken to the guy for all of an hour on a flight. Yes, she'd been inordinately attracted to him— felt a zap of chemistry she hadn't felt before—but she could chalk that up to her vulnerable state right now. She was raw, with her emotions tender and close to the surface. After this ordeal with Barry was over, she would get stronger.

The emcee moved closer to Troy in a loud crackle of gold taffeta, which carried through the microphone. She keyed open the cuffs and he tucked them into his tuxedo pocket. He kissed her hand before taking the mic from her.

"Ladies and gentlemen," he said in that same carefree voice that had so enticed Hillary earlier as he'd calmed her nerves on the plane, "I'm pleased to be a part of such a generous outpouring tonight—all in the Robin Hood spirit and not a single computer hacked."

There was no denying it. The crowd loved him. They all but ate up his irreverence and charm. All except Colonel Salvatore. He seemed—skeptical.

"As you're all aware, I'm not known for playing by the rules. And tonight's no different." He motioned to the reserved woman who'd won the bidding battle. "My assistant here has been placing bids for me so I'll have the opportunity to pick the lady of my choice for the weekend."

Gasps, whispers and a couple of disgruntled murmurs chased through the partiers.

"I know—" Troy shrugged "—not completely fair, but I can't be accused of driving someone else to pay more since I took the burden of the highest bid upon myself."

Madame Emcee leaned in to the mic. "And it is a quite generous donation, may I add." She nodded to Troy. "But please, continue."

"Since we're all here in support of a worthy cause, I hope my request will be honored by the woman I choose. After all, it would be a double standard if this bachelor auction didn't work both ways."

His cocky logic took root and cheers bounced from person to person like beach balls at a raucous Jimmy Buffett concert. Troy started down the steps with a lazy long-legged lope, microphone in hand. The men and women around Hillary whooped and shouted louder while Troy continued to speak into the mic. He paused at the first row, then moved on to the second and the third, playing the crowd like a fiddle as each woman wondered if she would be chosen. The spotlight followed him farther still, showcasing every angle of a face too handsome to belong to someone who couldn't be trusted to use that charm wisely.

Abruptly, he stopped.

Troy stood at the end of row five. Her row. He stood beside Colonel Salvatore. The older gentleman—her contact—scowled at Troy.

And why not? He was making it difficult for her to stay low profile this weekend, which was what she'd been instructed to do. But then he couldn't possibly know how much trouble he could cause just by bringing the spotlight to this row.

Troy extended his hand and looked Hillary straight in the eyes. "I choose you."

Three

Her stomach fell as quickly as her anger rose, which was mighty darn hard and fast. What game was he playing now? She had no clue.

She did know that every single pair of eyes in this room was glued to her. She looked farther—and crap—her horrified face was plastered right there in full color on the wide screens.

Undaunted, Troy dropped to one knee.

Damn his theatrical soul.

"Hillary—" his voice boomed through the speakers "—think of the children and their scholarships. Be my date for the weekend."

She wanted to shove him on his arrogant ass.

Troy shifted his attention to the colonel. "I assume you won't mind me stealing your date?"

The colonel cleared his throat and said, "She's my niece. I trust you'll treat her well."

Niece? Whatever. Sheesh. This was nuts.

A steadying hand palmed her back. Salvatore. Her skin turned fiery with embarrassment. She turned to him for help.

Salvatore smiled one of those grins that didn't come close to reaching his pale blue eyes. "You should dance, Hillary."

Right. She should get her feet moving and then people would stop staring at her. Determined to feel nothing, she put her hand in Troy's—and still her stomach did a flip. She was not sixteen, for crying out loud. Although his grip felt so warm—callused and tender at the same time. Her body freakin' tingled to life. She'd always prided herself on being in control of her emotions. The second she'd found out what an immoral creep Barry was, she'd felt nothing but repulsion at his touch.

She knew Troy was a liar, a crook and a playboy. Still her body sang at the notion of stepping into his arms and gliding across the dance floor.

Plus, he'd just bid nearly ninety thousand dollars to spend the weekend with her. Gulp.

The pianist began playing. A singer in a red dress cupped the microphone and launched into a sultry rendition of a 1940s love song.

Troy tucked her to his side and led her to the center of the empty dance floor. The spotlight warmed her already-heating cheeks. His silk scarf teased her hand as he held it against his chest and swept her into the glide of the music. She should have known he would be a smooth dancer.

She blurted out, "Is there anything you don't do well?"

"I take it that's not a compliment."

"I don't mean to be rude, but I'm here to work this weekend, not play games."

"Believe me, this is no game." He pulled her close.

She inhaled sharply at the press of his muscled body against hers. He wasn't some soft desk jockey. He was a toned, honed *man*. Her mouth dried and her pulse sped up.

"Just relax and dance." His warm breath caressed her ear. "And I promise not to sing along. Because, in answer to your question, I'm tone-deaf."

"Thanks for sharing. But it's not helping. You can't truly expect me to relax," she hissed, even as her feet synced perfectly with his. His strong legs brushed ever so subtly against hers with each dance step. "You just told a roomful of people and a pack of reporters that you paid nearly ninety-thousand dollars to spend the weekend with me. Me. A woman you've known for less than a day. We've only spoken for an hour."

He guided her around the floor as other couples joined in. The shifting mass of other bodies created a sense of privacy now that all eyes weren't so fiercely focused on them.

"Well, Troy?" she pressed. "What are you hoping to accomplish?"

"Don't you believe in love at first sight?" He nuzzled her hair, inhaling deeply.

She stumbled, bumped into another couple, then righted her steps, if not her racing pulse. "No, I do not. I believe in lust at first sight, but not love. Don't confuse the two."

All the same, she couldn't help but draw in another whiff of his bay rum scent now that she was as close to him as she'd ever been. Swaying, she resisted the urge to press her cheek to his and savor the bristle of late-day stubble. The kind of slightly unshaven look that wasn't scruffy, but shouted *testosterone* to a woman's basic instincts.

But the music slowed and she rested her cheek against his chest, just over the silken scarf for a moment.

"Hmm." His chest rumbled with approval. "So you admit you're attracted to me."

Of course she was. That didn't mean she intended to tell him. "Correction—I was stating that you are simply attracted to me."

He laughed softly, spanning her waist with a bold, broad palm. "Your confidence is compelling."

"Not confidence, exactly." She leaned back to study his eyes. "Why else would you have gone to all this outrageous trouble to spend time with me? Although I guess you're so wealthy that perhaps the obscene amount of money doesn't mean anything to you."

He sketched his knuckles along her jawline. "I wanted the chance to spend time with you."

"Why not go about that the normal way?"

"Tough to do if I'd ended up as someone else's date for the weekend."

"How did you even know I was here?"

"I saw you when I was backstage. My assistant was here. Giving her instructions on what to do was as simple as a text."

"But the ballroom was full of people."

"You could have been in a football stadium, and I would have seen you," he said intensely. His fingers skimmed along the sensitive curve of her neck. "Now let's stop arguing and just enjoy ourselves—unless you plan to renege on the agreement you made in front of all these people. But I have to warn you, everyone will be very disappointed in you if you cost the charity eighty-nine-thousand dollars."

His touch almost distracted her from his manipulative words.

She clasped his wrist and placed his hand back on her shoulder. Her bare shoulder. Maybe not such a good idea after all. "People won't like *you* very much either if you don't follow through on your assistant's bid."

"Everyone knows I've never cared what other people

think of me." His fingers caressed her subtly, enticingly. "But you do care about people's opinions. Rejecting the bid, refusing to play along, causing a scene could all damage your credibility as an event planner—"

"Oh stop it." Stop teasing her. Touching her. Tempting her. "We both know I'm not going to cause a scene, and you're going to pay the charity. How about we shut up and dance in peace?" While she thought about what to do next. At least dancing with Troy gave her an easy excuse to check every face on the dance floor.

He tut-tutted. "My mother always said it isn't nice to tell people to shut up."

"You are really infuriating."

"At least you aren't indifferent."

"That's safe to say." She huffed a hefty exhale. "I want to get this date out of the way so I can go back to my real reason for being here this weekend."

"To check out the chef."

"Right, the food."

Something shifted in his eyes, then his expression cleared again. "Our date is for the whole weekend."

An entire weekend of his touch? His humor and charm? Even with her real reasons for being here, it seemed she didn't have a choice on that. So she could either fight him or use this situation to her advantage.

She could be his "bought for the weekend date," and she could use that role to mingle with everyone, see if she could catch a glimpse of the mystery man Barry had claimed was his business partner. No one would question why she was here and if Colonel Salvatore hadn't liked the idea he would have objected when Troy asked her to dance. Now, people would be too focused on who she was with to worry about why she was here. He would actually make the perfect cover.

All she had to do was resist the overwhelming urge to pull him into a dark corner and kiss him senseless.

Troy had been trying to figure out how to get Hillary away from the crowd for the past two hours.

And yes, he wouldn't mind having her alone after one hundred and twenty-two minutes with her pressed against him, either dancing or tucked by his side as they sampled the array of tiny desserts. The soft feminine feel and minty scent of her was damn near driving him bonkers.

Except he had a plan. He'd already executed the first part through the bidding war. Salvatore's scowl had shot daggers his way all evening, a price worth paying. Hillary could still make her identification, and she would have him as a bodyguard, even if she didn't know it.

He guided her along the pastry line, then over to the drinks table—seltzer water with lime for them both—then out on the balcony where tables were set up. Lights were strung and twinkling, the sounds and smells of the lake carrying on the wind. He picked the table against the wall, overlooking the rest of the small outdoor area and out of clear view of the security cameras.

They could sit beside each other, shielded by the shadows. No one would approach without him seeing them first, and she could watch the party, even though she didn't know they were on the same side. His instincts told him she was honest, but he couldn't risk telling her of his affiliation with Salvatore until both he and Salvatore were certain of her innocence.

Bluesy jazz music drifted through the open French doors. A saxophone player had joined the pianist and singer. All of the musicians tonight were big names who'd donated their talent to the event. One of them was even a buddy from reform school and a Salvatore recruit, as well. This place was crawling with money and agendas.

Including his own.

He took his seat beside her, the handcuffs in his pocket jingling a reminder of his earlier fantasies about cuffing them together—all night long. He tipped back his glass and allowed himself the luxury of studying her out of the corner of his eye. There was no way to hide a woman like her. Sure she wore a simple strapless black gown, her hair clasped back on one side. Yet in a place full of women in designer gowns and priceless heirloom jewels, she stood out from the simplicity of her presence alone. Her unassuming grace, the way she didn't seek the spotlight—and yet, it followed her. She drew the light.

She drew him.

Troy watched her over the top of his glass. "Are you still angry about the auction?"

Slowly, she placed her seltzer water back on the shiny steel table and stirred the lime around deliberately. "I'm upset that you didn't tell me the truth on the airplane. I don't appreciate being lied to."

"I didn't lie." He'd been careful with his words.

She looked up sharply. "You left out parts. You quibbled about your identity." Her freckled nose crinkled ever so slightly in disgust. "Quibbling is the same as lying."

She sounded like Colonel Salvatore. He cursed softly.

"What was that?" She arched a brow, again just like his mentor.

"If I'd told you my full name on the plane, would you have spoken with me during the flight?" He leaned forward, taking her cool hand in his, the minty scent of her carrying on the late-night breeze. "Or if you did speak, would it have been the fun, easy exchange we shared?"

She stayed silent, but she didn't pull away.

"Exactly." He thumbed the inside of her wrist, enjoying the satiny softness of her skin, the speeding throb of her pulse. "I wanted to talk to you, so I didn't pull out a calling card that says hey, I'm the Robin Hood Hacker."

"Okay, okay—" she chewed her bottom lip, which glistened with a simple gloss, all of her makeup minimal "—but can you at least acknowledge that you deliberately misled me?"

"I did." He clasped her hand with both of his and squeezed once. He was making progress. Getting closer. Anticipation thrummed through his veins in time with the bluesy music. "And I'm sorry that has upset you, because honest to God, from the moment I saw you on the plane, I've just wanted to spend time with you. I want you to see *me,* not my Wikipedia page."

She released her bottom lip from between her teeth. "You make a compelling argument."

"Good. Then consider this. We're both here for the weekend. So let's make the most of it. Don't think past Sunday. I'll be patient through all your visits with the chef."

"You don't have to."

"I'm in Chicago because I'm obligated to be here. You've made a dull weekend much more interesting." His eyes lingered on the way the stars and lights brought out streaks of gold in her sleek red hair. His fingers ached to thread through each strand. "If we hang out together for the rest of this gala, we don't have to make awkward conversation with others."

"Better the devil I know than the devil I don't?"

"I can live with that if it means I get to spend more time with you."

Her midnight-blue eyes narrowing, she traced a finger

over the top of their clasped hands. "Are you seriously hitting on me?"

"Yes." And for once he wasn't holding anything back.

"You must be really hard up."

"Or just h—"

"Don't even say it."

"Hungry for your company."

"You're not funny." Her mouth twitched anyway.

"Yes, I am. But it's not something I take pride in. I'm a smart guy, and intelligence is a genetic lottery. What really matters is how I use those winnings."

She swayed forward just a hint. "There's sense in some of that egotistical ranting of yours."

He canted closer until only a sliver of air separated them. He waited. Her breath puffed faster and faster with the quickening rise and fall of her chest. Her pupils widened as she met and held his gaze.

Then her lashes fluttered closed. All the invitation he needed.

Taking advantage of their shadowy corner, Troy slanted his mouth over hers, testing the soft give of her full lips. Tasting the lingering lime flavor of her drink. He squeezed her hand more firmly and claimed her. Completely.

He slid his arm around her shoulder and deepened the kiss, teasing along the seam of her mouth until she opened for him. Her sigh filled him with a surge of triumph. He'd been imagining this since the second he'd clapped eyes on her on the airplane. She didn't just melt, she participated, stroke for stroke.

His fingers tangled in the silky glide of her hair along her shoulders. The strands clung to his fingers with a snap of static and something more snapping through his veins.

There was chemistry here, a connection and crackle he burned to explore along with the curve of her hips, her breasts. He wanted to kiss the crook of her arm, behind her knee and find the places that made her go weak with pleasure. This weekend presented the perfect opportunity to indulge in the countless fantasies exploding to life in his brain.

Her hand flattened to his chest, her fingers gripping his silk scarf and bringing him even closer.

His heart ramped up at the strength of her passion. And the thought of her tugging that scarf off, of peeling the rest of their clothes away and touching him without the barrier of fabric… A possessive growl rumbled deep inside him, almost pushing him over the edge.

He pulled himself from her before he took this too far in such a public setting. She gasped, then looked around quickly.

Her eyes wide, she pressed the back of her trembling wrist to her mouth. "That was…"

"Damned amazing."

"Not a good idea."

"I thought you might say that." But given her reaction to him, he wasn't daunted in the least.

She flattened her palms to the table and drew in a shaky breath. "You've got to understand, I have exceptionally crummy taste in men. It's like I have a radar for finding the most dishonest, untrustworthy guy in the room. So the fact that I like you makes you very dangerous for me."

"You like me." He nudged her loose hairpin back into place. "But, wow, you sure know how to throw a guy hope and smack him back down again at the same time."

"I'm sorry, but it's true, and honestly—" she looked around nervously "—now's also a really horrible time for me to even think about dating."

She seemed to be searching for an escape route, but then he knew that she also needed to stay here, at the party.

Watching. Just as he did. So, pressing her to stay at the table shouldn't be too tough.

He wanted to kiss her again. But he would settle for hearing the sound of her voice, which was more amazing than even the professional singer and musicians back in the ballroom.

"Tell me more about these horrible men you chose."

She started to stand, to leave. "I don't appreciate being made fun of."

He stroked her arm, the heat of their kiss still firing through him. "Stay, please. I'm serious. I want to learn more about you. Unless you have somewhere else to be?"

Pressing two fingers against her temple as if combatting a headache, she looked through the doors at the crowded ballroom, then shook her head. "I should stay until...the chef is free."

"Then pass your time with me. Tell me about the losers."

She turned slowly back to him. "Fine, if you insist." She held up three fingers. "In high school, I dated three guys. One cheated on me." She tucked down a finger. "The other was just using me to get to my best friend." She tucked down another. "Number three liked to mix vodka in his sports drink and dumped me in the middle of the homecoming dance. And the pattern continued on through college and the few times I've risked the whole relationship gig as an adult. I'm some sort of a scumbag magnet."

She said it all dispassionately, as if she'd built a defense against the hurt, but somehow, he knew it was an act. Guilt pinched inside him over the things he wasn't telling her, that he wasn't authorized to tell her. His intermittent work for Interpol depended on him keeping up a carefree, jet-setting lifestyle. But if she ever found out his real reason for being here, she would have to know that for once, someone was actually putting her welfare first.

"Hillary, it's not nice to call me scum."

"I'm sorry, really, but you must be if you're drawn to me. Or maybe it's because I'm drawn to you." Her pupils widened again in response, just as they had right before he'd kissed her.

"Or maybe you're just going through lots of frogs until you find your prince."

Her laughter reached out to him on the night air. "You're mixing up your fairy tales. You're not a prince. You're Robin Hood."

He winced. "God, I hate being called that."

"Robin Hood's been a beloved fella throughout history." She toyed with a lock of her hair. "He took care of the less fortunate. Exposed corruption."

"He wasn't in it for the glory."

Her praise was making him itchy.

"So it's the adoration you object to." She tapped his wrist, already showing a bruise from where he'd first fought the handcuffs earlier. "That's actually rather honorable."

"Watch it. You're falling under my scummy spell."

"Right." She inched her hand away. "Thanks for the reminder."

"I just want to keep you safe from me." He winked.

She rolled her eyes. "I'm twenty-seven. It's time I looked out for myself."

"Does that mean you're going to stop fighting the notion of being my date for the weekend?" This whole weekend would be so much easier if she went with the flow. Easier, yes, but he also couldn't deny he found bantering with her exciting.

Intoxicating.

"I thought the auction was for tonight?"

"No, you didn't." He took her hand again. "But nice try." He kissed the inside of her wrist, lingering.

Her throat moved with a long swallow. She shot to her feet. "About the weekend, I do have to work. I can't spend every waking moment with you."

"I'll just hang out while you work. I can even sample some pâté, give you my opinion on petits fours. My friends say I'm quite enlightened." He slid his arm around her shoulders, pulling her against him so quickly she forgot to protest. "I'm amazingly footloose, too much money and not enough to do. So I'm all yours."

"That's not a good idea." As they moved away from the table and entered the hallway, she glanced over her shoulder, back at the ballroom.

"Why not?" Because if the way they'd danced together was any indication, they could be very, very good together.

She weaved past two women whispering on their way to the restroom, jewel-encrusted clutch purses in hand. "You'll be bored."

He stopped in front of the gilded elevator and jabbed the up button. "Let me make that call. I really can help you, you know." He chose his words carefully, so she would think he meant the chefs, but so she would also realize he could get her more access overall. "If you're with me, you will meet more people, make more connections for your entertaining business."

She looked up at him through narrowed eyes. "Do you think everyone's Machiavellian?"

"I *know* they are," he answered without so much as blinking. "And knowing that makes life easier."

"Troy?" She touched his silk scarf lightly, her blue eyes darkening with…sadness? "That's no way to live your life."

She swayed into him, and he wondered how the hell he'd gotten closer to her at the moment he'd been trying the least. Something about Hillary Wright had him off balance, as it had from the start.

Right now, he wanted nothing more than to head up to his penthouse suite and make love to her all night long. To tell her again and again how damn perfect she was. To show her she could trust he was one hundred percent into her. That he was a man who didn't want to take anything from her. He just wanted to give.

The elevator slid open.

Colonel Salvatore stood alone inside, mirrors capturing his scowling reflection. He held Hillary's little black clutch bag in one big fist. "I've been looking for the two of you."

Four

Hillary's high heels darn near grew roots into the plush carpet as she stared at Colonel Salvatore glowering at her from the elevator.

She couldn't seem to make herself move forward and end this evening with Troy. An amazing evening. Unconventional, sure, but fun. He'd surprised her with an engaging mix of arrogance, humor, intelligence and perception.

Plus, he kissed like molten sin.

She forced her feet to drag forward without pitching on her face. Inside the elevator, she held out her hand for her thrift-store purse. "I must have left it at the auction. Thank you for keeping it safe."

Silently, Troy stepped in after her, and she realized he must be curious about Salvatore even though he'd written off the man as her "uncle" just before he'd whisked her away to dance. She searched for the words to explain without saying things she shouldn't.

"Troy, this is my friend, Colonel—"

"No need, Ms. Wright," Salvatore interrupted. "Troy and I know each other well."

Something dark in his voice, an undercurrent she didn't comprehend, sent shivers down her spine. She looked from one man to the other. Troy slid in the key card to access the penthouse floor and the colonel kept his hands behind his back. She reached to press the button for her floor.

Salvatore shook his head as the doors slid closed. "We're all going together. It's time the three of us had a talk."

Together?

Ding. Ding. Ding. The floors went past.

These two men more than just known each other. Suddenly she realized that Troy was somehow tied into her reason for being here. Given his sketchy background could he be part of Barry's mess, too? Her stomach plummeted even as the elevator rose.

Although she could swear she'd never seen him with her ex-boyfriend. So many questions and fears churned through her head, stirring up anger and a horrible out-of-control feeling. All her life, she'd tried to play by the rules. She'd worked hard to get ahead and somehow she kept screwing up.

The elevator dinged a final time, opening to a domed hallway with brass sconces and fresh flowers. A door loomed on either side, leading to two penthouses. Troy angled left, guiding them inside the three-room suite that sported a 1920s Great Gatsby opulence.

Any other time she would have enjoyed examining the tapestry upholsteries and dark polished woods—not to mention the breathtaking view from a wall of windows overlooking the Windy City. Skyscrapers and the lake blended together in a mix of modern prosperity with a layer of history. She loved cities, craved the bustle and excitement—the ultimate contrast to how she'd grown up. She rubbed the silver cow charm on her purse and turned to face the two men.

Colonel Salvatore paced with his hands behind his back, his heavy steps making fast tracks over the Persian carpets in the living area. Troy leaned lazily on the bar, flipping a crystal drink stirrer between his fingers.

The silence stretched until Hillary was ready to pull her hair out. "Will someone please tell me what's going on?"

"Fine." Salvatore stopped abruptly. "I expected better from both of you. While you two were playing footsie on the balcony, our guy was slipping away. My sources say he left sometime this evening and is probably already on a private jet out of the country."

Her legs folded and she sank onto the edge of a camel-backed sofa. "*Our* guy?"

Pivoting sharply, Salvatore pinned Troy with a laser glare. "You really didn't tell her *anything* about your role here? Damn it, Donavan, why is it you chose now to follow the rules when you've rarely concerned yourself with keeping me happy in the past?" His sigh hissed between his teeth as he shifted his attention back to Hillary. "Troy Donavan's in Chicago for the same reason you are. To help ID Barry Curtis's associate."

Of course he was.

She'd known the truth on some level, from the moment those elevator doors slid open and Colonel Salvatore said he was looking for both of them. Except, up to the last second, she'd been holding out hope—foolish hope—that she was wrong. Apparently her bad-boy radar was in full working order.

Troy knew about her reason for being here and hadn't said a word to her. He'd made her believe he really wanted to spend time with her. She must have looked so ridiculous to him, talking about needing to see the chef. It had all been a game to him, playing along with her. Likely he'd been keeping this from her even on the airplane.

She forced her attention back to Salvatore's words. For better or worse, she still had to get through this weekend in order to reclaim her life.

"The guy we're after is insanely good at staying away from security cameras. It's as if he has an inside scoop. But I would still like the two of you to review the recordings of tonight's events, make use of Troy's exceptional tech skills and see if you can find even a glimpse."

She struggled to sort through so much information coming at her so fast. "Why do you need both of us to identify him?"

Troy snapped the crystal drink stirrer. "Yes, Colonel, please do enlighten us, because I've been wondering the same thing."

"Some things in life are on a need-to-know basis and neither of you need to know why I chose to play it this way. Troy, my tech guy has forwarded you all the security footage from tonight. I hope to hear good news from you both by morning." He nodded to Hillary. "Your luggage has already been brought here so you can change out of your formal wear."

Share a suite with Troy? She eyed the two doors leading to bedrooms. Where was the colonel staying? "And if we find who we're looking for in the video feed right away, we can all go home? This is over?"

"Troy will contact me in my suite across the hall. Once we've reviewed what you found, you'll be free to leave. If anyone sees you leaving the hotel, let the partiers here think you're spending your weekend together somewhere else."

"You're just sending Hillary back to D.C. unprotected after making her a target?" Troy snorted. "Think again."

A target? Surely, he was exaggerating.

"And don't you think she was every bit as much a target before? Helping us is her best shot at getting back a normal life. Good luck convincing her to do anything your way after the masterfully foolish way you've pissed her off," Colonel Salvatore shot over his shoulder before walking out the door.

The door clicked. Then clicked twice more as Troy secured all of the locks, sealing her inside with him.

Hillary shot to her feet and charged over to the panoramic window, suddenly claustrophobic and needing to embrace the open space of the outside. "I can't believe I was such an idiot."

Troy walked up beside her, hands stuffed in his tuxedo pockets. He didn't look surprised. And why not? He'd been playing her from the start.

"Damn you, Troy Donavon." She smacked her palm on the glass. "I was kicking myself for falling for your act on the plane. I knew better than to trust you, and still I bought into your line of bull only a few hours later. You must have been laughing the whole time at how gullible I was."

"Hey, I'm the good guy. There's nothing wrong with your instincts." Broken stirrer in hand, he tapped the glass right by her hand. "And I can promise I was never laughing at you. I just wanted to keep you safe."

She folded her arms over her chest. "How are you a good guy? I'm working with the colonel to get myself out of trouble because of a stupid choice I made in who I trusted. If the colonel's coercing you to be here as well, that isn't exactly a vote of confidence for the man to keep me safe."

"Let's just say he's a friend and he needed my help—

all of which I'm sure he will confirm." Troy leaned closer, the heat of him reaching out to her in the air-conditioned suite. "When I saw you and realized what you were walking into, I thought you could use some… reinforcements."

"But you lied to me. Again, after the auction." And that hurt, too much for someone she'd just met. "On the dance floor, and every second on the balcony when you didn't tell me you knew why I'm here. When you kissed me. You lied by not explaining you're here for the same reason. You played me for a fool."

His deep green gaze glinted with so much sincerity it hurt. "I wasn't playing you, and I never, never thought you were foolish. My only concern from the second I saw you on the plane has been protecting you from any fallout."

"And seducing me? Is that part of protecting me?" The memory of his kiss steamed through her so tangibly she could swear it might fog the window.

He stepped closer. "Protecting you and being attracted to you don't have to be mutually exclusive."

She pressed a hand to his chest to stop him, that damn silk scarf of his teasing her fingers, making her burn to tug him even nearer. "Doesn't that break some kind of code of ethics?"

"I'm not a cop or detective or military guy or even a James Bond spy." He tossed aside the broken drink stick he'd been holding and pressed his hand over hers. "So, no. Seducing you doesn't interfere with my ethics."

"You're just…what? Please do explain." She stared into his eyes, hoping to find some window into his soul, some way to understand what was real about this whole crazy evening with him.

"I'm a concerned citizen with the power to help out, as you are." His voice rang true, but there was a cadence to his answer that sounded too practiced. There had to be something more to his story, to why he was here. But from the set of his jaw, clearly he didn't intend to tell her.

"Then *why* did you kiss me?" To have that toe-curling moment tainted was just the final slap.

"Because I wanted to. I still do." He didn't lean in, but his fingers curved around hers until their hands were linked. The connection between them crackled all over again, even without the kiss.

God, what was wrong with her?

She snatched her hand away. "Well, that's damn well never going to happen again." She backed away from him and his too-tempting smile. "Would you please set up your computer while I change? We have work to do. I would like to finish as fast as possible so we can say goodbye to each other and to this whole horrible mess."

Hillary locked herself in the spare bedroom and sagged back against the six-paneled door. Crystal knob in hand, she propped herself up. But just barely.

As if the day hadn't promised to be stressful enough, she'd been blindsided by Troy again and again.

She scanned the room, her temporary sanctuary with flock fleur-de-lis wallpaper and a dark mahogany bed. Whereas the sitting area had been wide-open with a wall of windows, this room was heavily curtained, perfect for sleeping or curling up in a French, art deco chaise by the fireplace.

For now, she needed to focus on her suitcase, which rested on an antique luggage rack at the end of the carved four-poster bed. She pitched her clutch bag on the duvet and sifted through what she'd packed for something appropriate to wear. What did a person choose for an evening with a guy she wanted, but needed to hold at arm's length? Confidently casual, with a hint of sparkle for her bruised pride—

Her phone vibrated inside her clutch, sending the purse bouncing along the mattress. She raced to grab the cell—and saw her sister Claudia's phone number.

Claudia had stayed in Vermont with her husband and her three kids, where she taught school and watched out for their mother. Her older sister was the "perfect" person, the strong one who met life on her own terms. She never hid from anything or anyone. She admired her sister and her ability to let go of the past enough to move smoothly into her own future.

Claudia would have never been fooled by someone like Barry.

Hillary thumbed the on button. "Hello, Claudia."

"Is that all you have to say? *Hello, Claudia?*" her sister said with more humor than worry. "Hillary Elizabeth Wright, why haven't you returned all seven of my calls?"

She tucked the phone under her chin and unzipped the side of her evening gown. "I've only been gone a day. There's no need to freak out."

"And what a day you've had, sister," Claudia said, pausing for what sounded like a sip of her ever-present Diet Coke. "You should have told me."

"Told you what?" She shimmied down her dress and kicked it to the side in a pool of black satin.

"That you know Troy Donavan—*the* Troy Donavan, Robin Hood Hacker, billionaire bad boy."

Hillary stopped halfway stepping into her jeans. "What are you talking about? I don't *know* him."

Now who was quibbling with the truth? But she needed to stall and gather her thoughts.

"Then you have a doppelganger, because there are

photos of you with him all over the media. Your Google numbers are through the roof."

Oh great.

Of course they were. She should have known. She yanked her pants on the rest of the way. "I just met him earlier today."

Was it only one day?

"Nuh-uh, sister dear. That story's not flying. He bid a *hundred thousand dollars* for a weekend with you?"

"Eighty-nine-thousand dollars, if you want to be technical." She tugged on a flowy pink poet's shirt. "The reporters must have rounded up."

"*Eighty. Nine. Thousand. Dollars.* Ho-lee crap. I can't get my husband to foot the bill for a waffle cone at the ice-cream shop."

"Billy's a great guy and you've been head over heels for him since you sat beside him in sophomore geometry class."

"I know, and I adore every penny-pinching part of him since he's so generous in other ways." Claudia purred over the phone not too subtly. "I'm just living vicariously through you for a minute. It's nice to fantasize about no mortgage and no diapers. So, spill it. I want deets. Now."

"It's crazy." Hillary fingered her silver chain belt link by link. "I'm sure he's just bored and I said no, which he took as a challenge."

"Then keep right on challenging him until you get some jewelry."

"That's an awful thing to say." She hooked the belt around her waist loosely.

"Ahh," her sister said knowingly. "You like this guy."

"No. I don't. I *can't.*" She flopped back on the four-poster bed, staring up at the intricately carved molding

around the tray ceiling. "I haven't known him long enough
to draw that kind of conclusion."

"That hot, is he?"

"Hotter."

"You lucky, lucky lady." Claudia paused for a long gulp
of her drink. "Did you have a crazy one-night stand with
him?"

"God, no." Hillary sat upright. "Since he bought this
weekend with me, sleeping with him would feel…cheap."

Still, her mind filled with images of lying back with
him on this broad bed until her fingers twisted in the lacy
spread.

"I hate to be the one to break it to you, but eighty-nine-
thousand dollars isn't cheap, sister."

"You know what I mean."

"I do. I'm just teasing." The phone crackled with the
sound of her shuffling the phone from one ear to the other.
"Would you have slept with him if there hadn't been the
infamous auction?"

"No. Definitely not." She hesitated. "I don't think so."

"Wow." Her sister's teasing tone faded. "He really has
gotten to you."

"He's—" a knock sounded on her door "—here. I need
to go."

"Call me. Just check in to let me know you're okay."
Claudia's voice dripped with big-sister concern. "It's been
a tough year for you."

"For all of us." Their father had died of a heart attack
in his sleep. Their mother was in rehab—again. And then
in her grief, Hillary had lost herself in a relationship with
Barry. It was time for luck to swing over to the positive
side. "Love you tons, but I gotta run."

She disconnected and reached for the door. Now, she

just had to make it through the whole night without thinking about how Troy's kiss brought her body to life in a way Barry's never had.

Love you tons.

Hillary's voice whispered in Troy's head as he watched her walk deeper into the suite's living room. Who had she been talking to on the phone while she changed clothes?

She'd been buttoned-up sexy in her power suit on the plane. She'd been gorgeously hot in her strapless black gown.

And now she was totally, approachably hot in tight jeans and a long pink poet's shirt with a slim silver chain belt resting low on her hips. She made comfy look damn good.

He pivoted away hard and fast, shoving up the sleeves on his button-down—he'd changed into jeans, too. On the coffee table, he'd fired up his laptop. Now he just needed to log on to the secure network to retrieve the colonel's video feed.

How like the old guy to make sure Hillary was royally pissed off before leaving her here for the rest of the night. Colonel Salvatore had definitely gotten his revenge over the auction stunt.

They'd played back-and-forth games like this since school. Troy would reprogram the class period alarms. The colonel extended evening study period by an hour, which pissed off Troy's classmates, who rained hell down on him in other ways.

Usually the mind games and power plays with Salvatore were fun. But not tonight. At least having Hillary here in his suite made it easier to keep an eye on her.

Troy called to Hillary without looking up from the keyboard, "I ordered coffee and some food in case it turns into a long night."

"I'll take the coffee but pass on the food. Let's not waste time." Her bare feet sounded softly along the Persian rugs. "We have a job to do."

"I've wired my laptop into the wide-screen TV so we don't have to hunch over a computer. The images will be larger, nuances easier to catch." He'd also run the pixilation through a new converter he'd been developing for use with military satellites.

"That looks high-tech, but it makes sense you would have the best toys."

Toys? He wasn't dealing in Little Tikes, but then he wasn't into bragging, either. He didn't need to.

His "toys" spoke for themselves. "You might want to reconsider the food. This will take a while. It's not like watching footage of the night once and we're done. There are different camera angles, inside and outside. We'll be reliving the night five or six times from different bird's-eye views."

"Are *we* on there?" She gripped the back of the chaise.

"We will be. Yes." Would she see how damn much she affected him? Good thing he was in control of what played across that screen.

"What about out on the balcony? The kiss? Is that one on camera for anyone to see?"

"I'm also fairly good at dodging security cameras when I choose." He glanced at her, took in every sleek line of her long legs as she walked to the room-service cart. "I can assure you. That moment was private."

Her footsteps faltered for a heartbeat. "Thank you for that much, at least."

"You're welcome." He grinned and couldn't resist adding, "Although, there's still the film of us dancing so close it's almost like we're—"

"I get the picture. Turn on the TV." She poured a cup

of coffee from the silver carafe, cradled the china in her hands and curled up on a vintage chaise.

He sat on the sofa, in front of his laptop. He split the TV screen into four views. "We can save time using the multiple views on some of the sparser scenes, then go back to single screen for the more populated cuts."

"Why is it that so few people have seen this guy?" She blew into her coffee.

"It's not that so few have seen him. It's that they're all afraid to talk." He fast-forwarded through four squares of empty halls, empty rooms. "You should be afraid, as well."

"Why aren't you?"

"I'm afraid for you. Does that count?"

He slowed the feed of cleaning and waitstaff setting up. Caterers. Florists. Just because their informant said the guy would be at the party didn't mean he couldn't be using a cover of his own. Troy clicked to zoom in on a face with the enhanced pixilation software that could even read the bar code still stuck to the bottom of a box of candles.

Glancing left, he checked for a reaction from Hillary, but nothing showed in her expression except pleasure over the sip of coffee. He took in the bliss in her eyes over a simple taste of java. What he wouldn't give to bring that look to her face. He turned back to the TV mounted over the fireplace.

Even keeping his attention on the screen and computer, he was still hyperaware of Hillary sitting an arm's reach away. Every shift on the chaise, every time she lifted the mug of coffee to her lips, he was in tune to it all.

The air conditioners kicked on silently, swirling the air around, mixing the smell of java with her fresh mint scent. Was it her shampoo or some kind of perfume? He could picture her in a bubbling bath with mint leaves floating around her....

"Troy?"

Her husky voice broke into his thoughts.

He froze the image on the screen. "Do you see something?"

"No, nothing. Keep running the feed." She set aside her china cup and saucer with a clink. "I'm just wondering... How did you meet up with Colonel Salvatore? And please, for once, be honest the first time I ask a question."

She wanted to talk while they watched and worked? He was cool with that. He could share things that were public knowledge. "The colonel was the headmaster at the military boarding school I was sent to as a teenager. He's since retired to...other work."

"You still stay in touch with him?"

"I do." As did a few other select alumni. "Let's just say I'm obligated to him for the life I lead now, and he's calling in a favor."

She slid from the chaise and walked to the room-service cart. She rolled it closer to him and poured *two* cups.

A peace offering?

She set down a cup and saucer beside his computer. "What was your high school like?"

"Imprisoning." He didn't bother telling her about his no-liquids-around-computers rule, especially when the computer was equipped with experimental software worth a disgustingly large amount of money. Instead, he lifted the cup and drained half in one too-hot gulp.

"I meant, what was school like, what was your life like before you were sent to reform school?"

"Boring." He drank the rest of the coffee and set aside the empty china.

"Is that why you broke into the DOD's computer system?" She sat beside him, her drink on her knee. "Because you were bored?"

"That would make me a rather shallow person."

"Are you?"

"What do you think?"

On the screen, the auction area began to fill. He manipulated the focus to capture images of people with their backs to the cameras, reflections in mirrors, glass and even a crystal punch bowl.

She leaned forward, her slim leg alongside his. "I believe you're probably a genius and a regular academic environment may not have been the right place for you."

"My parents sent me to the best private schools—" again and again, to get kicked out over and over "—before I went to the military academy."

"You were bored there, too."

Did she know she'd inclined closer to him?

"Teachers did try," he said, working the keyboard with one hand, draping his other arm over the back of the sofa. "But they had a class full of students to teach. So I was given lots of independent studies."

"Computer work." She set her cup on the far end of the coffee table. "Alone?"

Hell, yes, alone. All damn day long. "The choice was that or be a social outcast in a class with people five or more years older."

She tapped the pause key on his laptop and turned toward him. "Sounds very lonely for a child."

"My social skills weren't the best. I was happier alone."

"How could the teachers and your parents expect your social skills to improve if they isolated you?" Her eyes went deep blue with compassion.

He didn't want her pity. Frustration roiled over how she'd managed to slip past his defenses, to pry things out of him that he usually didn't share. He snapped, "Would you like to tutor me?"

She flinched. "You seemed to have mastered the art of communication just fine."

Anger was his fatal flaw. Always had been. He leveled his breathing. "I have the brotherhood to thank for the social skills."

And the anger management.

"The brotherhood?"

He reached for the keyboard again, setting the screen back into motion, losing himself in the technology of manipulating the image. "Military reform school was a sentence, sure, but I found my first friends there. They were people like me in a lot of ways. I learned how to be part of a pack."

"Military reform school—so they had issues, too?"

"You mean criminal records."

"I'm not judging." She leaned back until her hair slithered along his arm. "Just asking."

Was she flirting? What was her angle? Why was she asking more about him? Regardless, he wouldn't miss out on the chance to reel her in, and perhaps win back her trust.

"A lot of the guys in the school were there because they wanted a military education prior to going into the service." He wrapped a lock around his finger, unseen behind her back. "Some of us were *sent* there to learn to be more self-disciplined."

Touching her hair, just her hair and nothing more, required all the self-control he'd ever gained. But nothing could will away the blood surging south, the hot pounding urge to undress her.

"And you formed a brotherhood with those people, rebels like yourself?"

"I did." That much he could say honestly, and without

mentioning the whole Salvatore/Interpol connection. "To-gether, we learned how to play within the rules."

She nodded toward the image of him on the runway at the bachelor auction, taking the mic and crowing to the audience about how he'd played them. "You don't look particularly conformist to me."

"You should have seen me back in the day." Hair always too long for regs and an attitude he'd worn like his own personal uniform.

"Do you have pictures of yourself from that time stored somewhere on this computer?" She leaned forward and he let go of her hair quickly.

"Sealed under lock and key. Trust me, you'll never find any old yearbook photos of me."

"Hmm…"

She went silent again, and he wondered what she was thinking. He clicked the computer keys to freeze on the frame of the ballroom filling the screen. She leaned her head on his shoulder.

His body went harder, if that was even possible. He almost reached to pull her over, kiss her again, tuck her underneath him and—

"Troy, there's a photo of me sitting on the Easter Bunny's lap."

What? She was giving him conversational whiplash. "What's so bad about that?"

"I was thirteen."

"Aww…" Now he understood. She'd been trying to make him feel better by sharing her own secret embarrassment. So sweet, he didn't have the heart to tell her he'd left those concerns behind him a long time ago. "Your mom made you."

"Hell, no." She froze the image again and angled sideways to face him full-on. "I was there because I wanted to believe. In the Easter Bunny. In Santa. In the Tooth Fairy. I was teased in school until I learned it was best to keep some things to myself. There wasn't a Sisterhood of the Tooth Fairy at my junior high."

God, she was freaking amazing. After all the ways he'd lied to her, quibbled, maneuvered, whatever, she was still worried about him being hurt by some slights back when he was a kid.

He gathered up a fistful of her hair. "You really are too awesome for your own good."

"Compliments will not get me into your bed," she said, her lips moving so close to his they were almost touching.

His fingers tangled in her hair, he stared into her blue eyes, which were deepening with awareness. "What if I came to *yours*?"

Five

The feel of his hand in her hair, his fingers rubbing firm circles against her scalp, offered a sensual mixture of setting her nerves on fire and melting her all at once. Right now, she wanted to be the type of person who could just lean into him for more than a kiss and damn the consequences. She wanted to do something she'd never done before—have a one-night stand with a virtual stranger. He was so close their breath mingled until she couldn't tell if the coffee scent came from him or from her.

"I told you we were never going to kiss again."

"I heard you. I was there, remember? While I enjoy the hell out of kissing you, it's not mandatory for going to bed together. Admit it," he growled softly, "you're tempted."

"I'm tempted to eat all the marshmallows out of a box of Lucky Charms, but that doesn't mean I intend to do it."

"Never?" he challenged.

"Okay," she conceded. "Maybe I did it once. Doesn't mean that was a smart thing to do."

"Then how about a kiss just for a kiss's sake, so you can prove to me whatever we felt downstairs was a fluke."

A fluke? Oh, she already knew what she'd felt, and it was real. That didn't mean she intended to jump into bed with a guy just because the kiss rocked her socks. Perhaps that was the lesson Mr. Have It All needed to learn. She could turn the tables, knock him off balance with a mind-numbing kiss and show him she could—and would—still walk away. Excitement pooled low in her belly at the thought. She trailed her fingers along his forehead, over the eyebrow with a slash of a scar through it, then cupped his jaw in her hands.

With slow deliberation, she took his bottom lip between her teeth, tugging before teasing her tongue along his mouth. His eyes glinted emerald sparks of desire, and then she didn't see anything. Her eyes closed, she sealed herself to him, her mouth, her chest, her hungry hands and hungrier body.

This kiss was different than the reserved connection on the balcony where there'd been the threat of interruption. Here, they were alone. She was free to explore the breadth of his shoulders, the flexing muscles in his arms as he hauled her close.

Her breasts pressed against the hard wall of his chest. Her nipples tightened to needy buds against him, hot and achy, yearning for the soothing stroke of his tongue. A tingling spread inside her, so intense it almost hurt. She wriggled to get even closer, shifting to sit on his lap, straddling him. And...

Oh. My. She arched into him, against the rigid length of his arousal pressing so perfectly against her.

A purr of pleasure clawed up her throat, echoed by his

growl of approval. Apparently this was a language optional make-out session.

His hands slid from her hair, roved down her back and slid under her bottom. In a fluid move, he flipped her onto her back and stretched over her on the sofa. The weight of him felt good, so very good, intensifying every pulsing sensation. The fabric of the sofa rubbed a sweet abrasion against her tingling nerves.

She hooked a leg over his, throwing back her head as he kissed along her jaw and over to her ear. His hot breath caressed her skin with the promise of how good that mouth would feel all over her body. She tipped her face, shaking her hair back and giving him fuller access as he tugged on her earlobe with his teeth. In an out-of-control moment, she flung out an arm to steady herself. Her fingers clenched the coffee table—

Sending her full china cup clattering to the ground.

Troy froze, then looked to the side sharply before sweeping his computer away from the spilled coffee. The rush of air along her overheated body brought a splash of much-needed reason. What the hell was she doing? She'd only just met the guy and already she'd kissed him twice. She'd wanted to show him how she could kiss and walk away, and she'd ended up beneath him.

Gasping, she swung her feet back to the ground, her toes digging into the plush Persian cotton. The rush back to earth was slower than she expected; her senses were still on tingling alert. Giving in to the temptation to kiss him hadn't been her best idea. She should be focused on the video feed, on finding Mr. Mystery Cohort as soon as—

Squinting, she studied a far corner of the screen, just a hint of a flashy gold ring that looked familiar, with some kind of coin embedded on the top. The fog of passion parted enough for her to process what was right in front of her eyes.

"Troy, hold on a second." She grabbed his shoulder. Her fingers curled instinctively around him for a second before she pulled back.

"What's wrong?" He looked over his shoulder.

"On the TV, can you play with the image for me? There…" She pointed to the top left corner as he righted his computer and sat again. "Can you find a reflection of the face of that guy wearing the ugly gold ring?"

"Of course I can." He dropped back onto the sofa with his laptop, his hair still askew from her frenzied fingers. She seriously needed to rein in her out-of-control emotions.

She clenched her fists against the temptation to finger comb his hair back into place and focused her attention forward. In a flash, the picture zoomed in, with a clarity that boggled her mind. Whatever software he had beat the hell out of anything she'd seen on *Law & Order* reruns. The picture moved and inverted as he shuffled the views, pulling up reflections off a number of sources until…

Bingo.

"That's him," Hillary said, standing and walking closer even though she didn't need any further confirmation. "That's Barry's business partner."

Two hours later, Troy leaned in the open doorway to Hillary's room as she packed her small suitcase.

After she had ID'd the face in the video feed, they'd contacted Salvatore. Troy had only caught one glimpse of Barry Curtis's cohort at a regatta race in Miami, but he agreed the face fit what he remembered. Now Salvatore was off making his calls to contacts. Since they had a face to run through international visual recognition systems, hopefully soon they would have a name. An honest to God lead, a trail to follow. They would have the guy in custody soon.

But in the interim, Troy needed to make sure no backlash came Hillary's way for bringing down a multibillion-dollar international money laundering operation. He needed to keep her in his sights. And lucky for him, thanks to the bachelor auction, going their separate ways wasn't going to be that easy to accomplish. Aside from the fact that everyone in that ballroom had seen them together, the tabloids had snapped photos that were already circulating around the blogosphere. Follow-ups would come their way, questions on how they'd spent their weekend together. She couldn't just duck out of sight, and he couldn't let her stand alone and vulnerable in the spotlight.

He had to admit, time with Hillary would not be a hardship in the least.

Thanks to a pair of killer high heels, her already-amazing legs looked even more train-stopping. Her black tank top and wide belt drew his eyes to every curve he'd felt pressed against him earlier. Curves he was determined to explore at length someday in the not-too-distant future.

He might be completely the wrong man for a rose-colored glasses chick, but that last kiss from Hillary made it impossible for him to turn away. She would be his. The only question was when.

Now that their first goal of the weekend had been accomplished, he would have time with her to figure that out. She might think she was going home to D.C., but he had other plans. He just needed to persuade her.

Hillary flicked her damp ponytail over her shoulder. "What's wrong, Troy? Aren't you happy? We helped them identify the guy." She zipped her roll bag closed. "He won't be able to rip people off anymore. You delivered justice today."

"He's not in custody, and he's smart." Troy shoved away from the door, taking her question as an invitation to enter her bedroom in the shared suite. "If he realizes you're the one who identified him… No, I'm not ready to celebrate yet."

"I'll be fine." Her confidence was hot.

Too bad it was also misguided.

"You're too damn naive about this. You're going to take time off from work and come with me. I know a great, low-profile place where you can put your feet up and relax until this all blows over."

"That he-man act may work with some women, but not with me. I'm going home. The whole reason I came to Chicago was to ID this guy so I could go back to the job I love." She hefted up her suitcase.

He thought about taking the bag from her, but a tug-of-war would likely make her pull back all the more. He sat on the end of the chaise by the window. "You can't return to D.C. Not yet. You need to lie low until the authorities bring him in."

"That's a rather open-ended timeline." She dropped the bag to the ground and sat on it. "I can't just duck out of my life indefinitely."

Good. At least she wasn't walking out the door. "The colonel assures me it will be a week, two weeks tops. Take emergency leave—say you've got a sick mother."

"Sick mom? Really?" She crossed her feet at the ankles. "You think up lies easily."

"Say whatever the hell you want." He tapped the toe of her high heels with his Ferragamo-clad foot. "But let me help."

"No, thanks." She tapped him right back. "I can take my own vacation without you."

His foot worked up to her ankle. "Can you just walk away from this?"

Her lashes fluttered for an instant before she said, "It's just physical reaction."

"Is that such a bad thing?"

"It can be." She pulled her foot back and crossed her legs.

Gorgeous legs. Miles long. The sort made for wrapping around a man's waist.

"Then come away with me for a week, err on the side of caution." He winked. "I promise to come through for you."

"Argh!" She stomped both heels on the carpet. "Can't you just talk to me? Drop the charming, polished act and just speak."

His grin spread. "You think I'm charming?"

She shot to her feet and grabbed her bag by the handle. "Forget it—"

He stepped in front of her. "I'm sorry. I just... I don't want you to leave. What the hell do you want from me?"

"Honesty. Why are you pushing so hard when this is already settled? Our work here is done, and I'm not a defenseless kid."

"Hillary, damn it..." He struggled for the words to convince her when she'd hamstrung him by telling him not to use any charm. Kissing her again wouldn't gain him any traction right now, either. "You confuse the hell out of me. I'm worried about you, and hell, yes, I want to make love to you on the beach in every continent. But I also want time with you."

"Honestly?"

"As truthful as I know how to be. Spend a week with

me. Be safe. Get me out of your system so you can return to your regular life without regrets."

"What makes you think you're in my system?"

"Really? Are you going to look me in the eye and tell me you don't feel the attraction, too? And before you answer, remember I was there when we kissed."

"Okay, I'll admit there's…chemistry."

"Explosive chemistry, but it's clear neither one of us is ready for something long-term. So let's let whatever this is between us play out before we return to our regular lives."

She studied his face, and he could have sworn she swayed toward him. But it was just her head moving back and forth.

"I can't, Troy. I'm sorry." She backed away, pulling her roller bag with her. "I'm going home to Washington, to my normal, wonderfully *boring* life."

Ouch.

There wasn't a comeback for that.

Stunned, he watched her walk away. She was actually leaving, opting for her everyday job in D.C. rather than signing on for the adventure of following their attraction wherever it led. Some might call it ego for him to be so stunned, but honest to God, he was floored by the power of their attraction. He knew it wasn't one-sided. That she would turn her back on the promise of something so unique, so fantastic—so very much *not* boring— blew him away.

He wasn't sure exactly why it was so important to him that he follow her. The attraction. Keeping her safe. The challenge of her saying no. Maybe all three reasons.

Regardless, she'd vastly underestimated him if she thought they were through. If she wouldn't come with him then he would simply have to make do with helping her hide out in the nation's capital.

* * *

She'd actually done it. She'd walked away from Troy Donavan.

That made her either the strongest woman in the world—or the most afraid. Because the thought of spending the next week or two with Troy was the scariest and most tempting offer she'd ever received. Walking away hadn't been easy, and she still didn't know if that made her decision to do so right or wrong.

Her roller bag jammed in the revolving door.

Figured.

She yanked and yanked until finally the door bounced back and released her suitcase. Freed, she stepped outside the hotel, scanning for a cab. She would worry about the expense of changing her ticket return date later.

Of course it was raining, turning an already-muggy early morning all the more humid and dank and overcast. Four more aggressive commuters snagged cabs before her. Exhausted, frustrated and close to tears, she sat on her suitcase again.

"Need a ride?"

Hillary almost fell off the bag.

"Colonel Salvatore?" She steadied herself—darn heels she'd vainly chosen because of Troy. "I'm just trying to catch a cab to the airport."

Her eccentric contact again wore a gray suit and red tie, his buzz-cut hair exposed to the elements. She couldn't help but think about Troy's linen fedora and all the thin-brimmed hats he wore in the photos of him that filled the press.

"Then let me take you. I owe you that, as well as arranging for your change in flight plans."

Resisting would be foolish, and she really did need to leave before she raced back up to Troy's suite—which she couldn't even do since she didn't have a penthouse key card. "Thank you. I gratefully accept."

A driver was already opening the doors to a dark SUV with tinted windows. She slid inside for what had to be the most awkward car ride of her life. Colonel Salvatore didn't speak for their whole drive through the city to Chicago's O'Hare International. He simply typed away on his tablet computer. After five minutes of silence, she focused her attention on final views of the city slicked with rain. Who knew when or if she would return?

Her eyes drifted over to study the colonel, the former headmaster of Troy's military high school. Troy had said he "helped out" but how deeply did that connection go? She'd been working with local authorities when she met the colonel.... None of it mattered. Time to put the past— Barry— behind her and start fresh.

Right?

But once they reached the airport, the SUV didn't stop at the terminal. "Colonel?"

Holding up a hand, he focused on whatever he was working on at the moment.

"Sir," she pressed as the muffled sound of jet engines grew louder, closer, "where are we going?"

He clapped the cover closed on his tablet. "To the private planes. I'm taking a personal jet."

"But I'm going to D.C. Regular coach status is okay with me."

"You have options."

"I've done what you asked me. It's time for me to go home."

"Troy will follow you because he's convinced you need watching until we have everything neatly tied up."

A thrill shot through her before she could steel herself,

an unstoppable excitement over the thought of seeing him again after all. "He's free to go where he chooses."

"Or you could go with him to someplace…different."

Confusion cleared, like the mist rolling away to reveal the line of private jets beyond the colonel's. "He's in one of those planes, isn't he? Is it his personal aircraft or is he waiting inside yours?"

"You're a quick one. Good. Troy needs someone sharp to keep up with him." He nodded toward the row of silver planes nestled in the morning mist. "Mine's next in line, and yes, the one closest is Troy's private aircraft."

"You expect me to just hitch a ride with him? Don't I need to check in or something?"

"I've okayed everything with the pilot. You have your luggage with you." He smiled for the first time. "Admit it. You're tempted to spend time with him. So why not go away with him for a week?"

She bristled at his confidence. "You're awfully sure of yourself."

"Just hedging my bets," he said so matter-of-factly that they could have been discussing breakfast—not the idea of her hopping on a near stranger's plane to go God only knew where.

"You have an answer for everything."

"I study people and make calculated decisions based on how I believe they will react." He straightened his already-impeccable red tie.

"And you're calling me predictable." How could he when she didn't even have a clue what to do next?

"I just bargained on you doing the right thing for Troy."

"The right thing for *Troy?*" That brought her up short. "What are you talking about?"

"I gave you credit for being smarter than this."

She leveled a steady gaze at him and wished she could

wield something a little harsher. She was at the end of her patience here, exhaustion and emotional turmoil having worn her out. "You're not a very nice man."

"But I'm effective."

"Please, get to your point," she snapped. "Or I am leaving."

"I have to agree with Troy that life would be easier and less complicated for all of us if the two of you took a remote vacation. Running around D.C. is too obvious a place for you to be when there is a rich and powerful individual still at large who has reason to be quite unhappy with you and Troy. And if Troy follows you straight to your home, anyone who might be upset over this sting will be able to find Troy, too…. Do I need to keep spelling out all the extremely uncomfortable scenarios for you?"

Her skin went cold. She'd been worried about her future—as in her freedom—but she'd never considered that white-collar criminals might resort to force. "You're not playing fair. And what did you plan to do with me once I ID'd the guy? Did you have a plan to keep me safe?"

"I had hoped we would have the man in custody, and when he got away, I assumed you would be leaving with Troy, based on seeing the two of you together."

The attraction was that obvious to others? "Well, you guessed wrong, and now you're telling me *I'm* responsible for Troy's safety? That's your job, isn't it?"

"I'm doing my job right now. I'm saying what has to be said, for both of your sakes. Get on his plane. By letting him think he's protecting you, you'll be protecting him."

She hesitated.

His eyes flickered with the first signs of something other than calculation or cool disdain. He looked like he actually…cared. "Ms. Wright, please, be the first person in Troy's life to put his interests ahead of your own."

His words sucker punched the air right out of her.

Whether or not his words were genuine or calculated, he'd found a means of coercion so much stronger than force. For whatever reason, she had a connection to Troy, a man she'd only known for a day. He had an influence over her emotions that she couldn't explain.

Maybe it was because she understood what it was like not to have anyone put her first in their lives. Or maybe it was the memory of all he'd told her about his time in school. Or maybe it was that she wanted more kisses.

Whatever the reason, she was climbing on board that airplane.

Dropping his hat on his head, Troy slid from the limo outside his aircraft just as the colonel boarded his Learjet. Ironic. Apparently everyone was getting the hell out of Dodge.

He tugged out his briefcase and jogged through the light rain to the stairs. Once he made it inside, he would need to confer with the pilot about changing their flight plan, rerouting for D.C.

Even with the delay, at least he could work since his plane was a fully outfitted office and completely familiar. He'd built a pod he could move from the hold of any aircraft to another, with an office, a small kitchenette and sleeping quarters. Some seemed surprised at the lack of luxury, but he didn't need the trappings. He had what was important to him: his own portable technological nirvana.

He ducked through the hatch inside and stopped short.

Hillary. Here. On his private jet.

She lounged at his desk, her iPad open in front of her. Early-morning sunrise streamed through a window and outlined her in an amber glow.

Amber glow?

Good God, this woman was turning him into some kind of a poet.

She spun the chair to face him. "I assume that was an open invitation to go with you, but don't gloat. It's not an attractive trait."

He placed his briefcase on the white leather sofa and pulled his hat off. "Well, I certainly wouldn't want to do anything that would make me unappealing to you."

"Good. We're on the same page then." She returned to her iPad and started typing.

"Everything okay?" He resisted the urge to offer her one of the tablets he had on board, prototypes beyond anything the public had seen yet.

"I'm sending a couple of emails to rearrange things at work so I can take an emergency vacation for personal reasons." She looked up. "I'm not comfortable with a convenient 'my mom is sick' lie."

"Fair enough." He placed his hat on his desk in front of her.

She closed her iPad. "Just so we're clear, I'm here for safety's sake. Not for sex."

God, the spark in her eyes made him hot. Although now might not be the best time to point that out.

"Can't be much clearer than that."

"Good. Now where are we going?"

"Monte Carlo."

"Monte Carlo?" she squeaked, her composure slipping. "What about passports?"

"Taken care of. If you recall, when the CIA first questioned you, they required you to turn over your passport to ensure you wouldn't flee the country. Now that you're in the clear, you can have it back. We'll make a brief refueling stop in D.C.—your passport is already there waiting to be picked up." While Hillary talked, he pulled out his phone and typed instructions to his assistant and Salvatore to make sure her passport *would* be there.

"And what about clothes for me to be gone that long? Appropriate for that locale and weather?"

"Got it covered." He dashed off another text to his assistant before tucking his phone back inside his suit.

"You were that confident I would join you? I'm not sure I like being that predictable."

"Hillary, you are anything but predictable." He scooped up his hat and dropped it on her head, sliding his fingers along the brim.

"Why Monte Carlo?"

"Why not?" He tugged her by the hand to sit on the sofa beside him. He flicked the seat belt toward her and they both buckled in for takeoff.

"Do you live your life that way?" She touched his hat self-consciously. "With a perpetual why not?"

"Works for me." Right now, he was living for the day he saw her wearing that hat and nothing else.

"Why Monte Carlo?" she repeated.

Because he had backup there, and he needed help from someone he could trust. Sometimes, the brotherhood reached out to each other, without Salvatore in the mix. This would be one of those times.

Of all his military school friends, Conrad Hughes, the very first person he'd met on the first day of school, would understand how a woman messed with a man's head. Conrad wouldn't judge. "I'm touching base with a friend who can help cover our tracks. Ever been to Monte Carlo?"

She took off his hat and dropped it on his lap. "I went to Atlantic City once."

"Did you like it?"

"Yes, I did."

"Then you're in for a treat beyond anything the Tooth Fairy would shove under your pillow." He put his hat on, tugged it over his eyes and stretched out to nap.

Six

Monte Carlo was everything she'd imagined—and more.

They'd landed at an oceanside private airstrip near the Ports de Monaco, where a limo awaited them. A thrilling ride later, along the Mediterranean coastline, they'd arrived at a casino that overlooked a rocky cove and packed marina. The beige stucco resort, while clearly pristinely new, had a historical design with Roman columns and arches, statues and sculptures spotlighted in the moonless dark.

Deep inside, there were no windows, but plenty of lights so bright it was impossible to tell day from night. Troy walked through without stopping at the check-in desk. She didn't bother asking questions. She'd already seen how regular rules didn't seem to apply to him.

The air was filled with the cacophony of machines, bells, whistles and gambling calls, but more than that, she heard music, laughter and the splash of a mammoth fountain. Her high heels clicked along the marble mosaic tiles as she and Troy weaved through the crush of vacationers. A mix of languages came at her from all directions, a little like mingling in some of the D.C. parties she'd planned.

Except eyes followed them here. People whispered and pointed, recognizing Troy Donavan.

He pulled off his signature hat. "Let's try our luck once before we head up. Your choice. Cards? Roulette? Slots?"

Exhaustion took a backseat to excitement. Monte Carlo had been in her top ten fantasy places to visit as a kid. She'd researched it, dreaming of James Bond and Grace Kelly. But photos and movies and tabloids just didn't capture the vivid colors, clashing sounds, exotic scents. She'd even fantasized about a fascinating man on her arm, and the reality on that count far surpassed any dreams.

"I'm a little underdressed for cards or roulette." She swept her hands down her jeans.

"You're welcome anywhere I say you are."

Ooooh-kay. "I'm good with a slot machine."

"Fair enough." He guided her to a line of looming machines with high leather bar stools in front.

He offered his hand as she settled in place. Tokens? She'd totally forgotten about getting—

A woman in uniform stopped beside them, smiling at Troy. "*Bonjour,* Mr. Donavan," she said in heavily accented English. She passed him a leather pouch. "Compliments of the house. Mr. Hughes sends his regards."

"*Merci, mademoiselle.*" He opened the pouch and Hillary caught a glimpse of tokens, chips, key cards and cash. He pulled out a fistful of tokens and extended his open palm to Hillary.

"Only one token, thanks. For luck before we go to our rooms to freshen up."

Hillary plucked a single coin from his hand and hitched

up into the chair. *Ching,* she set the lights flashing and waited for the results.... Troy stood behind her, leaning in ever so slightly until his bay rum scent mixed with the perfume of live flowers.

She'd given up trying to understand how she could still be so drawn to, so aware of, a man she knew led a secret life and wouldn't hesitate to stretch the truth if he thought it was "for her own good." Here she was in Monte Carlo and all she could think about was how glad she was to be here with Troy. For the moment, at least, she would embrace the adventure. She would revel in the sensations and refuse to let herself get too attached.

The slot machine ended on a losing note, and she didn't even care. She was here, and her nerves all tingled as if she'd hit a jackpot.

Chemistry. What a crazy thing.

She smiled over her shoulder at him, which brought their mouths so close. She could see the widening of his pupils, see every detail of the scar through his eyebrow. Her breathing grew heavier but she couldn't seem to control the betraying reaction that gave away just how much she wanted his mouth on hers again. She froze, waiting for him to make a move....

He simply smiled and stepped back, offering his hand for her to slide from the high bar stool.

"Whenever you're ready," he said.

Her breath gushed out in a rush. Disappointment over that lost chance for a quick kiss taunted her. She put her hand in his. "Thanks. Or should I say *merci?*"

His hand warmed her the whole way to the elevator, which was made mostly of glass, for riders to watch the whole casino on the way up. Her stomach dropped as the lift rose. She'd always prided herself on being so practical in her plans for her life, but the way she wanted to be with Troy was completely illogical. And now they were as far away from Salvatore, chaperones and intrusions as possible.

What did she want from this time with him while they waited for the all clear from Salvatore?

The answer came to her, as clear as the elevator glass—so smudge-free she almost felt like she could walk right through and into the open air. She wanted to learn more about Troy—and yes, she wanted to sleep with him. She needed to sort through his charm to find out what was real about him, then figure out how to walk away without regrets and restless dreams once she returned home.

The elevator doors slid open as she once again headed to a hotel suite. With Troy.

He palmed her back and guided her into the luxurious, apartment-sized space with a balcony view of the marina. High ceilings and white furniture with powder-blue accents gave the Parisian-style room an airy feel after the heavier Gatsby tapestries of their Chicago penthouse. She stared out at the glistening waters as the bellhop unloaded their bags and slipped away quietly.

Troy walked through her peripheral vision. "Something to drink before we head down for dinner?"

"I didn't sleep at all last night and while you may have had an amazing nap on the plane—" damn his nonchalant soul "—I did not. I just want room service and a good night's rest. Can we 'do' Monte Carlo tomorrow when I'll be awake enough to enjoy it?"

"Absolutely." He tossed his hat on the sleek sofa before walking to the wet bar. "What would you like to drink?"

"Club soda, please," she answered automatically. "Thank you."

He poured the carbonated water into a cut crystal tumbler, clinking two cubes of ice inside. "That's not the first time you've turned down alcohol."

"I told you before." She took the glass from him, fingers brushing with an increasing familiarity. "I don't drink. Ever."

"Have I been around long enough to hear the story yet?" He rattled the ice in his own soda water.

Why not? It wasn't a secret. "My mother was an alcoholic who hit rock bottom so many times she should have had a quarry named after her."

"I'm very sorry."

"It's not your fault."

He brushed her shoulder, skimming back her ponytail. "I'm still sorry you had to go through that."

"I learned a lot about keeping up appearances." She sipped her drink and watched boats come in for the day and others head out with lights already blazing for night travel. "It's served me well in my current profession."

"That's an interesting way of making lemonade out of lemons."

Enough about her and her old wounds. The point of this time in Monte Carlo, for her, was to learn more about him.

She pivoted to face him, leaning against the warm windowpane. "What about you?"

"What do you mean?" he answered evasively.

"Your childhood? Tell me more about it."

"I had two parents supremely interested in appearances—which meant I never had to learn how to play nice. They were always ready to cover up any mistakes we made." His eyes glinted wickedly as he stared at her over his glass.

"Us?"

"My older brother and I."

"You have a brother? I don't recall—"

"Ahh…" He tapped her nose. "So you did read my Wikipedia page."

"Of course I did." She'd been trying to find some leverage, since this man tipped her world about seventeen times a minute. "It doesn't mention your brother."

"Those pages can be tweaked you know. The internet is fluid, rewritable."

She shivered from more than the air conditioner. "You erased your brother from your history?"

"It's for his own safety." He stared into his drink moodily before downing it.

"How so? What does your brother do now?"

"He's in jail." He returned to the bar and reached for a bottle of scotch—Chivas Regal Royal Salute, which she happened to know from event planning sold at about ten thousand dollars a bottle. "If the other inmates know the kind of connections he has, the access to money…"

She watched him pour the amber whiskey into a glass— damn near liquid gold. "What's he in prison for?"

"Drug dealing." He swirled his drink along the insides of the glass, just shy of the top, without spilling a drop.

"Did your parents cover up for him?"

"Periodically, they checked him into rehabs, before they took off for Europe or China or Australia. He checked himself out as soon as they left the continental U.S." He knocked back half an inch.

"You blame them."

"I blame him." He set down his glass beside the open bottle. "He made his own choices the same way I have made mine."

"But drug dealing… Drug addiction." She'd seen the fallout of addiction for the family members, and as much as she wanted to pour that ten-thousand-dollar bottle of booze down the sink, she also wanted to wrap her arms around Troy's waist, rest her head on his shoulder and let him know she understood how confusing and painful his home life must have been.

"Yes, he was an addict. He detoxed in prison." He looked up with conflicted, wounded eyes. "Is it wrong of me to hope he stays there? I'm afraid that if he gets out…"

Her unshed tears burned. She reached for his arm.

He grinned down at her wryly. "You and I probably shouldn't have children together. Our genes could prove problematic. Sure the kids would be brilliant and gorgeous." He stepped back, clearly using humor to put distance between them as a defense against a conversation that was getting too deep, too fast. "But with so much substance abuse—"

"Troy," she interrupted, putting her club soda down slowly. This guy was good at steering conversations, but she was onto his tactics now. "It's not going to work."

"What do you mean?"

"Trying to scare me off by saying startling things."

His eyes narrowed, and he stepped closer predatorily. "Does that mean you want to try and make a baby?"

She cradled his face in her hands, calling his bluff and standing him down, toe to toe. "You're totally outrageous."

"And you're outrageously hot." He rocked his hips against hers. "So let's have lots of very well-protected sex together."

She brushed her thumb over his mouth even though the gesture cost her. Big-time. Her body was on fire. "Abstinence is the best protection of all."

"Killjoy." He nipped the sensitive pad of her thumb before stepping back. "I'll go downstairs and leave you to your rest then. Order anything you want from room service. Everything you'll need is in your room. Enjoy a bubble bath. God knows, I'll be enjoying thinking of you in one."

He scooped up the bottle of Chivas on his way out of the suite.

Great. She'd won. And never had she felt more completely awake in her life.

He sure as hell wasn't going to get any sleep tonight, not with Hillary sleeping nearby.

Without question, he intended to make love to her. But not tonight. He had business to take care of, ensuring he covered their trail and that she was safely tucked away. Then, he would be free to seduce every beautiful inch of her taste by taste, touch by touch, without worry that some criminal would come looking for her.

First, he needed to find Conrad Hughes.

Luckily, the leather pouch included a key card to Conrad's private quarters. At last count, Conrad owned seven, but the one in his casino was his favorite and his primary residence since he'd split with his wife.

The second the elevator doors parted, Conrad was there, waiting. Of course he'd seen Troy coming. Nothing happened in this place without the owner knowing.

"Hello, brother." Conrad waved him inside, brandy snifter in hand. "Welcome to my little slice of heaven."

Conrad Hughes, Mr. Wall Street, and Troy's first friend at the military reform school, led him into the ultimate man cave, full of massive leather furniture and a gigantic television screen hidden behind an oil painting. There was a sense of high-end style like the rest of the place, but without the feminine frills.

Apparently, Conrad had stripped those away when he and his wife separated.

Troy held up the Chivas. "I brought refreshments."

"But you didn't bring your lady friend. I'm disappointed not to meet her."

"She's changing after our trip." Images of her in the spa tub were a helluva lot more intoxicating than anything in the top-shelf bottle he carried. "I figured this would be a good chance to speak with you on my own. Check in, catch up and whatnot."

They had a long history together—two of the three founding members of The Alpha Brotherhood.

Conrad had been a step away from juvie when they'd met in reform school. His crime? Manipulating the stock market, crashing businesses with strategic infusions of cash in competing companies, manipulating the rise and fall of share prices. He would have been hung out to dry by the court and the press, except someone stumbled on the fact that every targeted company had been guilty of using child laborers in sweatshops overseas.

Once the press got hold of that part of his case, he'd been lauded as a white knight. The judge had offered a deal similar to Troy's. Through the colonel's mentorship, they'd learned to channel their passionate beliefs about right and wrong. Now they had the chance to right wrongs within the parameters of the law.

Their friendship had lasted seventeen years. Troy trusted this man without question. And now was one of those times he would have to call upon his help.

His wiry, lanky buddy had turned into someone who looked more like a pro athlete these days than a pencil-pushing businessman. The women had always gone wild over Conrad's broody act—but he'd only ever fallen for one woman.

Conrad had gone darker these days, edging closer to the sarcastic bastard he'd been in the old days. A sarcastic bastard with dark circles under his eyes and a dining tray full of half-eaten food. His friend looked like he'd been to hell and back very recently.

Troy sprawled in a massive leather wingback chair across from Conrad. "I need to tuck Hillary away for a week or so, but I don't want anyone looking for us."

"Is this Salvatore-related or just a need for personal time with a lady friend?"

Conrad was one of the few people on the earth he could be completely honest with. "Started as the first, became both."

"Fine, I can handle things from this end."

Troy trusted Conrad to do what was asked, but he wasn't quite as clear on Conrad's methods, and these days, Troy was more careful about life. Right now more than ever, he couldn't afford to let his impulsive nature take over. Control was paramount.

"Want to share how you intend to do that?"

"Because you're worried I can't handle it? I'm hurt, brother, truly wounded." Conrad drained his drink and poured another.

"Because I want to learn from the master."

"Nice salve to my ego." He smirked. "But I get it. A woman's involved. You can't just leave it all to trust. I can cover for you."

He thumbed on the wide-screen TV and a video of Hillary with Troy at the slot machine played. "I assume this little snippet here was a public display for gossipmongers and the press or you would have used my secure, private entrance."

"Of course it was." He and Conrad had secret access to each other's homes around the world at any time. Yes, he had wanted people to see him with Hillary here, and he should have realized Conrad would have already intuited his plan. "Kudos to your security people for capturing my good side."

"My casino staff aims to please." Conrad cleared the screen. "I'll loop some reels on the security tapes of you, play with the technology so it looks like you're wearing different clothes on different days. My secretary will submit some photos to society pages. The world will think you're here kicking up your heels like a carefree playboy with his next conquest."

"Thanks." He stifled a wince at the word *conquest*. Somehow Hillary had become…more. "I appreciate your help."

"Your plane trip here will cement the story. It would help if you forwarded me some photos from the different airports."

"Consider it done." And that quickly, business was taken care of, which only left the personal stuff. "How are you, brother?"

"I'm good."

"You look like crap. Have you slept recently? Eaten a meal?"

"Who turned you into the veggie police?"

"Fair enough." Troy lifted his drink in a toast. "Just worried about how you're doing since you and Jayne split."

Even the woman's name made Conrad curse.

The breakup had been a surprise to everyone who knew them and so far neither of them was spilling details. Even the social pages had been strangely quiet on the issue and God knows, if either had been cheating, some telephoto lens would have caught something.

Not that his friend would have ever cheated on Jayne. The two had been crazy in love, but a restless traveler didn't work well with a white-picket-fence woman. And those middle of the night calls to assist Colonel Salvatore probably hadn't helped, either.

Conrad rolled his glass between his palms. "Jayne took a job in the States."

"She's a nurse, right?" he asked, more for keeping his friend talking than a need to know.

"Home health care. My altruistic, estranged wife is taking care of a dying old guy, even though she has millions in her checking account. Money she won't touch." His hands pressed tighter on the cut crystal until something had to give. Soon. "She hates me that much. But hey, by all means, don't let my catastrophe of a marriage turn you off of relationships. Not all of them end up slicing and dicing your heart."

He flung his glass into the fireplace, crystal shattering. He reached for the bottle.

"Dude, you really need to lay off the booze. It's making you maudlin."

"And mean. Yeah, I know." He set the bottle down again. "Let's play cards."

"Believe I'll pass tonight. I prefer not to have my ass handed to me." And truthfully, he was itching to get back to Hillary now that he'd taken care of business. But he couldn't leave until he was sure his buddy would be okay.

"You're no fun. And after I did you this great favor."

"Hey, we could play Alpha Realms IV."

"So you can hand me my ass? No, thanks." He thumbed the television back on. "What do you say we catch—"

A sound at the door cut him off short and they both shot to their feet. Hillary stood on the threshold with the leather pouch in her hands and a master access key card in her other hand. "Alpha Realms IV? Really? How old are you two? Ten?"

Conrad set aside the bottle slowly, a calculating gleam in his eyes that had Troy's instincts blaring. *Mine.*

"Ah, so this is Hillary Wright in the flesh. Or should I call you Troy's Achilles's heel?"

Seven

Hillary stood self-consciously in the open archway leading into what could only be described as the man cave to end all man caves.

She'd finished her bath and her meal only to find she'd discovered her second wind. She'd put on a chic yellow silk dress and gone in search of Troy. The guard outside her door had informed her that the leather pouch was her golden ticket to whatever she needed at the casino. Then her own personal body guard had escorted her here to find Troy and his buddy, the casino owner.

Good God, there was a lot of testosterone in this room. Whereas Troy was unconventionally handsome, edgy even, his buddy was traditional: tall, dark, buffed and broody.

Personally, she preferred edgy.

"I'm Conrad Hughes," the dark-haired Adonis extended a not-so-steady hand. "Mr. Alpha Realms's best friend."

Troy hooked an arm around his shoulders. "And he's a perpetual liar, so disregard anything he says."

Like the part about her being his Achilles's heel?

Conrad simply laughed. "As for being ten, yeah. We're men. We're perpetually ten in some aspects."

In which case, she should probably just go. "I'll just leave you to it. I'm sorry I bothered you."

Troy grasped her elbow. "Hold on. I'm done here." He glanced over his shoulder. "Right, bud?"

Nodding once, Conrad said, "We're good. Now go, have fun. What's mine is yours. Nice to meet you, Hillary."

She was back in the elevator with her guard excused before she could register being ushered out. "I think you and your buddy Conrad both need to sleep it off rather than play video games."

"I'm not drunk. Not even drinking anymore beyond the one I had in the room and one when I came down here." He brushed his lips across her forehead. "You're welcome to check my breath."

She tipped her head to his, their mouths so close. And as she looked deeply in his eyes, she could see he was completely sober. He hadn't lied. He'd controlled himself. There hadn't been some "out with the boys" bender. He was here for her, and that was definitely more intoxicating than alcohol.

"I'm not sure I understand you."

"Hillary, the last thing I would do is show up drunk in our room. You have understandable issues on the subject. If I stumbled in sloshed I would be less likely to score."

And that fast he eased the tension that had been growing too heavy and fast for her.

Laughing, she strode ahead of him out of the elevator, back at their suite. "Oh my God, did you really just say that?"

She glanced over her shoulder and caught him watching her with unmistakable appreciation.

"I did. And you're a little turned on." Walking behind her, he stroked a finger up her spine. "Admit it."

Hell, yes. She was burning up inside from a simple touch along her back.

"I'm a little exasperated." She bantered right back without brushing his hand away. Funny, how she was becoming more and more comfortable with his hands on her. Maybe too much so.

"Let's see what I can do about that."

She spun around, hand on her hips. "Seriously, are you suffering from some kind of Peter Pan syndrome? You crack jokes at inappropriate times and you still play video games."

"I develop software, yes."

Her thoughts screeched to a halt. She was learning fast to pick apart his words since he had a deft way of dodging questions with wordplay. "Not just video games?"

"Did I say that?"

There was something here. "Why do I get the sense you're toying with me?"

"Maybe because I would like to toy with you, all night long." His hands fell to rest on her shoulders. "But we need to leave Monte Carlo first thing in the morning so you really should get some sleep."

"We just got here. I thought we were going to play." Is that what she wanted? To play? All she knew was that she didn't want to say goodbye to him, not yet.

"We didn't come here to play. We came here to get you out of the public eye." All lightheartedness left his gaze and she saw the cool calculation at the foundation of everything he'd done. "First thing in the morning, we're going to leave through Conrad's private entrance. The world will think we're here in Monte Carlo somewhere, in case anyone's looking."

"Where are we really going?"

"To my house."

His house? She struggled to thread through his rapidly changing plans. "Didn't you say you live in Virginia? Doesn't that defeat the whole purpose of lying low?"

"I said I'm from Virginia. I do have my business based there, the corporate offices. But I have a second home where I get away to do the creative part of my job—or just to get the hell away, period."

With each word he confirmed there was so much more to him than she'd realized. She hadn't looked below the surface, not really. Maybe because the steady logical man in front of her made the charming playboy all the more appealing. "Where would that be? Who knows where we're going? I'm all for hiding out, but there needs to be someone to look for us if we fall off the planet."

"Smart woman. I respect that about you." He cradled her face in his hands, thumbs grazing her jaw, the calluses rasping over her tingling skin. "I assume you trust Colonel Salvatore."

"As much as I trust anyone these days. The whole trust thing is…scary."

"Good. Those concerns are there to keep you safe in life." With a nod, he stepped away. "We'll make a pit stop at Interpol headquarters in Lyon, France, and update him personally on our way."

"On our way to where?" Her eyes followed him as he walked toward his room without pressing her to accompany him. Which of course only made her want to go with him all the more.

"Costa Rica. But before we get there, I have a surprise."

* * *

Dinner in France?

Hillary was blown away by Troy's incredibly thoughtful surprise. He'd remembered her wish to talk to the chefs in Chicago, and he'd taken that dream up a notch.

Some of the finest chefs in the world worked in Lyon. She'd expected to zip into Interpol and be whisked right out of the country. But Troy had given her a hat of her own and sunglasses, changed his signature fedora for a ball cap and they'd become typical tourists in a heartbeat. After an early dinner, he'd suggested a sunset walk at the municipal gardens—*Jardin botanique de Lyon*—in the Golden Head Park. *Garden* didn't come close to describing the magnificence of everything from tropical flowers to peonies and lilies, to a massive greenhouse with camellias over a hundred years old.

The scent alone was positively orgasmic.

His hand wrapped around hers felt mighty damn special, too.

Holding hands while walking in the park was something so fundamental, so basic anywhere in the world, yet she strolled with a world-renowned guy in France, no less. Still, he made it seem like an everyday sort of date.

And there was no question but that this was an honest-to-goodness date.

Of course, this was the guy who'd cut his teeth on breaking into the Department of Defense's network. Who was he, this man who ran in such high-profile circles but appreciated simple things? A man who worried so deeply about his brother, even as he pretended to cut himself off from deeper feelings with a carefree attitude?

Troy was getting to her, in spite of all her wary instincts shouting out for self-preservation. She wanted for once to find out the yearnings of her heart could be trusted.

She leaned in to smell a camellia. "Why did you do it?"

"Do what?" His thumb caressed the inside of her wrist.

"Really?" She glanced sideways at him through her lashes. "Doesn't everyone ask you about it?"

He brushed an intimate kiss along her ear. "Why did I break into the Department of Defense's computer system?"

"Yeah."

"I told you already." His mouth flirted closer to the corner of her lips. "I was bored."

"I'm not buying it." She spoke against his mouth.

"Then you tell me. Why do you think I did it?" Pulling back, he held her eyes as firmly as he held her hand.

She studied him for a second before answering honestly. "I think you want me to say something awful so you can get pissed off."

"Why the hell would I do that?" He scowled.

"And yet, you're getting pissed anyway, which gives you a convenient wall between us." She tapped the furrows in his forehead.

He backed her against a roped-off area. "You want more? Walls down, total openness and everything that comes with that?"

"You'll only find out if you answer." She smoothed aside the long hair on his forehead, his normally cool-guy 'do pushed down by his ball cap. "If you don't want to tell me the real reason, just say so, but it's unrealistic to think people—especially people close to you—wouldn't want to know."

"You're close to me?" He linked both arms around her, bringing her closer.

"Aren't I?" Butterflies filled her stomach as she thought about how close she wanted to get, how deeply she wanted to trust Troy.

His arms fell away and he backed away a step. "Okay,

fine…" He whipped off the cap and thrust his hands through his hair before jamming the hat on his head again. "Everyone says I had this altruistic reason for what I did, but honest to God, I was unsupervised, spoiled and pissed off at my parents for not—hell, I don't know."

"You did it to get their attention." An image of him as a boy started to take shape, one that tugged at her heart. She suspected there was more to the story but that he was only going to tell her at his own pace.

"I wasn't five." He steered her out of the way of an older couple snapping photos of flowers, touching her with such ease, as if they were lovers. "I was fifteen."

"But you weren't an adult."

"Lucky for me or I'd have been in prison." He stuffed his hands in his suit pockets. "Hell, if I'd done the same thing today, even as a teen, I wouldn't have gotten off so easy."

"So the brotherhood, the guys like you at the military high school, they were really more of the family you never had."

Defensiveness eased from his shoulders. "They were."

"The casino owner? He's a brother?"

"What do you think?"

Her mind skipped to the obvious question. "What did he do?"

He hesitated for an instant before shrugging those broad shoulders that endlessly drew her eyes. "It's public knowledge anyway. Remember the big fluctuation in the stock market a little over seventeen years ago?"

"No kidding?" She gasped. She'd only been about ten at the time, but her teachers had used it in a lesson plan on government and economics. Newscasters and economists still referred to it on occasion. "That was him?"

She sank down on a park bench as other tourists milled past.

"He accessed his father's account, invested money, made a crapton. So his dad let him keep right on investing." He sat beside her, his warm thigh pressing against hers. "But when he caught a couple of his dad's friends assaulting his sister..."

"He crashed the friend's business?"

Troy stretched his arm along the bench, touching her, taking part in more universal dating rituals. "He did. And once he was in the system, he uncovered a cesspool of companies using child laborers overseas. The press lauded him as a hero, but he never considered himself one since his initial intent was revenge."

"So even though what he did was wrong, he had an emotionally intense reason for it, as did you."

"Don't try to glorify what we did. Any of us. We all broke the law. We were all criminals heading down a dark path that would have only gotten darker if we hadn't gotten caught." He tugged a lock of her hair, bringing it close to his face and inhaling. "There was this one guy—a musical prodigy—whose parents sent him to reform school instead of to drug rehab."

She turned on the bench, sliding her hand under his suit jacket to press against his heart. "That had to be painful for you to see, because of your brother."

He didn't answer, just stared back at her with those jewel-tone green eyes, and she wondered if he would kiss her just to end the conversation. She wouldn't stop him.

Then something niggled in the back of her brain. "I think what you did had something to do with your brother."

He looked down and away.

"Troy?" She cupped his face and urged him to look at her again. "Troy?"

"My brother failed out of college, enlisted in the army, then got busted and sent to jail." He held up a hand. "I'm not defending Devon. What he did was wrong. But there were others in his unit dealing, and two of them got off because their dads were generals."

Her heart broke over the image of a younger brother dispensing justice for his older brother.

"Once I got into the system, I stumbled on other… problems…and I decided I might as well do a thorough job while I was in there."

"Wow…" She sagged back. "You sure set the world on its ear."

"The irony of it all? My dad used his influence to keep me from serving time." He bolted to his feet. "Time's up. We need to head back to the airport."

He didn't take her hand this time. Just clasped her elbow and guided her back out of the gardens. His expression said it all.

Date over. There would be no kiss at the door. And honestly, as vulnerable as she felt right now, she could use a little emotional distance herself.

On a plane leaving Lyon, France, Troy knew he should be pleased with how his meeting had gone today with Salvatore at Interpol Headquarters. His plans were falling into place. Hillary was safe. The world believed they were sharing a romantic week in Monte Carlo. No one except the colonel and Conrad knew about their true destination as they flew through the night sky.

Costa Rica.

They would be there by sunrise. He should be pleased, but still he felt restless. Unsettled.

Hillary was snoozing in the sleeping compartment. The transferable pod made his location less traceable as he came and left in different crafts, while still having all of his personal comforts available.

He preferred his life simple, although he couldn't miss the excitement in Hillary's eyes over dining in France. She'd told him from the start that she'd chosen her job to get away from her rural roots, that she was looking for glamour and big-city excitement. He could give her that, and he wanted to. Although he could do without more soul-searching, like what they'd done in the gardens. But he also wondered how she would feel about his more scaled back lifestyle in Costa Rica. He knew his life was not what anyone would call simple, but amidst the travel and business, he preferred things to be…less pretentious, less complicated.

Maybe those days in the military school had left an imprint on him in ways he hadn't thought about before. At the academy, all he'd had was a bunk, a locker trunk and his friends. He'd lived that way even after leaving school and growing his hair again, even with clothes as far from a military school uniform as he could make them. He'd kept his world Spartan, when it came to letting new people into his life. Until now.

Right now, he felt like that fifteen-year-old kid whose life had been turned upside down, leaving him on shaky ground as he figured out who to trust.

Troy tossed his uniform hat on the bottom bunk along with his day planner, pissed off, as usual, and he was only six months into his sentence. "What the hell are you doing here?" he asked Conrad, who was pretending to be asleep.

Conrad called from the top bed. "You're blowing my cover."

"What cover?"

"That I missed formation because I fell asleep," he said,

his voice echoing in the barracks, which were empty other than one other guy who actually was snoozing. "What's your excuse for blowing off a mandatory formation?"

"I got my ass handed to me in trig class today. Just didn't have the stomach to get ripped again by Salvatore because of imaginary spots on my brass buckle."

Conrad extended an arm with his spiral notebook, marked Trigonometry. "Be my guest. Can't help you with the buckle, though."

"Thanks."

Conrad dropped the book and Troy caught it in midair, accepting it without hesitation. He'd helped Conrad out last week with hacking into a news site for stock returns. The limited computer access hadn't been quite as tight as they'd claimed. Except in one realm. "How is it that I can get into any system except where they keep their tests?"

"Uh, hello, they know you're here." His arm arced down and he swatted Troy with a pillow. "They must be paying Bill Gates a fortune to keep that out of reach."

"Funny." Not. It was frustrating being confined to this place. He flopped back and started thumbing through Conrad's notes. Notes that were damn near Greek. "Must be nice being a friggin' math genius."

"If I was a genius I wouldn't have gotten caught. I would be at some after-homecoming dance getting blown by a debutante who gets off on the fact that my old man is rich enough to buy me a Porsche for my sixteenth birthday."

"I think you wanted to get found out."

Conrad ducked his head to the side, looking down. "You think I wanted this? You're nuts. Why did you do it?"

"I'm not sure. 'Mommy' and 'Daddy's' attention instead of a new toy? Fame and recognition? Who knows? The court-appointed shrink just says I'm antisocial." And

how damn weird was it that now, here, he finally had a real friend. "How did you get caught?"

"*I let a female knock me off my game. I got sloppy. It's my own fault. Women have always been my weakness. Take it from me, man. Never let a woman be your Achilles's heel.*" He ducked back to rest on his own bed again. "*But you, you never do anything you don't mean to.*"

In his six months here, he'd never seen Conrad's confidence shaken.

"*Sure, I do, Hughes. I blurt out crap all the time that I don't mean to say. Teachers really hate that, by the way.*"

His buddy laughed, shaking off some of the darkness. "*So I see every day. You do take the attention off the rest of us, and for that, we thank you, man.*"

From the far corner, the guy he'd thought was asleep jackknifed up and threw two fistfuls of brass buckles across the room. "*Do you think you two could hold it down? Take the belt buckles, just go and let me sleep in peace. I've got some sort of stomach bug. Leave or you might catch it.*"

Stomach bug? The loser was probably coming down off something. He was some piano prodigy who'd been busted for drugs and shipped here.

Troy tossed a belt buckle. "*No, thanks, Mozart. I'll pass on Marching 101.*"

"*Really, dude—*" Mozart swung his legs over the side of his bed, holding his stomach and wincing "*—if you would stop worrying about being a moody whiner all the time, you could learn something. To infiltrate the system, learn to work it from the inside. Use those brains of yours to play the game. Polish your damn brass.*"

Conrad did that uppity sneer thing he had down to an art form. "*You're actually telling us to kiss ass, Beethoven? Because you sure as hell don't.*"

"Exactly." Mozart/Beethoven *grabbed the Pepto-Bismol from his bedside table. "There are other ways...."*

Troy scooped up a remaining buckle and tossed it from hand to hand. "You make people laugh. Good for you. That's your gig. You're a people person."

After guzzling a quarter of the bottle of stomach meds, he swiped his wrist over his mouth, smearing away the pink stain. "Studies say that a sense of humor is the true measure of intelligence."

"Just because you took that psychology class, Bach, don't think you can trick me into doing things your way by playing mind games."

"Whatever. I'm offering you a new tool for your arsenal." Mozart/Beethoven/Bach—*aka Malcolm Douglas—shrugged, stretching back out again. "It's up to you if you want to take it."*

"Knock-knock jokes, Douglas?" Troy tossed the final buckle back. *"Are you for real?"*

Douglas applauded. "See, that was well-played sarcasm. You've got potential."

The door exploded open across the room.

Colonel John Salvatore stood framed in the opening. "Gentlemen, you'd damn well better be hurling right this second or you will be by the time I'm done running you."

Troy shoved up from his computer workstation and pushed open the door to where Hillary slept. Curled up on her side, she hugged the wool blanket he'd picked up on an African safari. Her red hair splashed an auburn swath over the white Egyptian cotton. His hand itched to cup the curve of her hip. He ached to slip into bed and lie behind her, tucking her body into his. He would wrap his arm around her waist, the undersides of her breasts resting against his skin. He would breathe in the scent of her shampoo, stay right there until she woke up and rolled into his embrace, inviting him to indulge in more.

Indulge in everything.

He wanted Hillary in his bed for real, not just to sleep, and he had wanted that since he'd first seen her. But he needed to have his thoughts in order, be in control of himself. He wasn't the impulsive teen anymore who blasted through security firewalls without thinking of the consequences.

And as he thought this through, he was beginning to realize his preference for keeping things simple wasn't going to work with her. She was the type of woman that asked for, demanded, more from a man. She had a way of getting him to talk that no one had managed before. Maybe because she wasn't some groupie who glamorized what he'd done. Even when she didn't agree with his choices, she listened. She wanted the real story.

That was mighty damn rare and enticing.

As he watched the even rise and fall of her chest as they powered across the ocean toward the Costa Rica coastline, he couldn't deny it any longer. He would do anything to sleep with her. Anything.

And he would need everything he'd learned from Salvatore, from Hughes and from Douglas to win her over.

Eight

His Costa Rican getaway wasn't at all what she'd expected.

She slid out of the Land Rover, sounds of the tropical wilds wrapping around her. The chorus of isolation, of escape, echoed. Birds and monkeys called from the dense walls of trees. His home rested on a bluff, with a waterfall off to the side that fed into a lagoon. Wherever he looked out from his home, he would have an incredible view.

Sure, it was a pricey pad, without question. But not in a flashy way. She'd expected a sleek beach place with gothic columns and swaths of gauzy cabanas on a crystal-white beach.

Instead, she found more of a tree house. The rustic wooden structure was built on stilts—which made sense for surviving fierce storms. Built in an octagonal shape, its windows provided a panoramic view of not only the water but also the lush jungle. Splashes of blooming colors and ripening fruits dotted the landscape like tropical Christmas lights.

This wasn't a beach vacation place for parties. This was a retreat, a haven for solitude. There wasn't even a crew of servants waiting. She carried a travel bag while Troy unloaded their luggage. He'd been strangely pensive since their flight, studying her like a puzzle to figure out.

Although she was probably looking at him in exactly the same way.

He glanced over. "Elevator or stairs?"

"Stairs," she said without pause, "I wouldn't miss a second of seeing this from all angles."

Climbing the winding wooden stairs, she drew in the exotic perfume of lush fertility seasoned with salty sea air. The spray of the waterfall misted the already-humid morning air. She cleared the final step to the wraparound balcony.

The man who would choose this type of home intrigued her, and she suspected the house would only get better. She wanted to believe that, as if the house was an indicator of the real Troy. It was ironic that after she'd fought so hard to leave the isolation of the farm, that somehow this secluded place felt amazingly right.

He ran his fingers along a wood shingle, and it opened to reveal an elaborate panel of buttons and lights. He'd keyed codes into elaborate security gates along the drive to the house. Apparently there was a final barrier to breach. He pressed his palm to a panel and the front door opened.

She stepped into a wide space full of rattan sofas and chaise lounges with upholstered cushions of deep rusts and greens. With the windows, it seemed as if the inside and outside melded seamlessly. No period pieces or antiques.

Just well-constructed comfort.

Troy tapped another small panel on the inside wall and

the lights came on. "There are multiple bedrooms. You can choose which suits you best. We're on our own here, so no worries about where the staff might sleep."

Music hummed softly; ceiling fans swirled. "Is the whole place wired like a clap on/clap off commercial?"

"A bit more high-tech than that, but yes. I may dress better these days—" he sailed his hat toward a coat tree with perfect aim "—but I'm still the same computer geek inside. The whole place is wired for internet, satellite, solar panels."

"Everything here is fresh. I thought there wasn't a staff?" The place had clearly been serviced, from the fresh basket of fruit on the kitchen island to the thriving plants climbing toward the vaulted ceiling.

"There isn't an official crew here. Not full-time, anyway." He set their luggage by a sofa. "A service comes in once a month to air the place out, dust the knickknacks. Fill the pantry before I arrive. Then they leave. I come here for solitude."

"But you brought me."

"Yes, I did," he said from beside the fireplace, one foot braced on the stone hearth. "That should tell you how important you are to me."

The seriousness of his statement caught her off guard. "Does that line usually work with women?"

"Your choice. Trust me or don't."

And that's what it all boiled down to for her. Trust. The toughest of all things for her to give. "Could I just give you my right arm instead?"

He shoved away from the wall. "What do you say we take this a step at a time?"

With each step that brought him closer, her temperature rose, her desire for him flamed even as wariness lingered. "What do you mean?"

"Rather than jumping all-in, you can test the waters, so to speak." He lifted a strand of her hair, sliding it between his fingers with slow deliberation.

"Test the waters how?" Like make out on the sofa? Play strip poker? Progress to third base? Nerves were stirring her into a near hysteria, because if her body ignited when he was just touching her hair, there wasn't a chance in hell she would be able to hold out against a full-out touch. And there was nothing and no one here to stop them.

He let her hair go shimmering free. "Go swimming, of course. So which will it be? The pool or the waterfall?"

Hillary stripped out of her travel clothes, a dress she'd slept in on the plane. She needed a shower, but since they were heading to the waterfall... She would just take shampoo with her.

Her suitcases waited at the foot of the bed, but the open doors on the teak wardrobe showed rows and shelves full of clothes, all her size.

He truly had prepared for her visit. What would he have instructed buyers to choose for her? She thumbed through sundresses, jeans, shorts, gauzy shirts—and a half-dozen swimsuits with sarongs. Two-pieces and one-pieces, giving her choices.

One-piece, for sure. She tugged out a basic black suit and stepped into it before reaching for the phone to check in with her sister. Her hand half in and half out of her bag, she paused. What did a call from Costa Rica cost? And would it be traceable, thus risking their safety? She should probably check with Troy on that.

She yanked on a matching cover-up, then stuck her head out the door. "Troy?" she called out. "What're the rules on phoning home? I meant to call my sister while we were in France, and I, uh, forgot."

Their date had so filled her mind, she'd lost sight of everything else.

"Use the phone by the bed," he answered from somewhere around the kitchen. "It's a secure line."

"Thanks, I'll only be a minute."

"Take as long as you need." The sound of cabinets opening and closing echoed. "The only rules here are that there are no rules, no schedules."

She slid back into the room, the easy exchange so enticingly normal, so couple-ish. Plus a ka-billion-dollar vacation home and a world-renowned computer mogul she'd met while they both helped international law enforcement solve a case.

Yeah, totally normal.

And how would she even know "normal" if it bit her on the nose? She certainly hadn't seen a lot of healthy relationships in her life.

Sagging onto the edge of the bamboo-frame bed, she dialed her sister's number from memory. Since there was only an hour's time difference, her sister should be awake. The ringing connection was so clear, she could have been calling from next door. Of course Troy had crazy good technology.

"Uh, hello?" her sister said hesitantly, probably because the caller ID wouldn't have been familiar.

"It's me, Claudia, not a telemarketer."

"God, Hillary, it's great to hear your voice. How's Monte Carlo? Are you winning a fortune? The photos of you are gorgeous, by the way." The sound of Claudia sipping her signature soda filled the airwaves for a second. "I've been saving everything I can get my hands on and downloading the computer articles so you can see it all when you get home. We could have a scrapbooking weekend to organize everything."

Monte Carlo. Their cover story. Telling her sister everything would only worry her so she simply said, "Thank you. You can show me when I visit next."

"We could both be in our retirement rockers by then. Try to make it sooner."

"Fair enough. I promise." She always promised, but when push came to shove, somehow something always interfered.... And why? Her sister was wonderful; her brother-in-law was a great guy. She loved the kids. Their family was actually an example of how a healthy family *could* work. Had she avoided them because it was painful to see everything she didn't have? "I just wanted to check in and tell you I love you. I'll send the kids cool T-shirts."

"How about just have fun with that überhot guy. He beats the hell out of Barry the Bastard Cutthroat."

"He does. He really does. I'm actually getting some of that R & R you're always telling me I need. We're going swimming in a few minutes."

"Please tell me you're wearing a sexy two-piece so I can continue to live vicariously through you."

She looked down at the conservative black swimsuit with the simple black cover-up. "Um, sure."

"Atta girl. You deserve to play, date, flirt. Everything doesn't have to be intense. Enjoy the chase. Love you, but I have to run to clean the guest room."

"You're having company?"

"Uh...yeah. Listen, I really need to go. The kids are killing each other over who gets the last packet of gummies. Bye—" The phone connection cut off.

Phone still pressed to her ear, Hillary eyed the open wardrobe and that stack of bathing suits.... She tossed the receiver down and bolted across the room. Before she could change her mind, she tore off the black suit and snatched up an aqua-colored bikini, crocheted with flesh colored lining. It was suggestive and sexy and something she never would have dared pick out for herself.

If it had been the only suit on the shelf, she might have been angry. But there was such a wide range to choose from, this wasn't forced on her. The store tags on everything made it clear the items had been bought for her.

And she felt good wearing it.

She pulled on the frothy cover-up that matched, the nearly sheer silk sliding seductively over her skin like a lover's kiss. She arched up on her toes to snag a beach towel from the next shelf up. The white-and-black patterned cotton slid down in a tumble all around her, a huge towel made for sunbathing. She whipped it forward to refold...

What in the world?

Blinking, she looked again and sure enough, Troy had somehow, someway ordered a towel with a big Holstein cow pattern. No way could this be coincidental. The man was too smart and too observant. He had to have noticed her cow-patterned luggage tag and the silver pin on her evening bag.

Her sister was right. Things didn't have to be intense. She could play. Flirt. This wasn't an all-or-nothing proposition. A guy who gave cow towels definitely understood the lighter side of life. Her bruised heart could use some soothing after all she'd been through the past month.

Cow towel cradled to her stomach, she charged through the door, ready to meet her adventure head-on.

Troy needed to give his assistant a big fat bonus.

Palm flat against the kitchen counter, he took his time staring at Hillary from head to toe. There were no words other than *wow*—just wow—for how mouthwateringly hot she looked. The sea-green, almost-sheer cover-up rippled over her skin like waves of water, touching her in all the places he ached to caress.

He'd told his assistant to order a variety of clothes for any occasion. His only specific instruction had been to include a few cow-patterned accessories for fun. His assistant had been smart enough not to question or laugh.

That's why he paid her well.

He cleared his throat. "Did you find everything you need?"

"And more." She held up the cow-patterned towel. "This is amazing. Thank you."

"Thank my assistant. She did all the work."

"I'm guessing that she didn't decide on her own to pick out a beach towel with a bovine theme."

"I may have given her some direction. I'm glad you like it." He couldn't wait to see what she thought of the other surprises he'd ordered for her.

His own personal mermaid walked toward him, stealing a little bit of his sanity and will with every long-legged stride. Her eyes slid over him, lingering on his black board shorts and plain white T-shirt with the sleeves cut off.

She held up a small beach tote. "Do you mind if I wash my hair at the waterfall?"

He slid an arm around her and pulled her flush against him. "You can do any damn thing you want to."

"I do believe that's a compliment." She shook her hair back to glide down her spine.

"All that and more." He placed a floppy sun hat on her head before reaching for his straw fedora.

Hooking an arm around her shoulders, he grabbed his own bag of supplies for their morning—food and more towels. He guided her through his house and out onto the balcony. Her jaw dropped in awe, her feet slowing as she looked around her. For a moment, he saw his house through fresh eyes. Somewhere along the line, he'd lost sight of the details, just seeing the place as home.

The space widened into a veranda with a hot tub and a sunken pool built up to the edge. In spite of his carefully cultivated playboy reputation, he didn't take much time off. Even when he came here, he worked. Enjoying a morning at a waterfall with Hillary was an indulgence for him.

"Troy, this is incredible." Kneeling, she played her fingers through the crystal water. "I've seen infinity pools before but nothing like this one. With the way it's sunk into the balcony, it's like the pool is suspended in mid-air. What an architectural wonder. Did you come up with the design?"

"I had an idea in my mind for something like this, but I had to leave it up to the experts to make it happen. I have an architectural contact. He's more of an artist, actually."

Standing, she shook her hand dry. "One of your school pals?"

"Not this time." He slid his arm around her waist and started down the winding stairs that led from the house, down the bluff and toward the lagoon. "The architect is the stepbrother of my business partner. He had the place built from all regional materials. Most of the wood comes from Guanacaste trees…the fabrics are local weaves—"

"Whoa, hold on." She touched his stomach lightly. "You have a business partner?"

"In my software company, yes." Their flip-flops slapped each wooden plank on the way. "He provided the start-up funds."

"But I thought you came from old money? The press all said your father—" She stopped short.

"That my father bought a big company for me." He pushed past the sting of her assumption. He'd long ago accepted there were people who would always see him as a trust-fund kid. He could live with that, especially since it helped him when Salvatore needed him.

"What's the real story?"

He glanced over at her, surprised she asked. "A school friend provided an infusion of start-up cash to get things rolling. So I can't claim I did it all myself."

"I'm guessing your friend earned his money back many times over."

"Our company has done…well." Troy plucked a blue bloom from a sprawling Gallinazo tree and tucked it behind her ear.

Smiling, she touched the flower as a toucan flapped on a branch above. "You said his stepbrother designed the place. Who is this architect?"

"Jonah Landis."

"Of *the* Landis family?" Her eyebrows shot upward. "The stepbrother…is a Renshaw? Wow, you do have connections."

The Landis-Renshaw family were financial and political powerhouses. They understood his intense need to protect his privacy.

This place offered the ultimate in seclusion, with nature's soundproofing of a roaring waterfall and chattering monkeys.

His feet slowed as they reached the secluded lagoon. He set his bag on a mossy outcropping and tossed his hat on top, kicking off his sandals. He peeled his T-shirt over his head and—

Hillary stood on the edge of the shore in a bikini that glued his tongue to the roof of his mouth. Her smile was pure seduction as she backed into the water, bottle of shampoo in hand.

His erection was so damn obvious in his swim trunks, immediate, total immersion in the waterfall would be the best course of action. He climbed up the nearest rock ledge and dived in.

He parted the water with his hands, swimming closer and closer to Hillary. Her aqua-colored suit blended with the shades in the water until she appeared naked. Just what his libido needed. Yes, he wanted to seduce her. But he wanted to be in control when he did it.

Right now, he felt anything but in control.

He surfaced next to her and plucked the shampoo bottle from her hand. "Mind if I help?"

"Knock yourself out." She gave him the shampoo and disappeared underwater. The flower in her hair floated free. She shot back up again, her hair drenched and slicked back.

He squeezed shampoo in his palm then pitched the bottle back to shore. Facing her, he smoothed the shampoo along her soaked auburn locks. "How was your sister?"

The feel of her hair in his hands struck a primal chord deep inside him.

"Busy. As usual. She has the husband and kids and the big farmhouse. Our parents' old house, actually." Her head lolled back into his hands. "Where are your parents now?"

"I honestly don't know or care." His fingers clenched the rope of sudsy hair in his hands.

Her head tipped to the side as she studied him through narrowed eyes. "I didn't mean to upset you."

"Nothing upsetting about it. Just facts. You left home. So did I." Stepping behind her so she couldn't read his expression, he worked up the lather, massaging along her scalp. "Go ahead and say what you're thinking."

"I still keep in contact with my mother."

"I'm glad for you."

"I'm sorry for you. And I'm sorry I even brought this up."

"Don't be sorry." He slid his soapy hands along her shoulders, down her arms. Her silky skin sent lust throbbing through his veins, made him ache to peel away Hillary's suit and explore every soft inch of her rather than talk about his damn family. "My folks are living happily ever after, soaking in the sympathy of their friends over the huge disappointments their children have been."

"You're a billionaire, a successful software entrepreneur. You've turned your life around." She started to shift around to face him, but he stopped her, bringing her back flush against him instead. "They should be proud."

Her voice hitched, and she relaxed against him, her bottom nestled against his erection.

"I'm a self-centered playboy," he said against the top of her head, breathing in the scent of her minty shampoo. "But of course I do outscore my jailbird brother."

"What made him start using in the first place?" She reached back to cradle his cheek. "Where were your parents then? Or when he was in rehab?"

"We're adults. We take responsibility for our own actions." His heart pumped faster the harder she pushed the subject.

"But you weren't adults then."

Enough.

Enough of her trying to rationalize his past so he fit her mold of morality. He gripped her shoulders and turned her around to face him, needing her to see him, him as he really was. "We were old enough to know right from wrong and we both chose to do the wrong thing. There are consequences for that."

"Were the two of you close?" She clasped his wrists and just held on, her touch gentle but firm.

"We alternated between hating each other and being best buds. He sent me care packages at school—almost got me expelled with some of the crap he included." The memory made him smile...for a second, anyway. "I visited him in rehab to return the favor. A lot of the families there had reasons for what happened—abuse or depression leading to drug use. My brother had the same excuse I did. He was bored."

She squeezed his wrists. "I'm sorry, but I'm not letting your parents off that easily. At the very least, they were neglectful."

This conversation wasn't going the way he'd intended and this outing sure as hell wasn't going the way he'd planned.

"Troy—" she stepped closer, leaning into him "—tell me something...happy. Surely you've got some positive memories with your brother. You're a good person. I know the colonel and your brotherhood were there when you needed them, but there had to be some kind of foundation for that goodness inside you."

He wasn't sure he bought into her line of reasoning, but if it would get her smiling again, he would dig deep for something. "When we were kids, we had a nanny. When our parents weren't around we would even call her Mom."

"She sounds sweet." Hillary gifted him with a smile.

"She was tough as nails, just what two out-of-control boys needed. She was one step ahead of our pranks—and the first to reward us when we behaved."

"Reward you how?"

"Take us to baseball games, swimming at the lake, building tree houses and forts." And until now he hadn't thought about how his home here echoed those early tree houses—on a grander scale. "She even got us a couple of puppies and taught us how to take care of them."

"What kind of puppies?"

Hillary's breasts brushed his chest as they stood toe to

toe. He would keep right on happy talking for this kind of result.

"Pound puppies, of course. She told us a person's worth isn't measured by pedigree or looks. It's not about what something costs." She'd been a smart woman. He'd learned a lot from her, life lessons that stuck. "I picked a lab-bulldog mutt and my brother chose a shepherd mix."

Her smile faded. "You said you went to boarding schools, before the military school. What happened to the dogs? Did your nanny watch them?"

The water chilled around him. "When I was eight and my brother was ten, our parents fired the nanny."

"Because you were going to boarding school?"

His eyes closed. "Because they overheard us call her Mom." Her gasp pushed him to add wryly. "At least we knew she would take care of our dogs."

"Your parents gave away your dogs, too?" There was no escaping the heartbreak in her voice with just the two of them, out here alone.

He plastered on his best smile. "Damn, you asked for a happy memory. Sorry about the detour."

Sympathy shone in her eyes, along with a glint of something else. Determination. Her cool hands splayed on his chest as she stepped between his legs in a message of unmistakable seduction. "What do you say we make a great memory now?"

What the hell?

Now she wanted to make love? After he'd damn near opened a vein? Or *because* he'd opened that vein?

Realization dawned. She was feeling sorry for the kid he'd been, and was probably acting out of stirred-up emotions. He should tell her no. Wait until she was thinking clearly.

But then he'd never been particularly big on playing by the rules.

Nine

Hillary's heart was in her throat. The revelations about Troy's childhood had touched something deep inside her. She'd planned on being with him when they walked out here to the waterfall, but she'd underestimated how much he could move her. She'd deluded herself into thinking she could have a simple fling with him.

Somehow, Troy had gotten under her skin in only a few days. A few days that felt like a lifetime. She splayed her hands across his hard muscled chest sheened with water.

Troy cupped the back of her neck, his pupils dilating with arousal. "Are you seducing me?"

"Are you seducible?" She trailed her fingers down his chest.

"Totally."

He cupped her face and kissed her, openmouthed and without hesitation. She met him just as fully, wanting everything from him, determined to rock his foundation as surely as he did hers.

The taste of morning coffee lingered on his tongue. She wrapped her arms around his neck and kissed him right back, her mouth, her hands, her whole body in the moment. Finally, allowing herself to feel everything, no holding anything in reserve for later. There was no later. Everything inside her screamed *now*.

The water swirled around her, around them both, each bold caress of his hand sending the fresh currents over her. Her feet slipped on the slick stone floor and he steadied her with his hands under her bottom. The strength of his hands thrilled her. The rasp of his callused fingertips along her skin doubled the pleasure of his touch. She sketched her foot up his calf, then hooked both her legs around his waist.

The sun shone down on her head and her shoulders, but the sparks behind her eyelids had more to do with the man than the rays. And then they sank slowly underwater. Bubbles swirled around them as the rest of the shampoo left her hair. His mouth still over hers, he pumped his feet again and again, swimming backward until the suds stopped. For once, she surrendered control and let his strength carry them through the clear waters of the lagoon.

He broke the surface and she gasped for air against his shoulder. Their bodies fit, their legs brushing underwater in tantalizing swipes. She leaned into him, sealing them skin to skin.

His erection pressed against her, a solid welcome pressure against the ache building inside her. His hand braced between her shoulder blades, and she let her head fall back as he lavished attention along the exposed curves of her breasts. His mouth worked over her, teasing her through the swimsuit fabric until she reached a fever pitch.

Her hands fell away from his shoulders, and she reached behind herself. She untied the bikini strings at her neck. He smiled against her skin and made fast work of untying the rest. The scraps of aqua fabric floated away. The rippling surface brought her nipples to even tauter peaks.

He tucked an arm behind her back, tugging her hair gently until she arched farther for him, easing her breasts from the water. His mouth skimmed over one then the other, kissing and plucking as he bared her to the morning sun. He dipped his chin in the water and took her nipple lightly between his teeth, rolling and suckling, tugging just enough to send her writhing against him. Everything was brighter here, pristine when seen through the glistening droplets of water spraying from the falls. She felt like she was part of a fantasy or story or film.

From the start, she'd been drawn to Troy. They'd been leading up to this moment. Regardless of what happened afterward, she would regret it if she didn't experience today to the fullest. She wanted him inside her. Now.

She grabbed his shoulders and raised herself up again, sliding her legs to the rocky floor, pressing her body flush against his. "Do you have birth control? A condom? Because if I'm not mistaken, we're both one instant away from losing it."

"Back at the house," he murmured against her mouth. "Condoms are back at the house, damn it."

"Then we need to get there. Come on…"

He brushed his bristly, unshaven face against her cheek, whispering in her ear, "Or, we can take our time here, carefully, safely, still very pleasurably."

Possibilities swirled through her mind like the spiraling whirlpools rippling around the jutting rocks. "What exactly did you have in mind?"

He swiped his hand through the water, stirring the current between her legs until finally he cupped her. "I could touch you here." He clasped her wrist. "And if you're so inclined, you could—"

She palmed the length of his erection, stroking down, down, down and then up again, learning the thick, impressive length of him. "Is that what you mean?"

"Uh…" His head fell back and his throat moved with a slow gulp. "Yep, you're right on target."

With a deft hand, he untied the strings along her hips and the rest of her swimsuit floated away. She reached to grab it and he clasped her hand.

"I'll get you another suit just like it if you want, but right now I have more ideas for us."

His fingers slid between her legs, searching, teasing, finding the right places and pressure against the nub of nerves. Pleasure coiled tighter inside her, building. The buoyancy of the water held her up, and good thing it did, as her knees were quickly turning to jelly.

She tugged at the waistband of his trunks, her hands clumsier than she would have liked, but he was wreaking havoc with her equilibrium right now. He slid two fingers inside, crooking them just enough to send sparks exploding behind her eyelids….

To hell with taking off his shorts, she reached inside and found him, thick and long, all for her. She explored him with her hands, stroking his throbbing erection until he growled primitively in her ear. She gripped him a bit more firmly, the water slicking her hand as she worked him every bit as intensely as he tormented her. He took her to the edge, so close to fulfillment, then shifted his hands away deliberately, sipping along her neck, whispering against her skin how much he wanted her. How desperately he wanted to make her come apart, until she cried out and sank her teeth into his shoulder from the burning ache to finish.

He scooped an arm under her bottom and lifted her, walking with her toward the shore and she thought, yes, finally they would go inside and make love on his bed. Or the sofa.

Or hell, a sturdy table would suffice right now.

He kissed her, his tongue thrusting and sweeping until her eyes closed and she lost herself in the bliss of him. Step by step, he moved closer to the shoreline, until they were waist-deep in the water. His hands spanned her waist and he lifted her. She opened her eyes, disoriented, confused.

The water dripped from her skin as he set her on a moss-covered stone outcropping. He pressed her backward until she lay along the smooth, earthy rock with her legs draped over his shoulders while he still stood in the water. His intent became very clear a second before he closed his mouth over the core of her.

Her arms flung wide and dug into the mossy carpet. His tongue stroked and soothed, circling and pressing. His hands glided up her hips then over her breasts, doubling the sensation as he toyed with her. Still, she squirmed to get closer, closer still as she burned for him to finish even as she wanted the liquid fire to continue forever. Each thrum of her heart accented the pulsing pleasure growing stronger and stronger until she couldn't hold it back any longer.

She cried out her release, no holds barred. Their complete isolation gave her the freedom to ride the orgasm through each blissful aftershock. Her fingers scraped deeper into the moss, her back bowing upward as Troy laved every last sensation from her body until she collapsed, her bones all but melting into the stony outcropping.

A light breeze whispered over her bared flesh, bringing her back gust by gust. Troy lifted her off the rock and into the water again, body to body.

"Hmm…" She hummed her pleasure at this most perfect moment, but had to ask. "What about you?"

"We'll get there." Sliding an arm under her legs, he cradled her against his chest and started toward the shore. "I'm not worried."

"Where are we going?" She leaned into him, resting in his arms. Her body was all but a muscleless mass after the explosive orgasm he'd just given her.

"Back to the house before you're too sunburned to enjoy the rest of what I have planned for you."

"Smart man." She threaded her fingers through his hair, loving the length, enjoying everything about this unbelievably unique and special man.

Something insanely out of control was happening to her, and as much as she'd told herself she had crummy judgment in men, right now she felt like she'd merely been passing time until this man came into her life.

Troy carried Hillary up the winding stairs, back to the sprawling pool area. Every step he prayed for the self-control to wait until they made it back to the house. The press of her naked curves against him was damn near driving him insane with the urge to drop to the ground right here, right now and thrust inside her, out here in the open air, on the lush earth, with the scent of crushed foliage and flowers all around them.

Except he needed protection. He couldn't forget about keeping her safe in all realms. He'd stocked condoms everywhere in the house and on the patio, but he hadn't thought to pack them in their picnic lunch.

But honest to God, she'd caught him unaware down there. He'd planned to swim with her, wow her with his home. Except she'd been the one to wow him with how she'd melted over a lame story about his brother and puppies.

But then Hillary had been surprising him from the start. The only predictable thing about Hillary was her unpredictability, and for a smart guy used to figuring things out at least twenty-five steps ahead of the rest of the world, he was enjoying the hell out of the unending surprises she doled out.

And if she kept that up with her mouth on his chest, he was in danger of losing his footing, sending them both crashing down. If he rolled on the ground with her for even a second, he would lose control. Totally. Damned, though, if he could bring himself to tell her to stop what she was doing with her tongue.

Finally—thank heaven—he reached the pool area built into the balcony. He set Hillary down on a lounger, double-sized and covered by a gauzy cabana.

She reached up to cup his face. "Please say you have condoms here."

"I do." In the table by the lounger. He stretched out over her.

She skimmed her foot up and down his calf, which brought the heat of her more fully against his erection straining like hell to get out of his boxers.

"You sure were confident in your plan, Troy."

"Confident in how damned hot we both get the second you walk into the room, or into my thoughts."

"That's actually pretty romantic."

"I'm trying." Now probably wasn't the time to tell her he'd taken the edge off in the shower the night before. But he was grateful he'd done so, because no way in hell was he going to waste this chance with her on some quick trigger finish. He would be in control, damn it. Holding himself in check at the waterfall had been worth it. "And as for being confident about today? Not exactly. I'm never certain of anything around you. You surprise me on a regular basis. So while you were changing, I stored condoms in about a dozen different places."

"Why not by the waterfall—or in a beach bag for when we went to the lagoon?"

"You surprised me." And they'd improvised well.

He had no complaints about the appeal of carrying this fiery-haired beauty—*his* fiery-haired beauty—up to his lair. He was damn glad for the privacy and security that allowed him to roam the grounds freely with her. The couple who serviced the home lived five miles away, and they never came unless he called. No one would get past the wired gates without his say-so.

He and Hillary had free run to do whatever, whenever they wanted here.

"*I* surprised *you*?" She tugged the hair along his neck gently. "Very cool. Because you've been surprising the hell out of me since the second you talked your way into the seat beside me on the plane."

"Any objections?" He slipped his hand between them, gently rolling her nipple between his thumb and forefinger.

"Only that you're talking a lot, and I have better plans for your mouth right now, like using those teeth to tear into a condom wrapper."

He pressed his thigh between her legs until she moaned. "I do like a woman who knows what she wants."

"In that case, this time, I want control."

Power plays were cool by him since they were both going to be winners here. "I'm all yours."

"Well, we can start by getting rid of your board shorts." She tugged at his waistband and together they sent his swim trunks flying into the pool.

Her eyes and hands went to his hips, then curved around his arousal. He passed her one of the condoms, and she sheathed him with torturously slow precision that threatened to send him over the edge, here and now, with the monkeys laughing at his lack of restraint. But then she'd vowed this was about her turn to be in control.

Rolling with her, he shifted to his back, bringing her on top of him. She straddled his hips and lowered herself onto him inch by inch, stretching, accepting him into her body. He guided her with his hands on her hips, thrusting into her over and over as they found their rhythm. Her husky purrs of pleasure spurred him on, made him want to bring her over the edge again. He cradled her breasts, and she rewarded him with a breathy gasp. He couldn't take his eyes off the beauty of her. The way her hair slithered over her shoulders as she rode him. How her breasts moved in his hands.

The pleasure on her face.

With each stroke, he claimed her as his, again and again. Or maybe she was claiming him. Right now, all he cared about was that he had her. And he would have her over and over this week. The thought of losing this, of losing her, ripped through him, and his fingers dug into her hips, guiding her harder and faster, watching for the signals that she was close to completion, as well.

A flush rose up her chest.

The pulse in her neck throbbed faster.

Her head flung back, auburn hair streaming as she—

Yes. He thrust into her a final time, the silken vise of her body pulsing around him as he came, powerfully and completely. He pumped into her one last time and wrung yet another cry of pleasure from her. His arms went around her, gathering her as she melted onto his chest. He kissed her forehead, tasting the salty dots of perspiration along her brow. Their sweat-slicked bodies sealed and holy hell, he was in trouble.

For the past seventeen years he'd told himself he was done with family. Only claiming a group of brothers equally as cynical and world-weary as he was.

Today, with Hillary, he wanted more.

Three days later, Hillary reclined against Troy in the bubbling hot tub, mint leaves floating around them and scenting the night air. She'd had more sex since arriving here than she'd had in her entire life.

Okay, perhaps a slight exaggeration, but she certainly had never been this satisfied. Troy's meticulous attention to detail, his determination to study every possible way to make her come was mighty enticing. She'd never had a man this devoted to giving at least as much pleasure as he received. Sagging back against his chest, she let the pulsing jets work their magic on her well-loved muscles.

She tipped her head back to look at him, taking in his now-familiar face. "Thank you for my cow towel."

"You already thanked me," his voice rumbled against her.

"And for the big fuzzy cow slippers."

"Wouldn't want your feet to get cold at night." His hands slid just under her breasts, massaging her ribs, her stomach, soothing and arousing even though her body was too exhausted to comply.

"Coffee definitely tastes better in a cow mug." She twisted to kiss his shoulder, right over the spot where she'd nipped a little too hard earlier. He had a way of driving her crazy like that. "Although the hula cow by my toothbrush was a little strange, but it made me laugh."

"Then I've done my job well."

She'd laughed herself sore when she'd realized all the

computers—and there were many in his house—had Holstein cow screen savers.

"You've been very generous and thoughtful—and fascinatingly original."

"God forbid I ever be boring." His strong fingers worked along her thighs. "Would you like a black-and-white diamond pendant to go with your collection?"

"You're being outrageous." Outrageous—and so charming she didn't know how she would go back to the real world again, where this fantasy would fade. Because she knew without question, the fantasy always faded.

"Damn, does that mean I have to take it back to the store?"

What was he saying? Something about a diamond cow necklace? "You didn't actually…"

"You'll have to wait and see, won't you?" His massaging hands slid between her legs, arousing her again after all.

As her knees eased apart, she realized the fantasy was going to live a while longer.

Troy propped his feet on his desk using an upgraded video phone that could put the competitors under if he released it. He still hadn't decided.

Sometimes it was better not to upset the order of things. Leave the market alone for now and save the technology for a time it might make a significant difference rather than just adding yet another upgrade for folks to buy while tossing out products still in perfectly good working order.

All the same, he enjoyed his toys and kept the best of the best here in his own personal, techie version of a man cave. More than just a wall of computers, he had shelves of parts and storage, old and new. For now, he focused on his video call. His brother—the military school kind—

was on the other end of the conversation, still wearing his rumpled tux from the concert he'd given the night before.

"Mozart, I appreciate the help. You're the man, as always."

"It's all good, my friend." Malcolm Douglas popped an antacid in his mouth then set aside the plastic jar—already half-empty. Troy's musical protégé buddy had come a long way from his days at the military reform school—but he still had a finicky stomach. "Consider the favor done within the hour."

The casino cover story was starting to grow stale. Some might begin to suspect the truth, since Troy wasn't renowned for staying in one place for any length of time. Salvatore assured him they had leads; they were on the guy's trail, just a little longer.

But Troy wasn't willing to sit back and bet on it. Backup plans were always in order. So he'd sent photos to online magazines and gossip blogs of him with Hillary having a candlelit dinner. Spliced in with some older photos of him with Malcolm taken last month, the press and the public—and anyone else watching—would think they were in New York City, that they'd had dinner followed by attending a concert.

"Congrats on the latest gig, by the way. Not too shabby playing Carnegie Hall."

"Minor compared to what's going on in your world right now." Malcolm brushed off praise as he always had. "The new woman in your life is smokin' hot. A California dime, no doubt."

"Thanks, and careful. That's my 'ten.'"

"Hey, just sayin'." His buddy continued to push Troy's buttons for fun. It's what they did.

"Note to self, no more candlelight photos for Mozart."

Malcolm pointed. "I'm not talking about your romantic dinner pics, buddy. She's rocking the fluffy robe."

Troy spun his chair around fast, feet back on the ground. Sure enough, Hillary stood behind him in her robe, her eyes wide. "Are you talking to *the* Malcolm Douglas?"

Jealousy spiked, fast and furious and irrational. He forced himself not to go all caveman just because the woman he cared about happened to be a groupie for this generation's cross between Harry Connick Jr. and Michael Buble.

Tearing his eyes off Hillary, Troy pivoted back to the screen. "Gotta run, pal. Thanks again for the help. I owe you."

"And I will collect. Count on it."

The screen went blank.

Strolling deeper in the room, she angled her head to the side, auburn hair still tousled from sex and sleep, then more sex and sleep. "Your brothers run in high circles. The friend who helped you at the casino and now him." She gestured to the empty screen. "There sure are a lot of you."

"I wouldn't say 'a lot' of us exactly." He rocked back in his office chair. "That would make us so...cookie cutter."

"Trust me, no one would ever call you cookie cutter." She held up her hand, a platinum necklace with a white-and-black diamond cow charm dangling from her fingers. "You are one hundred percent original."

He grabbed her wrist and tugged her into his lap. "Now that is the hottest thing you've ever said to me."

"I must not be holding up my end of the seduction then." She wriggled in his lap until she settled.

"You're killing me here. I need an energy drink."

"Which I'll be happy to get for you if you'll make me one promise."

"What's that?"

"I adore the necklace and gladly accept it. But from here on out, dial back on the extravagant gifts. Okay?"

"Fair enough."

He slid the necklace from her hand. He swept aside her hair and hooked the chain around her neck. He might not be the most romantic guy in the world, but he prided himself on his originality, and he would do everything in his power to obliterate the memory of Barry Curtis.

He pressed a kiss to the latched chain.

She glanced back at him, their mouths and eyes so close they almost touched. "What are you thinking?"

"Something a smart man wouldn't say." A wry smile tugged at him.

"What do you mean?"

"Why would you want to know if I've already warned you it might upset you?" Standing, he set her on her feet, cow slippers poking out from the hem of her robe.

"Because…" She tugged his T-shirt holding him closer. "If you really didn't want me to know, you would have said something like…'nothing' or 'I'm thinking about breakfast or what goofy hat I'm going to buy next.'"

"You think my hats are goofy?"

"I'll answer you if you answer me."

Ah, what the hell? Might as well. "I was thinking about you and your jackass of an ex-boyfriend. I was wondering if you're still in love with him."

Whoa? Wait. That wasn't exactly what he'd been thinking. He'd just wanted to be sure she was over him. The *love* word hadn't entered his mind. But now that he'd gone there with the conversation, there was no going back.

She sank down into his empty chair, confusion on her face as she studied him. "Looking back, I can see I was never in love with him. I was definitely infatuated—very infatuated." She grimaced, fingering the diamond necklace. "Dazzled a little. But I like to think I would have seen through the glitz to the real guy underneath at some point."

He leaned back against a table of surveillance prototypes, listening. Hoping for what, he wasn't sure.

"What can I say?" She shrugged. "I told you right from the start that I have a history for picking bad guys. Eventually, I figure it out. In this case, Barry's arrest just sped up the realization process."

Usually he rocked at being analytical underneath all the jokes, but right now it was tougher than usual. Still, he forced himself to sift through the words. She didn't love Barry Curtis.

"Okay, then. I can live with that."

Too bad one realization led to another. She doubted her ability to choose the right guy to love, period.

Leaning her elbows on her knees, she pinned him with her eyes. "How can you be jealous when you've only known me a few days?"

"Who says I'm jealous?" Lame answer for a smart dude.

"Really? You want to try and bluff?" She laughed... then realized her robe was gaping. She straightened fast and held the part closed. She was shutting down and if he didn't do or say something fast, he could lose headway in his goal of... What?

He knew damn well what. It didn't matter how long he'd known her. He was certain. He wanted her in his life. Permanently. But he wasn't sure she was ready to hear that yet. She might not have loved Barry, but she'd been burned badly by the relationship.

The timing needed to be right. He couldn't afford to screw this up.

So he shoved away from the table and stalked toward her, at least letting all the possessive feelings show. "I'm not jealous so much as pissed off that the bastard hurt you."

He pressed his hands on either side of the chair, bringing their faces nose to nose. "I want to beat the crap out of him then hack his identity and wreck his credit. Got a problem with that?"

A slow smile spread over her face. "No problem at all." She tugged his bottom lip between her teeth. "And just so we're totally clear, I think your hats are sexy as hell."

Ten

Her time here was surely coming to a close.

Hillary floated on a raft, warm waters of the infinity pool lapping over her. She watched Troy swim the length of the pool. Lights underwater illuminated him powering through the depths, while the stars twinkled above on a cloudless night.

She and Troy had all but lived outside and at the lagoon since they'd arrived five days ago. They'd taken walks—made love in the forest—shared exotic delicacies—made love in the cabana. Learned personal details from political views to a shared preference for scary movies. Eventually they'd made their way inside to dodge the rain, enjoying a horror film in the theater-style screening room.

Like a real date.

But real life intruded often enough to keep her from getting too comfortable, too complacent, too eager to believe in something beyond the fantasy. Daily calls from

Salvatore let them know he was getting closer. Barry Curtis's accomplice had been tracked slipping over the channel into Belgium. They were on his tail and expected to catch him at any time.

What amazed her most was how easily Troy and Salvatore had maneuvered this whole situation while keeping things anonymous. Calls from her sister indicated the public was eating up tabloid stories of Hillary and Troy gallivanting around the globe, wining and dining in a different country every night.

While she'd enjoyed their dinner in France, she had to admit, the time alone with him was more precious.

Troy surged to the surface beside her. "Hey, beautiful." He lifted her hand and kissed each fingertip. "We're going to be waterlogged by the time we leave this place."

"Is that a bad thing?" Especially given the attention he was lavishing on her hand at the moment.

"Not at all." He rested his elbows on the edge of her raft. "Just checking to make sure you're cool with how little time we've spent in an actual bed."

He'd been attentive, romantic, and she was so tempted to think there was more going on here. But she needed to remember this would end soon. Life back in D.C.—in the real world—would be different. It always was. Still, she would miss the peacefulness of this place.

She toyed with his hair, longer now that it was wet. "Sleeping in the cabana was romantic. And watching the sunrise on the balcony—amazing. The past five days have been better than any vacation I could imagine. You've got the perks of this place down to an art."

"An art? What do you mean?" He trailed the backs of his fingers along her breast, down her side and over her bare hip. They'd never gotten around to putting on clothes today.

She was totally naked other than wearing her diamond cow necklace.

"If you've never brought anyone here, where did you romance all those women you were linked with in the tabloids?" She hated the hint of jealousy leaking into her tone regardless of how hard she tried to tamp it down.

"Are you jealous?"

Hell, yes. "Curious."

"Everything in the tabloids? All false." His face was stamped with deep sincerity. "I was a virgin until I met you."

Snorting on a laugh, she rolled her eyes. "Right."

"Serious," he continued, with overplayed drama. "I've lived like a monk. My staff put saltpeter in all my drinking water so I could save myself until the day I met you."

She splashed him in the face. "You're outrageous."

"So you've told me." He snagged her hand before she could splash him again, his face truly earnest now. "Would you rather I detailed past affairs? Because that's all they were. Affairs. Not relationships. Not serious. And never permanent."

Her stomach fluttered at the turn in the conversation. "Is that what we're doing here? Having an affair?"

"Damned inconvenient time for an affair, if you ask me."

"Okay then, are we having an inconvenient affair?" Those butterflies worked overtime, so much so she couldn't even pretend she didn't care about his answer.

"What if I said this isn't an affair?" He pinned her with his eyes as they floated together in the center of the pool. "I saw you, and I had to have you."

The possessive ring in his voice carried on the wind. Exciting in some ways, and perhaps a hint Cro-Magnon in others.

"That sounds more like I was a piece of cheesecake on a tray at a restaurant."

He winked. "I do like cheesecake."

"Could you be serious?" She flicked a light spray into his face.

He tugged her in with him, and they pushed away from the float. Sliding deeper into the pool, she treaded water, face-to-face with Troy. She looped her arms around his neck and their feet worked below the surface keeping them both afloat.

"Do you want me to be serious?" His hands cupped her bottom, their bodies a seamless fit against each other. "Because I can be, very much so. Except I get the sense that the timing is off, and if I tell you exactly what I'm thinking, you'll run."

His perceptiveness surprised her. She'd spent so much time enjoying his lighthearted ways and trying to remind herself this was a fantasy that would end, she hadn't considered he might be thinking of more after this week.

And he was one hundred percent right that the thought of life after Costa Rica scared her. "You're a very wise man."

Disappointment flickered through his eyes for an instant before his easygoing smile returned. "Then let's get back to having an inconvenient affair."

He sidestroked them to the edge of the pool. Her back met the tiled wall where his feet just touched the ground. He kissed her neck in the sensitive crook, paying extra attention to the place just below her ear that made her...*sigh*.

The hard muscles of his chest pressed to her breasts. Heat tingled through her veins, surging and gathering low. She explored the planes of his shoulder blades, his broad shoulders and his arms that held her so securely. He hitched her legs around his waist and started walking toward the semicircle of concrete stairs, kissing her every step of the way.

Climbing the stairs, still he held her. The air washed over their damp bodies. Goose bumps rose along her skin, every bit as much from Troy as from the night air. She tangled her fingers in his hair, loving the unconventional, uncut look of him.

With her legs looped around his waist, he carried her into the spacious house. Through the living area where they'd made love on a chaise lounge with the windows open. Past the kitchen counter where they'd had breakfast and each other. And down the hall to his bedroom where they'd yet to spend a night under the covers together.

He lowered her onto the towering carved bed draped with mosquito netting, like another tree house inside the ultimate tree house. The rest of the room was sparse, with only a wardrobe and a mammoth leather chair by the window. He presented such a fascinating mix of wealth and Spartan living.

But right now, she didn't want to think about his decor. Only feel. "This whole week has been a fantasy."

"You like fantasies?"

"What exactly do you have in mind?"

He eased back to his feet and went to the wardrobe. He tugged out his tuxedo jacket and shook it. Something rattled in the pocket. He pitched the jacket to her and she fished inside to find...

"Handcuffs?" She spun them on a finger. "Do you carry these around as a regular accessory?" Her mind filled with sensual possibilities, games she would only play with someone she trusted, and yes, at some point she'd learned to trust him. A scary thought, if she let herself ponder it for too long. So she again focused on the moment, on Troy and on the pleasure they were going to give each other very, very soon.

"They're from when I was auctioned off. I tucked them in my pocket and forgot about them until you mentioned fantasies." He closed the wardrobe, the dim lamplight casting a warm glow over his lean naked body. "The cuffs would have ended up at the cleaners when my tuxedo went in to be dry-cleaned, but we rushed out of the hotel so fast I never got around to it."

"The bachelor auction and the way you turned it around was quite a stunt." She'd been drawn to him then, in spite of her frustration over how little he'd told her on the plane.

He knelt on the edge of the bed, moving up the mattress until he covered her. "The auction was uncomfortable as hell, but it worked out well."

"I have to confess…" She stroked back his still-damp hair, the scent of mint and furniture polish riding the humid air. "I was jealous of your assistant, before I knew who she was, when I thought she'd won a weekend with you."

"Jealous, huh?" He hooked two fingers in the other side of the cuff, tugging lightly. "Feel free to elaborate."

"I was hoping plastic surgery chick would win."

"She wouldn't have," he said confidently. A drop of water from his wet hair spilled on her overheated flesh, trickling between her breasts.

Her nipples tightened from just that one droplet. She shivered in anticipation of how much more there was in store for them.

"The bidding could have gone much higher."

"I still would have won." His eyes blazed with flinty determination. "My assistant was authorized to do whatever it took."

"Just so you could choose me?" How far would he have gone?

"I didn't believe Salvatore was doing enough to protect you." He linked fingers with her, the handcuffs clasped in their joined hands. "I had to come up with a way to keep watch over you and that seemed the easiest way."

His words about safety chilled her, reminding her of their reason for being here in the first place. While she didn't doubt he was attracted to her, would they have ended up here on their own? Would he have pursued her had he just met her on the street? Old insecurities niggled.

"Spending eighty-nine-thousand dollars was easy?" She attempted to hide her unease with a joke like he did so often. "Why not hire a bodyguard? It would have been cheaper."

"You know how you said you were jealous of my assistant?" He held both her hands, pressing them into the mattress, his erection thick against her stomach. "I felt the same at the thought of turning you over to some security guy."

She arched up into him, enjoying the heat flaming hotter in his eyes. The scent of native flowers drifted on the breeze through the open windows, providing an intoxicating moment when she realized just how aware she was around this man.

A sense of power pulsed through her, and she embraced it, needing to feel in control of something here. "The attraction between us was pretty instantaneous."

"Once the auction rolled around, I was so damn happy to see you out there in the audience." He grinned down at her. "And then I was so turned on I had to keep my hands in front of me."

Now that would have made headlines. "I thought that was just because of the handcuffs."

"Oh, it was the handcuffs all right." He squeezed her hand in his, still holding the handcuffs. "Thinking about ways that you and I could use them had me sweating bullets. Which brings us back to fantasies."

"You've had fantasies, about me and handcuffs?" The simmering heat inside her flamed to life. "What exactly would you like to do with those handcuffs?"

"I wouldn't want to shock a Vermont farm girl."

"Please…" She tugged the handcuffs from him and dangled them in front of his face. "Shock me."

Troy had never been one to turn down a challenge.

And the challenge in Hillary's eyes was one he very much looked forward to fulfilling. He snapped one cuff around her right wrist and the other around his left, so they were shackled while facing each other. The past five days with Hillary had been beyond incredible, and with time running out, he hoped he could cement their bond before they left.

She blinked up at him in surprise. "I thought you were going to cuff me to the bed, Viking style."

"Then I did surprise you." He sketched his hand along her breast, which brought her hand to herself, as well.

She slid her free hand between them to stroke him but he manacled her wrist and pinned it against the bed.

"Troy," she said, writhing against him, the ache inside her building, "I want to touch you, too."

"We'll get around to that. We have all night." And if he had his way, they would have even longer.

"Who says you get to be in control?" She pressed back, knowing there was no way she could actually win in a contest of pure muscle, but maybe she had a chance in the battle of wills. "My. Turn."

He laughed softly against her, the puff of air along her

breasts sending fresh shivers down her spine. Then he rolled to his back, taking her with him. "Consider me at your command."

Her smile of pure feminine power launched a fresh flood of testosterone pounding through him in answer. Her hands still linked with his, she kissed her way over his chest, lingering and laving her way down until…holy crap, her lips closed around him. His head dug back into the pillow as he lost himself in the moist and warm temptation of her mouth, the tempting sweep of her tongue. She shouldn't be able to take him to the edge so fast, but then nothing was as he expected with Hillary.

The only thing he knew for sure was that he didn't want this to end.

He tugged their cuffed wrists and hauled her upward, unyielding, and flipped her to her back again, the length of him pressed between her legs. The silky dampness of her let him know she was every bit as ready as he was. With his free hand, he tugged on a condom in record time and slid into her welcoming heat. He knew her body after all they'd done together, yet still he couldn't get enough of her. Of the soaring sensation of being inside her with the scent of their mutual arousal perfuming the air.

The link between them was real, damn it. Every bit as real as the handcuffs binding them together. She had to see that, to believe it. He just needed to be patient and work past her insistence that her judgment in men was off. He needed to win her trust.

She hooked her ankles behind his back and took him deeper inside her, rolling her hips and bringing them both closer to completion. He wanted to wait—he had to wait— for her. Gritting his teeth, he held back his release, until finally, thank heaven, her breath hitched with the special sound that preceded her…cries of completion.

His own control snapped and he thrust again deeper, shouting with his own release jetting through him. Again. And again. Until he sagged on top of her, just barely managing to hold the bulk of his weight off her by levering on his elbows. He rolled to his side, their hands still locked together. He flung his other arm over his eyes, his defenses stripped back until he was unable to hide from the secret he'd been holding all day.

Salvatore had called after supper. Barry Curtis's accomplice had been picked up trying to slip into Switzerland. Extradition was already underway.

Hillary was cleared to return to D.C.

While the morning sun climbed, Hillary rested her chin on her hands on Troy's chest. The handcuffs rested on the pillow beside her. She would have to remember to tuck them away to play with again on another day. The whole Viking scenario held a certain appeal.

She kissed his chin. "You most definitely are not a monk."

"Nice to know you noticed," he said, his fingers tracing lazy circles on her back. "Have you checked under your pillow?"

Her hand went to her diamond necklace then over to her pillow. She tumbled underneath and her fingers closed around... Metal? She closed her fist around something square and pulled out...

"A cowbell?" Laughing, she rolled to her back, clanging the copper bell.

"Everything's better with a little cowbell."

"I can't believe you got this."

He rolled to his side, eyes on her face intensely, like he was looking for something. "You said I couldn't buy you extravagant gifts, so I've been working within your system."

"It's sweet. Really." She kissed him quickly. "I can honestly say I have never gotten one before."

"What till you hear my cow jokes. What do you call a sleeping cow?"

"A bull dozer."

"Okay, too easy." He threw a leg over hers, the ceiling fan stirring the mosquito netting. "Mooo-ving on."

She groaned.

"Why do milking stools only have three legs? Because the cow has the udder."

She swatted him with a pillow, the cuffs clattering to the floor. "That's awful."

"I know. I went through a lot of corny jokes at school until I learned the nuances of humor."

Something shifted inside her at those words, at the image of him "learning" to be funny, trying to fit in as he was tossed from school to school, his parents abdicating their roles in his life.

He flung his arms wide. "What? You don't have any ammo to toss back? Roll out the computer geek jokes. Take your best shot. I'm bulletproof. More than that, I'm a bullet catcher."

"You're a cocky bastard." But she sensed he hadn't always been that way. But saying as much would take them to a serious level she wasn't ready for, not yet. So she scrounged for a joke…. "Ethernet—something to catch the Ether Bunny."

"Oh," he groaned. "Talk about bad. You're a rookie."

She pushed for more, determined to keep it light and make the most of their time here before he told her they had to leave. "The truth is out there…if only I had the URL."

"Better."

"There are ten types of people. The ones who understand binary code and the ones who don't."

"Ahh," he said as he sighed, pulling her close. "Now you're making me hot."

She splayed her fingers over his chest, traced four scratch marks she'd left earlier. "You're crazy."

"That's very possible."

A darkness in his eyes unsettled her. "I was joking."

"I wasn't. This genetic lottery thing…" He tapped his temple. "It's enabled me to do some incredible things with my life. But sometimes it fails me on the basic things in life, things that everyone else has and takes for granted."

So much for staying away from deeper subjects. She should have known there was no hiding, especially not with Troy. And she found she actually wanted to know. She needed to understand him. "Such as?"

"A family. One that functions and talks to each other and eats Sunday dinners together."

"Troy," she gasped, gripping his shoulders insistently. "You can't blame yourself for your family friction."

"I played my part. You know, I could have just sucked it up and gone to medical school like my father wanted. It wouldn't have been that difficult for me academically," he said with confidence but not arrogance. He hooked his finger in her necklace, sliding it back and forth. "I could have done some kind of research gig where I wouldn't be around people."

God, he was breaking her heart here. "I don't know where in hell you got this idea that you're not good with people. You're charming and funny." She covered his hand on her necklace. "A total original."

"Like I said, it's a game I learned and I'm cool with that."

"Not a game." She shook her head. "I think maybe you learned to share parts of yourself, in a way others can understand."

She pressed her mouth to his before he could argue with her, her heart tumbling over itself with love for this man and sadness that she would soon have to leave him behind.

Eleven

Troy stood on the balcony, cell phone to his ear, trying to outtalk the monkeys and birds yammering in the trees. "Thanks for the update, Colonel. Glad to know Curtis is finally spilling his guts."

"It's a race between the two to make a deal. International money laundering doesn't sit well with the authorities. And stealing from disadvantaged kids' college scholarship funds plays even worse in the press." Salvatore's heavy sigh carried through the airwaves. "When are you and Hillary Wright coming in this morning?"

"Not this morning. But soon." When he got around to telling her.

"Donavan," the colonel said in the suspicious headmaster tone he'd honed over the years. "You've informed Hillary that all's clear. Right?"

"Of course I will, tonight." He leaned back against the rail, splinters snagging on his board shorts.

"Ah, Donavan." Salvatore all but tut-tutted at him. "How can a man so smart be so damn stupid?"

"Thanks for the vote of confidence, sir." Troy gripped the balcony harder, splinters digging straight into his palms. "If that's all, how about you roll me to the bottom of your on-call list?"

Salvatore's mocking laugh faded as Troy hit the end call button and set the cell on the rail.

Time was running out. Even the cackling monkeys in the trees seemed to be mocking him for being an idiot. Salvatore was right; he couldn't keep Hillary here indefinitely. He would take her home and just ask her out like a regular guy once they returned to the States.

Except he'd never done the "regular guy" gig all that well.

He heard Hillary's near-silent footsteps approaching a few seconds before she placed her hand in the middle of his back, her fingers curving in with familiarity.

"Was that good news on the phone?"

"Yeah…" He looked down at the lagoon where he'd made love to Hillary for the first time. Would she come back here or was this some fantasy escape for her, one that would be over and done when she was back home? He would tell her after lunch. She would still be back before the end of her hastily scheduled vacation. He needed to use this last pocket of time to seal the deal. "Work stuff. Mergers. Money. Boring office crap."

Hillary slid in front of him, wearing a floral sarong knotted over her breasts, a flower tucked behind her ear. She had sun-kissed cheeks and an ease to her that hadn't been there before they'd come here. When they returned, would she wear those buttoned-up suits like armor to keep him out?

"I would think you'd be happy." She sketched her fingers over his forehead. "You look worried."

"I am happy." He nodded, trying to shake the whole gloom-and-doom air weighing down his mojo. What the hell was up with that? He was the guy of the fedora hats and cool scarves.

She toyed with the string on his board shorts. "Let's take brunch up to the roof today. I think it's the only place where we haven't made love yet."

The vision of her with the waterfall in the background, mist in the air, wild outdoors all around them, took his breath away. He couldn't lose her. He needed to bind her to him before they left, ensure they had a future.

"Do you ever think about having kids?"

Hillary leaned back, her eyes wide. "Are you trying to tell me the condom broke?"

"No! God, no." Although the thought of a kid with Hillary didn't scare him as much as it should.

A sigh moved visibly through her. "Then that seems to be a rather premature question." She slid her arms around his waist. "Shouldn't we figure out if we're going to see each other after we leave here?"

"Lady, that's a given." At least he hoped it was. And if not, he intended to make it one. "And as for the kid question, I didn't say *our* kids, I said kids. Period. When people date—like we're talking about doing when we get back to the States—then they discuss their views on life stuff. Like having children."

"Okay," she said slowly, her voice wary, "then yes, sometimes I think about it."

"And your verdict?"

Why the hell had that jumped out of his mouth now? Her answer mattered to him, more than he was comfort-

able with. He was supposed to be romancing her to seal
the deal, not freaking her out with a full-court press.

"Honestly, Troy, the thought scares the hell out of me.
What do I know about being a mom?" She spread her arms
wide before tapping his chest. "And you mentioned genetics once. What about that? What if between our genes and
the patterns we've seen, our kids... I mean... Ah, hell."
She shoved against his chest. "Why are you bringing this
up now? We should be talking about whether to go out
for pizza or steak."

He shifted away from her, leaning back against the balcony. "I always thought I would adopt."

His answer stopped her. She turned to face him again.
"Really?"

"Sure, once I found the right woman to spend my life
with, because I don't know that I'm up to the task of parenting alone."

"And you would adopt because of the genetics fears
you talked about?"

"In part, maybe. But I also figure I have all of this
money and flexibility and there are kids out there without homes. Maybe I could just say to hell with worrying about someone getting into trouble and go ahead and
adopt a troubled kid. Help them turn it around, give a kid
the same break I got."

"You would do that?" She came back to him, leaning
a hip against the rail. "Take in a child you already knew
had problems?"

"If I had a biological kid who got into trouble like me
and my brother did, I wouldn't just write him or her off."
Memories of fights with his dad reverberated in his head.
"And by problems, maybe I would take in a kid with medical problems, someone overlooked. I could pay for any-

thing that kid needed. And hats. Lots of little hats for the kid."

Her eyes welled with tears as she touched his cheek. "Are you for real? Or is this an act to make women love you?"

"Would you believe me even if I said every word is true?"

He pushed back a wince at how he'd delayed for a day in telling her they could leave Costa Rica. He hadn't lied, he'd just...

Quibbled.

That's what Hillary would call it, and she wouldn't be forgiving of what she considered a lie. But how could he let her go not knowing if she'd agree to see him again?

"The thought of believing everything you're saying scares me. The fantasy is so much easier." She pulled a wobbly smile. "Even with the handcuffs."

"You're worried I'll hurt you." Even the thought of anyone hurting her made him want to haul her in and hold her tight.

"Remember when we talked about your happy childhood memory?" She folded her arms over her chest. "When my sisters and I were little, we would ride around on the tractor with Dad. He told us we were princesses and that was our chariot. It was fun to pretend."

"If you loved the farm so much, why were you so hungry to leave?"

"Because I realized all those times on the 'chariot'— that was just to protect the queen while she was toasted." She wrapped her arms around herself tighter, all but putting a wall between them.

"He was protecting his kids, you mean," he said, trying to put a positive spin on things, to give her something happier to hold on to.

"If he'd been protecting us, he wouldn't have enabled her. He loved her, but he was scared of her. He was scared if he pressed her to change, she would leave him." She stopped and held up her hand. "Whoa. Wait. I screwed up that happy memory exchange, too. Anyhow, I left the farm, but I don't hate it. I still go back to visit—my sister lives there with her family now that our dad's gone. Mom lives in an apartment—when she's not in rehab."

To hell with distance. He hauled her against his chest again. "I'm sorry for all you've been through. I can see how that would make you wary. But you can trust me, Hillary—"

His cell rang on the porch railing.

She looked quickly at the phone. "You should get that."

"Ignore it."

"It could be important."

Sighing, he snatched up the damn phone, knowing she was right. His assistant's name scrolled across the caller ID. If this had anything to do with Hillary's safety, he couldn't afford to ignore it.

"What?" he barked into the phone, resenting the intrusion of the outside world. "This better be important."

"It is. Hillary Wright's sister is going crazy trying to get in touch with her. Says it's something to do with their mother."

In the privacy of her room, Hillary cradled the phone and dialed her sister. After the intense conversation with Troy, she needed her space to face a call about her mother.

Why in the world did he have to bring up kids now? So early in their relationship? She was still adjusting to being in love with him. And then he had to roll out those incredibly enticing images of him as a dad, of him opening his life and heart to a kid who desperately needed a family. He was making her think he might want a future with her. Had she willingly signed on for another heartbreak by coming here with him?

The ringing in the phone receiver stopped and her youngest niece started chattering into the phone, "Aunt Hillary, Aunt Hillary, Grandma's moving in with us!"

Shock froze her. Her sister had always been softer where their mother was concerned, but she couldn't have actually caved on this. What about the children? "Could you please put your mommy on the phone?"

"Okeydokey. Love you, Aunt Hillary."

She clutched the phone tighter. "Love you, too, sweetie. See you when you come to Washington for your family vacation."

The sound of her niece shouting, "Mommm, telephone, Aunt Hillary," sounded in the background. Footsteps grew louder, then the rustling of the phone being passed over.

"Hillary?" her sister gasped into the phone.

"Claudia, what is going on there? I got an emergency SOS to call and now I hear Mom's moving in with you. Are you nuts?" All her fears and frustrations poured out in nervous babbling. "This is taking the codependent thing a little far, don't you think? You can't really expect to have her there with your children, can you? Maybe you don't remember what it was like, but I do."

"Hillary," Claudia interrupted. "Slow down, okay? I need to tell you something and it's a tough one."

"I'm already sitting." But she scooted farther back on the bed, nerves frothing in her stomach. "What's wrong?"

"While Mom was in the rehab clinic, the doctors found out she has a mass on her liver...." Claudia paused, her voice catching. "It's cancer, Hillary, and it's bad. End stage. The doctors say she has a couple of months left, tops. Her apartment isn't an assisted living type of setup. She has nowhere else to go."

Shock numbed Hillary as she absorbed the last thing she'd expected to hear. She'd spent her whole life figuring out how to cope with having an alcoholic mother. She'd never thought about how to cope with not having her mother at all. "I'm coming to Vermont."

"You don't have to rush right away—"

"Yes, I believe I do." She leaped from the bed, trying to deny the voice whispering in her mind that she wasn't running to her mother.

She was running away from Troy and the fear of him rejecting her love.

Troy stood in the open doorway of Hillary's room watching her pace frantically around, throwing clothes into her suitcase. From her tense shoulders to the sheen of tears in her eyes, he knew.

"I assume it was bad news on the phone."

She nodded tightly, folding her cow towel quickly and pressing it on top of everything else in her roller bag. "It is." She sat on the case and zipped. "My mother is ill, very ill. She has liver cancer. She doesn't have long left. I need to go home now and help my sister get Mom's affairs in order. We have to set up hospice, so many details."

She ticked through the to-do list efficiently. Even in a sarong, she could still harness the buttoned-up suit-type organization. She all but wrapped herself in competence.

"Oh God, Hillary." He pushed away from the door, reaching for her. "I'm sorry. Is there something I can do to help? Doctors? Specialists?"

She stopped in her tracks. "Actually, I do need something. I need for you to be sure my family won't be in any kind of danger if I'm there."

Ah, hell. She thought they still had to hide out here, away from Barry Curtis's accomplice. He could almost hear Salvatore's mocking laughter in his ears, followed by an *I told you so* for not letting Hillary in on the news sooner.

He took her hands in his. "No worries on that front. Actually, we're cleared to leave anytime."

"Really? Did they catch the mystery guy we identified in the surveillance footage?" Confusion chased across her face. "Are we sure there won't be retaliation against us for making the identification?"

"They have him in custody. Barry Curtis is talking now. They are in a rush to outconfess each other, so Interpol doesn't need our testimony." And he was damn grateful he didn't need to worry about her safety, although he knew now he would never stop being concerned for her. "We're just icing on the cake for them."

"That's awesome, and crazy convenient in the timing." She pressed a hand to her forehead, then, slowly, realization dawned in her eyes. "That call this morning, the good news, it wasn't about work was it? It was Salvatore."

"Yes, it was." He couldn't deny it.

"Why didn't you tell me? When did he find out?"

He hesitated a second too long.

Disillusionment flooded her face, followed by anger. "You knew before this morning, didn't you?"

Resolution settled deep in his gut, along with the urge to kick himself for being worse than an idiot. "I heard late yesterday afternoon."

"Why? Why wouldn't you tell me?" Pain laced her every word. "Why would you let me worry and wonder? It's almost like you kidnapped me, handcuffing me here with a lie."

"I intended to tell you today. I just wanted to enjoy a final night with you."

"That wasn't your decision to make." Her eyes went cynical as she backed away. "But then maybe you already knew that. Consciously or subconsciously, you sabotaged this relationship because you don't want the reality, just this tree house fantasy."

"Damn it, Hillary, that's not true. Give me a chance to explain." He gripped her by the shoulders.

But her body was like ice under his hands.

"I only have one question for you, Troy." She met his gaze unflinchingly, beautiful and so vulnerable. "Why couldn't you have just been honest with me? Why did you have to go to such lengths to break my heart?"

Her words stabbed him clean through. He'd vowed over and over that his intent was to protect her and yet he'd done the thing guaranteed to hurt her most. There wasn't any excuse he could make. No matter how much he'd worked on his people skills, he hadn't learned all the lessons he needed now.

She shrugged free of his hands. "That's what I thought. There's nothing left to say." She unhooked the diamond charm necklace and dropped it in his palm. "Please, just take me to Vermont and then get out of my life."

Twelve

She'd come full circle.

Locking her rental car, she strode up the flagstone walkway leading to her childhood home, her body more than a little weary from her day of travel, her argument with Troy. After they'd fought, he shut down. He'd offered her his plane to see her mother and then he'd disappeared into his computer-filled man cave.

And now she was home. The countryside was dark, other than lights on the house and barn and another marking the entrance to the dirt driveway.

But even in the dim light, she knew her way by heart. Her sister hadn't changed much on the two-story clapboard farmhouse, not even the black shutters. There were a few extra flowers in the garden and more toys in the yard—a bike lying on its side, tire swings spinning in the wind, and a fort built into the V of a sprawling oak tree. A sign hung on the front with *No Boys Allowed* painted in bright red letters.

Not a bad idea.

She couldn't get past feeling like a fool. After telling herself a million times Troy was a playboy and she had a radar finely tuned to find jerks, she'd still made the same mistake. She'd trusted the wrong guy.

But damn, he was so good at the game. He'd romanced her in a way no man had even thought of trying, dazzling her with contrasts. One day they were dining in France and another day picnicking off fresh fruit from the trees around his Costa Rican retreat. Who gave a woman a cowbell as well as a charm with exclusive black diamonds?

A genius playboy, that's who. He'd told her he'd studied how to be funny, how to charm and weave his way through society, yet somehow she'd never considered he was using those skills to manipulate her into going to bed with him in less than a week. She wanted to pound her head against a tree.

Or collapse on the front stoop and cry her eyes out.

Her older sister pushed through the front screen door, hinges creaking. They could have been twins born seven years apart, yet they'd taken two such different paths. As much as Hillary had scoffed at anyone staying on this farm, her sister definitely appeared to be the wiser one.

Claudia opened her arms and hugged her hard. They'd been close as kids, taking care of each other. What had changed? When had she quit helping her sister?

Hillary stepped back and hooked an arm with Claudia. "Where are the kids and hubby?"

"Asleep, but looking forward to seeing you in the morning. Where's your Robin Hood Hacker Hunk?"

"Long story. Can we save it for later?" When she could talk about him without crying? Like maybe sometime in

the next decade. "I'm sorry to have kept you up so late…
I'm sorry I left you to take care of everything with Mom
and Dad."

"You don't have to apologize for anything." Claudia
squeezed her sister's hand on their way up the steps they'd
climbed countless times. "You're living your life. That's
what grown-ups are supposed to do."

"Are you living yours the way you want? With Mom
staying here?" She needed to hear that she hadn't totally
wrecked her sister's life by bailing.

Claudia tugged open the creaky screen again. "No one
wants to have an alcoholic mother in and out of rehab clin-
ics. And I'm sure you don't want to have to keep footing
the bill because I'm too cash-strapped with three kids to
feed. We both do what we can."

"Writing the check is easy."

"Ha! So says the woman who doesn't have a kid in
braces." Her sister guided her through the house, toward the back guest room. "Come on. Mom tried to stay
awake to see you, but she's on a lot of pain medication.
She drifted off about an hour ago."

Only a few more steps and they would be outside their
mother's door, where she slept.

"I'll see her in the morning then. We could all use a
good night's sleep." Hillary turned quickly, stopping in
the kitchen, a traditional wide-open space with a six-seat
oak table in the middle. "I appreciate your trying to make
the distribution seem fair, but I still feel guilty. Like I've
run away."

"We're both children of an alcoholic. That leaves a
mark on the way we deal with things." Claudia snagged
a caffeine-free Diet Coke off the counter, popped the top
and passed it to her sister before getting one for herself. "I
lean toward the whole codependent gig, and you lean to-

ward avoidance. We're both trying to do better, to be better. I figure as long as we're both still trying, then there's nothing to be gained from beating up on ourselves."

Hillary leaned against the tile counter, sipping the Diet Coke. "It seems so strange that she came here to die when she always swore she hated this place, that the boredom drove her to drink."

"Honey," her sister crooned squeezing her arm, "you gotta know that was just an excuse."

Hillary looked around the kitchen with all its windows showcasing the wide-open space…much like Troy's place. "It's really pretty here."

"Yes, it is." Her sister smiled serenely, tipping back her can of soda.

"You can say 'I told you so' if you want." She deserved everything coming her way after she'd been all but snobby about the place. Until this moment, she'd never really seen her home without the dark filter of her mom's bitterness.

"I'm not a gloater. You should know that about me." Her sister tapped her can against Hillary's.

"I do, which is probably why I offered to let you lord it over me, since I knew you wouldn't."

"That's convoluted logic."

"I picked it up from the best." Another thing she'd learned from Troy this week. How could so much happiness and pain be mingled together?

Her sister cocked her head to the side, brow furrowed. "You can love here and love somewhere else, too. That's okay."

Hillary nodded. "I'm starting to understand that." She looked around at the children's art on the fridge, at the cow clock on the wall, and found the words falling from her mouth in spite of the burn of tears behind her eyes. "Troy has this place in Costa Rica, and it's amazing. But not because it's flashy. His home is actually very rustic— with a lot of high-tech gadgetry of course, but the look of the place is earthy. It's *real*."

"Sis, I gotta confess, this is a stretch. You're comparing Costa Rica with Vermont? No offense to my beloved home state, of course."

"I know, I know, I've thought the same thing." Her jumbled thoughts from this whole crazy week started coming together in her mind like puzzle pieces…. She'd been using the farm as an excuse for her own unhappiness. On some level, she must have known that or why else would she have insisted on carrying little cow talismans as reminders of home? Her childhood hadn't been perfect, but it hadn't been all bad. There were good memories, too. Life wasn't clear-cut or black-and-white like the spots on a cow.

Had she been missing the boat on her career, as well? Focusing on the glitz at the expense of depth? Did she really want to spend the rest of her life planning parties? Troy had found simplicity and meaning underneath all the wealth. She'd been so busy judging Troy, she hadn't considered her own superficial choices. Her narrow view of the world had likely led to her previous bad choices in men.

But she should have realized Troy was different. Special.

She set her soda on the counter. "I'm trying to say a place's beauty isn't about the trappings. It's about appreciating it exactly as it is."

"That's pretty profound, actually." Her sister stood beside her, leaning back against the counter, quietly waiting.

So much more effective than if her sister had pressed.

"The media paints Troy as this arrogant, urbane guy." She thought of that first time she'd seen him on the plane. "It's a face he puts on for the world, and honestly that persona is sexy as hell."

Her sister raised one eyebrow and waved for Hillary to keep talking.

"But the real person underneath it all is infinitely more fascinating." So much so, she didn't know how she would ever get over him.

"You're in love with him."

"Completely," she answered without hesitation.

"Then why isn't he here?"

Such a simple question.

He wasn't with her because…?

She'd pushed him away. Yes, he'd lied to her. He wasn't a perfect man. God knows, she wasn't perfect, either. Just because he'd screwed up, that didn't mean everything about their week together had been false.

Life wasn't all or nothing for either of them. They would need time together to build a relationship, to learn to trust each other. She understood that now.

But would Troy understand it, as well—if she got a second chance to tell him?

"You owe me for this, Colonel." Troy rocked back on his heels, jamming his fists in his tuxedo pockets to keep from punching a wall in frustration over having to hang out at a black-tie fundraiser.

Less than two weeks had passed since he and the colonel had come to Chicago, and already the man was calling again, asking him to show his face at this dinner dance for some reason he'd yet to disclose.

In D.C.

Which happened to be the last place on earth Troy wanted to be since it reminded him of Hillary. He just wanted to go back to Costa Rica and lock himself in his man cave for some serious alone time. Except he couldn't go back to Costa Rica, not when he'd made love to her in every corner of the place, his home so full of memories he'd been climbing the walls without her.

Salvatore clapped him on the back as the jazz band fired up a Broadway show tune. "Actually, I don't owe you a thing. The way I remember it, you owe me."

"Our agreement didn't include back-to-back gigs." Even if this one was a good cause, hosted by Senator Landis to raise money for the area Big Brother program for at-risk and foster kids. "In spite of my playboy rep, I do have to work."

"Just pretend for a couple of hours, then your time will be your own for at least…oh, let's say six months." Salvatore held up his hand. "I promise."

Troy angled to the side for a waiter carrying a silver tray of appetizers to pass before saying to the colonel, "With all due respect, you lie."

Salvatore adjusted his red tie. "I take offense at that. Lying is a very dishonorable trait."

Troy ground his teeth. Had the colonel been hired by Hillary to call attention to all his flaws?

Then as if conjured from his thoughts, he saw her across the room. *Hillary*. She wore a simple black dress with complete elegance, outshining every other woman in the room. His fist clenched the diamond pendant tighter—her necklace—that he'd been carrying around in his pocket since she left him on the island. What were the odds he would see her at the first place he went after leaving Costa Rica?

The odds were off the charts, in fact.

"Damn it, Colonel." He glared at Salvatore. "Did you set this up? You want me to crawl back to her? She made it clear she doesn't want me. She doesn't trust me. That's all there is to it."

"Bull."

His head snapped back. "What did you just say?"

"You heard me. You're a smart man. A genius, actually, part of why I work with you. But you're also manipulative. You use that brain to trick people into doing what you want, while making them think it was their idea. Another reason you're a great asset to my team. But that kind of game playing does not go over well in relationships."

"I have friends."

"Who play by your same convoluted—sometimes sketchy—rules." Salvatore gripped him on the shoulder in a move that was almost…fatherly? "Here with Hillary, you had a chance at a normal, healthy relationship, and you blew it. Any clue why?"

"You seem to have all the answers today. You tell me." And God, he actually meant it. He wanted help, to find a way to get her back because the past days without her had been pure hell.

"I can't give you all the answers. If you want her bad enough, you'll figure this one out on your own. Which you can do if you use that genius brain of yours and think." He tapped Troy's temple. "Why are you here when she's here?"

"Because you set us up."

Salvatore shook his head. "Think again."

With a final pat on Troy's shoulder, the colonel faded into the crowd.

Could Hillary have actually called the colonel and asked for his help? Why would she have reached out to Salvatore rather than him?

That answer was easy enough. He'd made himself inaccessible to everyone except Salvatore. He'd hidden away in his cave and used all his techie toys to make himself unreachable.

Hillary had told him from the start she had trust issues

and he'd pushed that one inexcusable button. It was almost like his subconscious had self-destructed the relationship. For a man of reason, that was tough to swallow.

But love wasn't about logic. Hell, his feelings for Hillary were definitely not anything rational. He just loved her, and he wanted her. And he intended to do everything in his power to win her back.

Click.

The cool metal wrapped around his wrist. He barely had time to register the sensation before he looked up and found Hillary standing beside him.

Click.

She locked the other handcuff around her wrist.

Hillary hoped the smile on Troy's face was for real and not an act for the crowd. A spotlight focused on them as she led him across the ballroom floor. The partiers applauded while the senator took the mic from the lead singer in the band to thank Troy Donavan for his very generous donation.

That part had been Salvatore's idea—when she'd contacted him begging for help in finding Troy. She'd been surprised to learn from Salvatore that he and Troy actually worked together on a more regular basis—but it made sense. She'd already realized there was more to the man she loved than the superficial. And even as a teen, he hadn't cared what the world thought of him. He'd been out there crusading in his own way. She was glad now that she hadn't known before about his work with Interpol. That would have made it too easy to trust him. She wouldn't have had to search her heart and open her eyes.

Salvatore had even made her a job offer she found more than a little tempting...leave her D.C. position and sign on to freelance with Interpol. She and Troy had a lot to talk about. Thank goodness Salvatore had worked out a plan for her to speak to him. Granted, something a little less high profile would have been easier on her nerves. But Salvatore had insisted this would work best.

Hillary searched for a private corner, but there were people everywhere. Finally, she tugged him down the corridor and into a powder room—and, as she'd hoped, the presence of a man chased both of the occupants out. She passed the bathroom attendant folded cash and said, "Could you give us ten minutes alone, please?"

Laughing under her breath, the attendant ducked out into the hall. Hillary locked the door after them and turned back to Troy only to find herself at a loss.

She'd been so focused on getting him alone and making her gesture meaningful. She'd even planned at least three speeches...all of which flew out of her head now that she was face-to-face with him. So she gave herself a moment to just soak in the beloved sight of him, here, with her again.

God, he knew how to wear a tuxedo, with the white silk scarf and fedora. He stole her breath as well as her thoughts.

Troy held up their wrists. "You sure do know how to make an impression."

"I wanted to make sure neither of us could run away this time."

"Good move." He stroked the inside of her wrist with his thumb. "How is your mother?"

The past couple of days had been hectic, getting her mom settled in with hospice home care, talking during her lucid moments. "She and I have done a lot of speaking again. We're finding a way to make peace." As much as was possible, but they were trying. "But that's not why I'm here tonight. Troy, I want to tell you—"

He pressed a finger to her lips.

"You know what? Hold that thought." He cupped her waist and lifted her onto the bathroom counter next to a basket of rolled-up hand towels. "I need to say some things to you first. Any objections?"

Smiling hopefully, she held up their cuffed wrists and jingled the cuffs. "You have my undivided attention."

"For starters, you left this." He pulled his free hand from his pocket. Her diamond cow necklace dangled from his fingertips. "It belongs to you."

A smile played with her lips and her heart. "I'm guessing there aren't a lot of women on the lookout for one of those."

"It's a one-of-a-kind, made for a one-of-a-kind woman." He reached behind her neck, taking her cuffed hand along as he latched her necklace in place again.

The charm still carried his heat as it rested against her chest.

He clasped their hands between them. "You've taught me a lot, Hillary Wright."

"What would that be?"

"I've prided myself on being fearless in business, fearless in standing up for a cause, even if it lands me in hot water." He linked hands with her. "But I botched things when it really counted. When it comes to relationships— when it came to the way I handled things with you—I haven't grown much beyond the kid who hid in his computer room rather than risk having people let him down. I betrayed your trust, and I'm so very sorry for that."

There hadn't been many people in his life teaching *him* how to trust when he was growing up. "The fact that I'm here should tell you something. I forgive you for not telling me right away, and I hope you'll forgive me for running rather than talking through things."

"Thank God." His throat moved in a long slow swallow.

His eyes slid closed, and she realized how, in spite of his grins and jokes, he really was sweating this every bit as much as she was. She mattered to him.

She rested her forehead against his.

Troy threaded his fingers through her hair. "You're a hundred percent right to demand I pony up my one hundred percent where you're concerned. You deserve it all, everything, and I want to be the man who makes that happen for you. I need to tell you something else, about Colonel Salvatore and—"

"Your freelance work with Interpol?"

"How did you…? He told you, didn't he?"

"Yes, he did, when I asked him to help me find you."

Troy eyed her warily. "And you're not upset with me for not explaining it myself? I know how important trust is to you."

"I'm assuming that kind of work isn't something you just go around sharing with people right away, but you'll have to clue me in on the nuances since it looks like I'll be signing on with the colonel, as well. He says his recruit list needs some estrogen."

For once, she'd stunned Troy into complete silence. His jaw went slack, and he started to talk at least twice, only to stop and shove his hand through his long hair. Finally, he just smiled and laughed. He wrapped his unshackled arm around her and spun her once before setting her on her feet again.

"God, I love you, Hillary. No questions or doubts in my mind, I am so in love with you." He kissed her once, twice then held on the third time until her knees went weak. "You know I'm going to want to be with you on any assignment so I don't go crazy worrying. Maybe I should be more laid-back, but when it comes to you—"

"You already are everything I could want, and of course we'll be together, always, so I can watch your back," she said against his mouth, her heart so full she could barely breathe. "I love you, too, Troy, my totally original man. Mine."

"Yes, ma'am, I am." He kissed her, firmly, intensely, holding for at least seven heartbeats. "I intend to work on being the best man possible for you each and every day." He sketched kisses over her forehead, along her eyes, finishing on the tip of her nose. "I'm a smart man, you know. I'll figure this one out if you'll give me the time."

"How much time were you thinking about?"

"A lifetime."

She took his hat and dropped it on her head. "It just so happens, that totally works for me."

* * * * *

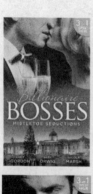
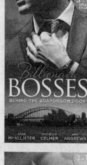

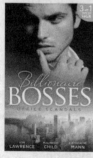
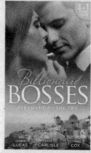

The World of
MILLS & BOON®

The World of
MILLS & BOON®

HISTORICAL

Awaken the romance of the past
6 new stories every month

MEDICAL ROMANCE™

The ultimate in romantic medical drama
6 new stories every month

MODERN™

Power, passion and irresistible temptation
8 new stories every month

By Request

Relive the romance with the best of the best
12 stories every month

WORLD_ M&B2b